N.J. YOUNG

Evernight Publishing

www.evernightpublishing.com

N.J. YOUNG

DEDICATION

For Eric—my perfect combination of love, laughter, and friendship.

DOUBLE DOWN

Ozark Magic, 1

N.J. Young

Copyright © 2015

Prologue

Isabel Craig stared at the fresh mound of dirt on top of her grandfather's grave, and shivered in the fall breeze. She reached down and adjusted one white carnation that had slipped from its bouquet. Even now she still felt the need to take care of him, wanting everything to be just so.

She'd known this day was coming, but that knowledge hadn't kept her heart from breaking. Her grandfather had been her only family since her parents had died when she was in college. He had been the person she could always talk to during all of her twenty-six years, no matter what the issue. He had always known what to say.

Now she was alone.

Izzy blew out a breath. The day wasn't over yet. She'd greeted everyone at the cemetery and had accepted all of their kind words of condolence. She knew she had friends that cared about her, but right now it didn't feel like enough. She shivered in the fall breeze and then jumped as a hand rested on her shoulder. She hadn't heard anyone approaching.

"Hey, sweetheart." Graham's arm went around her shoulders and with that one touch she felt more at peace. "I wanted to make sure you were okay."

Sheriff Graham Nolan was over six feet of hard muscle. He towered over Izzy's small five-and-a-half-foot frame. Graham looked at her, his deep gray eyes heavy with concern and worry. He was in his familiar navy sheriff's uniform and jacket. His wavy dark brown hair almost reached his collar, and his close-cropped beard just drew more attention to his full lips.

Izzy had been zombielike all day. She wished she could just cry and get her emotions out. Instead, she was numb. But now that Graham was here, she felt something inside her break, and the tears came. They spilled from her blue eyes, and she hugged herself tighter, turning into his open arms.

"I-I'm fine," she said, but her shaky voice betrayed her words.

Graham unzipped his jacket and wrapped his arms around her, tucking her in close to his warm body. "You're not fine. You're shivering."

Izzy's arms wound around Graham's lean waist, and she instinctively rested her head against his chest. She rarely got to touch him this way and she relished the opportunity, loving how safe she felt in his embrace.

"You know, you don't have to be so strong all the time," Graham said, his cheek resting against the top of Izzy's head. "You've taken care of your grandpa for the last three years. It's time for you to lean on someone."

Izzy shook her head, even as she leaned into Graham. It felt so good to be held, surrounded by his heat. She could hear his heartbeat, smell the musky scent of his soap.

Her brain told her she should walk away. But this was where she wanted to be, in Graham's arms. She knew he didn't love her the way she loved him, but right now, she didn't want to let go.

"I don't know what to do now," she whispered. "Besides managing grandpa's resort, my entire focus has been taking care of him, making sure he ate, took his medication, went for his chemo…."

After Izzy graduated from college with a degree in hotel management, she had moved back to Magic. The plan had originally been for her to take over the Lakewood Resort so her grandfather could retire. After suffering from a bad cough that refused to go away, Richard Craig had finally gone to the doctor only to discover he had lung cancer. Just like that, she'd become the manager of the hotel and her grandpa's main caregiver.

Izzy took a shaky breath. "I've known this time was coming, but I'd been so busy trying to keep him comfortable I never thought about what I was going to do with myself after he was gone."

Her tears started again and Graham's arms tightened around her, holding her close as she cried. She heard him murmur soothing words, his lips finding the top of her head. Even in her grief, she reveled at the intimate gesture.

"It's going to be okay, Iz. There are so many people who love you. We are all here for you."

After a few minutes, Izzy's tears finally began to slow, and she focused her attention on what Graham was saying. *People who loved her?* His words finally started to register. Did that include him? She sniffled a bit and looked up.

Only inches from his face, she could see how his gray eyes revealed flecks of dark blue that sparkled like sapphires. They were full of concern for her—and possibly something more. Something darker. She sucked in a breath as his callused hand came up to cup her cheek, her body now fully aware of how close they were, and how firmly his body was pressed against hers.

"Hey, is everything okay?" the voice of Tessa Lawson broke through Izzy's spell, and she almost stumbled as Graham immediately released her.

"I'm sorry, I didn't mean to interrupt," Tessa continued. "I just didn't want you driving." Shooting a quick glance at Graham, Tessa reached out her hands and took Izzy's. "I'm going to take you home, and as soon as Andrea can ditch her asshat of a husband, she'll join us." Tessa was always one to tell it like it is. As much as Izzy loved her friend, she was frustrated that Tessa chose this time to disrupt a rare moment of connection with Graham.

"No, Tess, you really don't have to. I wanted to finish talking to Gr—" Izzy turned toward Graham and was sad to see him already walking away. The small spark of hope she'd felt immediately fizzled.

Tessa's face tightened and her eyes narrowed at Graham's retreating figure. "It's okay, sweetie. Come on. I have a ton of food at your place, complete with ice cream. And there's also wine if you decide to go that route."

Izzy was familiar with Tessa's love of red wine, and was quite certain there were bottles of cabernet, merlot, and pinot noir waiting at home. Izzy wasn't a huge drinker, but right now, ice cream and wine sounded like the perfect dinner.

Izzy turned to take one last look at Graham as he reached his patrol car. He didn't look at her as he got in. Izzy swallowed the lump in her throat before looking back at Tessa.

"Yeah," she said hoarsely. "Yeah, let's go."

****

Graham started up his car and watched Izzy cross the cemetery lawn and get into Tessa's SUV. It had nearly killed him when he caught her standing over her grandfather's grave alone. She'd looked so vulnerable, so lonely. She sparked every protective instinct he had. And shit, when she'd started to cry, he almost lost it. Her uncle should have been there offering her comfort. The bastard hadn't even stayed for the service.

As he watched Tessa's car drive away, Graham had to resist the urge to follow the women. If only Izzy knew how much he loved her. Graham shook his head. He was no good for her. He was staying away *because* he loved her. He couldn't give her what she needed and would only end up hurting her. He'd discovered the hard way that it just wasn't in his makeup to be able to love Izzy the way she needed to be loved. He wouldn't put her through the heartache.

At least there was some solace in the fact that her friends, Tessa, Andrea, and Jillian would take care of his girl.

"Dammit, no." Graham rested his head against the steering wheel. He had to stop thinking of Izzy as his. There had been a time when he thought he could be around her and easily resist. That time was long gone.

This was exactly why holding her the way he had was dangerous. She'd felt so small, her tight little body flush against his. He'd tried not to think about the way her pert breasts had pressed against him, or how she smelled of lavender.

She had looked up at him with those wide blue eyes and that wavy blonde hair curling around her face, and Graham had wanted nothing more than to suck that quivering bottom lip of hers into his mouth. He'd practically shoved her away from him so she wouldn't feel his hard cock resting against her.

What the hell was he doing? Her grandfather's body wasn't even cold and he was imagining her in bed. But that wasn't anything new. It seemed like no matter how hard he tried to avoid it, Izzy invaded his thoughts.

He'd wanted to kiss her so badly only moments ago. What would happen if he just threw all caution to the wind and took her? He would put his handcuffs to good use so he could make sure Izzy was properly restrained as he pleasured her body. The thought of her naked and held down made him grow even harder. He would run his hands all over that smooth, creamy skin. He wanted to taste her everywhere. He would make her come over and over again with his mouth. What would she sound like? Taste like? Would she scream when she came? He wanted her screaming and whimpering and begging. Oh, she would be *begging* him to fuck her.

Graham jumped as his phone buzzed, dragging him out of his own head. His grip on the steering wheel was so tight that he was surprised it hadn't snapped into pieces.

"You're killing me, Isabel Craig," he muttered as he dragged the phone from his pocket, checking the display. *Chris Nolan*. Graham hit the decline button. Today was certainly not the day he wanted to deal with his twin brother.

Since moving to St. Louis four years ago, Chris had only come back to Magic to visit their mother, Lily. Clenching the phone, Graham thought of his brother and the damn utopian ideals he used to have about relationships. Chris had finally seen the light when a woman had come between them and shattered those ideals. For letting that happen, Graham would never forgive himself.

The two of them had gone from being close to barely speaking. But he couldn't blame his brother, could he? Graham deserved to be alone. And he certainly didn't deserve Izzy.

Tossing his phone on the passenger seat, he started the car. He drove back to the station trying to figure out how the hell he was going to get Izzy Craig out of his head.

Chapter One

Two weeks later

Chris Nolan settled into his suite at the Lakewood Resort and lay down on the bed to take in his surroundings. The subtle elegance of the suite surprised him. The plush carpet was a deep chocolate, and the gleaming walnut entertainment center sported a 56-inch flat screen. Although slightly dated, the room, as well as the entire hotel, had been well maintained. *Yep, this place definitely had the potential to be a great resort.*

The marina here used to be so much fun when he was a kid. He had such fond memories of paddle boating with his brother, and of his mom teaching them how to water ski. Chris had been raised in Osage Beach, which was across the lake from Magic—about forty-five minutes when you had to drive around the lake rather than cut across via boat. While he was familiar with Magic and its surroundings, he hadn't spent a lot of time here aside from those summer moments with his family.

Chris sank back into the mocha-colored down comforter on the bed. Mergers and acquisitions certainly wasn't his dream job, so he was happy at finally getting an assignment that excited him.

The firm's newest client wanted to buy the Lakewood and expand the small resort, then add a few luxurious amenities to attract more high-paying customers. Once Chris secured the purchase of the land, he could get rid of all those trees and do something about that huge, wasted acreage. Maybe an outlet mall. This town needed something more than just a lake view to draw the tourists.

Right now, he was just happy to be back. The lake area was his home, and he couldn't count the number of times over the last four years that he'd almost quit his job and moved back. What kept stopping him? Pride? Regret?

Chris felt his cell phone buzz. "Nolan," he answered.

"Give me good news, Chris." His boss's nasal voice whined in his ear, and Chris rolled his gray eyes. After he sealed the acquisition, he knew the top VP spot at Waddell and Stevens was his to slide into. When Chris started at the firm four years ago, he had wanted to achieve VP level before he hit thirty. Now he was twenty-nine, and could make it just under the wire. The only problem was, he didn't know if that's what he even wanted anymore.

"Mr. Stevens, it's a piece of cake. This location is more than perfect. I haven't had the chance to check out the entire property yet"—Chris looked out the window at the huge expanse of trees—"but there's plenty of room for a golf course and a shopping area. This place could be a gold mine."

"Perfect." Stevens's excitement radiated over the phone. "Remember, we are on a very tight timeline. Our client is anxious to get this deal wrapped up so he can get started on the expansion. He needs to have a signed contract within two weeks to be able to secure his top investors. Just find the owner and get it done. You have a brother down there, right? That would be a good place to start. Maybe he knows her." Stevens had done his homework.

Chris stiffened as he thought of his identical twin, Graham. He had only seen Graham a handful of times in the last four years, and their brief meetings had been tense. Several calls to Graham over the last couple of weeks had been fruitless. Frustration washed through him. He'd just wanted to let Graham know he was coming to town, but his brother had not returned even one of his calls.

"I can do this on my own. No need to involve my brother."

"Well, word has it that this girl, Isabel Craig, is a pretty thing, so you can do what you do best—charm her pants off." Stevens chuckled. "Hell, if your reputation's everything it's cracked up to be, you can get her to promise you anything after that."

Chris could practically hear Stevens leering through the phone. The older man was right. He did have a reputation as quite a womanizer, but that wasn't a bad thing, was it? He liked sex, and he certainly didn't have a problem turning on the charm when necessary. He'd bedded down with some previous clients to push a deal along. If this Isabel Craig was cute, that would definitely be a preferable way to charm her into signing on the dotted line.

"Nolan, I've given your number to our client. Expect to hear from Mr. Jacobs by tomorrow. He wants to keep in close contact with you so you can give him daily reports on how things are moving along down there."

After wrapping up his call and promising to give Stevens constant updates, Chris sat and stared at his phone. He'd entered Eric Jacobs into his contact list, but wasn't overly thrilled at dealing with the man. They'd only met once in Stevens's office. Jacobs was a big fellow with graying hair and a full beard. He'd seemed perfectly dull and nondescript at the time, but there was something about him that Chris couldn't quite put his finger on, something that just rubbed him the wrong way.

Nolan, you're too stressed. That's your problem.
Running a hand through his hair, he moved to look out the window. He should really climb into his car and drive by the station to let Graham know he was in town. On the way into Magic, he had stopped to see his mom, and Lily had stuffed him full of grilled cheese sandwiches and chocolate chip cookies.

Chris smiled at the thought of his mother. She had always doted on her boys, especially since their father had passed away when they were sixteen. Lily had worked hard to make a good life for them. Now it was Chris's turn to take care of her. Unfortunately, Lily always refused the money he tried to send her. Chris had finally just opened an account in her name and deposited money in it every month. He was going to make sure his mother was taken care of one way or another.

His brother was a different story. Chris knew Graham had been upset recently. They hadn't spoken in months, their relationship strained, but Chris still had that damn "twin sense," as their mom had always called it. He'd told himself he needed to check in on Graham and find out what the hell was going on.

He missed his brother. He and Graham had been as close as two brothers could be when they were kids. They had been close until they had let a woman come between them, and now Chris didn't know if they would ever get back the connection they had once shared.

Scrolling through his phone to find Graham's number, Chris hovered over his name and sighed. He just wasn't in the mood to deal with Graham's moodiness tonight.

Tomorrow. First thing tomorrow.
Shoving his phone back in his pocket, Chris decided to head down and check out the bar. The place hadn't seemed too busy when he'd checked in, but there

was always hope of finding a pretty woman hanging around, someone who maybe wanted to keep him company for the night.

****

The sun was setting on the St. Louis skyline as Claude Stevens put his phone down and looked at the man sitting across his desk. He hoped he had done the right thing in sending Chris Nolan to Magic. He knew the boy was talented, and Claude really hoped he could close this deal. It wasn't often they had a client as demanding as Eric Jacobs. Normally, Claude would have sent someone more experienced, but since Chris knew the area, that gave him the upper hand.

"Mr. Jacobs, you don't have a thing to worry about. Nolan is the best. He'll close this deal before you know it. The Lakewood is as good as yours."

Jacobs sat in the soft brown leather chair with his legs crossed and picked an imaginary piece of lint from his dark suit. "He'd better, Stevens. I really don't want to have to take matters into my own hands."

What exactly was that supposed to mean? Flustered, Claude responded, "Uh, no, no. You won't have to at all." He started to launch into Chris Nolan's past acquisitions to prove his capabilities, but Jacobs ignored him, rising from the chair and heading toward the door. "I'll be in touch."

Claude stared at the door after it closed behind Jacobs. He really hoped Chris wrapped this up quickly. There was something about Eric Jacobs that made his skin crawl. The man put on a pleasant front, but Claude was a good judge of people.

Jacobs supposedly represented a holdings company, but Claude didn't trust that the man was all he was cracked up to be. When Claude looked into the eyes of Eric Jacobs, there was a coldness there that almost scared him. No, Claude certainly did not want to deal with the man any longer than he absolutely had to.

****

Martin Craig waited until he returned to his hotel room before peeling off the fake beard, toupee, and glasses—all the trappings that made him Eric Jacobs. Looking in the mirror, brown eyes stared back at him out of his bronzed face. He always made sure to keep his skin tanned to a healthy glow. Even though he was graying at the temples, he knew he didn't look 52.

Martin scrubbed a hand over his face as he thought about his niece, well, his half-niece. He was determined she not find out he was the one behind this deal. If she knew that, she would never sell to him.

The land in Magic, Missouri was rightfully his. It should have gone to him once his half-brother Richard died, but dammit if he hadn't left it to his fucking granddaughter. Martin had been enraged. The last he knew, Richard was planning to leave a decent sum of money to the girl and the land and resort to him. Now the girl had it all. All of the land and all of the oil underneath it.

She was well aware she was sitting on almost half a billion dollars in oil, and her grandfather had been, too. Four years ago, Martin had talked his brother into hiring an oil surveyor to do seismic testing on the land. The final geophysics report concluded the land was insanely rich with oil. He'd been dumbfounded when Richard had merely shrugged and said no one was going to ruin the resort and start drilling on his land. *What a fucking idiot!* Richard could have had millions. But Martin was smart. Knowing Richard had terminal cancer, he'd bided his time. He certainly hadn't expected the bastard to hang around another four years, though. Martin knew that if he just waited, then the land would be his.

Except it *wasn't*. Here it was, four years later, Richard dead, and that stupid girl had everything that belonged to him. Two weeks ago, Martin had made her the same offer he'd made Richard, but just like her grandfather, she had refused. She had no desire to ruin the resort, she'd said. Martin was tired of waiting. He wanted his land and his money. He deserved it. That girl certainly didn't.

Picking up his phone, Martin decided to check on his back-up plan in case the land acquisition didn't work out as he'd hoped. He was pleased when Ramiro answered immediately.

"Mr. Craig. Are you ready to let me to take care of your little problem?" the younger man's gruff voice said.

Ramiro had worked for Martin Craig for nearly a decade. Sometimes there were problems in business that seemed insurmountable. When that occurred, Ramiro was able to eliminate them quickly and without a mess.

"Not yet. I've given Nolan two weeks to do this his way. If he can't get it done in my timeframe, I'll have you step in."

Ramiro sighed. "I don't know why you're letting that pretty boy handle this. I'm already here, and I've made more connections than he has. It would be easy for me to eliminate the problem."

"I don't need your opinion, Ramiro," Stevens said firmly. "This is different than your usual jobs. I know people in that little town. This girl is related to me. If Nolan can seal this and we can avoid bloodshed, then I don't have to worry about any suspicion falling on me. Besides, that boy can charm the pants off of any woman who gets within a twenty-mile radius of him. I think he'll come through."

Ramiro snorted. "Two weeks. Call me if Pretty Boy can't do it."

The line went dead before Martin could reply, making his jaw clench. He was going to have to spell some things out for Ramiro. The man was forgetting who was in charge, and Martin wouldn't have it. As soon as this job was done, they were going to come to an understanding. And the job *would* get done.

Of course, Chris Nolan didn't know the real reason Martin—or Eric Jacobs—wanted to acquire the land. He thought his client wanted the land so he could expand the resort and tap into the big business around the Lake of the Ozarks. He knew Nolan could make the deal, but he seemed like too much of a boy scout for Martin to trust him with the truth, and his boss Claude Stevens wasn't much better. Too damn honest. Didn't they realize that in big business, you had to get your hands dirty?

Martin sat down at his laptop and pulled the Isabel Craig file up on his computer, staring at the girl's picture. She had blonde hair, which must have come from her father. But it was the eyes that struck Martin. She had her grandfather's large blue eyes. She was thin, which made the eyes seem larger. Martin almost felt a pang of regret when he saw his brother's eyes staring at him out of this girl's face. He didn't want to have to hurt her. After all, she was family, and he wasn't a monster. But if she didn't sign the contract... well, then it just couldn't be helped.

Two weeks. The land would be his one way or the other.

****

Isabel Craig sat at a table by the bay window, taking in the view she loved so dearly; the way the sunset glinted off the trees, making them shimmer like gold and red jewels. One more month and the trees would be bare, but Izzy was going to enjoy every moment of the beautiful fall foliage. With a quivering lip, she thought of how much her grandpa loved this time of the year. *Deep breath, Izzy. Don't lose it again in the middle of The Lounge.*

"Two rum and cokes. And I had Milo make them both doubles," Andrea said with a little wink as she sat down and pushed a drink in front of Izzy. She then reached for the laptop on the table and pulled up a spreadsheet as Izzy studied her. Andrea had been her friend and assistant manager since Izzy arrived in town three years ago. Her fingers flew over the keyboard as she added to the list of supplies they needed for the annual Costume Ball.

Staring at her friend, Izzy found herself wishing she could help Andi. No one could stand her husband, nor could they understand how Andrea could be happy. But not wanting to lose a friend, Izzy stopped prying about the situation long ago.

Andrea paused and pushed a strand of long brown hair behind her ear. She looked up at Izzy, her deep chocolate eyes awash with concern. "What? What's wrong?"

"I'm sorry. I didn't mean to stare, Andi. I was just thinking." Izzy picked up her drink and took a long sip. "Whoa," she said, choking. "That's more like a triple, not a double."

"Well, you could probably use it. I'm worried about you, Iz. You've done nothing but work 24/7 for the last two weeks. You need a break."

Reaching out to the centerpiece, Izzy turned the miniature jack o'lantern to face her. "Maybe after Halloween. Right now, I just want to get through the party."

The Costume Ball was a huge event every year, and a big draw for tourists and locals. It was always a lot of work, but Izzy usually enjoyed it. This year, it was bittersweet. She couldn't help but think of how this would be the first Ball she'd attend without her grandfather. Tears blurred her vision.

"Oh, sweetie," Andrea reached over and clenched her hand. "Please talk to me. You're still grieving. It would help if you let it out."

Shaking her head, Izzy took an even bigger sip of her drink. "I'm fine. Really. I know it's going to take time. I really do. This is what I need. Working. Planning the party." She sucked in a deep breath, feeling the alcohol already hit her brain. "Staying busy helps me to cope."

"Are you going to move back into the cabin?"

Richard Craig's cabin sat on a hill about half a mile from the resort. He had lived there for twenty years and Izzy had lived there for the last three years taking care of him. On the day after the funeral, Izzy had moved all of her belongings into a room on the second floor of the Lakewood. She just couldn't deal with being at the cabin by herself.

"I haven't decided yet. I mean, maybe I'll move back in at some point, but not now. The only time I spent there with Grandpa was when he was sick. That's all I think about when I'm in the cabin. And I don't want to remember him like that. Does that make sense?"

Andrea squeezed her hand. "Of course it does. Of course."

With a deep breath, Izzy turned her attention to Andi's laptop and moved over so she could see the screen.

An hour later, Andi closed the computer, and both women were pleased with the preparations they'd made. All the food and decorations were now planned out, as well as their costumes. Next, they just had to start placing supply orders.

"Why don't you join me for a drink before you head home?" Izzy asked.

Andrea's face tightened as she looked at her watch. "Oh! I didn't realize it was so late. I really have to go!"

"It's only 7:00." Izzy laughed. "What are you talking about?"

"You don't understand. Brian doesn't like it when I—"Andrea stopped suddenly. "I just have to go. I'll see you in the morning, okay?"

Izzy frowned, but didn't stop her friend as she gathered her things. Andrea leaned over and gave her a quick kiss on the cheek before she raced out of the restaurant.

Draining what was left in her glass, Izzy looked out at the night. The trees were swallowed by the darkness, but she could make out the lights on the boats that bobbed on the water. People out for dinner cruises, lolling on the lake.

"Nolan!" Izzy heard the bartender boom as someone strode up to the bar, and she immediately jerked her head around to look.

Her mouth dropped open as the gorgeous man walked through the door of the hotel bar. Her heart usually skipped a beat whenever Sheriff Graham Nolan walked into the room, but today, Izzy was pretty sure her heart had galloped right out of her chest. Frowning, she studied his profile as he smiled at something the bartender said. He'd shaved. That was weird. Graham hated to shave. And his brown hair was shorter than last time she'd seen it. This was much more of a clean-cut look than the tousled waves that usually brushed his collar.

She turned, looking out the window again. As much as she missed Graham, she didn't know if she had the emotional strength to deal with him right now.

Her finger absently traced the rim of her rum and coke and she let her mind wander to Graham, sneaking glances at his incredible denim-encased backside as he talked to Milo at the bar.

Graham had been so tender with her when her grandfather had passed away. But just when Isabel thought they were finally making a breakthrough, he had backed off again. She could still feel how he'd put his arms around her and held her as she cried, lightly stroking her hair until her sobs had eased. And then when she had wanted to talk to him, he had walked away. Just like always. Those few brief moments were enough for her to miss him desperately, to crave his touch.

Izzy snuck a look back at the bar and her mouth went dry. Graham had turned, and he was staring right at her. A corner of his mouth tipped up in a slow smile before Izzy realized she was staring back. She quickly turned back to her table and looked into her rum and coke as if it held all the answers. She desperately hoped he hadn't seen her blush.

****

Now that is what I'm talking about. Chris's mouth practically dropped open when he spotted the gorgeous blonde sitting by the window. She was turned so she could look out at the lake, and Chris studied her openly.

Her ivory skin glowed in the light from the jack o'lantern on her table. She looked to be petite, but she had full breasts. Her wavy hair stopped at about the middle of her back, and as he watched, she reached up to absently twist a strand around her finger. He wondered if she ever wore it in a ponytail. He loved ponytails. He could wrap it around his hand and hold it with a firm grip while he guided her toward his—

"Here you go, Nolan," Milo said, setting a pint of Boulevard beer in front of him. Shifting in his seat, Chris realized how uncomfortable his jeans had become.

"Dude, do you know who that is? She's gorgeous."

Snorting, Milo just shook his head. "What the hell is it with you Nolan boys?"

Narrowing his eyes, Chris asked, "What the hell is that supposed to mean?" Sipping his beer, he watched Milo shake his head. The men had been friends since second grade, so Chris was pretty good at reading his old friend.

"It means that even when you're not trying, you and Graham manage to choose the same girl."

Coughing on his beer, Chris tried to take a breath. "You mean she's—are you trying to tell me she's Graham's?"

Cocking his head slightly, Milo thought for a moment. "Well, I don't know if I would define her as being his, but I will say that he doesn't have eyes for anyone but her."

"Hey, barkeep! A beer over this way!" said a voice from the end of the bar.

Milo rolled his eyes and mumbled, "Barkeep. Fuck, I hate tourists."

After Milo walked away, Chris turned again to look at the blonde and was pleased to find her staring right at him. He smiled slowly at her, and almost laughed as her eyes flared briefly before she spun back toward the window. *Well, that is the look of a woman who's interested if I ever saw one.* Maybe Graham *was* interested in her, but the way she was looking at Chris told him she might not feel the same way. In fact, he'd love nothing more than to explore the heat in those big eyes. Picking up his beer, he took a deep breath. "Here goes nothing."

****

"Hello, beautiful," said that familiar warm, velvet voice, as Graham sidled up to her table.

Izzy almost jumped because she hadn't realized he had moved so close. She glanced up and realized he was staring down at her with a slightly amused expression.

Get it together, Izzy!

"This is a surprise." Izzy slowly looked the man up and down, taking in his dark jeans and light blue button down shirt that set off the blue flecks in those steel-gray eyes. She smiled appreciatively, enjoying the sight of his big muscular body in something other than his sheriff's uniform.

When Izzy looked into Graham's face, she frowned slightly. It was so weird to see him shaven. She'd never seen him without the close-cropped beard he always wore. It constantly invaded her thoughts because she couldn't help but wonder how that beard would feel when he kissed her mouth. Would it be scratchy when he put those full lips on her breasts? Or when he moved that gorgeous mouth lower, would he—

Izzy sucked in a breath, trying to rid herself of the sexual thoughts. It was pointless, right? She shot a glance up to Graham's face and saw his amused expression. Oh no, how long had she been sitting there studying his entire body?

"I like your look," she blurted out, gesturing up and down his body.

Graham's smirk turned into a wide grin revealing perfect white teeth. Oh, that smile sent a jolt of electricity right through her body every time. He pulled out the chair next to hers and moved it closer to Izzy before sitting down. Leaning forward so his face was a couple of inches from hers, he said, "Well, I *love* your look, sweetheart."

Izzy's pussy clenched in response. She loved it when he called her sweetheart. Was he actually flirting with her? What had gotten into him? The two times she had dared to flirt with him, he had looked at her like she was a piranha ready to bite his head off, and then he'd put up that wall he'd built so effectively around himself, shutting her out completely. The one time she had been so brazen as to ask him to dinner, he had quickly refused, then ran away so fast, he'd nearly left skid marks.

But he wasn't running now.

****

Chris reached out his hand to introduce himself, "Hi. I'm—"

"All right, Nolan, here's your scotch," interrupted the booming voice as the tattooed bartender set his drink down on the table at the seat next to the blonde. "Don't forget to tip me."

Chris smiled at Milo, saluting him with his middle finger, but the man just laughed. "That hurts, Nolan. Seriously," he said, shooting a wink at Izzy.

"Can I get you another drink, Miss Izzy?" Milo asked. "Another spiced rum and Diet Coke?"

"Uh, no. No, I'm good, Mi. Thanks. I think I'm going to head up to my room soon, and I don't want to wake up with a headache tomorrow."

Chris's entire body heated up at the visual of Izzy slipping in between the sheets of her bed. He wondered if she slept nude, and he thought of sliding his hands over her, feeling that petite body next to his.

"Okay, darlin'. You just let me know if this joker gives you any trouble," said Milo, slapping Chris on the back before heading back to the bar.

Chris sat next to Izzy and took a sip of his drink as he studied her. When she looked back up at him, he heard her slight intake of breath and realized he was staring at her with a look that probably conveyed how much he wanted to fuck her.

"Um, you know, I should really go," she said nervously.

Chris panicked slightly at the thought of her getting up and walking away. "Please don't go." He grasped her hand. "Stay and finish your drink with me."

Izzy glanced at him, chewing on her bottom. She looked as though a war was taking place inside her head. Finally, she said, "I suppose I could at least finish my drink." Chris blew out a relieved breath as he watched her turn to look out the window. "I do love this time of night," she said wistfully. "The lake right after sunset, when the moon is rising. It's so beautiful."

"It is beautiful," Chris said, gazing at her. "But I'm looking at something more beautiful than the view." He ran his thumb over her knuckles, pleased at the way she jumped.

Izzy looked back up at him and blushed furiously, but her eyes heated up. There was a hunger there for him. Chris was certain of that.

Yanking her hand away from his, Izzy gripped her drink tightly. She studied the amber liquid in her glass, swirling it around. It almost seemed to Chris like she was trying to make up her mind about something.

Chris's hand felt like it ignited when he'd touched her. He could feel the intense heat between them. He watched her look at his hands still resting on the table, and then up to his face. Her eyes were hooded and dark. She felt it too.

"I can't do this," Izzy whispered. "I'm so confused, and right now I just don't have the energy to try and figure out what's happening here."

Chris's heart clenched at the vulnerability in Izzy's voice. "I'm sorry if I came on too strong. Really, I just wanted some company while I have a drink."

He meant it. There was no doubt he was straining to get inside of Izzy, but he didn't want to scare her. He didn't understand what he was feeling right now, and was taken aback by the electricity that seemed to sizzle through him when he touched her.

She eyed him warily. Even though Chris was giving her an out, he was sure the desire on his face completely betrayed his words. He resisted the urge to reach out and twist one of those blonde waves around his finger.

"What exactly are you doing here?" she asked, her voice breathless as she tried to avoid his gaze.

Chris studied her intently, watching her pink-stained cheeks, the way her eyes kept sliding away from his. He would bet every penny he had that she was sexually submissive, and his cock hardened as he thought of her kneeling before him, presenting herself to him. He would hold her in his arms while Graham would—*Good lord, where had that thought come from?* He gave his head a shake to clear the thoughts and took a deep breath. *Slow down, dammit.*

"I'm here on business. How about you? What brings you here?"

"The Lounge, you mean? Well, it has been a long couple of weeks since my grandpa died, and Milo makes the drinks strong." She tried to smile, but it didn't reach her eyes.

Chris frowned as he really noticed the sadness in her eyes, and fought the urge to reach out and gather her close to him. Wow, he needed to back off. This lovely woman was vulnerable, and he certainly didn't want to take advantage of that. Yet, he felt a protective urge for her too. He hated the sorrow that was so evident in her face, and wanted desperately to take it away, to make her laugh.

"I'm sorry. I know this must be a very difficult time for you."

Izzy simply nodded and took a deep breath. Chris wanted to ask more about her grandfather, but Izzy forged ahead, obviously not wanting to talk about it. Chris knew what she was going through. He and Graham had lost their dad when they were sixteen. It helped having friends around you, but it didn't take away that sense of helplessness.

"So what kind of business do you have here exactly? Why aren't you staying in town?"

Ah, she must be wondering why he wasn't staying with his mom. At least she didn't ask why he wasn't staying with his brother—that had been Milo's first question. Chris just shrugged. "It's just easier here, I guess. Plus, it worked out perfectly because I got to see you."

Izzy's eyebrow went up as she looked at him quizzically. "Why are you playing with me?"

Why was she so convinced he was playing with her? What the hell had Graham done to her? "No games, sweetheart. I'll tell you anything you want to know about me. All you have to do is ask."

Izzy sat back and looked at him thoughtfully. "Really? And you'll answer everything honestly?"

"Absolutely," Chris said.

Izzy took a deep breath. "Why are you flirting with me?"

That surprised him. "Seriously?"

She blushed so beautifully, her eyes sliding away from his as her fingers nervously played with the edge of a napkin. "Never mind. I shouldn't have asked that."

"No, that's a perfectly reasonable question. It just amazes me that you would be at all surprised when a man flirts with you. We're going to have to do something about your self-esteem, sweetheart. You're incredibly beautiful."

She needed to know how incredible she was, how with one glance at her, she'd mentally brought him to his knees. He wanted her to know how desirable she was, wanted her to know what she did to him. So Chris decided to take a chance. She would either embrace it or slap him across the face. He leaned in so only Izzy could hear him.

"It's more than your beauty, though. It's the way your body screams to be fucked." He chuckled at Izzy's sharp intake of breath, and was pleased when she didn't pull away.

Taking that as encouragement, he continued. "I wonder how that full mouth of yours will feel when I suck on your bottom lip. Will you moan? How will you feel when I slide my cock into you? Will you stare up at me with those big blue eyes and whimper as I make you come? Or will you shut them tight and scream out your orgasm?" Chris inched closer, his breath caressing Izzy's neck. "I'll bet I can make you scream, sweetheart."

He felt a shudder go through Izzy's body, and he leaned back in his chair, shifting uncomfortably at his growing erection. Izzy looked down, noticing his problem, and he thought her eyes were going to bug out of her head. Damn, her innocence was so sexy. Her hands shook so badly that she clasped them together in her lap, twisting her fingers.

She swallowed hard and started to speak, but kept her eyes locked on her hands. "You...I mean I—I . . . but . . ." She clamped her mouth shut, and he smiled, watching her take a couple of steadying breaths.

"Look at me, Izzy," he said with a gentle firmness. "I want to see you."

She looked up into his eyes without hesitation. She stared at him for several moments before testing out her voice again. "You . . . want me?" she practically squeaked.

Chris shook his head in amazement. "We are really going to have to do something about your self-esteem. Why on earth does that seem to come as such a surprise to you?"

She held his gaze. "I just never thought that you would," she said softly.

Chris leaned into her again, his hand going up to cup her cheek, his thumb stroking over that full bottom lip. Izzy's eyes closed as she released a whimper from the back of her throat. Oh, that did things to him.

"I've been honest with you, Izzy. Now I want you to be honest with me. Can you do that?"

She opened her eyes as she leaned into his hand, which was softly stroking her cheek, her hair, and down her neck.

"Uh - yes." She swallowed visibly. "Yes, I can."

"Good. Then tell me something. Tell me what you want, Izzy. What do you want right now?"

This time Izzy didn't hesitate. "You," she said softly. "I want you. I've wanted you since the moment I saw you." Izzy leaned forward slightly, her lips a centimeter from his.

Chris marveled at this woman. She had an innocence about her, a trusting nature that made him want to shield her from the world. There was a sadness in her eyes that he wanted to take away. He wanted to bring her pleasure, make her forget everything except him.

His hand went around the nape of her neck, and her lips parted in anticipation a moment before he lightly touched them with his own. He felt her softly gasp at his gentle touch, and he took advantage of her open mouth to slide his tongue past her lips, opening, tasting.

He almost groaned at the sensation of her tongue tentatively gliding over his. Oh, she tasted better than he'd imagined, and his mind was spinning. Chris slanted his mouth over hers, causing a moan to escape from Izzy as he deepened the kiss. That moan surged through him, lighting up his soul.

A loud peal of laughter startled them both back to reality, and Izzy yanked away from Chris, her hand going to her slightly swollen lips as she stared in awe at him. Chris looked up to see three women come in and settle themselves at the large bar in the center of the room, talking and laughing loudly.

He looked back at Izzy, barely trusting himself to speak. "Upstairs?" he whispered, his eyes a silent plea for her to agree with him. She stared at him, and he could practically hear the wheels turning in her head. Chris leaned forward to put his hands on her upper thighs, and began to rub them lightly. "Please, Izzy. I want you.

Please stay with me tonight. Be with me." He meant it as a question, but it came out as more of a command.

No games, he'd said. He was making it very clear what he wanted. After a moment that seemed to last a lifetime, Izzy made the choice as to what she wanted, too.

She looked into Chris's smoldering gaze and nodded, reaching out a hand to tentatively take his. "Upstairs," she agreed in a soft voice.

Chris smiled, grasping her hand, pulling her up before anchoring an arm firmly around her waist. "Let's go," he said as he led her out of the hotel bar to the elevator.

****

Dangerous. Every time Izzy looked at Graham Nolan, *dangerous* was the word that came to mind. Not because he was a bad boy, not because he was too rough, or because she was afraid of him, but because of the way he seized her heart when he didn't even try. And Izzy's heart clenched when she looked at him now as he led her to the elevator, his arm around her waist, burning into her skin with his sensual heat.

She was so used to seeing him in his sheriff's uniform with that damn cowboy hat perched on his head. When he did take the hat off, his dark wavy hair was always unruly, falling to his collar. She wondered what business he had at the hotel that was important enough for him to shave and dress up. He almost looked like a different person.

She'd wanted him for so long, but not only for sex. She wanted to go down this path with him, but part of her was afraid that she wouldn't be able to recover when he'd had his fill. He was so good at drawing her close and then pushing her away. Most of the time, she didn't think he meant to do either. But it always hurt, nonetheless. Would he do it again? Would he push her away this time?

It was this thought that had her stopping in her tracks before they reached the elevator. Graham turned to her as she suddenly stopped. "Izzy? Baby, are you okay?"

"Um, yeah. I'm just…" She trailed off, looking down.

She immediately felt his finger underneath her chin, tilting her face up so he could look in her eyes. "You're just what? Honesty, remember?"

She nodded and swallowed. "Scared," she said finally. "I'm scared. Nervous." Saying the words out loud made it seem ridiculous. She was a grown woman. A twenty-six-year-old single woman about to indulge in sex with a gorgeous man. Sex! She had only had sex twice in her entire life.

"I'm sorry. I'm being silly," she said, shaking her head.

"No, you're not," he said, stroking her cheek with the backs of his knuckles. "You're being sweet, and honest. I'm glad you're talking to me. Tell me what you're scared of. Me? I would never hurt you. I need you to know that."

"I know." That's not what she was scared of. Her biggest fear was watching him walk away, but she didn't think now was the time to bring that up. Having Graham for a night would be better than never having him at all.

He reached down to take her hands, and she almost gasped at the hunger that was so evident in his eyes. Oh, she could feel her pussy throbbing for him. This would be worth it.

"We don't have to do this," he said softly. "We can walk back into The Lounge and have a drink, I can kiss you good night, and that can be it."

She knew he meant it. She looked into his chiseled face, enjoying the fact that she could see his features more clearly without the beard. His full lips, high cheekbones, the lone dimple that peeked out of his left cheek when he smiled. He may not be able to love her back, but he wanted her. He wanted her! Her heart leapt with joy even as her head told her this was a bad idea. She had wanted him so badly for so long. She had loved him for three years. Even if it was just for one night, she needed him. She didn't want to think about what happened afterward. She needed to feel his arms around her, feel him inside of her.

She shook her head firmly. "I want this." Izzy took the last few steps to the elevator and pushed the button before turning back to the gorgeous man before her. "I want you."

Chapter Two

Sheriff Graham Nolan leaned back in his worn desk chair and rubbed his hands over his face. It had been a long fucking day.

"Sheriff Nolan, sir, I'm all wrapped up here."

Bouncing into the room, Jillian smiled. After six months of working for him, she still insisted on addressing him formally, and after three months, he'd finally given up insisting that she call him Graham.

Not that he minded formality under the right circumstances. God knows he imagined Izzy calling him "Sir" enough times. Usually when he imagined that, he was also envisioning her handcuffed to his bed. Stifling a groan at the thought, he turned his attention back to his secretary.

"Sir? Are you alright?" Jillian asked, looking slightly concerned.

Pasting on a smile, Graham tried to rid himself of his usual Izzy sex thoughts. "Fine. Everything is fine, Jillian. Did Viv need me to come out?"

"No, no," Jillian waved her hand toward the phone. "I had a long conversation with her. I kept reminding her that even if you came out, you wouldn't be able to catch the ghosts haunting her house because they would slip right through the handcuffs."

Graham put his head down on his desk and sighed. Vivian Warner was a 65-year-old woman who was born and raised in Magic. She lived on the outskirts of town in a huge three-story house that looked like it was right out of the movie *Psycho*. As if that wasn't enough to scare people off, Vivian was convinced her house was haunted, and the ghosts were out to get her. Her house didn't scare everyone off, though. Izzy visited the woman often to make sure she had everything she needed, and she just loved the fact that Viv's house looked like something out of a horror movie.

Jillian continued. "She said that since it's nearing Halloween, the veil between the human world and the spirit world is much thinner. She said there's a better chance for you to catch the ghost because it might take human form. But she thinks the ghost is Cleopatra. I told her that Cleopatra wouldn't hurt her because she was suicidal, not homicidal."

Graham snorted, lifting his head. "And that worked?"

"Yep! That seems to be the key. Everyone tries so hard to convince Viv that ghosts don't exist. It's much easier to convince her that she has a good ghost and not an evil one." Jillian pushed her large glasses up on her nose, looking quite pleased with herself. "I even called Lane and told him not to worry."

Lane Warner, Vivian's only son, lived outside Kansas City in a small town called Preston, but called the station often to keep tabs on his mom and make sure she wasn't causing too much trouble. Graham laughed. "I don't know what I'd do without you, Jilly."

Jillian wiggled her eyebrows at him. "Good. That means I'm indispensable. Oh! Don't forget to call Milo back. He called when you were on the other line. Said it was important."

Graham promised to call Milo and watched Jillian scurry out the door. He looked at his watch: 8:00. Milo was working the hotel bar tonight. Dammit, he was probably going to ask Graham to come out for a drink. Tapping his fingers on his desk, he looked out the window. Would Izzy be around? He felt guilty for avoiding her since her grandfather's funeral.

The quiet intimacy they'd shared in those few brief moments scared him, but it was ridiculous to avoid her. His heart had been breaking as she'd sobbed in his arms. He wanted nothing more than to hold her forever, soothe her, and not let anything hurt her ever again.

Rubbing his eyes, he pushed down those feelings. The protectiveness he felt toward her was exactly why he pushed her away. If he got too close, he would hurt her, and he didn't want that. He couldn't do it. He cared too much about her. But dammit, she was getting harder to resist.

"Oh, sweetheart," he whispered aloud, running his hands through his hair. Suddenly a tingling jolt went through Graham's belly, so strong that it startled him. He knew that feeling. It was easy to tell when he had a feeling that belonged to his damn brother.

"Fuck. I'm horny and miserable, and Chris is getting lucky. Not fucking fair." Graham mumbled, reaching for the phone to call Milo.

The phone was answered on the first ring. "Lakewood Lounge," Milo's gravelly voice said.

"Hey man," Graham started. "I don't know if I can come out ton—"

"Graham!" Milo interrupted. "You have to get out here!"

Graham shot up straight in his chair, alarmed by Milo's urgency.

"What is it? Is it Izzy? Is she okay? What happened?" He was getting up, already grabbing his keys.

"No, it's nothing like that. She's fine."

Graham breathed a sigh of relief, until Milo continued.

"She's with your brother."

"My brother?" Graham asked, confused. "What are you talking about? Chris is in St. Louis."

"No. No, he's right here," Milo said. "And he was just making out with Izzy right before they took an elevator up to the rooms."

"What?" Graham bellowed into the phone.

"About twenty minutes ago. You'd better get your ass down here."

Graham was already ending the call before Milo could finish, and shoving the phone into his pocket, as he headed for his truck.

****

Chris unlocked the door to his room and held it open for Izzy. He could smell her lavender scent as she walked in, loving the way her wavy blonde hair tumbled down her back. He imagined how that hair would look with his hands fisted in it as she had that beautiful mouth wrapped around his cock.

Damn, he really needed to control those types of thoughts. Usually, he was good at maintaining control, but something about this woman made him feel distinctly out of control. The way she looked at him both thrilled and scared him, those eyes full of so much trust. He should have run. Normally if a woman looked at him like that, he would have. But Izzy was different. He was confused by the need to protect her, and the ache to take her to bed and fuck her until she was screaming her release.

Her nervous energy was palpable, the way she twisted her shaky fingers together and swallowed repeatedly. She'd been torn on whether to come up with him. Not because she wasn't turned on, but because he was pretty damned sure she wasn't the type of woman to go to bed with strangers. He really didn't want her to change her mind about him, though. *Play it cool, Nolan.*

41

"What are you thinking?" she asked, turning to look up at him with those wide eyes.

Chris reached out to brush a stray curl off her forehead, reveling at the way her breath caught when he touched her. He ran a thumb across her bottom lip, and almost groaned as he thought of the things he wanted her to do with that mouth. Even better, he thought about all the things he wanted to do *to* her.

Chris leaned in close so his voice was just a whisper against her ear. "I was thinking how good you must taste, the sounds you make when you come, and I was imagining how good it's going to feel when I'm inside of you."

Pulling back, he smiled as he saw Izzy's face. Her cheeks were flushed, and her lips were slightly parted, those big eyes staring up at him. His cock swelled, and he held back a groan. He couldn't wait. He had to taste her now.

Pulling her close, Chris leaned down to capture her mouth. He felt her tense, raising her hands to his chest. At first, he was afraid she might push him away, but as he sucked her bottom lip into his mouth, he felt her slight whimper against him, and her hands clenched the front of his shirt as her lower body leaned into him, pressing against his erection.

Her lips parted to allow him access, and he seized the moment, his tongue thrusting inside, tasting her sweetness. Izzy's arms drifted up around his neck as she returned the kiss, her tongue rubbing against his.

He pulled away and stared down at her flushed cheeks. "Do you want to tell me what you're thinking now?" he asked.

"I— I was just thinking how that kiss was so much better than I ever thought it would be."

Chris smiled. He didn't remember the last time anyone had made him smile so much. "And is kissing me something you've thought about a lot?" he asked teasingly.

Her flushed face grew even redder. "It is," she said seriously. "I've thought about it a lot."

Chris frowned at her serious tone, but she stepped away from him before he could respond, her fingers going to the buttons on her blouse. His mouth went dry.

Reaching out, he covered Izzy's small hands with his large ones. "Let me."

She stared at him for two heartbeats before she dropped her hands in his and let him lead her to the king-sized bed.

****

Shifting nervously, Izzy looked at the giant bed. She didn't have much sexual experience. She was twenty-six years old, but she'd only had two lovers her entire life. The first one had been a boyfriend during her freshman year in college who had been just as inexperienced as she had. The second one in her senior year had mainly been concerned about his own pleasure.

What if Graham was disappointed with her? What if she didn't know how to please him or what to do?

Before she could turn and run from sheer nerves, she felt his arms come around her from behind, wrapping around her middle. His chest pressed against her back, his warmth sinking into her.

"You seem tense, sweetheart. Do I make you nervous?" he asked, moving her hair away from her neck so he could nuzzle her nape.

Oh, even though he'd shaved, he had a five o'clock shadow that scraped against the sensitive skin of her neck. Her breath caught at the slight pain that sent shockwaves directly to her pussy.

"Yes," she breathed. Wait, what had he asked her? "No, I mean. No. You don't make me nervous."

He chuckled, and she felt his chest rumble against her back. She leaned into his strength, his arms tightening around her. His hot breath caressed her neck a moment before she felt the tip of his tongue.

"Oh," she breathed.

His gentle lips kissed along her neck nipping lightly, her skin sizzling where he touched.

"You're so responsive," he breathed against her. "Tell me, Izzy, are you sensitive everywhere?"

Before she could answer him, his hands moved from around her waist and up to cup her breasts. Her nipples hardened into pebbles before he even touched her. Cupping her breasts, his thumbs circled those hard peaks, the fabric of her blouse causing just the lightest amount of friction. At his light pinch on her nipples, Izzy's knees buckled, and she melted against him, arousal flooding her system so she couldn't even see straight.

Suddenly her feet left the ground, and she squeaked as he lifted her in his arms. As he laid her gently on the bed, she looked up to see the intensity in his eyes. He stepped back to pull his blue shirt off over his head without even bothering to unbutton it.

Oh, he was magnificent. Izzy had seen Graham without a shirt before when they'd both gone boating with mutual friends, but now she could openly admire the man in front of her without feeling like she had to sneak quick peeks at him.

He was utter perfection, with a sprinkling of dark hair over his well-defined chest. Izzy's eyes trailed to his ab muscles that rippled as he unbuttoned his pants, shoving them down. He stood in front of her now only in a pair of boxer briefs, and she had to stop herself from groaning as she looked at the notches at his hips. That had to be the sexiest part of a man's body.

Without thinking, she sat up and reached out a hand, her fingers tracing the notch at his right hip, causing his erection to twitch. Izzy smiled, pleased with the power she felt. Graham always seemed to render her completely defenseless. It felt good to be able to have an effect on him.

"You're killing me, Izzy," he groaned as she ran her hand over his ab muscles, wanting to feel every inch of him. Sitting up, she traced her fingers over his nipples, and gasped when his hand suddenly shot out and grabbed her wrist. "My turn," he said gruffly. And all of a sudden, she was on her back with his body half covering hers.

Izzy opened her mouth to say his name, but before she could talk, his mouth was on hers, his tongue plundering, waking up her body as if she'd been asleep her whole life. His tongue thrust into her mouth, mimicking what she wanted his cock to do. When he broke the kiss, she realized her blouse and her jeans were completely unbuttoned.

She blinked up at him. "How did you do that?"

His dimple flashed as he shrugged one shoulder. "Skill," he said with a wicked gleam in his eye.

She laughed, but the sound turned into a gasp as his fingers unhooked the front clasp of her bra, her breasts spilling free. Instinctively, Izzy put her arms up to cover herself, but he would have none of it.

"Oh no, you don't." He pushed her arms above her head, holding her wrists immobile with one large hand. She was shocked at how much his authority turned her on. Graham was always so gentle with her, but this side of him had her wet and aching.

"You're mine tonight, sweetheart," he said, his fingers finding a nipple, his thumb gently stroking the hard nub. "And I want to see what's mine. Taste what's mine."

His? She bit her lip to stifle a moan when he bent his head to take one hard nipple into his mouth, sucking firmly as his fingers found the other one, rolling it between his thumb and forefinger. Oh yes, she was most definitely his. Somewhere in the back of her hazy brain was the nagging question of why now? Why, after all this time, did he finally notice her now? And not *just* notice her, but claim her as his own. They should talk first, said the nagging voice. There were so many questions.

But as his teeth gently bit down on her engorged nipple, all thoughts fled from her brain, replaced with intense need.

"Oh God!" she cried out at the pain/pleasure. She had never experienced such arousal. She wanted to touch him and tried to yank her hands free, but his firm grip tightened on her wrists. The restraint only heightened her arousal, and she could feel her pussy flooding, wanting. She could only arch her back in an attempt to push her breasts up, seeking more attention. "Please," she whispered. "Oh, please."

"Please what, Izzy?" He lifted his head to look at her with his intense gray blue eyes. "Tell me what you want."

How was he so good at talking when her brain couldn't form a sentence?

"You," she breathed. "I want you."

He smirked. "You want me to do what, baby? This?" he said, circling his thumb around her nipple again.

"Please! More."

"More what? I want you to tell me."

If she wasn't already completely flushed with pleasure, she knew her face would be even redder. She wasn't good at talking dirty. It felt foreign to her. But any embarrassment she felt took a backseat to her desire. She would tell Graham exactly what he wanted if it meant that he would stop teasing her and take her now.

"I want your cock inside of me. Please. I need you. I feel so empty. I want you to take me and fill me up. I want to taste you when you—"

Her words were cut off by his harsh groan as his mouth slammed down on hers.

****

Chris couldn't deny this woman. God, she was so beautiful. His tongue toyed with hers as his hand went to her hip. It was time to get her out of these clothes, rid himself of the barrier that was separating him from this passionate woman. "Izzy," he breathed.

Her blue eyes were filled with arousal. She was so fucking responsive. And so incredibly starved for affection, leaning into his every touch, her breath hitching. How was it that no one had tapped into that incredible well of passion simmering beneath the surface of this gorgeous woman?

A lot of women had shared his bed over the years, but never in his life had he met one so reactive. Her body was close to exploding just from him playing with her breasts. Chris knew she would go off the second he touched her.

He wanted this to last, but he needed her so badly. Her creamy skin tasted like honey. He thought his cock was going to burst at the sight of her firm breasts, and those nipples that looked like small plump berries waiting to be devoured.

After making quick work of the rest of her clothes, he slid off his boxer briefs before sliding between her legs. Izzy's hands grasped his shoulders as she tilted her head up for his kiss.

And he took that mouth, demanding more from her now, devouring. Any willpower Chris had left was rapidly evaporating. He tore his mouth from hers, his voice rough. "I wanted to go slow."

Izzy's eyes gleamed. "Next time. We can do slow next time." She leaned up to his ear, nipping the lobe gently between her teeth. "But right now, I want . . ." She took a shaky breath. "I want you to fuck me."

"Fuck, baby, yes." That was all Chris needed. That beautiful assent from Izzy. How had he gotten so lucky to meet this incredible woman and have her want him? But she did want him, and he needed her now.

Sliding off the bed, he snatched his pants from the floor and fumbled in his wallet for a condom. Izzy's eyes focused on him as he ripped open the plastic with his teeth and sheathed himself quickly before climbing back between her legs. He was determined not to go too fast, and he knew if he let himself plunge into her like he wanted, he wouldn't be able to hold back. Instead, he rolled over on his back, taking her with him.

Grasping her hips, Chris moved her to straddle him, his cock pressing against the slickness of her pussy. Oh, she was so wet. He could feel her juices flowing as his cock slid up against her.

Looking up at her as if she were a goddess, he marveled at every move. She brushed her hair to one side before leaning down and pressing her mouth to his. No longer hesitant, no longer holding back, her tongue found his as her hips gently ground against him.

Groaning, he closed his eyes at the sweet torture. "Sweetheart, you really are going to kill me." Now he was the one begging. "I need you. Now." He pushed her back slightly so he could line himself up against her opening. "Fuck me, baby."

His hands went to her waist, and he held her steady as she lowered herself onto his cock. It took every ounce of willpower he had not to bury himself up inside her in one quick thrust, but he was determined not to hurt her. He looked into her face to see her eyes squeezed shut.

"No, Iz. Open your eyes. I want your eyes on me when I fuck you."

Her eyes popped open and locked directly onto his. Her warm hands centered on his chest to balance herself, as she slid his cock into her.

Chris threw his head back. "You're so tight. God, I've never felt anything so good." Her wetness surrounded him like a velvet glove, and he knew he wouldn't last.

Her pussy clenched around him as she fully seated herself. A slight grimace flickered over her face, and she immediately started to move, but Chris stilled her.

"Not yet, baby. Get used to me first."

She nodded and took a slow breath, making Chris smile. Brave girl, trying so hard to please him.

"Are you gonna talk to me?" he asked.

"I…" She licked her lips. "I just never imagined that it would feel…that *you* would feel . . ." She groaned as he flexed his cock inside of her.

Reaching up, he grasped her head gently and pulled her down to him, capturing her mouth. He kissed her deeply, feeling her body relax, her hips gently grinding against him. She was ready, and he was quickly losing control.

Holding on to her waist, Chris steadied her as she lifted herself almost all the way off his cock and slid slowly back down. Squeezing his eyes shut, he savored the sweet torture.

"Oh no. Eyes on me," Izzy breathed, mimicking his earlier words.

Chris opened his eyes, locking gazes with her as they began a steady rhythm. He rocked his hips up as she slid down on him, her movements becoming faster, her body tensing, her pussy grasping his cock.

He watched Izzy's face, and felt his heart clench. What had she done to him? He had known this woman all of an hour, and never in his life had he felt this kind of joy, such fire, such energy with anyone.

Trying to hold off was futile, as he felt the tingling in his balls start already. He moved his hand from her waist and slid it in between them, his fingers finding her clit.

Izzy's small hands clenched around his forearms, and he could tell she was close.

"I want to feel you come." Chris said, his thumb sliding over her engorged clit. He pressed firmly against the hard nub. "Come with me, Izzy."

He stroked twice before he felt her body go completely rigid, her eyes close tightly as the wave crested and swept over her. She threw her head back and cried out.

Her orgasm set off his own, and he felt the jittering tingle along his spine. He thrust faster and faster into her spasming body before his own muscles tensed, and he groaned in pleasure, emptying himself into the thin latex barrier that separated them.

Collapsing on top of him, Izzy's breathing was as ragged as his own, their heartbeats racing.

As the two of them floated back to earth, Chris reached up to stroke her hair. "Are you okay?" he asked, fearing that he'd gone too fast, been too rough.

"Oh, yes," Izzy sighed contentedly against him. "Yes, Graham, I'm perfect."

Chris's hand stilled in her hair. Graham? No, he didn't hear her right. He imagined that.

Izzy raised her head up from his chest, looking at him. "What's wrong?" she asked, concern showing in her eyes. "Graham, is everything okay?"

Chris lay there stunned, searching the face of the woman who had just trusted him, given herself to him, shared that incredible passion that simmered beneath her surface. Except she hadn't given it to him. She'd given it to his fucking brother.

He'd told her his name, hadn't he? He was sure he did. He thought back to the bar. He'd walked up to her table to introduce himself, and then . . . no, they had been interrupted. He'd never gotten out the words 'I'm Chris.'

He raised a hand to cover his face. "No. No. No. Oh, fuck!"

Izzy slipped off him, alarmed. "What is it? What's wrong?"

Before Chris could answer, there was a pounding at the door to the room, making them both jump. "Open up, you son of a bitch! I know she's in there! Izzy!"

****

Izzy sat on the bed, trying to wrap her brain around what was happening. "Graham?" That was Graham's voice at the door. But how could he be at the door when he—
She looked at the man next to her who was sitting up disposing of the condom. She felt horrified as the realization began to hit her. The business clothes, the clean-cut face. "Wait. You're . . ."

Chris sat on the edge of the bed, and turned to look at her with regret in his eyes. "I'm not Graham."

"Chris, damn it, open this fucking door!"

"Oh God! Ohmigod!" Izzy scrambled off the bed. What had she done?

"You're Chris. You're Graham's brother." She knew Graham had a brother, but a twin? No one had ever said the word "twin" much less "identical twin." Graham couldn't have fucking shared that little tidbit when he'd talked about his brother?

Scrambling to yank on her panties and blouse, she looked over to see that Chris had slipped his boxer briefs back on.

Chris sighed. "Yeah," he said grimly. "I'm the brother." He started to walk toward Izzy, but she backed up, and he stopped, cursing.

"Izzy, I didn't lie to you. I didn't know you thought I was Graham. If I'd know, I never for a second would have . . ." He trailed off, looking at the bed.

Tears stung her eyes, and she jumped again as the pounding on the door got louder, more threatening. Graham sounded like he was about to break through it with his fists.

"Dammit," Chris muttered and strode to the door, yanking it open, looking like he was ready for a confrontation.

Graham lunged through the doorway, his eyes shooting fire. Izzy's hands were shaking too much to button her blouse, so she closed it over her breasts. Graham took one look at her in her blouse and panties before rounding on his brother. His fist shot out so fast that Izzy doubted it even registered with Chris until after it connected with his face.

His head snapped back. "Son of a bitch, Graham! What the fuck?" Chris reached up to touch a finger to his bloody lip.

"Graham!" Izzy screamed, launching herself at him, grasping his arm with both of her hands before he could rear back and hit Chris again. "What are you doing?"

She'd never seen him look so angry. He turned to her, grasping her shoulders. She would have been scared, if his touch weren't so gentle on her, his eyes assessing her, as if he was looking for injuries. Even so, he gave her a little shake, that careful control slipping. "Izzy, how could you. . . No." He stopped himself. "We're not doing this here."

"Put your clothes on," he said, glancing down, his jaw clenching. "I'm getting you out of here, and then we're going to have a serious fucking talk about some of the choices you make."

Izzy followed his gaze, and sucked in her breath in embarrassment. Her shirt had fallen open again, completely revealing her breasts. Yanking away from Graham, she tried again to button her blouse.

Graham turned back to Chris, but this time his brother was ready, looking just as menacing. "You got one punch, Graham. Next time, I'm hitting back."

The two men simply stood glaring at each other, slowly circling like a couple of bulldogs about ready to pounce on each other.

"How dare you take advantage of her, you bastard. What are you doing here, anyway? Did you fuck everyone in St. Louis so you had to come back here?"

Chris's face reddened. "I did not take advantage of her. Damn it, I didn't know there was something going on between you two."

Looking at Izzy, his gaze softened. "Baby, I'm so sorry. I didn't know you and Graham . . ." He shoved a hand through his hair in frustration. "If I'd known you thought I was him . . ."

"There's not. We're not—" Izzy began, but she was interrupted by Graham.

"Wait. What? You thought Chris was me?" Graham asked, stunned.

Her face heated, and tears of humiliation stung her eyes as she looked between the men. Oh God, she'd never been so mortified in her life. Graham knew she wanted him. She'd never been good about hiding it. And now he knew she'd jumped into bed with his identical twin thinking it was *him*. She needed to get out of there.

Finally managing to work her fingers, she finished buttoning her blouse and yanked on her pants. She looked around for her purse, but Graham's hand closed around her wrist, turning her to face him. "Isabel Elizabeth Craig, you answer me!"

A strangled sound escaped Chris, and startled both Graham and Izzy. They both looked at him, and she saw that Chris's face had gone a bit pale.

"Isabel? Isabel Craig?" he asked.

Graham rolled his eyes heavenward. "How is it that you two didn't manage to exchange names before you started fucking? Wait, never mind. I don't want to know. Izzy, let's go." He yanked on her arm, pulling her toward the door.

"No!" Izzy pulled her arm from his grasp, anger beginning to replace her embarrassment. "I'm not going with you. Graham, what are you even doing here? You have no right to storm in here and act like I've done something wrong. I'm not your girlfriend."

"You're not?" The question came from Chris.

"Shut up!" Graham shot at his brother, and then looked at Izzy, searching her face carefully before speaking. "Sweetheart, I know you're not mine, but I do care about you, whether you believe that or not. I didn't want you falling into bed with someone who was going to hurt you."

"You make a lot of assumptions, little brother." Chris practically growled. "Besides, she is a grown woman, and you said it yourself. She's not yours. She can make her own decisions about who she wants to sleep with."

"You're right," Graham sneered back. "Me! She thought she was sleeping with me! Although how she thought I'd ever get this haircut, I'll never know," he said, flicking a finger at Chris's shorter hair.

"Fuck you!" Chris shot back, stepping toe to toe with his brother.

Izzy looked back and forth between the two men. She could easily see the difference now. It wasn't just the fact that Graham had a beard and slightly longer hair. The big difference was how the two men carried themselves. Chris held himself with a smooth confidence and charm that could melt a woman's heart. Graham looked dangerous, exuding a sexy intimidation. It's like they were two sides of the same coin.

Her head was swimming. She had to get out of there. She couldn't do this. Not now. Grabbing her purse, Izzy started for the door, hearing the men call her name as she opened it and ran down the hall.

****

"Damn it!" Graham smacked his hand against the doorframe. He turned to give his brother one last piece of his mind.

"What are you doing?" Graham asked as he saw Chris shoving his legs into his pants.

"I'm going after her. What the fuck do you think I'm doing?" Chris answered, looking around for his shoes.

"Like hell you are!" Graham was seething. He'd known Izzy wanted him, and he'd pushed her away countless times. What was she supposed to do? Be celibate for the rest of her life? He just couldn't handle the fact that she had jumped into bed with his brother.

Chris looked up at Graham warily. "What are you doing, Graham? You have this beautiful woman who is obviously in love with you, and you're pushing her away just like you push everyone away."

Fisting his hands at his sides, Graham tried to control his anger. "Don't psychoanalyze me. You don't know me anymore."

"Don't I?" Chris finished tying his shoes and pushed himself off the bed to face Graham. "I'd bet you haven't had a relationship since Alisha died."

Graham's jaw clenched at the mention of their ex-girlfriend. "I have been with women since then," he spat out.

"Been with women? Yeah, I'm sure you've fucked plenty, Graham. But have you let yourself care about anyone?"

"You're one to talk!" Graham yelled at his brother. "I'm betting you have a different woman in your bed every night. How is that working out for you?"

"I'm not doing this," Chris said, turning toward the door while yanking a T-shirt over his head. "You're obviously not going after her, so I will.

"I won't let you hurt her." Graham's words stopped Chris before he reached the door. He turned back to face his brother.

"I'm not going to hurt her, Graham. But I'm not just going to let her go either." Chris blew out a breath. "We always did have the same fucking taste in women."

Graham shook his head. "It's not like that between Izzy and me."

Chris snorted. "Bullshit. You forget I can feel what's going through you. I know how emotionally ragged you've been, and now it all makes sense."

"What makes sense?"

"Izzy," Chris breathed her name. "She's the one. You feel it, and it scares the shit out of you. It would also explain why I felt like I was half in love with her the moment I saw her."

Graham swallowed hard. He hadn't let himself think about loving Izzy. There were plenty of nights when she invaded his dreams, where he would let go and take her in his arms, and tell her what was in his heart. But then in the dream, her face always turned to Alisha.

Turning away from Chris, he looked out the window, wanting to hide the pain on his face.

"You can't hide it, you know," his brother said. "And you can't blame yourself about Alisha forever."

Graham snorted. "And how is it that you're so forgiving? I was pretty sure you hated me for what happened to her."

Graham thought back to the woman he and his brother had shared. She hadn't been the first one. In fact, it seemed like neither he nor Chris had ever been able to have a successful relationship without the other one. And then Alicia had decided she wasn't in love with Chris, but that she only wanted Graham.

"I blamed you for a long time," Chris said quietly. "But not for her death. I never blamed you for that. She loved you, not me. After I left, I wondered what I'd done to turn her off, or what was so special about you that she chose you instead."

"That's stupid. Most of the girls we . . . well, most of them always chose you in the end." Graham said, turning back to face Chris. "And I didn't love Alicia. You did."

"Yeah, and who knows. Maybe that was why she chose you. She was the type of girl who seemed to want what she couldn't have." Chris shook his head. "I wish I'd figured that out sooner." He shook his head, as if to clear the old memories. "It doesn't matter now. What matters is Izzy. Fuck. Isabel Craig. She owns this place."

Graham smiled, a sense of pride going through him. Izzy had run the resort for the last three years, ever since her grandfather started to go downhill, and The Lakewood was thriving.

But he wasn't going to go after her. Nope, he wasn't going to do it. He didn't want to lead her on, he thought, as he watched Chris leave the room.

Graham waited about two beats. "Dammit," he said, jogging out after his brother. "Wait up."

Chapter Three

"How fucking dare he be mad at me! Where does he get off?" Izzy stomped her foot on Tessa's carpet as she paced back and forth in the small living room. The apartment over the old library was cozy, but comfortable. The bright colors of the throw pillows and area rug were a perfect reflection of Tessa's vibrant personality. Since Tessa had revamped Magic's library into a popular media center, the city council had been happy to include the apartment as part of her employment package.

"I would love to continue discussing this, but sit your ass down before I hand you this glass of wine because I don't want it sloshed everywhere as you make another trek around the room."

With a sigh, Izzy accepted another glass of wine and plunked down on Tessa's sofa, curling her legs underneath her. "Thanks," she said, studying her friend.

Tessa's rich brown hair was pulled back in a ponytail, black glasses perched on her nose, and she boasted curves that Izzy would kill for. She envied Tessa's ability to remain calm under pressure. That was a trait that would come in really handy right now.

"I still don't understand what you're so upset about. I mean I honestly don't see the down side here. The whole thing is so damn hot!"

When Izzy glared at her, Tessa just steamrolled ahead. "I mean, come on! You had sex! And then Sheriff Dark and Dreamy finally showed some interest." Tessa pumped her fist in triumph. "It's about freaking time. I *knew* he liked you!"

Taking another large gulp of wine, Izzy tried not to giggle. Tessa had a way of looking at everything in a positive light.

"Now, I really want details. Let's hear about the brother. How was he? Was it awesome? Are they really identical? How big was his—"

"Tessa!" Izzy sputtered on her wine, but couldn't help laughing even as she felt the heat creeping up her cheeks.

"Oh, don't be embarrassed. You deserve to have sex. Hell, you haven't had sex in the six months I've known you, and God only knows how long it was before that."

"You know I was busy with my grandpa. I didn't have time for a relationship." Izzy felt a little pang of sadness, and wondered what her grandpa would think of her escapade this evening. She put a hand to her forehead, hoping he couldn't see her now. "I can't believe I slept with a stranger," she groaned.

"Oh no, don't you dare!" Tessa startled her with a sharp reprimand.

"Don't what?" she asked, pressing her fingers against her right temple in an effort to stifle the self-deprecating thought.

"Don't sit there and start judging yourself. I can see it on your face."

Enjoying another gulp of deep cabernet, Izzy could tell she'd better slow down as the fog rolled pleasantly across her brain. Pausing momentarily, she studied her half-full glass. If there was ever a time she deserved to be a little foggy, tonight was definitely that time. "Aw, screw it." Tipping her head back, she drained the contents.

"I wonder how long Chris will be here," she pondered, swiping the back of her hand across her lip to wipe off the wine mustache. "Maybe I can just avoid him until he leaves town." Except she really didn't want to. No one had ever made her feel like that before. She wanted Chris to hold her again, wanted him to touch her, wanted him to—

Tessa sat her glass of wine down, and snatched Izzy's empty glass out of her hand, setting it on the coffee table.

Her voice gentled as she took Izzy's hands in hers, sitting down beside her. "I know that look on your face. You are way too caught up in this black and white ideal you seem to have. You like Graham. And maybe you like Chris too. Sweetie, I love you. You know that. But you have been mooning over Graham for years, and it's ridiculous. He obviously has the same feelings for you.

"No," she held up her hand to stop Izzy from talking. "He *does*, no matter how much you argue. I, for one, am sick to death of the stolen glances and sexual tension between the two of you. Maybe this is finally the push he needs. I mean, he knows you wanted to fuck him now, right? That's a good thing!"

Tessa giggled as Izzy groaned in embarrassment, putting a hand over her face.

"And if our hunky sheriff is too much of a complete moron to finally make a move, well then, you're moving on . . . with his super hot brother!" Tessa wiggled her eyebrows.

Before Izzy could answer, her cell phone startled her. Her current ringtone of "So What" by P!nk was so loud it made her jump. She picked it up and looked at the display. *Graham.*

"That is like the fifth time he's called," Tessa pointed out. "Him realizing his feelings for you won't do a damn bit of good if you won't even answer his phone calls."

"I'll answer him." Izzy silenced her phone. "Just not yet. Tess, how can I talk to him if I don't even know what to do?"

After wanting Graham for so long, it seemed strange to think of someone else taking up residence in her heart. That was probably premature. She'd just met Chris, and she didn't know anything about him. How come Graham never talked about him? His mom had.

Lily was very proud of her boys, and talked about how sad she was that Chris lived three hours away. Too bad his mom hadn't mentioned the word "twin" at some point. She'd just assumed the brothers weren't close. But now, it was obvious things were way more complicated than that.

The differences between the two men were discernable . . . well, at least they were *now*. When Chris had walked into The Lounge tonight, she'd known he was different than Graham. Deep down, she'd known. It didn't make sense at the time to her, but she could easily see the differences now. As if one Nolan brother hadn't caused her enough heartache, she now had to deal with two.

Her phone buzzed again, and she sighed.

"Why don't you turn it off?" Rising from the couch, Tessa disappeared into the bedroom and when she came back out, her arms were filled with a huge pillow and a thick purple fleece blanket. "You need to get some sleep. Maybe you'll be able to think more clearly tomorrow."

Grabbing the bedding from her friend, Izzy began spreading the blanket over the couch. "I hope so."

Tessa grabbed her for a side hug, and Izzy embraced her back, resting her head on Tessa's shoulder. "I really hope so."

****

The Lounge was fairly crowded in the morning, converted from a bar and grill atmosphere to more of a family ambiance. White tablecloths covered the tables, and silver insulated pitchers of coffee sat on each one. Hotel guests gathered at the breakfast buffet lining one wall, filling their plates with scrambled eggs, hash browns and thick slices of bacon. Even though it smelled heavenly, Chris wasn't hungry. He sat at the bar, absently stirring sugar into his coffee as Milo approached.

With one look at him, Chris was really hoping he would be able to get through his morning coffee without getting another right swing to the nose. Not many people were taller than he was, but Milo stood a good two inches over him, and outweighed him by at least fifty pounds of solid muscle. Chris was pretty sure he wouldn't be able to win that fight.

"Don't tell me you're mad at me too," he grumbled, assessing Milo carefully.

The large man frowned, pulling himself up to his full height as he stepped into Chris's personal space.

"Isabel Craig is like a sister to me, Nolan. If you've done anything to hurt her . . ." Milo let the threat linger, narrowing his eyes in warning.

"I didn't do anything," Chris sighed warily. "Or at least I didn't try to hurt her." But he knew he had. He could still see the hurt and confusion on Izzy's face as she'd stormed out of his room last night. She was just supposed to be a pretty girl to warm his bed and maybe piss off his brother in the process. But she had turned out to be so much more. And now he had royally fucked it up.

Milo studied Chris's face, his anger turning to amusement. "Well, son of a bitch. You like her. How about that?" He slapped a meaty hand on Chris's back, almost knocking the wind out of him, and snagged a nearby pitcher to pour himself a cup of coffee.

When he came down to The Lounge for coffee, Chris hadn't expected to be scrutinized. He bit his tongue and glared at Milo, stirring his coffee so vigorously that some sloshed over the edge.

"Did you at least talk things through with your brother last night?" Milo asked, gulping his own coffee down black.

Chris snorted. "Hardly. After Izzy ran off, we tried to find her, but she wasn't in her room, and her car was gone. Hell, I don't even have her phone number. When I asked Graham, he just shot me the middle finger and stormed off." The fucker. What was Chris supposed to do, just walk away? Tell Graham to keep her? Pain shot through him at the thought, and he rubbed at his chest to ease the ache. No way. He'd be damned if he'd concede this time.

Taking a long glug of coffee, Chris wondered what the hell he was doing. He remembered the heartache he felt the last time a woman chose his brother over him. Did he really want to go down that road again? Did he really want to open himself up to that possibility again?

And then there was Izzy. Where the hell was she? He'd barely slept last night. Every time he closed his eyes, her face loomed in front of him. The way her blue eyes had flared when he was inside of her.

Milo sighed and pulled out his cell phone, shaking his head.

"What are you doing?" Chris glanced over at his friend, watching him scroll through the numbers on his phone.

"Taking pity on your love-struck ass."

Chris scowled as he began to argue. "I am not—"

"I texted you her number. Just promise not to go all stalker boy on her, or I really will have to kick your ass." Milo eyed him, and there was no doubt in Chris's mind that he meant it.

A grin spread across his face, as he picked up his phone and saved Izzy's number.

"And work things out with your fucking brother because I don't have the energy to watch you two fight over another woman."

Chris shrugged. "He claims there's nothing between them. I'm not his keeper."

A frown crossed Milo's face. "Yeah, well, you know Graham isn't famous for talking about his feelings. Just be careful, okay?"

Swigging the last of his coffee, Chris rose from his chair. "Always."

Now he just had to decide if Izzy was worth the risk of getting hurt all over again.

****

Graham listened to Izzy's outgoing voicemail message for the hundredth time and cursed as he hit 'End' on his phone. He missed landlines. Slamming a phone down was so much more satisfying than pushing a button.

"Dammit, Izzy, where are you?" he muttered.

"Hey boss, everything okay?"

Graham looked up as Jillian walked into his small office, stepping around the two leather office chairs across from his desk to set a cup of coffee in front of him. Her wild mane of bright red curls bounced with each step she took.

"Yeah," Graham said distractedly. "And I've told you that you don't have to bring me coffee," he said, as he picked up the cup and took a sip of the brew. He almost groaned in pleasure. "But you sure do make good coffee."

"Damn right I do." Jillian grinned in triumph.

As he drank his coffee, he watched Jillian straighten papers on his desk. His office was small, but Jilly kept it immaculately organized. In addition to his desk, a worn couch sat against one wall, and windows lined the other, allowing Graham to spy on Main Street. In this town, that was an excellent way to keep tabs on what was going on.

"Hey, you're friends with Izzy, right?" he asked his secretary in a way he hoped was casual and nonchalant.

"Izzy? Suuure," she said slowly, furrowing her brow with curiosity. "We've become really good friends through the book club. But you already know that, sheriff." She crossed her arms, looking at him for an explanation. Jilly didn't miss much.

Graham thought of their "book club" and had to bite his lip to keep from grinning at how Jillian's cheeks pinkened slightly every time she mentioned it. It wasn't a big secret in town that many of the women were members of an erotic book club. Graham had seen one of the paperbacks once when Jillian had left it on her desk, and it had practically made him blush. The cover had boasted a woman and four men. Four! What the hell would a woman even do with four men?

And Izzy read those books. A combination of jealousy and arousal shot through him. Arousal certainly wasn't a new feeling when he thought of Izzy, but jealousy was something that hadn't really entered his brain until the last twenty-four hours. He still couldn't get the thought of Izzy and Chris out of his head.

Even though he had argued with his brother, it felt good to have Chris here again, talk to him, fight with him. Chris had been right when he said Graham hadn't had a successful relationship without him. When they were young, it just seemed natural to share women.

Memories of their college years flooded his brain. Damn, but they'd had a lot of fun. He was surprised at how many women were quick to jump on the fantasy of bedding down with hot twins. The problem was that once the novelty wore off, there weren't many women who wanted an actual relationship with two men. They either preferred Chris because he was outgoing and charming, or they preferred Graham because they thought he was dark and brooding.

He wasn't good at putting on the charming front like Chris was. He never had been. That's why sharing had always worked well with the two men. He could be himself, and he didn't have to try to smooth out his rough edges. Chris was always there to do it for him.

There had been a couple of women that Graham had tried to have a relationship with on his own, but they quickly found out he didn't do likable and endearing. Even the women who wanted the "bad boy" got tired of him after awhile.

And there lay one of the biggest reasons he pushed Izzy away. They were friends. He liked seeing her, hanging out with her at the resort, going boating with her and Milo and Andrea. He knew she had feelings for him, and it was getting harder and harder to hide his feelings for her. But he wasn't about to screw things up with her. He didn't think he could handle it if he tried and failed at a relationship with Izzy.

His heart lit up at the way she looked at him, like he was her sun. What if he took things further with her, and she decided she couldn't deal with his moodiness? What if things between them became awkward and she disappeared from his life altogether? Or worse, what if something happened to her, and it was his fault?

No. Graham wasn't going to let that happen. They were friends, and it worked. If that was the only way he could have her, then he would take it. It was better than not having her at all.

But what if he shared her with Chris? He knew from those erotic books Izzy read, that the idea certainly didn't repulse her. Could she be happy with both of them?

No way. Chris fucked everything that walked these days. He'd be damned if he'd let his man whore of a brother touch Izzy again.

"Sheriff? Helllllooooo?" Jillian's voice interrupted his thoughts.

"Oh lord, Jilly, I'm sorry," he said, dragging himself back to the present.

"You were asking about Izzy." Her mouth quirked up in a knowing half smile. Yep, Jillian's curiosity had definitely been piqued.

"I was just wondering if you'd seen her. She hasn't been home since last night, and she's not answering her phone. I'm starting to get worried about her."

Tapping a finger against her bottom lip, Jillian scrunched up her face in thought. "Well, I know it's been total craziness for her getting ready for the Halloween party and all. Maybe she just needed a break. If she went out and tied one on with Tessa, I doubt she would have driven home. So maybe she's over there."

Graham started to panic. What if she'd had too much to drink? What if something had happened to her?

"Sir? You just went pale. Maybe you should—"

Graham was already picking up his phone dialing Izzy again before Jillian could finish her thought. As he listened to the phone start to ring, he heard the unmistakable sound of music. *So What* by P!nk. The song got louder as he heard the outside door to the police station slam open, followed by Izzy's loud curse.

"Dammit, Graham! Stop calling me!"

Relief flooded his system. She was all right. He felt almost weak as the worry drained from him. The relief was short-lived, however, as a very annoyed blonde ball of angry walked into his office, her eyes spitting fire.

Jillian looked back and forth between Izzy and Graham before backing up. "I think this would be a really good time for me to take my lunch. If anyone needs me, I'll be . . . . uh . . .not here. Bye!"

And with that, his secretary practically left skid marks as she ran out the door.

****

After watching Jillian make a hasty exit, Izzy turned back to Graham. Dammit, why did he have to be so beautiful? It would be easier to be angry with him if her mouth didn't water every time she saw him. *Stay calm and stand firm, Isabel.*

"Do you want to tell me why you decided to blow up my phone?" She walked toward his desk and waved her phone in front of his face.

Rising from his chair, Graham walked around to lean against his desk so he was only about a foot away from her. As he crossed one long leg over the other, his gaze flicked to her phone before returning to her face, and he assessed her for a long moment. After a moment, his face visibly hardened, and Izzy backed up as she saw him go from concern to anger.

"Where the hell have you been all night? Do you have any idea how worried I've been about you?" His deep voice was low and deadly calm, causing her to back up a step.

"It is none of your business where I was!" she huffed. "I needed time alone, and I certainly don't have to answer to you. There is no reason for you to call me fifty freaking times!"

Coming here was a mistake. She thought they could talk rationally, but looking at Graham told her differently. Well, she certainly didn't have to stand here and listen to him talk to her like she was a child. Shoving her phone in her purse, she turned to leave, and made it two steps before a strong hand on her shoulder stopped her. Strong and firm. She went still as she felt him move close behind her – close enough that the heat of his body radiated against her. Swallowing was becoming much more difficult, and she took a shaky breath trying to gather her thoughts.

"I was worried, sweetheart." His deep voice tried to be gentle, but she knew he was talking through clenched teeth. She could tell he was angry, but he wasn't mean – never mean, not Graham. "You ran out so fast last night, and then you didn't come home. I just wanted you to answer your phone and tell me you were okay."

No. No matter how concerned he acted now, she couldn't get over the humiliation she felt about the way he'd busted in on her and Chris the night before.

Stepping forward, out of his reach, she turned to look at him, lifting her chin. "Well maybe I didn't want to talk to you," she said, crossing her arms, not sounding nearly as defiant as she'd hoped.

Closing his eyes, Graham's mouth moved slightly as though he were counting to ten. When he opened his eyes, he spoke softly and deliberately.

"You could have been lying dead in a ditch for all I knew, Isabel." Calm and menacing. His tone sent a shiver down Izzy's spine. "You don't want to talk to me? Fine? But at the very least, you could show me some common courtesy."

"Dead in a ditch? What are you now- my father?"

Before she could catch her breath, Graham grasped her upper arms and gave her a little shake. His grip was secure, and although his touch was gentle, his hands were shaking.

"No, I'm not your father." She could see his control slipping. "But I guarantee you that if you were mine, you would not act like this." He bent his head closer to hers, the deep timbre of his voice washing over her.

"If you belonged to me, I would take you over my knee and spank that pretty ass of yours. I'd make sure you couldn't sit down until you learned not to put yourself in stupid situations."

If I were his? Izzy's mouth dropped open a bit. How the hell was she supposed to respond to that? And stupid situations? Was he talking about the fact that she'd stayed out all night or the fact that she'd bedded down with his brother?

His hands began to gently rub her arms where they'd squeezed, and his face was so close she could feel his breath against her skin, feel the tickle of his beard against her lips. Slanting her head in a subconscious invitation, she ran the tip of her tongue over her lips. A light groan escaped Graham as his eyes flared in response.

She had come into his office primed and ready to fight, but if there was one thing Graham was always good at, it was throwing her off balance. She became very aware of how close he was, his touch tingling her arms, the way his eyes began to smolder.

"Graham—" she whispered. *Kiss me,* she silently pleaded, her eyes drooping with growing desire. Every thought fled except the desperate need for his kiss, to feel his lips, to taste him. All she had to do was lean forward, just a little bit, and press her lips to his.

The instant she leaned in, his face hardened, and he dropped his hands from her as if she burned him. The moment was gone.

"You're not mine, though," he said stepping back, his mouth twisting with regret.

Her eyes stung as the hurt of his rejection hit her a moment before fury started to rise like a boiling tide. A little growl escaped the back of her throat, and before she could help it, Izzy stomped her foot. "No, I'm not yours. You have made that abundantly clear, *Sheriff.*" She said the last word with a sneer.

Three years. Three damn years was how long she'd been hiding feelings for Graham. She had taken all the hope, the disappointment and stuffed it deep down. But now it was bubbling to the surface. And she wanted a fight.

"What exactly is that supposed to mean, sweetheart?" he asked with amusement in his voice. "And did you just growl at me?"

Oh, the fact that he seemed amused with her made her anger boil over. "Shut up! We're not doing this anymore, Graham. Stop acting all concerned about me."

"Isabel, I am concerned about you. I'm concerned about every citizen in this town."

Ugh! Why did that just make her angrier? Was she really only just as important as everyone else? Did he just lump her in with the every other resident of Magic and not think of her as special? If that were true, he wouldn't care so much. That couldn't all have been an act.

"Really? Do you burst into everyone's hotel room when they're having sex?" she asked as if to prove her point.

His mouth thinned to a firm line. "If it's you, and you're having sex with my brother, then yes, I do."

"Why do you care? I'm not yours, you said so yourself. So cut the jealous boyfriend act." She ran a hand through her blonde hair, practically tugging it out of her face. "Jesus, Graham, you act like you don't even like me half the time."

When he reached for her again, she backed away a couple of steps so she was out of his reach. Her chin lifted again in defiance, and she crossed her arms over her chest.

"Not like you? Not like you?! Are you serious right now?" He looked almost incredulous.

"I am quite serious." She took a deep breath. "I came here today to get everything out in the open. I can't handle the back and forth. I just want to figure this out, Graham. Figure *you* out." She swallowed before she spoke again. "I have had feelings for you for a long time now."

"Sweetheart . . ." He said it as almost a warning.

"No. Please let me finish. I've had feelings for you for almost three years. I'm not super good at hiding that, so don't pretend like that comes as some big shock to you." Great, now her palms were sweating. Uncrossing her arms, she slid her clammy palms along the thighs of her jeans and re-crossed her arms, hoping she didn't look as nervous as she felt. The fact that he stood motionless in front of her except for those intense eyes studying her face certainly didn't help any.

"I feel like I've practically thrown myself at you, but you've pushed me away countless times. A rational person would just walk away if someone wasn't interested in them." She paced to his desk and back, unable to look at him directly any longer. "Maybe I'm just a glutton for punishment," she mumbled almost to herself.

"Isabel, stop." At his command she stopped dead in her tracks.

"Look at me." She immediately looked at his face. What the hell was that? Her body obeyed him before she could even consciously process what he'd said.

"Good. Now, talk to me." The look on his face made her stomach flutter, and that really pissed her off. The corners of his mouth tipped up just slightly, and she knew he liked her reaction to him. Hell, she was probably blushing.

"This is my point, Graham." She put her hands to her cheeks. Yep, they were warm.

His brow furrowed. "I don't understand. What's your point?"

" I've never been exactly sure of what your feelings are for me. Just when I think I am, you do something to throw me off." She lowered her hands. "And you're really good at that."

"Throw you off?" He shook his head. "I don't understand what you mean."

Sighing, she felt that damn ache in her temple starting again. "I mean you would do things like always shovel my walk when I was staying at the cabin. Every time it snowed, you were there at 5:30 in the morning. You didn't have to do that." He opened his mouth to speak, but Izzy stopped him. "I know it was you, so please don't deny it. I get up earlier than you think I do.

"And besides that," she continued, "you always showed up at the hospital and brought me food when I was sitting with my grandpa, and forced me to eat. You brought me an iPod with my favorite music on it." She'd even jokingly referred to it as their mix tape.

"Because I'm your friend, Izzy," he said softly. "That's what friends do."

Tears pricked Izzy's eyes. She cleared her throat, hoping her voice came out steady. "What about all the times you held me, all the times you lowered your head like you were going to kiss me, but then stopped?"

If she hadn't lowered her eyes, she may have missed the way his hands clenched into fists at his sides. Was she angering him? Or was he trying to keep him emotions in check? When she looked back up to his face, she saw that careful control that was always in place.

"Just because I find you attractive doesn't mean that this," he finally said, gesturing between the two of them, "would be a good idea."

"Because you don't like me? You don't care about me?"

"It's not that simple."

"Then explain it to me."

"Great idea, Izzy." A voice from behind her made Izzy jump. She spun around to see Chris standing in the doorway, leaning his shoulder against the frame.

"Graham, why don't you explain to her why you're so much of an idiot that you're going to let such an incredible woman go."

****

Chris couldn't stand it. He heard the plea in Izzy's voice when she talked to his brother. If he wondered at all what her feelings were before, there was no doubt in his mind now. She was in love with Graham. And he was too damn stubborn to do anything about it.

Now that she turned to face him, Chris's heart clenched at the sight of the pain in her eyes. How could

Graham do this to her and then look at her with such a blank stare. Jesus, didn't the bastard have a heart at all?

"How long have you been standing there?" Izzy reached up to swipe at a tear before it could fall. She was trying so hard to control the emotions he could see warring inside of her. When he stepped toward her, she backed up, looking at him warily. Scared little rabbit. What he wouldn't give to hold her and take away all the hurt he saw in those blue eyes.

"Long enough." He had come here to see what Graham's feelings were toward Izzy, and to figure out what his own next move was going to be. Well, fuck the rational planning. And fuck Graham too. He wanted to punch his brother for putting that look on Izzy's face.

Crossing the short distance between them, Chris ignored her uncertainty and put an arm around her shoulders, drawing her close to his side, as he stared at his brother. "You are an asshole of epic proportions."

"Don't." Graham sighed. "Chris, this has nothing at all to do with you."

"Oh, yes it does. I am not going to let you do this to her."

Graham threw his hands up in frustration. "Do what to her? I am trying to protect her!"

It's official. His brother was insane. "Protect her? From who? Me or you? Look at her! Am I the one who hurt her? Am I the one who put that look on her face? That was all you, brother."

Graham looked at Izzy with almost a pained expression. "I never meant to hurt you." And then he looked pointedly at Chris. "But I will be damned if I'm going to let you use her."

Before Chris could respond, Izzy let out a cute little growl. "Use me? For what? Sex? Maybe I want to be used! Maybe I want to have sex!"

She flushed even as she said it, and Chris's heart warmed a little more, remembering what they shared the night before.

"With me!" Graham shouted. "You wanted to have sex with me!"

Yanking away from Chris, Izzy started for the door. "I am not doing this again. I am not having this conversation."

"Whoa, little rabbit. Where are you going?" Chris rushed to stop her before she could reach the door. "I want to talk to you."

Graham came to stand in front of Chris before he could reach Izzy. "I am not going to let you use her, Christopher. She's not another one of your conquests."

"Get out of my way," Chris practically yelled, shoving Graham in the chest.

"Stop!" Izzy's scream silenced them both. "I have had it! You!" She shoved a finger at Graham. "I am tired of your flip-flopping. I am done! And you!" She then shoved said finger at Chris. "I don't know what your game is, but I'm not going to be used as some tool to make your brother jealous. As far as I'm concerned, you can both fuck off!"

And with that, Izzy stomped out, leaving both men staring after her with their mouths hanging open.

A moment later, Jillian walked through the door, holding a sack from Roxy's diner. "What the hell did you do to Izzy?" she asked before she looked at the two men. When she saw Chris, her eyes widened dramatically.

"Holy shit! You have a twin?" Jillian walked into the office, and slowly circled Chris, looking him up and down. "Wow, I always wondered what you'd look like without a beard, Sheriff."

Chris grinned at the curvy redhead as she looked him up and down. Graham just huffed and rolled his eyes. "Chris, this is my secretary, Jillian. Don't sleep with her."

Jillian gaped at Graham for a moment before regaining her composure. "Well, let's not get hasty. I *am* single."

If Chris had met Jillian twenty-four hours ago, he had no doubt he would've tried to get her into bed. But now, he barely saw how pretty she was. Izzy was the only woman he wanted. What the hell had happened to him?

"It's nice to meet you, Jillian."

"Oh, for crying out loud," Graham sighed, plopping down into his chair. "Jilly, can you give me a moment alone with my brother, please?"

Jillian excused herself with a wink in Chris's direction and shut the door behind her.

"Leave her alone," Graham ordered.

"Don't worry. I'm not planning to lay a hand on your secretary."

"Office manager!" Jillian shouted from the next room.

"Stop eavesdropping!" Graham shouted back. Then he pointed at Chris. "And I'm not talking about her."

Chris sat in the chair opposite Graham. "You're not keeping me away from Izzy. You don't want her. You've told me that, you've told her that. Everyone is quite clear on that fact."

Graham's jaw tightened. "You know damn well it's not that simple."

"Oh, I know that. I know you still feel so damn guilty over Alicia's death that you can't let yourself care about anyone else."

"Don't fucking psychoanalyze me," he said through clenched teeth.

Chris leaned back and assessed his brother. "I'm not stupid, you know. I know you want her. You know that I want her too. If you remember correctly, we were once very happy sharing."

A look of sheer panic crossed Graham's face. "That will NEVER happen again. Not with Izzy. Not with anyone."

Chris just shrugged one shoulder nonchalantly. "Fine. But don't expect me to hold back. I'm not giving her up because you have some misplaced sense of overprotection."

Graham's eyes narrowed. "Stay away from her."

"No."

"No?"

"No." Chris rose from his chair, starting for the door. "The days of you telling me what to do are long gone, Graham. I like her. And I'm going after her." He took one look back at his brother. "And you can't stop me."

Now what? Graham thought. How the fuck had everything gone so wrong? Izzy was so pissed at him. He'd succeeded in shoving her away, and now his brother was pursuing her. This day had truly gone to hell.

He was usually good at avoiding his inner voice that told him how stupid he was being, but today, that force was screaming so loud at him, Graham thought he was going to get a migraine.

She was going to get hurt. He just knew it. Chris was going to hurt her, but before he did, he was going to reap the benefits of bedding down with Izzy, and enjoying that hot little body.

"Dammit, dammit, dammit." Graham scrubbed his hands through his hair. This situation did not work for him at all. He didn't know what he was going to do, but he did know that continuing to avoid his feelings for Izzy

Craig certainly was not helping the matter. It was time to figure exactly what he was going to do about her.

Chapter Four

Closing the side door of the hotel behind her, Izzy breathed in the crisp morning air. She walked the short distance to the annex that contained her office, and enjoyed the crunch of leaves drifting across the sidewalk. The wind ruffled the trees, and she pulled her sweater a little tighter around her normal work attire of a long-sleeved black blouse and khakis.

Stopping in between the hotel and the annex building, she took a moment to admire the way the morning sunlight glinted off the lake. The hotel was situated on a portion of Izzy's land that jutted out into the water like a peninsula. The ideal location was one of the things she loved about the place. Almost anywhere you stood on the grounds of the Lakewood, you could look out and see the water. The only exception was the front side of the hotel, which faced the large parking area, surrounded almost entirely by her beautiful trees.

Enough time enjoying nature, Izzy. If she didn't place the supply orders this morning, then there wouldn't be much of a party.

An hour later, she rubbed her eyes and stretched in her office chair. The big bowl of Halloween candy called out to her, and she absently reached to grab a small chocolate bar as she mentally checked off the orders. Everything was on track for the Ball. The menu was confirmed with the chef, Milo had several spooky-themed concoctions he was mixing up for the party guests to imbibe, and decorations were being delivered that afternoon.

"Someone has an admirer!" Andrea's singsong voice interrupted her thoughts as she walked through the door, followed by the night manager Josh, who was carrying a giant fall-colored bouquet.

Izzy's chocolate-filled mouth dropped open as Andrea shoved folders aside on her desk so Josh could set down the huge bouquet. "What on earth? Andi, surely these aren't for me!" The arrangement covered half the space on her desk, and was full of peach roses, chrysanthemums, hibiscus, and sunflowers.

"Oh yes they are," Andrea said with an excited smile.

Josh grinned at the two women. "Here, there's a card." He reached out to pluck the card from the middle of the bouquet and handed it to Izzy.

Before she opened it, her brow furrowed at Josh. "What are you doing here? You don't come on duty until seven o'clock tonight. Shouldn't you be resting or entertaining ladies or something?"

Josh's tanned skin actually flushed as he shrugged a shoulder and handed her the card. Izzy felt a little bad about teasing him. Since they'd hired Josh a month ago, he didn't hesitate to work long hours if he thought she needed extra help. The poor guy didn't seem to have much of a social life, and Izzy couldn't figure out why with his dark good looks. Jilly and Tessa had taken it upon themselves to try to set him up with someone, but so far, he didn't seem interested in anything but work.

The heavenly scent of the flowers attracted Izzy's attention, and she couldn't stop herself from smiling before she'd even read the card. The only time she'd ever received flowers were from vendors or gracious hotel guests. That must be it. It was probably someone who'd had an exceptional experience at the resort.

"Read the card! Read the card!" The normally subdued Andrea was bouncing up and down like an excited schoolgirl.

Small neat handwriting adorned the card, and Izzy's mouth dropped open again as she silently read the message.

"I'm sorry we started off on the wrong foot. Please give me another chance. – C"

"Are they from Graham?" Andrea guessed, still bouncing. Izzy almost snorted at the thought. Even if she were in a relationship with Graham, he certainly didn't strike her as the type of guy who would send flowers. No, Graham was the type to cook her dinner and fix her car, but probably not flowers.

"Nope," said a voice from the doorway. "Wrong Nolan brother."

Andrea gasped and turned to gape at the gorgeous man leaning against the doorjamb. Chris looked relaxed in jeans and a button-down blue dress shirt. The cuffs were rolled up to almost his elbows, showing off the corded muscles of his forearms. The sight of him made Izzy's mouth water.

"Wow, you sure do have a gift for popping up at just the right time, don't you?" she observed wryly.

A wide grin spread across Chris's face revealing his perfect teeth, and accentuating his dimple. "It's a skill, baby."

Oh, that smile did things to her. "Andi, have you met Chris? This is Graham's brother."

It didn't take long before Andrea had her usual reaction when she came into contact with a dominant male. She blushed deeply and averted her gaze, her eyes finding the floor.

Before Izzy could speak for her friend, Chris stepped forward to take her hand. "I'm Christopher Nolan. I'm sure you've met my evil twin, but I'm the good one. You can call me Chris." Ever the charmer, he reached for Andrea's hand and lifted it to his lips to kiss the backs of her knuckles. "It's lovely to meet you, Miss. . .?"

"Andi." Her voice was barely a whisper. Josh seemed to quickly assess the uncomfortable situation and jumped in to help his shy co-worker.

"This is Andi. Andrea Lockhart Milton. She's the assistant manager for the resort. And I'm the night manager, Josh Capello."

Andrea snatched her hand away from Chris's, but not before her long sleeve fell back slightly, revealing a deep bruise on her forearm. Izzy frowned, and she noticed the way Chris's jaw clenched. He stared at her sleeve-covered arm even as he reached out to shake Josh's hand.

"Uh, yeah," Andrea said stepping away from him and still not meeting his eyes. "You know my brother, Reed. I think you knew him in school or something."

"Reed Lockhart?" Chris asked, his mouth falling open. "Oh my God, Andi?! Little Andi Lockhart? Last time I saw you, you were in braces." Chris's wide smile was back in place, showing off that gorgeous dimple. Andi's mouth tilted a bit, but her eyes darted around as if searching for an escape.

"I'd better get back to work." She moved to the door. "It was good to see you again," she said as she hurriedly rushed away.

Once she was gone, Chris looked from Izzy to Josh. "Is she okay? She seems awfully nervous."

"I'll go check on her," Josh said, already starting out the door. "It was nice to meet you, Mr. Nolan." He hurried off after Andi.

With a little frown, Izzy looked at Chris. "She tends to get a little shy around men. It's not you. She just gets a little freaked out sometimes." She gave a slow shrug, contemplating the situation. "Maybe you just make her nervous." But it seemed like more than that.

"And what about you sweetheart?" Chris asked, walking around the desk, so he stood close to where Izzy sat. "Do I make *you* nervous?"

His close proximity caused all other thoughts to flee from Izzy's head. She smelled the spicy scent of his aftershave, and felt her insides clench in response. She remembered that scent vividly, and knew it was stronger when she nuzzled against his neck. Suddenly it became harder to swallow.

Looking up, she saw Chris's knowing smile as he raised an eyebrow at her, waiting for her response.

"Uh, of course not. Of course you don't make me nervous." *Yes, he did!* Oh holy hell, did he ever. She clasped her shaking hands together and put them in her lap to hide the evidence that she wasn't the picture of calmness.

Amusement lit Chris's eyes. "I see," he said grinning. "Well, tell me Iz, do you like the flowers?"

Thank goodness he wasn't going to pursue that line of questioning. Izzy rose from her desk to face him, thinking he would move back to give her room. Nope, he didn't seem to care that he had completely hijacked her personal space.

Bending over her desk, she straightened the large vase so the flowers faced her, and smiled. She really did enjoy flowers. "They're beautiful. But you didn't have to do this. It's really not necessary."

"It is necessary. I wanted to apologize for the scene in Graham's office." His voice was sincere, but she just didn't know if she was ready to trust this man. The Nolan brothers were all kinds of complicated, and right now, that was not what she needed.

"Look at me, Izzy," he said gently, reaching out to lightly tug on a loose blonde curl.

She sucked in a breath, turning to meet his eyes, loving the way they held hers as he spoke, and the way they lit up as he smiled. "I like you. I'm not using you to make my brother jealous. I don't want you to think that. I also thought maybe the flowers might help you say yes."

Oh my, there were so many things she wanted to say yes to. She remembered the way her body had completely let loose in his arms. She would definitely say yes to that again. And if she remembered correctly, there was also his promise of his mouth on a very intimate part of her body. Yep, she'd certainly say yes to that too. Wait, no she wouldn't. She wouldn't say yes to that. Chris Nolan was one giant complication wrapped up in a super sexy muscular body.

"Yes to what?" Her breath sped up, and she could feel the heat warming her face. Yeah, it wasn't obvious at all what she'd been thinking about. She practically rolled her eyes at herself. She really needed to get better at hiding her emotions.

"To dinner." Other than the mirth in his eyes, Chris seemed nonplussed by the way her body responded to him. "I'd like you to have dinner with me tonight."

He was asking her on a date. Izzy felt her heart beat faster, even as her conscience frowned at her. She should stay away from him. She knew it. It wasn't a good idea to get caught in the middle of the two brothers, and that's exactly what she'd be doing. Even if Graham didn't have feelings for her, she did for him. And for Chris. Starting anything when she had feelings for two men was a bad idea.

"I would like to, but I really have to work. The Costume Ball is less than two weeks away, and there's so much to do." The excuse sounded lame even to her own ears.

"Before you say no, I need to apologize for something else. I want to make sure you are very clear that the other night wouldn't have happened if I'd known you thought I was . . ."

"Don't say it!" She plugged her fingers in her ears. "Seriously. I don't need to be reminded of how stupid I was."

"Not stupid. Just . . . hopeful. There's certainly nothing wrong with that. And please know that I certainly don't regret the night I spent with you. I just wish. . . there was full disclosure."

Chris moved forward to take Izzy's hand, bringing it to his lips. But this was nothing like the chaste kiss he'd pressed to the back of Andi's hand. Oh no, when he raised Izzy's hand to his lips, he slowly sucked the tip of her index finger into his mouth. His tongue swirled around it, sending shivery shockwaves directly to her pussy.

Oh, holy crap. She began to throb, and sucked in a breath as he moved on to the next finger. Once she realized she was panting, she jerked her hand away.

Trying to back away from him, she hit the side of her desk and lost her balance. He reached out to steady her as she stumbled, landing on top of a stack of file folders. *Smooth, Izzy. Real smooth.*

A deep laugh rumbled in Chris's chest. He was obviously enjoying the effect he was having on her. And that blue shirt he was wearing really did show off those dark sapphire flecks in his eyes.

"Sweetheart, just give me the chance to make you scream out *my* name," he said seductively, stepping in between her slightly parted legs, his hand going to her hip.

"I-I'm not sleeping with you," Izzy blurted out in her lust-filled haze, and wondered if he could tell there was nothing she wanted more.

His smile widened. "Who said anything about sleeping, baby?" Oh yeah, he could tell.

His head dipped to press a kiss to her exposed collarbone. How had her top button come undone? He was probably magic on top of everything else. Or else he was so hot that when he was near, her clothes just started to remove themselves. He was so close that his light and spicy scent washed over her, as the stubble on his face scraped along the sensitive skin at her neck. Suddenly, it seemed quite difficult to breathe. *When did it get so hot in here?*

"You – you know what I mean." Did her voice really sound that shaky? "I know what it must have seemed like the other night, but I'm not the kind of girl who just goes to bed with a stranger. I don't do that." Yeah, she wasn't sure how convincing she sounded when she was sprawled on top of her desk tilting her head back in hopes he would continue the journey along her neck with those soft lips.

Chris lifted his head, his smile fading. "I am well aware of that. Izzy, please know that I am not trying to pressure you at all." He backed up, and she suddenly felt cold at the loss of his warmth. "I know I come on strong, but when I say dinner, I really just mean dinner. We don't have to do anything you don't want to do. I'll take you to someplace nice. We can go to Osage Beach."

Osage Beach was a resort town on the other side of the lake, and a forty five-minute drive. It was more of a tourist trap than Magic, and boasted a lot more shops and restaurants.

As her fingers played with the edge of a file folder on her desk, she contemplated his offer. She had to eat, right?

"Just dinner?"

"Just dinner. I promise. Hands off," he said, holding his hands up.

The little pang of disappointment that shot through her really pissed her off.

"I'm not sleeping with you," she reiterated, not sounding nearly as convincing as she'd hoped.

Chris was trying not to smirk, she could tell. "You have made that abundantly clear."

"Okay, but we're not driving around the lake." The truth was she was afraid to be in a confined space alone with the man for that long. She might jump on him.

"That's fine. I can take you to someplace here in town. If we leave the Lakewood, that leaves Roxy's Diner, The Fishhook Grill, or various fast food establishments. Your choice."

"Hmm, well it is chicken fried steak night at Roxy's."

"Roxy's it is." Chris gave a small little fist pump in victory, and Izzy couldn't help but smile. "I'll pick you up at seven?"

Izzy lifted a brow. "Pick me up?"

"Of course. I'll swing by your room on the second floor and everything. I am a gentleman, after all."

She laughed. "Okay, seven o'clock." Just dinner, right? What was the harm in that?

The phone on Izzy's desk began to shrill, and part of her was very disappointed to end her conversation with Chris.

"I'll let you get back to work." Catching her off guard, he dipped his head one more time, his mouth brushing her lips in a soft kiss. Then he stepped back so quickly that Izzy would have lost her balance if she hadn't been leaning against her desk.

"See you at seven." With a little salute and a wink, Chris was gone.

And Izzy had a date. Oh, she sure hoped she knew what she was doing.

****

Graham thought about skipping dinner and just heading home. What a long fucking day. Collapsing into a deep sleep sounded heavenly right about now. Dustin, the sheriff's deputy, had been out of town for a wedding, but he was finally back. Thank goodness. Dustin worked the night shift, and Graham was looking forward to having a night of uninterrupted sleep.

His friend Theo Buchanan, the town PI as well as a former cop, filled in at the station when he could. Unfortunately, that wasn't enough. With all the tourists, the small lake area kept the Magic sheriff's department hopping. Graham really needed to hire another deputy, which meant he had to interview people. Definitely not something he relished. It was already hard enough to find people interested in the job within the limited population of Magic. The small community consisted of less than five hundred permanent residents, so the pool of applicants was slim.

The rumbling in his stomach distracted Graham from his thoughts. Maybe he would just walk across to Roxy's and grab some food to go. It was chicken fried steak night, after all. Maybe if he had a full stomach and a beer, he could just fall into a tired sleep without Izzy dancing circles around his brain.

Roxy's Diner was in an old building caddy corner to the sheriff's office. Roxanne Lewis had really fixed the place up from what it was when Graham was in high school. Graham had just been a teenager when she and her husband Charlie bought the old building and opened the diner. In fact, Roxy had given him his first job bussing tables when he was fourteen.

Here it was fifteen years later, and Roxy still made the best food around. She'd redecorated a few times over the years and brightened up the décor so it was inviting and homey. It was a huge draw for locals and tourists alike, and with the increased business, Roxy had recently talked about expanding.

The bell above the door jingled as Graham walked in from the cool night. Where it had been silent outside, the atmosphere in Roxy's was buzzing with customers. The place was full of people, there were mouth-watering smells coming from the kitchen, and music was blaring from the retro-looking jukebox in the corner. Teenagers packed the red vinyl booths at the front of the restaurant, and families and couples were spread out over the rest of the diner. Roxy's catered to everyone.

Graham noticed his friends Reed and Theo sitting at the counter, and the two men waved him over. Several people greeted the sheriff as he made his way over to the bar area to sit with his buddies.

The three of them had been friends since junior high. It was the weirdest thing to think that Reed, the boy who'd shed tears because his brother broke his skateboard, was now the town's well-respected doctor.

Theo was also a strange story in Graham's head. The boy who'd once spray-painted a phallic symbol on the side of the local high school now made his living both as a private investigator and by selling security systems. Graham had tried time and again to talk him into the deputy job, but Theo refused to do more than fill in when Graham needed him.

"It's a happening place in here tonight," Graham said as he sat down.

Reed smirked, his blue eyes twinkling as he adjusted his glasses. "Yeah, more than you know. . . . ow!" he exclaimed when Theo smacked his arm.

"What the hell is up with you two?" Graham asked.

"Us? Shouldn't we be asking you that? I didn't think you were one to back down, man. Apparently you're a lot dumber than you look." Reed was blunt to a fault and obviously would not be stifled.

Theo rolled his eyes at Reed, and scrubbed his hand through his copper-colored hair. "Jesus, dude. You're about as subtle as an elephant in a china shop."

"Hey sheriff, what'll it be?"

Graham turned his attention from his two friends and focused on Roxy who sidled up behind the counter with a pot of coffee. Her platinum blonde hair was perfectly coifed, and she wore bright blue eye shadow. On any other woman, it might look garish, but on Roxy, it just looked charming.

"No coffee for me tonight, Rox. I don't have to work the late shift."

Roxy raised a perfectly arched eyebrow. "Dustin finally get back?"

"Yes, thank God. I'm going to go home and get some sleep. As soon as I can get an order of chicken fried steak to go?" he asked hopefully.

"You got it, sheriff." Roxy sashayed off, and Graham turned his attention back to his friends.

"Now, what the hell are you two talking about? What do you mean backing down?"

Reed jerked his head sideways, motioning to the back of the restaurant. "See for yourself."

Although the diner was crowded, Graham looked up and immediately spotted the subject of Reed's comments. Izzy sat in the back corner booth. And Chris sat right next to her with an arm draped over the back of the seat. Seriously? He couldn't sit across from her? The idiot looked like he was trying to climb into her lap.

Graham's jaw clenched as he watched the couple. Izzy was laughing at something Chris said. She wore a pretty floral dress and a red cardigan that she'd left open, revealing a luscious swell of cleavage. Her hand was resting on the table, and his brother was toying with her fingers as he leaned in, talking close enough to her ear that her blonde hair touched his face. He was so close that Graham would bet he could smell that heavenly lavender scent that seemed to radiate from within her.

Wincing at the pain in his face, Graham realized his jaw was clenched so hard it was a wonder his teeth didn't shatter.

"Here, man, you look like you could use this more than me," Reed said, sliding his beer in front of Graham. "You want to tell us why your brother is enjoying the company of the lovely Miss Craig? I thought maybe the spidey twins were sharing again, but from the look on your face, I can see that's not the case."

Theo reached out a hand toward Reed with his palm up, and the doctor grimaced as he pulled out his wallet and slapped a twenty in his friend's hand. "Bloodsucker," he mumbled.

"Not my fault you keep making bets with me." Theo laughed before turning his attention back to Graham. "So, Chris comes back to town, and he's here what? Three or four days before he homes in on your woman?"

Graham took a deep swallow of beer and shot his eyes toward Theo. "Try three or four hours," he grumbled.

Both men looked at him with wide eyes for a moment before Reed let out a low whistle. "Damn. He sure doesn't waste any time."

"And Izzy is not *my* woman," Graham insisted, ignoring the way Reed snorted.

"You just keep telling yourself that, buddy."

Dammit, he really needed new friends. He sat in silence, listening to the buzz of conversation around him, while subtly shooting glances back at Izzy. Her breasts were truly perfect, and she couldn't have worn a dress that would have shown them off any better. Had she worn that on purpose to show off her breasts to Chris? Chris, who'd already had the pleasure of seeing those full breasts spill free, of touching them, tasting them, sucking those hard nipples into his mouth.

Fuck. Turning back around, Graham chugged his beer. He really shouldn't think like that. And why did he feel like he wanted to punch his brother? Their feud was pointless, but he didn't want to admit to himself that he was jealous. Jealous of the way Chris touched her with such intimacy. Jealous of the fact that he'd enjoyed a night inside her incredible, curvy little body, when that was something Graham had dreamed of countless times over the years.

Those dreams had become even more vivid lately, and every one of them starred Isabel, usually naked or in various states of undress. He'd never get used to the painful hard-ons he seemed to wake up with every morning, and his water bill was going to be outrageous with all of the cold showers he was taking.

A beeping sound startled him from his thoughts, and he looked up to see Reed grimace as he studied his phone. "Everything okay?" Graham asked.

Reed downed a glass of water and threw some bills on the counter. "Car accident. Drunk kids. It's a good thing I didn't have that beer. Looks like I'll be working tonight."

Graham started to rise too. He'd better head back to the station. Dustin could go work the accident and he could man the phones.

"No," Reed said, shoving him back down. "The accident was in Camden." Camden was the next county over, which meant Graham was off the hook. Reed on the other hand worked at the hospital that served the entire lake area.

Saying his good-byes, Reed turned to go, and Graham leaned back to once again look in Izzy's direction. His heart stopped as he locked eyes with her, and then he immediately looked away, frustrated because now she knew he'd been staring at her.

"I can tell you're not okay with… whatever that is," Theo said, jerking his head in the direction of the corner. "You have to do something, man. You can't keep going on like this."

"What do I do, though?" He had pushed Izzy away for so long, he knew he'd caused her pain, and he hated himself for it. Now he was afraid that no matter what he did, it was too little, too late. He sighed. "She's already made her choice."

"You never gave her a choice to make." Theo shook his head. "Don't be an idiot. Talk to her. Stop shoving her away. It's been too long, Graham. You're not dead, so stop acting like it."

Graham looked up into his friend's dark brown eyes and truly appreciated the concern he saw there. Theo had been there during his relationship with Alicia. He'd been there when she chose Graham over Chris. And he'd been there when she died.

"It's way past time to stop blaming yourself. It's time for you to live again." Theo slapped his shoulder in a manly gesture that offered both comfort and a declaration that he needed to get his shit together.

And Graham knew he was right. He couldn't just let Izzy walk off into the sunset with another man, even if that man was his brother. Nope, right or wrong, he just couldn't let her go. Maybe he was too late, but he wouldn't know until he tried. He had to fight for her, and it was definitely past time to start fighting. But first, he needed a plan.

"Here you go, sheriff." Roxy plopped a big sack down in front of him. "We had one piece of your favorite chocolate cake left, so I threw that in too, on the house," she said with a wink.

Roxy's chocolate cake was orgasmic, and Graham's mouth watered at the thought. He leaned over the counter and pecked a quick kiss on Roxy's cheek, enjoying how the older woman flushed. "You're the best, Rox."

"Oh now, you. Go on," she said and hurriedly walked away.

Theo grinned and shook his head. "You can make all the women swoon, can't you?"

"I don't know about that. Besides I don't really care about making *all* the women swoon." He looked back to see Izzy talking animatedly with her hands. "All that matters is one."

****

Izzy tried to look like she wasn't watching when Graham walked in, or like she wasn't admiring the way his dark uniform hugged his muscular ass. The way he perched on the diner stool really showed off that perfect behind. Oh, she wanted to bite his firm little tush. *Where the hell did that come from?* She shook her head.

The evening with Chris had flowed in a way she hadn't expected. He made her laugh, made her feel comfortable in a way she never had with a man before. So why did she feel guilty when Graham had looked up and locked eyes with her? It wasn't like he hadn't had every opportunity to further their relationship. If Izzy wanted to go out and have a fun evening . . . a date, then she should. Hell, she deserved to, right?

Chris traced slow circles on the back of her hand with his thumb. Damn, how could that make her heart flutter? And how was she supposed to reconcile the fact that she had feelings for two men? There had to be a way to completely block Graham out of her mind and her heart. But did she really want to? *Focus on the brother that actually returns your feelings. That's the smart thing to do.*

Chris had been a perfect gentleman all evening. Her defenses had been up, but when he knocked on her door promptly at seven o'clock and handed her a yellow rose, her favorite flower, her wall had started to crumble. He'd opened doors for her, and hadn't tried to touch her aside from the hand on her lower back as he'd guided her into the restaurant. That one small touch sent heat through her entire body.

Sure, he'd sat on the same side of the booth as her, but that was only so they could hear each other since it was so loud in the restaurant. Izzy enjoyed the rumble of his voice, the smile that played around his lips every time he talked about his mom, Lily. When he spoke about some of his past antics with his brother, he couldn't help but smile then too. She'd bet it wasn't conscious on his part, the way he glowed with admiration when he spoke of Graham, but despite their differences, she could tell that he truly loved his twin.

When Graham walked in earlier, she was half hoping that maybe he would come over and join them, but she stifled her disappointment when he walked out with his sack. Her heart ached a little that he didn't even come over to say hi. She really needed to get over her feelings for him.

As the new waitress shuffled up to their table, Izzy looked up with a smile. The girl's nametag read 'Sarah,' and the young woman seemed flustered as she balanced a tray of drinks. She began setting coffee down in front of them with shaky hands.

"Darlin', I'm sure you make outstanding coffee, but we didn't order any." Chris smiled, and the waitress flushed.

"Dammit. I mean dangit," she gasped. "Oh, I'm so sorry. I didn't mean to say that." She looked around to see if anyone had heard her.

Izzy smiled at the young woman. "It's okay. I've heard Charlie scream out a long stream of obscenities from the kitchen when he burns something, so I don't think anyone is going to care."

A nervous grin lit Sarah's face. "Thanks. It's just taking me awhile to get used to things. It's only my first week. Can I get you two dessert?" She sat the tray down, and pulled an order pad and pen out from her apron. "The special tonight is pumpkin spice cheesecake."

All of Roxy's desserts here were delicious, but anything pumpkin made Izzy's mouth water.

Chris chuckled. "From the look on her face, I'm going to go with yes. We'll share a piece of the cheesecake."

Sarah shuffled off, and Chris looked back at Izzy.

"Sweetheart, what do I have to do to get you to look at me with that kind of desire?" he said as he reached up to brush his thumb across her bottom lip, leaving a wake of tingles across her mouth.

He stopped suddenly and pulled his hand away. "Sorry, I told myself I was going to be on my best behavior tonight."

Flirting seemed to come very naturally for Chris. Even though she really did appreciate his effort to rein it in, she couldn't help but feel disappointed at the loss of his touch. Could he tell that he wasn't the only one trying to control himself? All he had to do was say the word, and she could lose herself. Falling into bed with him would be so easy, but she wasn't going to.

Crossing her legs, Izzy tried to smother the heat that seemed to be erupting between her thighs. She really was enjoying talking and getting to know Chris, so her nymphomania would just have to go on hold for a little while. She hadn't known what to expect from the evening, but it was going better than she'd anticipated.

"So tell me more about this Halloween party you're planning," Chris was saying. "The hotel guests seem very excited about it. I've heard it's the event of the year."

Clapping her hands together, Izzy practically bounced in her seat. "Oh Chris, it's so much fun!"

As she detailed some of the creative costumes she'd seen over the years, she wondered how he would look as a sexy cowboy. The thought of those large hands curling up a long rope made her teeth sweat.

As Chris stared at her mouth, his eyes seemed to droop a bit. Could he tell what she was thinking?

Swallowing, Izzy curled her hands in her lap and tried to focus on the conversation. "Uh, we always have prizes for the best costumes, and there are tons of party games for both the adults and the kids."

"I'd love to play some party games with you, baby." At his seductive tone, Izzy shifted in her seat. "Sorry," he said again on a sigh, running a hand through his hair. Taking a deep breath, he said, "Tell me more about the party. Really. And I'll try to keep the sexual innuendos to a minimum."

Biting her lip, Izzy hid her smile. "Well, Halloween is truly my favorite holiday. Horror movies, costumes, candy – everything about it is just awesome."

Her grandpa always had the best costumes. "Last year, Grandpa was the headless horseman." Izzy smiled fondly remembering how her grandpa had scared the crap out of Vivian at the Ball, but she also couldn't help the bittersweet tears that came to her eyes. It had been her grandpa's last big hurrah before he had really taken a turn for the worse.

"Oh, Iz, I'm so sorry. You must miss him so much." Chris's hand covered hers and squeezed. The small gesture wasn't sexual, but the intimacy touched Izzy.

"I'm sorry," she sniffled. "I don't mean to spoil our evening."

"Spoil our evening?" Chris shook his head. "What are you talking about? I'd love to hear about your grandfather. I want to get to know you, Isabel. That means I definitely want to know about one of the most important people in your life."

"Really?" she asked. Just when she thought she had Chris figured out, he threw her for a loop. He seemed like the type of guy whose main concern was having a good time, but the more she got to know him, she saw that was just a front for something much deeper.

He continued. "I know how hard it is to lose someone you care about. It helps to talk about them. It keeps them alive."

At the sorrow in his eyes, Izzy remembered how much compassion Chris's mom had shown her when her grandpa was in the hospital. Lily Nolan had talked about the husband she'd lost to lung cancer. Having someone who had been through it comforted Izzy, alleviated that feeling of isolation.

"Your mom used to come to the hospital a lot when my grandpa was sick. Most times, she brought cookies, but sometimes she would just sit and hold my hand. She told me a lot about your dad." She knew from those conversations that Chris's father had been gone more than ten years.

His misty gray eyes smiled. "Yeah, I'm sure she did. Sometimes I wonder how she managed to get through it intact after watching him suffer for so long. On top of losing him, she had two eighteen-year-old boys to deal with. I know we weren't the easiest kids."

"You're lucky you had your brother." Coping with her own parents' death at a young age had been more than she thought she could handle. She'd yearned for someone to lean on.

With only a slight wince at the mention of his brother, Chris smoothly transitioned the conversation. "What about you? You never really talk about your folks."

Izzy smiled a sad smile. "They were awesome. I was always really close with my mom. My dad was a journalist, so he was always traveling. A lot of the time, it was just me and my mom." Her mom had only been twenty-two when she'd been born. As Izzy had gotten older, the two had seemed more like sisters than mother and daughter. Then the unthinkable happened.

"When did you lose them?" Chris asked, then shook his head and squeezed her hand. "I'm – I'm sorry, baby. You don't have to talk about it if you don't want to."

"No, that's okay." Izzy took a deep breath before continuing. "We lived in Kansas City. That's where I grew up. When I was in college, my parents decided to drive down here for a weekend getaway. They loved Magic," she said nostalgically.

"The weather was fine in Kansas City, but it had started snowing down here. I guess they didn't look at a radar." She reached up to swipe at a stray tear. "By the time they got down here, the roads were pretty bad. You know how quickly the roads here can deteriorate in the winter."

The Ozark Mountains were full of twisty-turny roads. They could become quite treacherous in the winter. Aside from being slick and narrow, it was hard for plows to clear them effectively, just making things worse.

Chris nodded and squeezed her hand, waiting for her to continue. "They slid off an embankment not five miles from here. They were so close. If they'd just. . ." Izzy stopped. She wasn't going to play the what-if game. She'd done that numerous times over the years. What if they'd looked at a radar? What if they'd taken a different route? What if she'd come home that weekend instead of staying at school to party with her friends? Would they have gone at all?

She felt Chris's hand on the nape of her neck, massaging gently as his arm rested along the back of the booth. "We never know what's going to happen. And I know it's tempting to think about how things could have gone differently, but they didn't. All we can do is live for today, Izzy. Enjoy every day, every moment. It's too precious not to."

He was right. She looked up into his warm gray eyes, and before she could think about it, she leaned in and pressed her lips against his. He jerked in surprise, but quickly recovered, his hand tightening on her nape, holding her head still as his mouth slanted over hers.

"Ahem." The clearing of a throat had the two of them springing apart. Sarah was standing at their table holding a piece of cheesecake. "I'm sorry. I didn't mean to. . ."

"No, no, no," Izzy said hurriedly. "It's okay." Had she really just kissed him in public? She groaned inwardly. She was a little too old to be making out in the back booth of Roxy's Diner.

****

Chris took a bite of cheesecake, enjoying the flush on Izzy's cheeks. He could tell that she'd surprised even herself with that kiss. She was so sweet. And the vulnerability she'd shown when talking about her grandfather and her parents brought out protective instincts in Chris that he didn't even know he had. She'd been through so much pain, and all he wanted to do was make her happy, give her pleasure.

She deserved to be happy. She deserved the whole world. He could start by getting her more money than she'd ever hoped to have by selling the resort. Except even that didn't seem quite right anymore. He could tell by the way she talked that the Lakewood was more than just a hotel and a restaurant. It was a piece of her grandfather, and Chris didn't know if she'd ever want to let it go. He knew he didn't want to be the man to make her. But he thought he should at least touch on business before the night was over.

"What are your plans for the resort? Have you thought about selling it?"

Her eyes widened dramatically, and he felt guilty for bringing it up at all. "Sell it? No. My grandpa put his whole life into that resort. I could never sell it."

"That property is worth a lot of money, Izzy. You could get more for the resort than you probably realize." But she was already shaking her head.

"Nope. Never going to happen. I have an uncle – well, he's technically my great *half* uncle – who was really interested in the resort. I don't know him all that well. He's my grandpa's half brother, but he's like 20 years younger than my grandpa so the two were never close. Anyway, he showed up for the funeral, but he took off once he found out that my grandpa left the resort to me. He really wanted it. He contacted me afterward with an offer, but I told him the same thing. I'm not selling."

Well, that certainly took care of that. He didn't blame Izzy one single bit. If it were anyone else, Chris would push it. He'd go into his sales speech, start listing pros and cons, start talking money. In his business dealings, he was fairly good at getting people to do what he wanted, while getting them to believe everything was their own idea. But he just couldn't do that to Izzy. She was still grieving, but she was happy at the resort. He wouldn't be the one to take away her home.

Unfortunately that was going to leave him with a very unhappy client. Since Chris was familiar with the area, he happened to know there was a ranch for sale on the other side of the lake. It would be the perfect spot for a resort, and that side of the lake had more traffic. Perhaps his client would be open to that option when he realized Izzy's land wasn't available. Chris would have to work up a proposal.

He slid a sidelong glance at Izzy as she took a big bite of cheesecake and licked her fork. He had to shift in his seat as he felt his jeans tighten when he watched her mouth. It seemed like he was hard most of the time he was around her, but at the sight of her tongue slowly licking that fork, his cock literally twitched.

Not tonight, he mentally kicked himself. Take it slow. He took a deep breath. He really did need to take it slow, mainly because he had to figure out what he was going to do about his biggest problem of all – the fact that he was falling in love with her.

Chapter Five

"I don't want land on the other side of the lake!" Martin yelled into the phone. "Get your head out of your ass and do what I hired you for, Nolan!"

He pressed a finger to his temple as he listened to the Chris Nolan try to defend himself.

"Mr. Jacobs, if you would just listen to the benefits of having a resort closer to Osage Beach, I think you would realize that it would be more profitable than one in Magic."

"I am not paying you to come up with your own ideas. I am paying you to close the deal on the Lakewood. And if you can't do it, I will find someone who can!" With that, Martin ended the call. Picking up his crystal glass filled with three fingers of scotch, he whirled and flung it against the wall of his home office. The crystal glass shattered against the marble fireplace.

"Fuck!" he yelled to himself. He didn't know how things had gone so wrong. First, he'd lost the resort to that girl, and now the man who was supposed to be the master at acquiring property from anyone, seemed like he couldn't care less about closing the deal.

It was past time to take matters into his own hands. Hell, that should have been his first move. Experience had taught him not to trust other people to get things done. If Isabel couldn't be easily convinced to sell the Lakewood, then he would just have to make the thought seem more appealing.

Unfortunately, he still needed Ramiro for this task if he wanted to maintain a low profile. At least the younger man had proven helpful in the past. Bringing up Ramiro's contact information on his phone, Martin hit the call button. As always, Ramiro answered on the first ring.

"It's time for you to step in." He didn't waste any time, and he knew Ramiro had been in Magic waiting for instructions.

"Do you want me to take her out?" Ramiro asked as though he were discussing the weather.

Martin sighed. It would be so much easier if she were just out of the way, but she was popular in the community. Her death would receive a lot of attention.

Thinking of his options, he finally replied, "No matter what happens, suspicion can't fall on me. You have to understand that. If anything happened to Isabel, it would have to be an unfortunate accident. But if you can't make that happen, then maybe you could still give her some . . . . motivation."

"Motivation?"

"Yes. She doesn't seem at all interested in selling the property. Maybe something needs to happen at the resort so it's not quite so inviting for guests. If business started to go downhill, Isabel might decide it's not worth the hassle. What we need is the proper . . . incentive for her to sell. But if something happened to her before she could make the correct decision, well then, that would indeed be unfortunate."

He could almost hear Ramiro smiling through the phone. "Consider it done, sir." He disconnected.

Martin stared at the phone. He hoped whatever Ramiro had planned that he got it done quickly and that it had the desired effect. After waiting out his brother, he wasn't going to wait any longer. The land was his, and he needed to get Isabel Craig out of his way.

****

The ladder wobbled a bit as Izzy moved one step higher, orange streamer in hand.

"Jesus, Izzy! I told you to wait for me!" Milo rushed over, his big tattooed arms reaching up to steady the ladder firmly. "It would really give the resort a bad name if you fell and broke your neck in my restaurant."

It was three in the afternoon, and the two of them had been working since after the lunch rush to decorate The Lounge. Hazy gauze was carefully draped over various shapes of wire, giving the illusions of ghostly figures that would be highlighted by black lights the night of the party. Electric candles hung from the ceiling with thin wires so it gave the illusion they were floating. Some might say the streamers were unnecessary, but she didn't care. If she was going to decorate, she was going all out.

"There!" She attached the last streamer to a hook high above her head before slowly making her way back down the ladder.

"Nice!" She heard the raspy female voice from behind them and looked back to see Tessa doing a slow circle, admiring the decorations. "This looks amazing, Iz! You still have a week left before The Ball, and you're way ahead of schedule." Picking up a hand-shaped plastic glove filled with candy bars, she raised an eyebrow. "Nice touch."

The library, or media center, that Tessa managed was closed on Mondays, so it wasn't unusual for her to come in for lunch or a drink. Plus, watching the interaction between Milo and Tessa never got old. Izzy often wondered if they were going to take their flirting to the next level. Ever since Tessa moved to town, Milo hadn't been able to take his eyes off her. In fact, he really hadn't show much interest in anyone. Before his time in Special Forces, he'd been quite the ladies' man according to town gossip. But now, he didn't seem at all interested in making a move with anyone. Then again, neither did Tessa. The seemed to be the only two people who didn't notice how much the air sizzled when they were near each other.

As Tessa bent to study an intricately carved jack-o-lantern, Milo's blue eyes took in every curve of her body. With a sly smile, Izzy shook her head. Maybe she couldn't figure out her own love life, but that didn't stop her from wanting to give those two a push in the right direction.

"Come sit and have a drink with me." Tessa motioned to Izzy as she sat at the bar and patted a seat beside her.

Looking at her watch, Izzy perched on a bar stool next to Tessa. "I really need to go to the cabin and find some of my Halloween makeup so we can do an effective zombie look." Izzy had acquired quite the collection of Halloween makeup over the last few years, and the stuff lasted forever. She had also gotten really good at special effects makeup.

Milo smiled. "I always enjoy your costumes, Iz. It's amazing what you can do with liquid latex and YouTube."

"Come on," Tessa chided. "Have you taken a break at all today? Sit down for a second."

Izzy blew out a breath that ruffled her bangs. "Okay, one drink. Just one."

Milo walked behind the bar and leaned in so he was close to Tessa. "What'll it be, pretty lady?" The heat in Milo's eyes when he looked at Tessa almost made Izzy blush.

She watched as Tessa leaned in so her face was about an inch from his. "Do you think you could give me a screaming orgasm?"

Izzy had to bite her lip to stifle a giggle as Milo's mouth popped open, color rushing to his face. She didn't think she'd ever seen the big tattooed man blush before.

"Uhhh. . ." he stammered.

A wide grin spread over Tessa's face in triumph at the reaction she had elicited. "Yes, a screaming orgasm. It's vodka, Irish cream, and Kahlua."

"Oh, right. Of course," he said hurriedly, backing up. "I think we're out of Irish cream. I need to get a new bottle from the kitchen."

He immediately rushed off, holding a bar towel strategically over the front of his jeans, and it didn't take a genius to know what he was hiding. As soon as he was out of earshot, Tessa erupted into a fit of giggles, and Izzy shook her head, laughing.

"You know, you really shouldn't tease him like that."

"Oh, but it's sooo much fun. Tessa wiggled her eyebrows mischievously. "And speaking of hot guys, how are things going with your tantalizing twins?"

Groaning, Izzy walked around the bar to retrieve a bottle of water. "Things have not gotten any less confusing."

"Didn't your date with Chris go well?"

Nodding, Izzy related the events of their date, including the fact that Chris was a perfect gentleman, and made no attempt to come into her room when they got back to the hotel. He'd simply thrust her up against the wall and given her a mind-blowing kiss that curled her toes. Then he'd said good night. If that weren't confusing enough, Izzy related Graham's brief presence at the diner and the fact that her feelings were literally split between the two men.

"It should be easy to choose, right?" Izzy pondered aloud. "Graham couldn't be anymore clear about shoving me away. I just can't let my feelings for him go. But I don't want to let Chris go either." She leaned on the bar with her elbows, and began rubbing her temples. "I don't know what to do." Closing her eyes, she prayed for the answers to come to her.

"Oh sweetie, I'm sorry. I wish this were easier for you. I wish the choice was obvious."

Irish cream in hand, Milo walked up behind Izzy and reached for a glass. He seemed to have regained his calm and cool persona. "I'm not sure why you need to make a choice at all."

"Well, what am I supposed to do?" she asked, turning to look at him. "It's not fair to see both of them, or to have feelings for one when half my heart belongs to the other." Izzy drummed her fingers on the bar, even as Milo shook his head.

"No, you don't get it." He said as he reached for the vodka.

Tessa glared at Milo in annoyance. "Ohmigod, Captain Evasive, could you try being a little more specific?"

He began pouring Tessa's drink as he hid a smirk. "You two didn't know the Nolan brothers the way they used to be. They always dated the same women. Up until about five years ago."

"The same women? What do you mean? Like they took turns dating them?" That kind of competition definitely could have caused some tension.

"Nooo. . ." Milo drew out slowly as he poured the Kahlua. "I mean when they dated a woman, they dated one woman. Together."

A slow smile spread across Tessa's face. "Wooow. That is about the hottest image that has crossed through my head in I don't remember how long." She shifted her gaze to Izzy. "You are so damn lucky."

All the air went out of the room. The images that plagued her dreams of being in the middle of Graham and Chris could actually be a reality? "Wait a second. I think my head is spinning. Surely you're not saying what I think you're saying."

Milo just nodded while Tessa was the one who piped up. "Oh yeah he is!" She held up her hand to Izzy for a high five, but Izzy was too busy standing there with her mouth open.

Too many emotions were running through her head. Surprise was definitely one, considering the two men didn't even get along. But then the image of the two of them taking her together crossed her mind, and she felt her entire body heat up.

A laugh escaped her friend. Tessa pushed up her glasses as she assessed Izzy. "I think you just got it."

"So, so, it's—it's like book club?" She could barely get the words out.

"Oh yeah!" Tessa confirmed. "Except better because this is like reality." Thinking for a moment, a new wave of excitement overcame Tessa. "Hell, Izzy, think of the book reviews you'll be able to give. You'll know if some of this stuff is actually physically possible. Oh, this is awesome!"

Milo slid Tessa's drink to her as he rolled his eyes. "Can't you people read mysteries or something besides your lady porn?"

Chugging the drink, Tessa wiped her mouth with the back of her hand. "It is *not* porn. It is erotica! And some of the books are erotic suspense."

At Milo's raised eyebrow, Tessa crossed her arms over her chest. "What? You don't know."

Before Milo could respond with a quip, Izzy jumped in. "But they don't even like each other. They don't get along." Comprehension of the situation was just not fitting into her brain. "I can't imagine them sharing. It just doesn't make sense."

"Like I said, you didn't know them before, Iz," Milo said again. "They were close. Really close. They had been their entire lives. When they started dating the same women, no one really thought twice about it." Shrugging, Milo began to wipe down the bar with a towel. "It just seemed natural for them. They were happy."

"So what changed?" Izzy had already guessed that something must have happened between the two men, but with this new information, her curiosity was more than piqued. How had they gone from being so close to being worlds apart?

"That's not my story to tell, Iz." Milo shook his head.

"Oh, come on! You can't leave us hanging!" Tessa chimed in.

"You," Milo pointed at Tessa, "are a bad influence."

"Me? I am not, you tattooed barbarian!" And then they were off, exchanging barbs.

Grabbing her purse, Izzy decided to leave the two as they traded jabs.

"Hey!" Tessa's voice called after her. "I thought you were having a drink with me!"

Izzy didn't turn around, but just waved a hand behind her as she walked out. "I'll call you later!" Right now, she needed to process this new information and figure out exactly what she was going to do with it. If it were true, this put a whole different spin on things.

****

The police scanner crackled as Graham turned his car onto the road leading past Richard Craig's cabin and up to the resort. Izzy hadn't stayed at the cabin since her grandpa had died, the memories of his last weeks too painful for her. Graham completely understood, and knew it must be hard for her, trying to figure out how to adapt to things now. Besides, as independent as she was, Izzy didn't do well at being alone. Living at the hotel and being around people helped her heal. His heart swelled as he thought of her compassion for others.

Over the last few days, Graham had gone through several different speeches trying to cover what he wanted to say to Izzy. He'd wanted to talk to her since he'd seen her in the diner with Chris. It just took him a few days of practicing exactly what he was going to say and gathering his nerve.

Unfortunately, he still wasn't any closer to figuring out how to tell her what he felt. Hell, he still didn't quite know exactly how he felt. His feelings for her were so . . . intense. Something inside of him flared when he was near her, to the point where he felt almost out of control. That scared the shit out of him.

But what scared him more was not being with her at all. He couldn't watch her walk away from him. The thought of losing her caused a physical ache – an emptiness – somewhere deep inside of him that he didn't think he could live with. So where did that leave him?

He'd finally said 'fuck it.' He was just going to take her out to dinner and talk to her. Hopefully, he could form some semblance of . . . something coherent. It might help if he weren't as nervous as a fucking teenage boy about to talk to a girl for the first time.

Taking a deep breath, he slowed at the curve in the road. The fall leaves rained down from the trees that lined the main road. Normally he would admire the beauty, but today he was just trying to make it to his destination without losing his nerve and turning the car around.

Go slow and ask her to dinner. It's not that hard, Nolan. Still, what if she told him it was too late? What if she laughed at him? What if she was already in love with his brother?

As he drove past the cabin, he contemplated turning the car around again. Then he spotted Izzy's car. What the hell was she doing there? Surely, she hadn't decided to move back in.

Graham's insecurities fled as he pulled in. The crunch of the gravel drive signaled his arrival as he parked his car next to Izzy's in front of the cabin. His only concern now was checking on her to make sure she was okay.

He found the front door open, and raised a hand to knock when he heard muffled crying coming from inside. Panic washed over him and he rushed in. "Izzy! Izzy, where are you?"

The cabin was small, but the open layout made it seem spacious. A breakfast bar separated the living area from the kitchen, and a short hallway across from the kitchen led to two bedrooms. Graham didn't see Izzy, but noticed a box on top of the bar area. "Izzy!" Turning, he started down the hallway back to the bedrooms when she walked out.

"Graham?" her voice quavered, her eyes red, and fresh tears on her cheeks.

"Sweetheart," he breathed, and in an instant, he had crossed the short distance between them and gathered her in his arms. "Are you okay? What happened?" The anguish on her face caused his heart to hurt. He would gladly rip it out himself if it would spare Izzy pain.

"Nothing," she looked up at him with her big eyes. "It's just so silly." Weakly shoving at his chest, she tried to back away, but Graham held her tightly.

115

"What is? Talk to me, baby." He cupped her face in his hands, searching her eyes. Moving a few strands of hair from her wet cheeks, he searched her face carefully. He hadn't noticed she was holding something until she leaned back from him and he saw that she had a book.

"I was going through some of my grandpa's favorite books. I thought I'd take some back to the hotel to read." She backed away enough that she could open the book and pull out a bookmark. It looked like it was a laminated paper bookmark that a child had made. Izzy held it out to him, and he smiled at the child's drawing of a little girl holding hands with a man. It read 'To Grandpa, I love you more than forever. Love, Izzy.'

"He kept it." Her voice wobbled. "I made it for him when I was six, and he kept it." She swiped at another tear that fell. "It's ridiculous that this should upset me, I know." Tucking the bookmark carefully inside the book, she cradled the treasure to her chest.

"No, it's not. It's not at all. Why would you think it's ridiculous?"

"I just feel like I've been handling all the big stuff so well, and then something small hits me, and I go to pieces." She shook her head, biting her lip to stifle more tears.

Graham didn't say a word, but just opened his arms again and let her lean into him. "Let it go, baby. You can't bottle it up. You have to let yourself grieve, let yourself heal."

"I – I just don't know how," she whispered into his chest.

"Yes you do," he kissed the top of her head. "Lean on me. You can always lean on me. And it's okay to just let go. I'll always catch you, Iz." He closed his eyes, resting a cheek on the top of her head.

Choking on a sob, Izzy clutched him tighter. She buried her head in his chest and let out another sob, and then as if someone had pulled the cork from a dam, the tears let loose in a torrent. Strong hiccupping sobs flooded from her little body, and Graham held her tightly as she shook, her cries coming in waves.

He didn't tell her to stop or try to quiet her. He just held her and spoke in soft murmurs against her ear. "Let it go, sweetheart. I'm here. I've got you."

They stood that way for several minutes as he softly stroked her hair and her back, and eventually her tears eased, replaced with soft sniffles. Graham enjoyed the feeling of his arms around her, and hoped that didn't make him a bastard. Although he hated seeing her sad, it made him feel good to offer her some bit of comfort.

She was so good at putting on a strong front. This smart woman had a head for business, and a charming personality that could tame the most difficult hotel guest. She was kind and beautiful and funny and sexy. She was everything he'd ever wanted, and right now, she was in his arms.

When she finally lifted her gaze to meet his, he saw that the tears had faded, and her cheeks were slightly flushed. It reminded him of the day he'd held her at the cemetery three weeks ago.

"Graham, I—" She cleared her throat. "I'm sorry. I didn't mean to . . ." Suddenly she looked mortified. "Oh God, your shirt's all wet." Pushing against him, she tried to back away, but again he held her in place.

"Uh-uh. You don't get to be embarrassed or sorry. You needed to let that out, Iz." Reaching up with a rough hand, he caressed her cheek with the backs of his knuckles. He wondered if she even realized how she leaned into his touch. "I'm just glad I was here for you."

A little smile played at her lips. "I am too. But, what are you doing here exactly? I mean, I'm really glad you're here. It's just a surprise is all."

Reluctantly, he stepped back so he could look at her. "I came to see you. I was on my way up to the hotel when I saw your car."

"On your way to see me?" Her brow furrowed. "Is everything okay?"

Dammit, tell her how you feel. This is your chance. "Yes. Yes, everything is fine." He wanted to tell her what she did to him, how he needed her. The way his touch seemed to throw her off balance gave him courage, but here she was crying and upset about her grandfather. Deep down, he knew this wasn't the time to stumble through his conflicting emotions. There were so many things he wanted to say to her, but everything just went out the window. It wasn't the right time.

"Why don't I take you back up to the resort?" Maybe if he could get her back up to the Lakewood and buy her dinner, she would relax and they could talk.

But Izzy shook her head. "I can't go yet. I still haven't found the fake blood."

Graham almost snorted. "Uh – the what?"

The tilt of Izzy's little smile pleased him. "I originally came down here to get all the Halloween make-up." She gestured toward the large box on the counter. "I can't find the fake blood."

"And for Halloween, you're going to be. . ?"

"Tessa and I are going to be sexy zombies," she said, clapping her hands together. Graham laughed at the thought of her in zombie makeup. But the sexy part sounded promising.

Following Izzy over to the kitchen counter, he watched her dig around in the box as she spoke. "I really wanted to play *Night of the Living Dead* on the big screen in The Lounge the night of the party, but Milo is convinced it would scare the kids."

She rolled her eyes as Graham laughed. "Not everyone grew up with a love of horror movies, sweetheart."

Taking his hand, Izzy giggled and gave him a gentle pull toward the giant box of makeup and Halloween accessories. "Here, come help me find everything."

Thirty minutes later, she'd had found all of her makeup, and Graham was laughing at her stories of Halloweens past. It wasn't quite the afternoon he had originally had in mind, but he wouldn't trade this time with her. The smile radiated from her eyes, and Graham just hoped he had a little to do with the improvement in her spirits. Now he just needed to take a deep breath and ask her to dinner. It was time to discuss the possibility of a relationship between the two of them. And dammit, but he wanted to cross his fingers in hopes she said yes.

"Iz, I wanted to ask—" The buzzing of her phone caused him to trail off.

"Hold that thought one second," she said, answering the call. Immediately her smile widened as she listened to the person on the other end of the line. "Tonight? Sure." She giggled. "You will just have to wait and see what I'm wearing."

Fuck. His fucking brother. "Yep, seven o'clock. I'll just meet you downstairs." She finished the call and looked up at Graham as he reached for the jacket he'd lain across the back of the couch. "Where are you going?" she asked, confused. "I thought you had something you were going to tell me?"

It was stupid for him to be angry, but he was. He didn't know if he was angry with Chris, Izzy or himself.

"I have to go. I have things to do. I didn't realize it had gotten so late."

"Graham, please," she sighed warily. "Are you really that mad that I'm friends with your brother?"

"Friends?" he gave an unforgiving laugh. "Seriously, Izzy. You two are more than just *friends*. And yes, it fucking bothers me." The way she talked to Chris all breathy voiced made his stomach feel like he'd just swallowed a giant ball of jealousy, and he really hated it.

"Friends, Graham. We are friends. We're getting to know each other. And you are doing it again!" Her voice rose in frustration.

"Doing what again?" he asked, shrugging on his jacket.

"Acting like a jealous boyfriend when you said yourself that you didn't care about me."

"What?" his brows rose in surprise. "Izzy, are you crazy? I never said I didn't care about you."

"No," she said, rolling her eyes upward as if to recall his exact words from her memory. "You said we were friends, and that just because you were attracted to me, that it didn't mean anything."

Graham almost growled in frustration and scrubbed a hand over his beard. "We're not friends," he said in a harsher tone than he intended.

Her face fell, and he realized too late how that sounded. Fuck. "That's not what I mean, Izzy."

Hurting her seemed to be the only thing he was good at anymore. He had to get out of there before he caused total destruction. It didn't matter what he wanted for himself. He just couldn't cause her any more pain.

"Then what do you mean? Be honest with me, Graham. Tell me why you keep pushing me away."

She grabbed his arm as he turned to go, and he let out a frustrated sigh. This was a bad idea. What was he thinking, coming here to talk to her about his feelings when he knew she was dating Chris? Besides, no matter how much he hated to admit it, Chris could give her what she needed.

He looked her steadily in the eyes. "I'm not what you need, Izzy. As much as I want to be, I'm not. You need someone who's not going to hurt you." He shook his head in defeat. "Chris won't hurt you."

"You're contradicting yourself," she said with a stomp of her foot that he would have found cute if the situation hadn't been so serious. "You told me before that you had to protect me from Chris, and now you're telling me that he's the one for me."

"Yes." He nodded. "Iz, I know you won't understand this, but I can feel him – what he's feeling, I mean." He put his fingers to his eyes, not wanting to admit what he knew to be true. "I don't know in the beginning if his intentions were just to get you into bed, but I know the moment things changed, the moment it got deeper."

Not saying a word, Izzy just stared at him.

"Jesus, Iz, he's half in love with you." What he didn't say is that the intense feelings Chris had for her coursed through Graham's body along with his own. There would never been another woman in this world he would feel such an intense need for. "No matter what I think of him, he won't hurt you. I was wrong about that."

"And you will? You'll hurt me?" She asked incredulously.

He just nodded, his eyes still on hers. "I won't mean to. I won't want to. But it's inevitable. It's what always happens. I know you don't understand, but just know that I'm not going to let it happen to you. I don't want to take the chance of hurting you."

He watched her hands clench into fists at her sides. By the firmness to her jaw, he could tell that she had moved way beyond frustration and into anger. He couldn't say he blamed her.

"No," she said, her chin coming up.

"No?"

"You don't want me to get hurt, Graham?" Tears welled in her eyes. "You're hurting me now. Pulling away like this hurts me. Well, guess what? If there is one thing I have learned in the last few weeks, it's that life is precious, and if you're lucky enough to have people that you love, you have to hang on. You have to fight." A tear spilled over. "Don't I mean enough to you for you to fight for me?"

The determination in her face both thrilled and scared him. "Izzy, baby, it's just not that simple." He wanted to reach out, wanted to comfort her, make her understand.

She took a step closer. "It is that simple. You're not a coward, so stop acting like one. Stop running and talk to me. Tell me the truth. What happened to make you so damn scared?"

Her words knocked the air out of him. As much as he tried to hide his feelings, Graham felt stripped bare in front of her, as if she could see right through him. He stood toe to toe with her, looking down into the determined set of her face, her eyes full of emotion. "It's not that easy," he said again. "If I stay here, I'll—"

"You'll what?"

Shaking his head slowly, he turned from the intensity of her eyes. "Nothing." Taking a deep breath, he took a step toward the door. "Nothing, dammit."

He was startled when Izzy grabbed his arm firmly in her small hands, yanking him back with all the force she could muster. "No! You can't just walk away. Talk to me! Let me in!"

"I can't!" He felt his blood starting to boil the more she pushed. Why couldn't she just let him go?

"Why? Because you don't want me to get hurt?" She said it almost sarcastically, swiping at an angry tear. "Give me a better fucking reason than that!"

Graham spun around, his blood boiling over. "Because I'm fucking in love with you, and it scares the hell out of me!" he shouted.

Izzy's mouth dropped open, and she stepped back with a startled gasp, dropping her hands from his arm.

"Fuck!" Graham exclaimed, starting for the door again. He had to get out of there.

"You're just leaving?" she said in shock. "You can't say that and just leave."

"Yes. I can." Yanking the door open, Graham strode briskly to his car. He couldn't do this, couldn't get involved. If he took Izzy as his own and he lost her, he would never recover.

He stopped in his tracks. If he lost her? What was he doing? He was letting her go because he was afraid, but if he walked away, he would lose her anyway. And he didn't want to hurt her, yet he'd never seen so much pain on her face than when he walked away from her. So what the fuck was he doing?

She needed to know the truth – the whole truth. He wanted to tell her not only how he felt, but also about his past with his brother and their ex. Graham had been ready to make her understand. So what was stopping him now? He still wanted her. Fuck, he craved her. She was right. He was a coward. He was afraid of how she made him feel. He'd never felt like this about anyone in his whole life, and he didn't know how to deal with it.

Halfway between the cabin and his patrol car, he stood perfectly still. If he left now, he knew that was it. He couldn't keep doing this to her, couldn't keep causing her pain just because he was a jackass. Theo's words came back to him. *'You're not dead. Stop acting like it.'*

Turning to look back at the cabin, he saw her standing in the doorway, perfectly still, just watching him. He looked in her eyes, and he saw his soul, his future. It was time to stop being afraid. It was time to live. He couldn't let her go. Not this time. Not ever. This time, he wasn't walking away.

With determination on his face, Graham walked back to her in long, quick strides. As he got closer to her, Izzy stepped back. But Graham would have none of it. Never again would he let her pull away from him.

Reaching for her, he hooked one arm around her waist, pulling her to him, anchoring her body to his. The other hand tangled in her hair, cupping the back of her head, before he brought his mouth to hers in a punishing kiss. The parted surprise of her lips allowed his tongue access.

The taste of her was heaven. Graham's tongue slid over hers in a slow dance, his strong lips claiming her as his own. This was finally happening. He had dreamed of kissing her for so long. His mouth moved lower to nip at her jawline and trail kisses down her neck, her lavender scent intoxicating. Her breathing was ragged, little whimpers escaping her as he nipped along her neck. Good lord, the sounds she made caused his cock to go stone hard.

The slow steps he'd been taking as he kissed her had backed Izzy up to the breakfast bar that separated the kitchen from the living area. Leaning against it provided an anchor so Graham could press his hips against her. He smiled as she gasped, loving the feel of his erection against her stomach, wanting it closer, needing to be closer.

"Please don't stop," she breathed.

He lifted his head, gazing down at her with hooded lids. "Oh sweetheart, I have absolutely no intention of stopping."

****

Heat sizzled through Izzy as she felt Graham's erection pressing against her belly. Good God, he felt huge. In her hazy mind, she wondered if identical twins meant he and Chris were identical everywhere.

She lifted her arms to wrap them around Graham's neck and almost lost her balance as he suddenly stepped away from her. *Oh no, please don't let him stop again*. When he'd left just moments before, she felt her heart being trampled with every step he took away from her. She looked up at him in fear, but she saw his lids hooded and his mouth slack as his eyes washed over her. He wanted her. She swallowed hard, watching him shrug out of his jacket and toss it on the couch, followed by his holster, and then his shirt.

Admiring the ripple of his muscles as he moved, Izzy was desperate for the feel of that magnificent toned body against her own. She started to move forward to run her fingers through the dark sprinkle of hair across his chest, but he stopped her with one word.

"Strip," he said in a rough growl.

Her eyes widened as she stared back at him. "I – I beg your pardon."

"You heard me, Izzy," he said as he stood perfectly still staring at her. "You're wearing too many clothes. I want you to strip for me."

Usually a demand like that would have her protesting, but when Graham said it, she felt her pussy flood, her entire body trembling at the command in his voice. He noticed it too, she knew, as a slow grin crossed his face, his growing desire evident.

Still, she was self-conscious. Her body was oddly proportioned for her short stature. Her butt was too big, and she was pretty sure that her breasts were starting to sag. When she'd been with Chris, things had moved so quickly that she hadn't had time to think. But now, with Graham just standing back staring at her like he wanted to devour her, she didn't know if she could just –

"Sweetheart," he began stepping closer to her again, lifting a finger to run it down her cheek. She swallowed hard as his hand came to rest on her neck, his fingers enclosing around the front of her throat as if he was mimicking a collar. "There's one thing you need to be perfectly clear about. I like very much to be in charge in the bedroom. And I can already tell how much you like it when I take charge. Even if you don't know it yet, your body certainly does."

He was right. She could feel the throb of her heartbeat as her entire body surged toward him, as if he were a giant magnet attracting her every cell. With his hand in a non-threatening grip around her throat, she could feel his power over her, his authority.

"When I give you an order, I expect you to follow it, Isabel. If you truly don't want to do something, then just say 'stop.' If you say 'stop' then everything stops. Do you understand?" His thumb stroked the side of her throat, causing a groan of pleasure from deep with her.

Smiling at her response, Graham tightened his fingers briefly and released, leaving her feeling cold at the loss of his touch.

"You need to tell me you understand, baby. I need to know this is what you want." Although there was strength in the tone of his voice, his face held worry as he looked her, waiting for her response.

"So . . so . . 'stop' is like my safe word?" she finally asked, wrapping her mind around what he was asking of her. She licked her lips, heat pooling low in her belly as true understanding began to take hold. Safe word, direct orders. . . "You're a dominant," she breathed. "At book club, I've read . . ." she stopped, embarrassed.

Oh good lord, did she really want to tell him about the erotica that she read? Since her favorite book series took place at a BDSM club in Florida, she was quite familiar with the lifestyle. Well, she was familiar with it in books, anyway. Currently, she was reading a book where two men dominated one woman. The thought of Graham and his brother together, dominating her, having their way with her, made Izzy's knees go weak.

Graham's rich voice rumbled as he let out a low chuckle. "You read a lot of books, don't you sweetheart? Sure, we can call 'stop' your safe word, unless you'd like to pick a different word."

Izzy simply shook her head, staring at him, loving the way his eyes held heat and amusement. His mouth quirked up, and she knew there was a dimple hidden beneath that beard. Oh, she was finally going to feel the scrape of his beard on her breasts, on her stomach, on her . . . She almost moaned at the thought.

Wrapping an arm around her waist, Graham steadied her as the other hand cupped her chin. "Baby, I do not know what that look was, but I would really like to find out. I have got to start reading some of these books."

Gently caressing her face with those calloused fingers, he leaned in for a quick kiss. "I am dominant, although I wouldn't say I'm hardcore about it. I just like to be in control in the bedroom, and to occasionally use my handcuffs for more than just restraining criminals."

Her mouth went dry as she thought about him clicking cuffs on her, restraining her to the bed, climbing on top of her, taking her over and over again.

His face split into a slow grin as he twirled a lock of her hair around his finger. "I can see you like that idea." He tugged on the blonde curl and tucked it behind her ear. "But we'll save that for next time. This first time, I want to feel your hands on me, and your mouth on me. Tell me that's what you want too," he pleaded.

"Yes. Oh yes," she whispered, pressing into him.

"But first, you need to answer me, Iz. Do you understand what I said?"

"Yes. Yes, I understand," she said swallowing.

Nodding, he studied her face, her reactions. "And if I do something you don't like or don't want, what do you say?"

"Stop," she answered quickly. "I say stop."

"Good girl." Graham claimed her mouth again, his hand reaching up to caress her right breast. Her nipple hardened beneath the thin fabric of the blouse as he circled it with his thumb, causing her back to arch. He swallowed her whimpers as he pinched her nipples gently. He'd never seen a woman so responsive, so passionate.

"Too many clothes," he growled. He released her again, taking another step back. "Now I won't say it again, Izzy. Strip."

This time, her hands immediately went to the buttons on her blouse, her fingers trembling. It took a couple of tries, but she finally managed to slip the buttons through their holes, letting her black shirt slide down her arms and fall to the floor.

"Everything, Iz. I want you naked." His dark tone made her shiver, but she wouldn't deny him. Still self-conscious, Izzy felt strength in the intensity of Graham's hungry gaze over her body. She made quick work of the rest of her clothes. When she stepped out of her khakis and kicked them aside, she stood in front of him, reveling in the way his eyes worshipped her.

"You are so fucking beautiful," he murmured.

Part of her wanted time to stand still so she could savor this. She wanted this moment burned into her brain, the way he looked at her, the way it made her feel. But she wanted Graham so much, and she had waited so long that she couldn't stay still. She closed the distance between them, lifting her face for his kiss. He didn't deny her, his lips strong, demanding, as they took hers.

Her scalp lit up as one strong hand fisted in her hair, the other hand sliding down to her backside, squeezing and kneading, pressing her more firmly to him. Izzy broke the kiss to gasp for a breath. "Wait, wait. We have one problem."

"What?" he asked releasing her. "What is it, sweetheart?"

"You, sir, have too many clothes on." She reached for his jeans, anxious to see the rest of his body and take him in her hands.

Graham smiled wickedly, and Izzy didn't have time to register the fact that he bent down to hook an arm at the back of her knees. She squealed as he lifted her up and began carrying her down the hall to her old bedroom.

Burying her face in his neck, she enjoyed the softness of his beard, the warm spicy scent of his soap. She'd always thought his beard would be scratchy, but it wasn't. It was soft, with a light scrape over her skin that she found terribly erotic.

Encompassed in his rock hard arms, Izzy was almost frantic with need. His authority combined with the gentleness he exhibited as he laid her on the bright yellow comforter made her heart swell. She watched hungrily as he stripped off his jeans, and she heard a moan escape her lips as he released his engorged cock.

"You're the one who's beautiful," she whispered, sitting up on the bed to admire him. Graham was all tan, hard muscle. Just like his brother, his erect cock reached almost to his navel, but that was where the similarity ended. Where Chris was lean and muscular, Graham's muscles bulged, evidence that he worked out, and the slight bulk of him made him seem all the more powerful.

Izzy lifted a hand to run over his hard abs, enjoying the way he sucked in his breath, his stomach quivering at her touch. She was the one who felt powerful now, eliciting that reaction from him.

Her eyes widened as she watched him slowly stroking the large cock jutting out from the V of his thighs. He truly was beautiful. He already had a pearly drop of fluid on the tip. Gathering her courage, Izzy leaned forward and swiped her tongue over the head, causing a groan to escape Graham, his cock jerking in response.

"Sweet Jesus, Iz, you're going to kill me." His strangled voice came out on a harsh rasp.

Grinning up at him, she reached up to firmly stroke him with her hand, her other hand coming up to cup his balls, tight and heavy in the palm of her hand. She leaned her head forward once more, wanting nothing more than to taste his arousal on her tongue again, but Graham gently gripped her hair, pulling her head back.

"You don't have to do that," he said softly.

She frowned. "But I thought you wanted. . ."

"Your mouth on me," he finished. "Oh God, I do, baby. You have no idea how much. But is this something you want to do?"

She grinned, "What happened to ordering me around?"

He smiled back, "Okay, I can definitely do that." He playfully stroked her hair. "Tell me, Izzy, do you know how to suck cock?"

Her smile faltered. That's actually something she'd never done. It wasn't that she was opposed to it. She just had a limited amount of experience. Only one boyfriend had asked her to do it, but the act seemed almost too intimate, and their relationship had ended before she'd ever worked up the courage.

Graham frowned at her, "Oh God, you haven't done this before, have you?" He backed away, but Izzy's hands went to the back of his thighs, pulling him to her.

"Please, I want to. Please." She wanted this intimacy with Graham, wanted desperately to pleasure him in every way she could. "You just have to tell me what you like."

Sensing her nervousness, he quirked a smile. "Well, the only rule I have is no biting. Because I would really hate trying to explain that to Reed at the hospital."

She giggled, releasing the breath she didn't realize she'd been holding.

Leaning forward, she captured the head of his dick in a wet kiss, sucking lightly. He let out a strangled groan, his hands tangling in her hair.

"Yes," he hissed as she took more of him into her mouth. "That feels so good, sweetheart."

The soft skin covering the rigid steel of his erection tasted slightly musky. And the groans he made as she licked him from the base to the tip made this the best treat she'd ever. Looking up at him, she loved the way his eyes were closed in pleasure, his jaw relaxed.

"Just like that," he instructed as her tongue swirled around the bulging head. "Now, I want you to suck, sweetheart. Take me deeper."

Sliding her mouth down until he nudged the back of her throat, she began to suck, her cheeks hollowing as she lifted her head. She massaged his balls gently, and felt his hand tighten in her hair, the pleasure/pain spurring her on. She could taste more salty drops of fluid from his tip and knew he must be getting close.

"No. Iz, no," he groaned as his hips involuntarily surged forward. When she didn't stop, he gripped her hair more firmly, pulling her off of him.

"What?" she looked up into his pained expression. "What did I do wrong? I didn't use teeth. Isn't that the number one rule?" Biting the inside of her lip, she backed up in worry.

"You didn't do anything wrong," he said with a shaky breath, sitting on the bed next to her. Cradling her head, he kissed her swollen lips. "I just don't want to come in your mouth," he whispered against her. "I want to be inside of you. I want to come deep inside of you. I want to feel your pussy clench around me when you cry out my name. That's what I want," he said between little pecks.

Easing her back on the fluffy comforter, he put one knee between her thighs, covering her with his strong body. He captured her mouth, stealing her breath, possessing her, his tongue thrusting deeply, mimicking what she wanted his cock to do to her.

Her hazy brain couldn't form a thought. All she could do was feel, her skin hypersensitive as he released her mouth and began kissing down to her breast, the scrape of his beard sending little electric shockwaves straight to her pussy.

"Graham, please!" she cried out, her head writhing back and forth. "I need you. Please, I can't wait anymore."

****

The involuntary thrusting of her hips against him just about sent Graham over the edge. He wanted so much to take this slow, but all he really wanted to do was slam into her and take her for all he was worth. Not yet, though, not yet.

Kissing down her body, he sucked a nipple firmly into his mouth until it formed a hard peak. Circling it with his tongue, he enjoyed the way her hands clutched at his head, holding him to her breast, urging him on. Moving to the other nipple, he captured it between his teeth, laving it with his tongue as she cried out.

He dipped lower, trailing kisses to her belly button, circling with his tongue. He quickly learned that if he scraped his chin along sensitive areas of her skin, she moaned lightly, thrusting up at the light scratch of his beard. Enjoying her squirming, he dragged his chin against the line of her hip. At the same time, he reached up to cup her breast, loving the way it filled his palm, the hard nipple like a small pebble against his hand. He pinched it firmly, hearing her gasp as her body rose up.

He dipped lower until his mouth was even with her pussy. At the scent of her arousal, he thought his cock was going to burst. He leaned in to cover her vulva with his mouth, pulling back in a wet sucking kiss. Immediately her hands convulsed on his head as her hips arched up.

"Uh, uh, uh," he teased. Reaching up, he grasped her hands, holding her wrists firmly to her sides. "Be still."

She yanked her wrists against his hands, lifting her hips. Releasing one wrist, Graham brought his palm down in a light slap against her pussy. Fuck, he loved the way her legs jerked in response as she let out a startled gasp.

"I said be still, Izzy. I wanted to wait to restrain you until next time, but I'll do it now if I have to. Do you understand?"

"Yes sir, I'm sorry," she breathed mindlessly. She was so far gone already. It would be so easy to set her off. He was going to have to teach her self-control. But right now, he couldn't fault her for that. At the sound of her breathy voice calling him "Sir," Graham had to force himself to stop and count to three before he continued, his arousal almost overtaking him. Did she have any idea what she did to him? If he took her this second, he wouldn't be able to hold back, and he didn't want to scare her.

Holding her wrists immobile, he leaned in again, licking slow circles around her clit. He groaned just as she did, savoring her cream. She tasted sweet, a light honey flavor. "You taste so fucking good," he rumbled against her. He didn't think he would ever get enough of her.

All she could do was moan his name when he leaned in again, thrusting his tongue deeply into her vagina. He loved her little whimpers, loved the feeling of her hands fisting and jerking in his grasp, as little spasms shot like electricity through her body. He knew as soon as he attacked her clit, she would go off. But he didn't want that yet. No, he wanted to enjoy the pleasure torture of her body a little longer. With each swipe of his tongue, it seemed like her inhibitions fell away. She was writhing now, unable to remain still, and he loved driving her out of her mind.

Growling against her pussy, he thrust his tongue deeper, enthralled with how her body quivered from the vibration. Sucking in each of her labia, he trailed little bites along the sensitive tissue. When he began circling her incredibly swollen clit with his tongue, she let out a sound that was somewhere between a squeal and a cry. "Please, please, please," was all she could say over and over.

In what could be considered a reward or a punishment, he captured her slick clit between his lips, giving one strong suck to the engorged little nub before pulling back.

Kicking her feet against the bed in frustration, she thrust her hips against the air. Chuckling, Graham slid back up her body, moving her arms so he could pin her wrists against her head as his hips pinned hers to the mattress.

Her eyes shone with need and frustration. "Why did you stop?" she cried. Looking dazed, she was trying to catch her breath, her cheeks flushed. She looked almost drugged, and a sense of satisfaction washed over him. She was intoxicated with him, drunk with need, with want for him.

Leaning in for one hard kiss, he released her arms. "Look at me, Iz." He felt his heart swell as her eyes locked with his. God, how he loved this woman.

Her eyes searched his with wonder. In that moment, he knew that not only had she never performed oral sex on a man, but she'd never received it either. The thundering of her heart matched his own, and he leaned down to kiss her again before he backed away from her trembling body.

"No," she cried, sitting up. "Where are you going?"

Snatching up his jeans off the floor, he rummaged through his pockets. "A condom, baby. I need to get a condom." What he really craved was to thrust into her wetness with nothing between them, feel her silky body clench around him with no barriers. Soon, that would happen soon, but right now he had to protect her.

"I – I want to do it," she said reaching for him. His breath stopped for a moment as she took the condom from his hand. Brushing her hair back, she twisted her full mouth in concentration as she pinched the tip of the condom and rolled it down over his thick shaft.

"There." She leaned back, proud of herself, and looked up at him with a big smile. "You're not going to make me wait anymore, are you?"

"Not another second, baby." Pushing her back, Graham watched as she spread her thighs wide so he could settle in between them, and she lifted her hips to press her wetness against his cock.

"Slow, Izzy," he grasped her hips, holding her still. "Slow down." Above all else, he didn't want to hurt her. Arching up again, Izzy slid her wet pussy against his cock. All thoughts of going slow left his mind as his last shred of self-control snapped, his need for her consuming him.

Shifting slightly, he lined himself up with her vagina and paused. As soon as her eyes found his, he thrust deep. Izzy cried out, her pussy clenching around him as her hands gripped his shoulders, fingernails digging in.

"You're so tight," he groaned. She fit him like a glove, a soft velvet glove. Graham lifted his hips and slowly thrust himself back into her, deeply seating himself in her. Sliding into her felt like home, and he never wanted to leave.

****

Izzy felt so full, every nerve ending in her body lighting up. Everything inside of her was wound so tightly, she couldn't think. The desperate urge for release built fast and quick, but Graham found a slow deep pace, driving her out of her mind with need as she thrust up to meet his rhythm, trying to speed up, needing to come.

Pausing, Graham shifted slightly, adjusting himself, his hands going to the backs of her thighs to bring her legs up. Instinctively, she wrapped them around him. When he thrust again, he hit a spot deep inside of Izzy that caused her entire body to spark like frayed wire. Her eyes grew wide as her hands clenched spasmodically around his arms.

A wicked smile lit Graham's face. "That's it. That's the spot I was looking for." He thrust again and ground his pelvic bone against her throbbing clit.

Panting, Izzy thrust herself against him, her body rising to its summit. He thrust again so deep, and she was so, so close. The muscles of his biceps trembled beneath her fingers, and she looked into Graham's face to see his jaw clenched. With each thrust, he slammed into her hard, the force jarring her, sending her up higher.

The tingle of an orgasm started deep in her bones. She couldn't hold on, couldn't hold back. The sparks raced up her spine as she sprinted toward the edge.

"Baby, please. I need you to come for me. Come for me now." The muscles in his neck strained, and he thrust again, grinding his pelvis against hers. The sparks inside of her erupted into a flame that sent her soaring like a firework into the sky. Reaching that height, she detonated, her entire body bursting, shaking with explosive waves. And it didn't end. Her body involuntarily thrust against Graham, wanting more, needing more.

And he gave it to her in bone-shuddering thrusts. Somewhere, she heard a scream, and realized it was her own, a garbled version of Graham's name escaping her lips. When he gripped her hips tightly and thrust deeply, he held himself still and let out a roar, taking Izzy with him as he soared off that peak.

Never had she been multi-orgasmic, but her entire body shook, clenching around him, draining his cock as his thrusting slowed, bringing her down gently from her climax. Graham collapsed on top of her, and both of them gasped for air as they slowly drifted back to earth.

A few moments later, when he'd finally softened and slipped from her body, Izzy felt the loss, empty without him. When he rolled off, her hands went to him, holding him close. "Not yet. Don't leave me yet." She wanted to savor him longer. Just a little longer.

"I'm not going anywhere, sweetheart," he murmured contentedly against her ear. "Just give me one second."

He quickly disposed of the condom, and then gathered her close, pulling her next to him so he could cradle her in his arms. When her body cooled and she shivered, Graham reached down to snag a blanket from the end of the bed and pull it over both of them. She looked up at him with a little smile, and he kissed her slowly, sweetly. "Are you okay?"

Okay? She was perfect. A slow smile spread across her face, "Mmmm," she murmured as her eyes floated shut.

As she drifted off in his arms, she thought not only of Graham, but also of Chris. She wanted them both, and this had sealed it. She had to figure out a way to make this work, a way for all of them to be together. Her heart soared with hope for the future.

****

Toying with her hair, Graham watched Izzy as her breathing slowed and evened out. He was afraid he'd been too rough, but the harder he'd pushed, the more she seemed to let go, to lose herself. She really was everything he wanted.

Rolling on his back, he scrubbed a hand over his face. He wasn't so ignorant to think that everything was going to be sunshine and roses after this. There was still his brother to deal with. His brother who was expecting Izzy to be there at seven o'clock for a date. Somehow, she seemed unconcerned with this, which surprised him.

Graham's need for her had been the only thing he could think about. Now, he was afraid that this was just like years ago. He and Chris were in love with the same woman. Looking at Izzy's beautiful sleeping face, he knew that he couldn't let her go, and he would bet Chris wouldn't either. He tried to shake the thoughts free, to enjoy this moment with her. But no matter how hard he tried, he couldn't ignore the little nagging voice in the back of his head. *This won't end well.*

Chapter Six

'So What! I'm still a rock star. I'm having more fun, now that you're gone. . .' Graham woke to the sound of P!nk and realized Izzy's phone was trying to get her attention. "Sweetheart." He nudged her awake, and she opened her dazed eyes, blindly reaching for the phone.

Darkness had blanketed the sky outside, and Graham wondered how long they'd been asleep. Waking up with a naked Izzy next to him sent a jolt of adrenaline straight to his cock. The sheet fell beneath her breasts as she turned away revealing light pink nipples, and her gorgeous backside rubbed against his growing erection. Damn, he'd never be able to get enough of her.

Leaning in to nibble the back of her neck, he enjoyed her breathy little giggle that signaled her immediate arousal.

"Graham, the phone." Snatching her cell off the nightstand, she quickly leaned back into his embrace. But when she answered the phone, his smile disappeared as her body tensed, her face flaring in panic.

"What? What kind of emergency?" Sliding out of bed, Izzy began a frantic search for her clothes. She stilled midway toward the bedroom door, her face going deathly pale.

Fear seized Graham, but before he could reach Izzy, his own phone buzzed from somewhere on the floor. Crap, where had he tossed his jeans? He spotted them dangling off the rocking chair in the corner and sprinted over to dig out his phone.

"Nolan," he barked.

"Sheriff, you have to get to the Lakewood now." Dustin's voice shook slightly, causing Graham's anxiety to quicken. Normally Dustin handled any situation in town with a stoic resolve, often impressing others with his ability to remain calm. The fact that his voice betrayed his nerves set Graham on edge.

"What's happened?" he asked, yanking on his pants. Glancing over at Izzy, he saw that she'd headed into the small bathroom off of her bedroom.

"There's been a fire in the annex building – Izzy's office," Dustin said. "The firefighters are still in there, so I don't know how much damage there is, but we have everyone evacuated from the hotel."

"Shit! I'll be right there." Graham ended the call. Zipping up his jeans, he turned to holler at Izzy, but she was already standing in the doorway of the bathroom, wearing a short pink robe and clutching her phone. Her face was a ghostly white.

Crossing the room in a heartbeat, he pulled her into his arms. "It's okay, Sweetheart. I promise it's going to be okay." Rubbing her back in slow circles, he tried to ease the tension in both of them.

"A fire. My office." Tears pooled in her eyes as they darted around frantically, and she pulled away from him, shaking. "I have to find my clothes. I have to —"

"You have to calm down. Izzy, I will drive you to the hotel, but you need to calm down."

Her fingers trembled around her phone. "I don't understand. No one's been in there since this morning. I locked it up when I left. And the wiring wouldn't be a problem. Grandpa just had the annex built five years ago." Realization hit her, and she paused, her eyes widening. "Graham, you don't. . . you don't think . . . could someone have . . .?"

"Shhh," he soothed gently. "We're not jumping to conclusions. We'll go up there, and we'll figure it out. Together." At the trust on Izzy's face when she looked at him, he felt the urge to protect her grow deeper. "You're not alone," he said, cupping her face in both hands.

He gathered strength in the way she wrapped her arms around him and squeezed tightly. "Thank you," she mumbled against his chest.

****

The lights of two fire trucks beckoned to them, casting an eerie glow across the night. As Graham pulled his cruiser up to the main entrance, Izzy was struck by how the flashing lights from Dustin's patrol car illuminated the fifty or so hotel guests scattered about the front lawn.

Since she got the call from Milo, she'd tried to convince herself that maybe he'd been mistaken. A fire in her office just didn't make sense. But there was no mistake. The feverish buzz of conversations filtered through her window before the car even stopped, and the light scent of smoke singed her nostrils.

The deputy stood in the hotel entrance talking to Milo, and Izzy looked around for Andrea. If Josh hadn't been with her, Izzy might have missed her. The small brunette stood off to the side of the crowd with her arms wrapped around herself, looking like a turtle that was trying to withdraw into her shell. Josh's big body towered over her as he leaned in, speaking to her as he awkwardly patted her back.

Before Graham had even come to a complete stop, Izzy reached for the door handle. "Dammit, Izzy," she heard Graham behind her as she jumped out of the car and sprinted toward her friend. Unwinding her arms from around herself, Andi swiped at her streaked makeup and threw her arms around Izzy in a tight hug.

Josh stepped away, looking a bit relieved that someone was there to offer comfort, and Izzy had a fleeting thought that he was probably one of those men who lost all sense of speech the second a woman shed a tear. Reaching out, she squeezed his hand, grateful to him for staying with Andrea.

"Are you okay?" she whispered to her friend. "What happened? Was anyone hurt?" The questions tumbled out of her as she stepped back to look Andi up and down, searching for injuries.

"Everyone is fine, Izzy." It was Dustin who answered, walking up behind her. His long black hair, a trait of his Native American heritage, was swept back into a ponytail, and his midnight eyes held a look of concern. "No injuries."

He looked toward Graham as the sheriff stepped up beside her, winding an arm around her midsection in a protective embrace. Milo immediately put an arm around Andi's shoulders in a brotherly manner, and she leaned into him for support.

"We got lucky," Milo said, his face grim. "Thanks to Andrea."

Blinking, Izzy looked between Andi and Milo. "What do you mean?"

Josh stepped up, a firm set to his jaw. "If it weren't for her, no telling how many people would have been hurt."

"Yes, she really is a hero," Theo's voice was gruff as he walked up to join the group. Even in the darkness, Izzy could see her friend blush as her eyes cast downward, her body going rigid at Theo's approach.

"What did the fire chief say? Are we any closer to figuring out what the hell happened?" Dustin asked the PI.

Sighing, Theo shook his head, looking at Andi with wary eyes. "Andi, hon, we need to talk to you so we can get a better timeline of exactly what happened when you discovered the fire. Did you see anything? Anyone suspicious?"

A sense of security eased Izzy's worry, as she felt Graham's protective squeeze before he released her. "Not here," he said, eyeing a cluster of three middle-aged women who seemed to be inching closer to them, no doubt trying to see if they could hear anything to use as gossip fodder. "We need some place with more privacy."

"But – but I don't know anything." Andi's look of panic shifted from Theo to Izzy in a silent plea for help.

Even though she was shy, Andi's signs were easy for Izzy to read. The nerves. The fidgeting. The way her eyes darted around. The men needed to handle her with kid gloves if they were going to find out anything they didn't already now. If they pressed her hard, Andi would completely shut down.

Opening her mouth to speak, Izzy was about to tell Graham just that, when she saw a look pass between him and Theo, as if the two men were silently communicating. Taking a deep breath, Theo's tone softened.

"But you do," Theo said. "You were the first one on the scene. You yelled for Milo to call 911. Andi, you may have seen something that could help us, and you just don't know it. If you just talk to us . . ."

Graham's slight shake of the head stopped him. Pausing for a moment, Milo looked between the men and then slapped a meaty hand on Josh's back. "We need to go talk to some of the guests, and see if we can ease some anxiety."

"Uh, okay," Josh stammered. "How do we do that?"

"Ideally, with alcohol, my man," Milo grinned. "But since I can't get into my bar, why don't you just try smiling for starters."

Taking Josh by the elbow, he headed toward the nearby group of women. "Ladies," he boomed, "You're looking quite lovely this evening. Once we're back inside, I do hope you'll come join us in the lounge for our new firehouse cocktail. It's made with cinnamon whisky. Perfect for this evening, don't you think?" Milo had a hand on one of the women's lower back, and he led her away as she giggled, her friends trailing behind her. Josh followed, shaking his head at Milo with a look of admiration.

Turning back to Andrea, Graham didn't make a move to get closer or touch her. He only spoke in a gentle tone as if addressing an injured animal. "Why don't we go sit in the patrol car where it's warmer until we're cleared to go back inside?"

Shaking her head, Andrea hugged herself tighter, backing away from him.

Dustin leaned into Graham, speaking quietly, but Izzy picked up his words. "She's in shock, man. I'm going to go grab a paramedic to check her out before the ambulance takes off." At Graham's curt nod, the deputy headed over to the emergency personnel who were loading up their supplies.

"No one is trying to intimidate you," Theo said gently. "We just want to talk." He reached for her to guide her away, but Andi retreated so her back was up against the stone of the building. She looked terrified.

"Don't, Theo," she said in almost an urgent plea.

Izzy stepped in front of him, and saw that the look of determination on his face was clouded with hurt. You'd have to be an idiot not to see that there was something between Theo and Andi. She wasn't quite sure what, considering Andi was married, but still, there was something there. Unfortunately, whatever that connection was with Theo just seemed to make her more nervous.

145

Addressing both men, Izzy said, "If you want to talk to her, I'm going to be there too." She reached to take Andi's hand, offering her reassurance.

"Isabel. . ." Graham began in a warning tone.

"No, no it's okay," Andi's voice sounded stronger with the support of her friend. "I want Izzy here."

Looking at Theo, Graham gave a slight shrug, and Theo nodded his approval.

Dang, you really couldn't blame Andi for being nervous with these two hulking men, but all Izzy felt was protected. Even with the evening's events, Graham's presence exuded a sense of security. Theo's dark eyes assessed Andi with the same sense of shelter, vastly peaking Izzy's curiosity.

Before either man could address her, Andi looked at Izzy to speak.

"I don't know exactly what happened," she began. "I was just off work, getting ready to head home. I was just trying to find you." Pausing, Andrea swiped at another tear.

"It's okay, Andi, just tell us what happened. Take your time." Graham's dark chocolate voice was soothing.

"I— I wanted to make sure that Izzy received my message that the party game supplier wasn't going to be making their delivery until tomorrow afternoon." Taking a slow breath, Andi steadied herself and blew it out. "I stopped to talk to Milo for a couple minutes, and he said he hadn't seen you. It was six, so I thought you might still be in your office."

The annex not only housed Izzy's office, but also two other small offices, a large storage area and a conference room. The small building was connected to the lobby by a long breezeway, but it was far enough away from the main building, that the fire could have gotten out of control before anyone would have noticed it.

But she had fire detectors. They not only sensed smoke, but they visually sensed any sort of flame. Alarms should have been going off like crazy.

Anxiety seemed to send a shiver through Andrea as she crossed her arms in front of herself. "Izzy, when I stepped out into the walkway, I could smell smoke. I ran to the annex, and I – I tried to open the door. I was just so worried you were in there."

Clasping a hand over her mouth to stifle an emotion, Andi worked to regain her composure. "But it wouldn't budge. When I went around to the side of the building, I saw flames coming out of the storage room, and one of the windows busted out."

Squeezing her friend's hand tightly, Izzy nodded, encouraging Andi to continue. She may be shy, but she was a heck of a lot stronger than people gave her credit for.

Shaking her head, Andi resumed. "I – I was screaming your name. I should have gone for help immediately, but I took too long. The fire could have spread."

"But it didn't," Theo said. "It didn't because you were smart." He moved closer to wrap an arm around Andi's shoulders in what looked to be a friendly gesture, but she immediately stiffened.

A look of pain sliced through Theo's face for just a moment before he recovered, his expression evening out, as he dropped his hand from Andi.

Graham gently prodded Andi to continue her story, "So you grabbed the hose?"

Nodding, she continued. "The hose by the pool. I tried to put out the fire by aiming the hose in the window – through the bars. I thought I could do it maybe before it

147

spread. I was so stupid." She swiped at another tear, looking annoyed that they seemed to keep coming.

"Do not talk like that about yourself, Andrea! You are not, I repeat *not*, stupid." Theo's voice contained a steel edge that had both Andrea and Izzy looking up at him, their eyes widening.

She nearly missed the way Graham shot a look at Theo, and the slight shake of his head.

Blowing out a breath, Theo visibly gathered himself before he spoke. "According to Milo, you started screaming to high heaven. About scared everyone to death, but you sure got their attention. The staff at the front desk set off the fire alarm and started evacuating guests. Milo came to help her, and the two of them fought the fire until the firefighters arrived. Hell, it was almost out by the time they actually got there. Sure doesn't sound stupid to me, Andi."

Swallowing thickly, Izzy couldn't help but think how things could have gone horribly awry. What if Andi hadn't been there? "You really are a hero, Andrea." As the woman shook her head, Izzy hugged her fiercely. "You are. You're my hero. I don't know how I can ever thank you."

****

Seeing Izzy hugging Andrea made Graham want to envelop them both in a giant bear hug. When Andi and Theo had related the rest of the details of the fire, Graham's whole body had gone numb. Izzy could have been there. If he hadn't shown up at her cabin, and she'd gone back to her office, she could have been there when the fire –. No. No, he wasn't going to think of what could have happened. She was safe. She was safe for now, and Graham just had to make sure she stayed that way.

But there was still one thing bothering him. Izzy was staunch when it came to safety, especially fire safety. She had four fire detectors in the annex alone that were hard-wired in. They should have signaled the front desk immediately when the fire had started. Weren't they working? That sure as hell seemed like too much of a coincidence for all of them to be out at once.

After the men were convinced Andrea hadn't seen anyone else when she'd gone to the annex, Theo jerked his head for Graham to follow him. Leaving Izzy with Andrea while the paramedics checked her over, he walked over to the side of the building. The two men stood on a slight incline, high enough that they could easily pan the crowd of people.

Hands in the pockets of his jacket, Theo stood next to Graham taking in the clusters of hotel guests, some talking quietly, others casting looks of annoyance probably wondering when they'd be allowed back in.

"Graham, there's something I didn't want to say in front of Izzy."

"Arson, you mean? I already figured that. How bad?"

"More than just arson," Theo said, rocking back on his heels. "Someone threw a Molotov cocktail through the window of the supply room. With all the old files Izzy keeps in there, it must have ignited in no time flat. But that's not the worst part." Taking a deep breath, Theo said, "Graham, the door to the annex was barricaded. It was subtle, which may be why Andi didn't notice it."

Ice shards stabbed through Graham's gut as he tried to process what Theo was saying. His throat tightened. "Barricaded how?"

"Someone shoved small steel shards strategically around the door jamb. That's why Andrea couldn't yank it open."

Turning to look at Theo, he tried to grasp the situation. "Izzy's always in her office until six at least. And by that time of day, she's always by herself."

"Right," Theo agreed. "And I think there are several people who know that."

Graham voiced what they were both thinking. "If she'd been in there, she wouldn't have been able to get out. The windows in the annex are barred."

Nodding slowly, Theo agreed. "Graham, we're not just looking for an arsonist. This was attempted murder."

****

Humming to a tune on the radio, Chris turned on the road to the Lakewood. Spending all afternoon at his mom's, he'd proven he might have a future career in plumbing after installing her new water heater. He'd tried to call Izzy a few times to let her know he was running late, but there'd been no answer. Party planning seemed to be taking over the last few days, so that was most likely why she'd been too busy to return his calls. Still, he couldn't help the nagging feeling in his gut that something was wrong.

As he turned into the parking lot in front of the hotel, his system was flooded with the lights of a fire truck and two police cars, as well as several people milling about. All the blood seemed to drain from his body as he threw the gearshift in park and flung the door open, racing from his car.

Where was she? Panic surged through him. "IZZY!" Looking around, he shouted her name again, drawing the attention of several hotel guests who turned to look at him curiously.

"Chris?" Her sweet voice called to him from the edge of the crowd, and relief washed through him as he turned and spotted her standing with Andi.

"Oh baby," he ran to her, lifting her off her feet in a giant hug, burying his face in her honey blond waves. "Iz, what happened? Are you okay?" The way her body tensed in his arms worried him, and he pulled back to look at her. "Are you hurt?"

"No, no, I'm fine." But her eyes were looking behind him, and he turned to follow her gaze to Graham and Theo who were quickly approaching.

Putting his arm around Izzy, Chris straightened to address his brother. "Do you want to tell me what the hell is going on?"

Graham exchanged glances with Theo, and Chris gritted his teeth, recognizing that look. Graham was trying to figure out whether he should tell him the truth or throw up a smokescreen. He'd had the same look when they were kids and Graham had crashed his bike, and then lied about how the handlebar had gotten bent.

"No! Don't fucking do that. Don't keep secrets." Chris was frustrated, and the way Graham gritted his teeth just made his anxiety ratchet up a notch.

Graham sighed warily. "Alright, calm down, he said reaching for Izzy. But Chris tightened his grip around her waist. Why was Graham reaching for her? What was that about?

Disengaging herself from his embrace, Izzy backed away from both men and put an arm around Andi. He sure as hell didn't like the way she put distance between them, but now was not the time to address that. Turning his attention back to Graham and Theo, he listened silently as they filled him in on the fire. Even so, he could tell they were holding something back.

Before he could probe further, the fire chief strode out the main door and shouted in his megaphone for everyone's attention. "Ladies and gentlemen, the small fire we had is out, and there is nothing to worry about. We have the all clear, so you can return to your rooms."

A cheer went up, and Chris saw the relief on Izzy's face as people began to filter back in. Many people were smiling or downright giggling as they clutched the hand-written coupons for free drinks that it looked like Milo and Josh were doling out.

"There's Josh," Izzy said. "I'm going to help make sure everyone is settled and help hand out drink coupons for The Lounge."

"I'm going with you," Andrea said, her voice wavered, but she sounded strong.

"No," Izzy and Theo both said at once. Andrea pulled herself up to her full height of 5'2". "I am fine. I was upset, but I'm okay, and I want to help."

"Sweetie, you don't have to stay," Izzy said. "You were off hours ago. You should go home and get some rest."

Shaking her head, Andi looked like no one was forcing her to go anywhere. Good for her. The little mouse had some gumption.

"I'm staying," she said simply. "Please, Iz. I need to stay."

Pausing only for a moment, Izzy nodded. "Okay then, let's go."

After the women found Josh and headed inside, Chris turned back to his brother and Theo. "Do you want to tell me who the fuck set that fire?"

Graham looked taken aback. "How did—" He narrowed his eyes at his brother. "How the fuck did you know it was arson? Something you're not telling us, Chris?"

"No, dumbass. I was at Mom's all afternoon. Before I left, I went out to the office to see if Izzy wanted to have dinner, but she wasn't there. No one was in that annex, and I'm guessing it didn't fucking spontaneously combust!"

Graham sighed. "Look, the fire inspector is on his way, so we should know more soon, but . . ." He looked at Theo to continue.

"Molotov cocktail," Theo said shortly. "And you're right, no one was there. The problem is we're pretty sure that someone thought Izzy was in there. The door was barricaded."

As the realization hit Chris, his mouth fell open. He'd learned Izzy's routine quite well over the last week. She was usually in her office until six or later. She helped out at the front desk or in the bar in the early afternoon, and then she went to her office for the last couple of hours of the day to deal with anything pressing. It was a routine that rarely changed.

All the breath left Chris's body, and he felt as though he needed to struggle for air. "If the person who set the fire knew Izzy's routine, then they would've thought she was in her office." He shook his head in disbelief as he tried to grasp the situation. "Who the hell would try to kill Izzy?"

****

Later that night, Ramiro uttered a curse as he slammed the door to the hotel room he'd rented at the Lakewood and threw his jacket on the bed.

"Fuck!" This afternoon had not gone as planned. Not at all. He had fucked up. He should have made sure that Izzy was in her office before he set the damn fire. But she was a creature of habit. She was there at the same time every single day. How the hell was he supposed to know that this was the one fucking day she would change her routine?

Cracking open a window, he looked out at the small annex, and shook his head. It was swarming with people – the fire inspector, the PI, the deputy, and that damn sheriff. Ramiro was pretty sure that Graham fucking Nolan was to blame for getting Izzy out of the hotel that day since they had pulled up together after the fire.

Lighting a cigarette, Ramiro took a long drag, and then exhaled a stream of smoke out the window. He'd planned it out oh so carefully. Martin had wanted a distraction, but Ramiro thought it was ridiculous to waste time.

Since his room overlooked the small building where the offices were located, he'd hatched a brilliant plan. He could take care of Izzy without getting his hands too dirty. And he'd been so careful. He'd jimmied the lock early in the day and made sure all of the fire alarms were disabled. All he had to do was wait until she was in there, bar the door, and start the fire.

Dammit, how could he not have checked before he started the damn fire? How was he supposed to know that the little bitch would change up her schedule? She was in that office every fucking afternoon.

His phone buzzed, and he flicked his cigarette out the window before digging the phone out of his pocket to glance at the screen. Fucking Martin Craig. Martin hadn't known of Ramiro's plan to go ahead and get rid of the girl, so it would be easy to gloss over the fact that he'd messed up.

He hit the green button, "Ramiro."

"How is the distraction coming?" the nasally voice asked.

"Perfectly, of course," Ramiro lied. "There was an unfortunate fire this afternoon, took out the manager's office, and the supply room. It's going to be a big loss since the supplies for the upcoming Halloween bash were destroyed. In fact, they might even have to cancel it."

Martin's chuckle told Ramiro that the older man was pleased. "Well, that is unfortunate to hear," Martin leered. "Perhaps I should contact my niece and offer my sympathies."

"Yes, perhaps."

Then Martin was serious. "Watch the situation closely for a couple of days and give me updates. I need to know when she's the most vulnerable. That would be the perfect time to have Nolan strike and try one more time to convince her to sell."

"So no luck yet with lover boy?" This didn't come as a surprise to Ramiro. In addition to watching the girl, he'd also been watching the way Chris sniffed around her. He looked like a love-struck puppy dog, not like a businessman trying to close a deal. Shaking his head, Ramiro still wondered what Martin was thinking relying on the idiot.

"I will update you in the morning." The two men said their good-byes, and Ramiro turned from the window to fish out a small bottle of bourbon from the mini bar. He needed to come up with a new plan. If Nolan wasn't going to take care of the girl – and deep down Ramiro knew he wasn't – then it was up to him. And maybe he just needed to stop being so subtle.

He looked at himself in the mirror, his olive skin flushed with excitement, and he smiled as a new plan started to form.

Chapter Seven

Ouch! The pain in his fingers alerted Chris to the fact that he was biting his nails down to the point of bleeding. Dammit. Nail biting was his worst habit as a child, but it was something he was able to control now – usually. When his nerves weren't completely frayed, that is. He fisted his hands and stretched out his long fingers before typing furiously on his laptop, bringing up the list of hotel guests from the flash drive Izzy had given him.

Thank goodness she was so organized. All her records were backed up to a server at Theo's main office. Even though Izzy's office computers were gone, they could still access all of her information.

Sipping his lukewarm coffee, Chris glanced around the bar area of The Lounge from his table by the window. The helpless feeling of not being able to do anything had kept him awake most of the night. Sleep didn't seem to matter that much, though, when he was running on pure adrenaline.

When he'd driven up last night and saw the police cars and the fire truck, he'd gone completely out of his mind in the few moments it had taken him to find Izzy. The sense of panic when he thought she might be hurt . . . or worse . . . made him realize just how deep his feelings for her had become.

When Chris had told his brother he wanted to take an active role in the investigation, he'd been prepared for a fight. His mouth must have dropped to the floor when Graham had actually agreed. Turns out the two men shared the same goal – keeping Izzy safe. The more people there were looking into the fire, then hopefully the quicker they could find out who was trying to hurt her. And she was the only thing that mattered.

It was almost like he'd been living in darkness, and he hadn't even realized it until Izzy walked into his life. Her sunlight made the world seem brilliant, made him see things more clearly, especially just how unhappy he'd been before he met her.

Years ago, before he moved away, Chris and Theo had designed a computer program that could search multiple government databases and quickly gather someone's background information. The program was more thorough than anything currently on the market. And it was *mostly* legal.

By three this morning, Chris had familiarized himself with the updates Theo had made to the program. If a hotel guest set the fire, Chris would find out who and why. It was his responsibility to protect Izzy. She was his. At least that was how he felt.

Rubbing his eyes, he drained the last of his coffee. As tired as he was, his entire body hummed as his fingers flew over the keyboard. It felt damn good to be back in the world of computers rather than mergers and acquisitions.

Up until two weeks ago, he'd almost convinced himself he could handle a career in corporate America without losing his soul. But time in Magic had given him a fresh perspective. Moving away from his family and friends, living for nothing but work the last five years. Why had that ever seemed like a good decision? What had seemed important before, seemed irrelevant now. Funny how quickly things could change.

"Fresh cup?" Graham sat down across from him, handing him a steaming cup of coffee, and Chris smiled gratefully.

"How long have you been sitting here?" Graham asked.

Shrugging, Chris reached for three packets of sugar. "Couple hours, maybe." He'd only gotten an hour, maybe two, of restless sleep. But sleep could wait. Izzy's safety could not. "Izzy gave me the flash drive a few minutes ago so I can finally start combing through the guests."

His sweet Izzy. The circles under her eyes this morning were evidence that she hadn't slept anymore than he had. Although she'd attempted to cover those dark circles with make-up, Chris could see the exhaustion in her face, the worry.

"Where is she?" Graham was looking around the bar area, his tired eyes searching.

Chris gestured to the corner where papers, two laptops, and several coffee mugs were spread over a couple of tables. "She and Andi set up a mini office space in the big corner booth, but I haven't seen her for a little while. I think she's still with the party supply people. A couple of big trucks showed up first thing this morning, and since the main storage area was where the fire started, she and Milo are scrambling to find a spot for everything."

Graham scowled. "I wish to hell she would rethink this damn Halloween party."

Grinning, he thought of Izzy's reaction this morning when he'd suggested the same thing. "Not gonna happen, brother. And I wouldn't suggest it either. I did, and got a fifteen-minute lecture this morning on tradition and how our little spitfire isn't going to let the bad guys win." Despite his concern, he smiled at the thought of Izzy's passion, and so did Graham.

Chris watched his brother circle the rim of his cup of coffee with a finger. "She needs this, you know," Graham finally said. "It's been so hard for her, without her grandpa. Planning the Costume Ball has monopolized her time, but it has really helped her focus on something other than her grief." He sighed, his fist clenching. "When I find the person who did this. . ." He trailed off, his jaw tightening in a glower.

Chris lifted his hand in a wave as he saw Theo walk into the bar. He plopped down into a chair at the table. "Hey. You seen Izzy?"

"In the back," both men said in unison.

Theo blew out a breath, running a hand through his short hair. "I have a message in to the insurance adjuster. I was wondering if she's heard anything from him."

Looking at his watch, Chris leaned back in a long stretch. "Doubtful. It's not even nine o'clock."

Theo sighed, his eyes darting around the room for a server. "Who do I have to sleep with around here to get a cup of coffee?"

Pushing his chair back, Chris stood up and rolled his eyes. "Keep your panties on. I'll go get us a fresh pot."

****

Graham watched his brother walk away. With all the activity of the last few hours, he'd put off talking to Chris about their relationship with Izzy. *Their relationship.* When had he started thinking of it as one unit. *His* relationship with Izzy. *His, dammit.* Chris hadn't even known her for two weeks.

The problem was that it had been comforting last night to know Chris was there. When Graham had to work with the fire inspector and the arson investigator, it had been reassuring to know that Chris had been with Izzy, watching her, protecting her.

Running a hand over his beard, he blew out a breath. He'd thought he had it all figured out. Now, he wasn't quite so sure.

Strumming his fingers on the table, Theo's voice brought him back to the present. "Everything okay between you two?" He gestured in Chris's direction. "Since you're not punching each other, I'd say things seem better."

"Yeah, well, it helps that he seems dedicated to helping figure out who's trying to hurt Izzy." Just saying the words made his gut clench in dread. Izzy. So loving and caring and sweet. Who would want to hurt her? He looked around again, hoping she would appear in front of him, and thought about getting up to go find her. He just wanted to lay eyes on her. Just know she was okay.

"Yeah, it doesn't make sense to me. I've been racking my brain trying to figure out a reason why someone would want to hurt her. Maybe going through the hotel guests will give us something." Theo's finger thrumming on the table picked up speed, reflecting his increased anxiety.

"Hopefully we'll learn something since there's no fucking evidence so far." Letting go of his coffee mug, Graham rubbed his hands on his jeans.

"So nothing on the steel shards that were barricading the door?"

Shaking his head, Graham looked Theo in the eye. "Someone was very careful. No prints on the door or the shards. They could be bought at any hardware store, so that's no help. So far, forensics are getting us nowhere." As he thought about what they actually had discovered last, the sick feeling in his stomach hit full force. "I have to figure out how I'm going to tell Izzy the fire detectors were tampered with."

Theo's grim look echoed his own. They had both been there last night when the arson investigator discovered the wires in all four smoke detectors had been cut. Not only that, but the security cameras going out to the annex had been turned off. Someone knew exactly what they were doing.

"She's just had so much to deal with. Her grandpa, fielding all the offers on the place, and now this? It's not fair, man. She doesn't deserve this." Graham had to bite the inside of his lip to quell the stab of emotion. She didn't fucking deserve this.

The steady strumming of fingers on the table suddenly stopped, causing Graham to look up at Theo whose eyes were narrowed in concentration. "She's had a lot of offers on the Lakewood?"

Thinking back, Graham nodded slowly. "Yeah, since the land is surrounded by the lake, there have been a lot of interest over the years. I can't even count the number of people Richard had to deal with. But just in the last month, there have been three outside developers approach Izzy, plus her uncle."

The fear she'd actually sell the place and move away had been strong. The thought of Izzy leaving Magic, of not seeing her every day was unbearable. When she'd adamantly told him she would never sell the resort, he'd gone weak with relief.

"Her uncle? You mean that bastard who didn't even stick around for the whole funeral?" Theo asked with a tone of disgust.

The hard look that came over Graham's face was proof he felt the same way. "Yeah, the son of a bitch was interested in the will. He doesn't give a damn about Iz. As soon as he found out he didn't get what he wanted, he took off."

The bastard should have stayed. He was Izzy's only family. Thinking of his mother, Graham thought about just how lucky he was. Not all families were supportive. Some were downright cruel.

"So three other offers aside from her uncle," Theo said almost to himself.

Leaning back, Graham tried to follow Theo's line of thinking. "Yeah, but she's not interested. When I asked if she thought about selling, she said someone would have to drag her cold, dead body out of the place before she —." His entire body went cold.

Theo's eyes widened as they both seemed to process Graham's words at the same time.

"You don't think . . .?" Theo whispered.

"I think we just came up with a motive." *Fuck! How had he not thought of this before?* "There are plenty of people who want the resort. If Izzy wouldn't sell it to them, maybe they decided to take matters into their own hands." Graham rose from his chair, his entire body shaking. "If somebody really does want to kill her. . . . hell, this is the first thing that's made any sort of sense." Suddenly, a rage started to simmer in the pit of his gut.

"Take a breath, man." Theo could see his head was quickly spinning out of control. "Right now, this is just a possibility we need to look into."

Deep down, Graham knew it was more than a possibility. But even so . . . "Why would someone want the resort so badly they'd want to kill her? The offers have all died down. I haven't even heard of any new people who have been bugging her to sell." What the hell was he missing?

When Theo didn't answer, Graham looked up and followed his gaze to where Chris was standing a few feet away from them, pot of coffee in hand and his face as white as a sheet.

Turning to him, Graham tensed in alarm. "What? What's wrong?"

When Chris didn't say anything, Graham's panic began to escalate. "Christopher! Answer me!"

"I know," he practically whispered, visibly swallowing.

"You know? You know what?" Impatience was getting the better of Graham.

"I know who wants the Lakewood." Slowly Chris set the coffee down on the table.

Graham could feel his hands fisting at his sides, and was about to take a step toward his brother when Theo appeared in between them speaking calmly. "Why don't you two sit down," he said quietly. "That's not a request. I know you don't want to make a scene and upset Izzy any more than she already is." Theo smiled at the couple sitting at a nearby table, and said under his breath, "I'm serious. I will kick both of your asses."

Looking around, Graham noticed that a few people in the restaurant were already curiously looking in their direction. If the restaurant weren't so crowded, he'd just grab his damn brother and haul him outside. In fact, that might not be such a bad idea.

"I don't want to discuss this here." He jerked his head harshly toward the veranda. "Outside, Chris. Let's go."

Theo led both of the men over to the patio door leading out to the veranda. Since it was a chilly October day, there wasn't anyone outside. This would work. *There's no one here to see me kill him,* thought Graham.

As soon as the patio door closed behind them, Graham turned to his brother, dropping the friendly façade. "Alright, spill it."

He didn't like Chris's nervous look. He looked fucking guilty. "I— You know I'm in mergers and acquisitions, right? For Waddell and Stevens," Chris began.

"Yeah, what does your job have to do with this?" Graham asked, becoming more frustrated by the second.

Chris took a deep shaky breath before he spoke again in a rush. "A client hired my company to acquire the Lakewood. The client is desperate to buy the land from Izzy." Taking a deep breath, Chris closed his eyes. "I'm in charge of the account. I was sent here to try to get Izzy to agree to sell."

If Graham thought he felt rage before, he could now only see red at Chris's confession. This whole time, Chris had been playing her? Playing both of them? Just when the wall between he and his brother had started to crack a little bit? How could he have been so stupid? "You son of a bitch." The words came out menacingly as he took a step toward his brother.

Holding up his hands in surrender, Chris tried to reason with him. "Now Graham, listen to me. I wasn't going to pursue it. Izzy told me she wasn't interested in selling, and that was that. I didn't plan to —"

Seething, Graham began circling his brother like a lion circling his prey. "Did you set the fire? Was it you? Did you try to kill her?"

"What?! No! Of course not! You think I would hurt her? Are you crazy? I love—"

"No!" Graham shouted. "Don't you say that! You don't get to fucking say that!"

Putting a hand on Graham's arm, Theo said, "Calm down, man. Hear him out."

But Graham just shook him off. "Hear him out? Come on, this makes sense, right?" Jabbing an accusatory finger at Chris, he said, "You aren't in town two hours before you get close to her, trick her into sleeping with you. Now you're admitting it was because you were trying to play her. Was that part of your long game?"

"I didn't trick her. That's not what I—" Fisting two hands in his hair, Chris let out a frustrated growl, and turned to stalk to the edge of the patio, and then back again. "You're twisting my words."

"Graham, listen to me," Theo tried again, putting a hand on his shoulder. "I think we should sit down. Now that we know this, we can—"

"Shut up," Graham snapped, shrugging Theo's hand off for a second time. "I want to know what Chris has to say for himself. Better yet, if you're so honest," he said in a sarcastic tone, "what did Izzy say when you told her the real reason you were here?"

Chris's gaze dropped almost immediately, but not before Graham saw color bloom in his cheeks. "You really are a son of a bitch. You didn't tell her. You motherfucker." Letting out a growl, he took a step forward. He couldn't think clearly. The only thing he could think of was that Chris had come to town with the intention of hurting Izzy. No matter what he had or hadn't said to her, Graham knew she cared about his brother, and he knew how hurt she'd be when she found out the truth.

"No. No, I didn't tell her," he answered. "Look, dammit, I didn't plan any of this. When I saw Izzy that first night in the bar, Milo just told me you were interested in her. He never told me she owned the fucking hotel!"

Oh, this just keeps getting better, said the sarcastic voice that lived in Graham's head. "Wait a second. You knew I was interested in her? You knew she was mine and you went after her anyway?"

The anxiety over the last few days. . . over the last few years built up and exploded out of him. Before

Graham even consciously realized what he was doing, he fisted his hand and swung, catching Chris squarely in the jaw.

****

Leaning back against the wall of the walk-in freezer, Izzy shivered while watching Milo stack the last of the boxes.

"There," he said, putting his hands on hips and surveying his work. "Not my first choice as a spot to store everything, but we have the room in here, so why not?"

Sighing in relief, Izzy was just happy they'd figured out a place to put the rest of the food service supplies, as well as the games and prizes. "I'm sorry to take over your kitchen, Milo." Putting a hand to her head, she wondered for the hundredth time how long it would take to repair the annex. The supply room took the brunt of the fire, but there was so much smoke damage to the rest of it, that it would have to be gutted.

With a gentle hand on her back, Milo guided her out of the freezer. Oh, blessed warmth! Walking over to the furnace vent to the far side of the giant kitchen, Izzy stood over it, enjoying the rush of warm air.

Milo stood toe to toe with her. "This makes the most sense. Everything's in the same place, and it works out better since we won't have to drag it all over from the supply room. That just leaves the extra chairs, but Andi got that delivery pushed back so they won't be here until a few hours before the party starts." He crossed muscled arms over his broad chest. "Now, if I hear you apologize one more time for something that isn't your fault, or beat yourself up about anything that's been going on around here, I'll . . . well, you're not mine, so I can't take you over my knee, but I will certainly turn you over to Graham so he can."

Izzy's mouth popped open as an image of herself lying naked across Graham's lap assaulted her brain. Then realization hit, and she shook her head. Surely she hadn't heard that right. "Wait a second. You'll what?"

Saying nothing, Milo smirked as Andi walked into the room.

"Hey, did it all fit?" Andrea said, popping her head in.

Still staring at Milo, Izzy nodded mutely, then turned to look at a tense Andi.

"Iz," she began nervously. "I wanted to let you know that Graham and Theo just showed up. You might want to get out there. Graham and Chris make me . . . anxious when they're together."

Anxious? I know the feeling. In the last twelve hours, things had spun so far out of what she'd had planned. Being with Graham yesterday had been a high like she'd never felt. Even with the trauma of the fire, Izzy still had to admit that this morning just seemed a little brighter with the knowledge that he loved her. *He loved her.*

Then she thought of Chris. Yearned for Chris. Since their first night together, he had been trying so hard not to push her, taking the time to get to know her. Izzy had decided what she wanted, and that hadn't changed. One Nolan brother was mind-blowing. Two of them – well that just made her complete. It felt right. She just had to convince them.

Originally, she'd planned to talk to them both this morning and lay it all out, but now . . . well, now there was even more in the way. But maybe that shouldn't matter. She could talk to them anyway, and they could deal with this investigation together.

Except the way Andi was twisting her fingers back and forth caused a seed of worry to start in Izzy's stomach. "They're not fighting again, are they?"

Milo smirked. "When *aren't* they fighting? That seems to be how they exist with each other anymore," he said sadly, shaking his head. "I wish you knew them before they were like this."

Izzy frowned, wishing Milo would tell her what had happened to drive the two men apart. She knew she had to find out from Graham and Chris themselves, but right now, she really didn't feel like poking the bears.

"Well, things seemed to be going well, but then the two of them got a little heated," Andrea said, crossing her arms in an effort to stop twisting her hands. "I don't know what they were talking about, but Theo guided them outside so they were away from guests."

Izzy didn't miss the way Andrea's eyes flared when she mentioned Theo's name. "Well, thank goodness for Theo. That's the last thing we need, the Nolan boys scaring the guests." Walking briskly out of the kitchen, she really hoped this was just their usual bickering. Even so, she'd had just about enough of that. "I swear I'm going to call their mother down here so she can bang their heads together," she mumbled.

Izzy stopped short when she reached the dining room. Every eye in the place was trained on the patio doors, and some guests were on their feet, inching closer to the distinct commotion that could be heard coming from outside.

"Oh shit," Milo muttered, moving past her, and jogging toward the patio. When he opened the door, Izzy and Andrea gasped in unison as they saw Chris stagger backward with blood on his face.

"Oh my God," Andrea exclaimed, clasping her hands over her mouth. She hated confrontation, but Izzy didn't. The only thing she felt was pissed off, and couldn't wait to give those two a piece of her mind. She couldn't believe the two of them would cause such a disruption in The Lounge. Graham was the sheriff, for crying out loud. What on earth could cause so much drama? Stomping over to the patio, she was ready to jump in the middle of the fray, but stopped at the door when she heard their voices.

Milo had a firm grip around Chris's shoulders from behind, and Theo was using what looked like all of his strength to hold back Graham who was practically spitting fire.

"How could you do this, you motherfucker? She trusted you! How could you hurt her like this?" he shouted at Chris.

"Hurt her?" he strained against Milo's hold. "You're the one who has flip-flopped for the last three years. You had all that time, and don't decide to make a move until I'm interested in her?"

"Izzy is not a fucking competition!" Graham roared.

"I didn't do anything!" Chris shouted back, reaching up to wipe a smear of blood from his lip. "So I knew you were interested in her? Big deal. It's not like she belongs to you, little brother. You didn't show one iota of interest in her until I did. So maybe you're the one who's using her!" He jabbed an accusatory finger in Graham's direction. "Maybe you're the one that's playing games. You treat her like a toy that you don't want to play with until someone else does. And then you throw a fucking tantrum."

"I am going to kill you!" Graham shouted as he tried to lunge free of Theo's arms.

"Damn it, stop!" Theo yelled, using all of his strength to hold Graham back. "Can't you two calm down and discuss this like adults?"

"I know all I need to know. You already admitted that you know I was interested in her, or you never would have approached her in the first place!"

"I never fucking said that!" Chris shouted, trying to break free.

"You tricked her in to bed!" Graham continued. "You let her think you were me so you could trick her into fucking you, and it worked, didn't it?!"

There was an audible gasp of spectators behind her, and Izzy clutched a hand to her mouth, a wave of nausea rolling through her. She could feel every eye in dining room on her. Now, every person there knew the intimate details of her sex life, but that wasn't the worst part. No, that wasn't the worst part at all.

The men on the patio went silent at her squeak and turned toward the door, seeing her for the first time. Graham's face fell, as the realization of what he'd just said seemed to hit him full force.

Chris shrugged out of Milo's grasp, walking toward her. "Sweetheart, I —"

"No, don't!" Izzy held her hand up to stop him and took a step back.

"You heard her," Graham growled, yanking away from Theo and walking toward her. "Don't go near her."

"Stop!" Izzy shouted, putting up her other hand. "Both of you stay away from me!"

"But— but, Iz. . ." Graham started.

"No." Tears pricked her eyes as she shook her head. "No, you don't get to talk to me. Neither one of you," she said looking between them, her vision blurring.

"But I have to know. Chris, is it true? You acted like you didn't know who I was. But you knew that I . . .

that Graham . . ." She shook her head, disbelievingly. "Did you lie to me?"

"Izzy, it's not that simple, I —"

"Is it true?" she cried.

Chris's face grew a sickly pale and he nodded. "Yes. Yes, I knew Graham was interested in you. It doesn't matter, though. I would have approached you anyway. . ."

"But the fact that you thought I was Graham's girlfriend sealed the deal? You thought if you could talk me into bed, you could get laid, and it could be a big 'fuck you' to your brother?" She'd trusted him. She'd fallen in . . . no, no, it was all a lie. She couldn't love him.

From the look on Chris's face, Izzy knew she was right, but she needed to hear it. "Answer me!"

Chris simply nodded. "Yeah, something like that," he mumbled.

Swiping angrily at the tears streaming down her cheeks, she turned her attention toward Graham. "And you. He's right, isn't he? You weren't interested in me at all until he came to town."

"Sweetheart, that's not true." Graham's voice was quiet as he inched forward.

"Stop." Izzy almost whispered, backing up. "Just stop. I tried for years to get your attention, Graham. Three years, and you didn't want to have anything to do with me. But the second you think your brother is interested in me, then it turns into some sort of game you have to win." She was just some prize. He wanted to beat his brother and win the toy. He didn't love her. It was all she could do to stand upright, her knees shaking so bad that she thought she might collapse.

"No!" Graham exclaimed. "No, it's not like that!"

She shook her head. She had to get out of there. Anywhere else. *But first, keep it together, Izzy.* "I just don't know what to believe anymore. I don't know who I'm supposed to trust." She took a deep breath and raised her chin. She would be strong. Her heart was breaking, but she would be strong. "But I can't trust you. Either of you. And I can't do —" She gestured toward each of them. "I can't do whatever this is."

Turning, Izzy strode through the dining room, head high, as a room full of onlookers silently watched her.

Chapter Eight

Stomping away from the crowd around him to the edge of the patio, Graham uttered a long stream of curses. How could she think he didn't love her? He wouldn't toy with her emotions. . . *Fuck, that's exactly what he'd been doing all this time, though, wasn't it?*

Facing the lake, he watched a rowboat in the distance, slow but sure, a constant steady motion. Fall leaves floated around him as he focused on that boat, trying to steady his breathing and rein in his temper. If he could just talk some sense into Izzy, he could get her to understand his feelings for her. Okay, so maybe he'd needed a kick in the pants in the form of his brother to finally make him see it, but that didn't mean his feelings for her weren't real.

Turning around, he crossed to the doors, ready to find Izzy and plead his case, but Andrea moved in front of him, blocking his path.

"Andi, please get out of my way," he said with a sigh.

Standing up straighter, she lifted her chin. "N-no," she stuttered. Color rushed to her cheeks as the small woman stood her ground in front of him. Graham knew just how timid Andrea was, but right now she tried her best to put on a tough face. She wasn't about to let him pass.

He wasn't the only one who noted her nervousness. Stepping up to support her, Theo stood close enough that his big arm brushed her shoulder, lending her his strength. "Graham, you've got to let Izzy go right now. I think emotions are way too high." Theo looked between him and Chris. "You both need to calm down before you try to talk to her."

Graham shot a glare at his brother. "He doesn't need to do anything with her. He . . ." Then he stopped himself and blew out a breath, scrubbing a hand over his beard. Dammit, he knew Theo was right, but his blood was boiling.

He was angry that Izzy had walked away without hearing him out, he was angry at the danger against her, he was angry at his brother for trying to take her from him, but most of all, he was angry at himself for not cherishing her the second he laid eyes on her three years ago. Why had it taken him so damn long to realize what was right in front of him?

"Alright, fine," he conceded. "I'll wait down here until she's ready to talk. I won't go after her." He saw the way that Theo and Milo exchanged a glance.

"What?" he asked, his back going up.

It was Milo who answered him. "Look, man, I think it might be best if you took off for now. Just give her some time to cool off. She's going to have to come back down here to work, and it won't help if you're lurking in a corner somewhere watching her. You can talk to her later."

Graham was stunned. Leave? When she was in danger? When he turned from Milo, he saw the smirk on his brother's face, and had to stop himself from lunging at his twin again.

Milo obviously noticed it too because he smacked Chris in the back of the head. "Ow!"

"You too, lover boy," Milo said. "She doesn't need either one of you sniffing around. Go calm down. I suggest you go talk this out, but if you decide you want to kill each other, just don't do it here."

They were right. Graham didn't want to admit it, but he knew they were right. He shook his head. "I'm not going to leave her by herself while she's in danger."

"Dude, look around. She's not alone," Milo answered, crossing his arms over his broad chest. "Nothing's going to happen to her while I'm here."

Theo nodded. "It's okay, man. We're all here. We're watching out for her. I'll set up my computer in The Lounge and just work from here."

Unable to come up with another reason to argue, Graham blew out a breath in concession. "I'm not trying to be difficult. I just want to make sure she's okay."

"I'll go up," Andi said quietly. "I'll go stay with her so she's not alone."

Graham looked gratefully at her. "Thank you, Andi."

Then he turned, scowling at his brother who stood dabbing at the blood still coming from the corner of his mouth. Graham's tone became harsh. "He's leaving first." Yeah, that probably sounded immature, but he didn't care.

"I want to make sure Chris is nowhere near Izzy before I leave." Lifting his chin at his brother, Graham practically dared him to argue.

"Fuck you, man," Chris said without much fight. "No matter what you think, I never tried to hurt her."

Stepping up, Theo put a hand on Chris's shoulder. "Stop, you two. Go cool off. Talk to each other.

"I'll leave, but I'll be damned if I'm talking to him," Graham seethed.

With a curse, Chris turned, stomping through The Lounge. The stares and whispers of those left in the restaurant continued as Graham followed him out.

****

"Go away!" Izzy yelled at the knock on the door. She sat cross-legged on her bed, dabbing at her eyes with a wad of tissue. She couldn't talk to Graham or Chris right now. . . couldn't even look at them.

She was such a fool. She thought they'd really cared about her. After Milo told her they'd shared women before, she'd been under the misguided assumption that she could have both of them. In actuality, that should have made her realize that they were just going to rip her heart in half. All they cared about was outdoing each other, winning. How could she be so foolish?

The knocking came louder this time. "I said go away!"

"Iz, sweetie, it's us," came Andrea's soft voice.

Taking a shaky breath, Izzy slid off her bed and headed for the door. "Define *us*, exactly."

"OMG! Open the damn door, Iz. I have wine!" Tessa.

Opening the door, Izzy was greeted not only with Andi and Tessa, but also Jilly who embraced her in a giant hug. "And I have barbecue because I'm betting you haven't had lunch yet."

She'd skipped breakfast, and although food was the last thing on her mind, Izzy's stomach rumbled as she smelled the heavenly aroma of barbecue.

She sniffled slightly. "Are there ribs in that sack?"

Jilly's grin grew wide. "Oh, you know it, baby!" Her red curls bounced as she walked over to put the barbecue on plates, and Andi and Tessa led her to the large couch in the sitting area of the room.

The buzz of her women's conversation reminded Izzy just how lucky she was to have three such wonderful friends. Even though she felt like her heart was breaking into pieces, she knew these three women would always be there to help put her back together.

"Oh no, don't cry sweetie. It's going to be okay." Jilly sat next to her, wrapping both of her arms around Izzy.

"I didn't even realize I was crying," she said with a weak laugh, leaning against Jilly, as Andrea sat down on her other side and grabbed her hand.

Tessa sat in the chair opposite them, and poured them each a glass of wine before adjusting her glasses. "Men are assholes, Izzy."

She snorted a laugh. "Thank you for those wise words."

"I'm serious," Tessa continued. "It doesn't matter how rich, how smart, how good-looking they are, when a woman comes into the picture, all the blood rushes to their dicks, and none of them are able to rub two brain cells together."

As defeated as Izzy felt right now, she could easily get on board with the 'men are assholes' theory. "I'm such an idiot. I've known Chris for less than two weeks. How could I think he would care about me so fast? And Graham? I should have known there was something more to his sudden change of heart. I was just so happy he wanted me, so happy that he was finally coming around." The burning behind her eyelids started again and she pressed fingertips to her eyes to stem a new swell of tears.

Rubbing her back, Jilly tried to ease her tension. "If it's any consolation, I really don't think he was trying to hurt you. I know how it must look, but Izzy, I've worked for Graham for almost two years. I've seen the way he looks at you, the way he talks about you, the way he touches you so possessively. He's in love with you, Iz, and he has been for a long time. He just wasn't ready to admit it."

177

The ache in her chest made swallowing hard. "It doesn't matter now. Things are so screwed up. The two of them were at each other's throats down there. I'm not getting in between them, especially when they just see me as one big competition."

"And just why not?" Legs crossed, Tessa studied her while swirling her glass of wine. "Why can't you just let yourself fall, enjoy them both?"

"Come on, Tessa, think about it." She wouldn't even let a kernel of hope take hold. "If I let myself fall head over heels for both of them, what happens when one of them loses interest?" As much as it hurt now, it was better for her to walk away because she didn't think she could handle the pain when they decided they didn't want her. "I'd bet as soon as Chris realizes I'm not worth all this trouble, then Graham won't want me anymore either," she said quietly.

Tessa smiled, "Izzy, your self-esteem sucks. Neither of those men is going to change the way they feel about you."

"She's right, Iz," Andi said calmly. The other three turned to look at her as she spoke. "You know the thing about being shy and staying in the background is that I tend to be invisible."

As the women began to protest, Andi held her hand up to stop them. "No, just listen. I feel like I go through each day, a lot of times, with people barely seeing me. Sometimes it's frustrating, but one thing I've come to realize is that the people who matter see me." The corners of her mouth tilted up in a slight smile.

"Graham has always seen me, always talks to me, and always helps me." Turning to look pointedly at Izzy, Andi squeezed her hand. "And so does Chris. Yesterday morning when you were meeting with the food vendors, Chris spent twenty minutes helping me carry in supplies and put them away. He didn't even ask. He just saw that I needed help and stepped in. Izzy, he's kind. They're both kind. Everyone around here goes on and on about how different the Nolan brothers are, but they're not. They both have good hearts. No matter what else they have going on, that's all that really matters."

"I can't believe you're all taking their side," Izzy argued. But even though she didn't want to admit it, she'd seen the goodness emanating from both men, and knew deep down that Andi was right.

"I'm not taking their side," Andrea said quietly, patting Izzy's leg. "I know you feel hurt, but don't close yourself off. Sure, they're acting like idiots, but they're both crazy about you. Love is so rare." Andi averted her eyes as they became wet with tears. "Don't shut the door on the opportunity for love just because a guy acts like a – a —"

"Douche canoe," Tessa supplied.

Despite herself, Izzy grinned at Tessa's assessment. "I hear what you're saying, I do. But even if the two of them were perfect, how could I ever choose between them?"

"Who says you have to?" Jilly asked. "You know they used to share, from what I hear. I got the lowdown from Stacey, the bartender at the Fishhook." Bartender and town gossip should be Stacey's full title.

"I know. Milo told me." And why hadn't she asked either Graham or Chris about it? Despite the fire, she could have addressed it. "I just don't know if I'm ready for something like that."

"I can get you ready! I found a video on Tumblr of double penetration." Tessa started tapping at her phone. "Wait 'til you see it, Iz. It's hot!"

The tension in the room seemed to decrease exponentially as Tessa and Jilly began giggling. Reaching for her glass, Izzy just shook her head. "Good lord, if you're going to bring up porn on your phone, I think I need more wine."

Jilly and Andrea both moved to crowd Tessa as they peered at her phone, and Izzy couldn't help but laugh as Andrea's eyes grew wide. Her friends definitely made her feel better. Unfortunately, she wasn't any closer to deciding what the hell she was going to do about the two men in her life.

With her grandpa gone, the feeling of loss was so great. Part of her wanted to take a chance with both men, wanted to believe the things they'd said to her, but she was scared. What if she took a chance and lost? She didn't know if she'd be able to recover from that.

****

The split of the wood was satisfying as Chris swung the axe once more. After driving aimlessly around the lake and reaching no resolution about anything, he decided to head to his mom's house. At least here, he could do something productive even if all of his problems and worries continued to spin vicious circles in his head.

Rolling his shoulders, he winced at the sore muscle in his arm. Not quite as sore as his face was going to be tomorrow, he thought as he ran a hand over his bruised jaw, but at least he'd managed to get in one good punch. Gripping the axe firmly, he swung again, picturing his brother's face as he enjoyed the loud, satisfying crack of wood.

"Honey, I think I'm going to have enough firewood for the next two winters. You can stop anytime," said his mom, walking out onto the back deck of her cabin and sipping a steaming mug of coffee.

Just the sound of Lily Nolan's voice was enough to ease a little bit of the anxiety in Chris. His mom was in her mid-fifties, but easily looked ten years younger. Her chestnut hair was peppered with silver, and she had the same steel blue eyes that Chris shared with his brother. Lily loved her boys fiercely, and he deeply regretted the pain he and Graham had caused her by not speaking to each other over the past few years.

"Are you ready to tell me what happened? And what exactly it has to do with your brother?" Lily's worried eyes assessed her son, and Chris was filled with regret at the thought of disappointing his mother again.

With a deep breath, he laid the axe down against the tree stump beside him. Rolling his shoulders, he felt the trickle of sweat down his back instantly cooling in the fall breeze. "Not really. I just made a mistake, Mom. Again."

"Come here, baby. Talk to me." She held her hand out, and Chris took it, walking with her to sit on the wooden steps of the deck. Looking around the back yard, he wondered how much he should tell Lily.

The large tree in the center of the yard still held the old tire swing he and Graham had played on as kids. He could still remember the time when he was eight and decided to see how high he could swing before jumping off. When he'd cried hysterically after spraining his ankle, Graham had been the one who had picked him up and carried him into the house.

Wiping the sweat from his brow, Chris looked down at his dusty jeans. "When I left town, I was so angry, Mom. With Alicia for hurting me. With Graham for always having the confidence that I seemed to lack. And I was angry with me. For being a coward and not having the strength to see things through no matter how they turned out. I just ran away."

Lily rubbed his back, "Oh, honey, you didn't run away. You were trying to find yourself. You and Graham were always linked, like two sides of a coin. That wasn't a bad thing when you were kids, but I know it got to be hard on you."

Patting his knee, she spoke to him in that comforting tone that always worked to calm him down. "But you were so dependent on each other that you never took time to figure out who you were as an individual. I wish you'd left on good terms with Graham, but aside from that, I think the time apart was something both of you needed." Leaning back, Lily took a sip of her coffee. "And now I think it's time for you to come home."

Chris let out a laugh that held no humor. "Unfortunately, I think I've already screwed that up, too."

His mom smiled knowingly at him. "With Izzy, you mean?"

Chris's eyes widened in surprise. He hadn't said anything to his mom about his feelings for Izzy. But of course his mother knew. How did moms always know everything without you having to tell them?

As if to answer his unspoken question, Lily just laughed and said, "Magic is a small town, dear. I may live outside city limits, but I still make it to that library – or media center – every week. You know, I think Tessa keeps that place in business by supplying everyone with updates on the town gossip. And if there's anything she leaves out, then you can swing by the Fishhook and get it from Stacey."

Taking another sip of her coffee, Lily eyed him speculatively. "So, do you love her?"

A grin slowly spread across his face as he thought of Izzy. He'd asked himself that same question many times over the last couple of weeks, and he'd come to the same conclusion time and again. "Yeah. Yeah, I love her." It felt good to admit that out loud. Unfortunately, it made the stab of pain even worse. "But I'm pretty sure she hates me. She hates me, and she doesn't even know all the reasons she should."

Leaning back against a deck rail, Lily crossed an ankle over her other knee. "Honey, I've known Isabel Craig for years. I seriously doubt she hates you."

"Mom, you have no idea how badly I've fucked up."

"Christopher, language!" Lily said on a laugh.

His face reddened. "Oh, lord, sorry Mom."

"Why don't you tell me what you did, that you think was so bad?"

A feeling of shame filled him as he thought of the reason he'd come back to town. But then, he'd felt ashamed of himself for a while, and not only for coming to town with the pretense of trying to buy the resort from Izzy.

He'd bottled his feelings up inside for so long that he'd almost forgotten how to let them out. Graham was always the person he'd talked to before, and he felt like he hadn't had anyone to talk to – truly talk to – for so long. With his mother's caring face looking at him, something inside of him broke like a dam, and the words just came flowing out.

"Before I left here, there was a moment, a brief moment, when I thought everything was perfect. I thought I was in love with Alicia and that she loved me. I had a brother who was my best friend, and I was ready to go into business with Theo and focus on the security software we were developing. Everything was awesome." And then it wasn't.

He felt his fists squeezing together, heard the pain in his own voice. "And then it just fell apart. Alicia chose Graham. And it didn't even matter to me that he didn't want her back. I hated him for it, hated her. I didn't know how to get past it, Mom, so I just ran. I went to St. Louis and took this stupid job. Mergers and acquisitions. Jesus, I didn't even know what the hell that meant. I just knew I could make a lot of money. I thought that would solve my problems. If I were richer than Graham, more successful, I'd be happy, right? I'd 'win.'" He made air quotes with his fingers for emphasis.

Lily smiled sadly, "I always told you that money can't buy happiness, but I'm guessing you figured that out all on your own."

"Yeah. Too late, though, I'm afraid." And he hadn't quite figured it out on his own. No, it had taken one petite blonde with wide blue eyes to help him see what it truly meant to be happy. "Mom, the reason I came back to town is because I have a client who wants to buy the Lakewood. I was sent here to make the deal with Izzy." He looked at his mom, expecting to see shock or disgust toward him, but he only saw kindness in her eyes.

"And what did she say about selling the resort? What did she say when you approached her about it?"

"I never really did."

Lily smiled knowingly. "Really? You've been here two weeks. From my understanding, you've spent a lot of time with Isabel. And you haven't told her why you're here. Why not?"

Chris could tell by the look in his mother's eyes that she already knew the answer. "I fell for her, Mom. I fell for her, and nothing else mattered. I'm not going to try to take her home away, and I don't even want to try." He sighed in defeat. "Not that it really matters anymore. I seriously doubt I even have a job to go back to at this point."

"I see." Studying her son, Lily tapped her chin thoughtfully. "And how do you feel about that exactly?"

How did he feel? For the first time, he really thought about it. "Relieved." The word slipped out without him really thinking about it. And it was the truth. He was relieved. In the last two weeks, he'd spent time with his mom, started to become friendly again with his brother until today, delved back into the security software with Theo that he'd abandoned, and most of all, he'd fallen in love.

"Sweetie, you seem to have a good handle on things. Now you just need to keep moving forward."

"I don't even know how to do that, Mom," he said slowly.

"Yes you do. You move forward. That's the only direction God gave us. A good start would be shedding the things that make you unhappy, and then make things right with Graham and with Izzy. Tell her the truth."

"Mom, Izzy's not going to believe one word I have to say, and how can I blame her? And Graham?" Rubbing his eyes, Chris just shook his head. "Graham would just as soon kill me if I show my face anywhere near Izzy."

"Oh, I wouldn't be too sure about that." She patted his knee, looking at a spot behind him. Turning to follow her gaze, he was shocked to see Graham standing there, leaning his shoulder against the frame of the backdoor.

"How long have you been standing there?" Chris stood, expecting a fight, a continuation of what happened earlier at the hotel.

But Graham just shrugged calmly. "Long enough," he said quietly. "Can we talk?"

Exhaling a breath that Chris didn't know he'd been holding, he just nodded, surprised that his brother wasn't trying to blacken his eye.

Lily rose from the porch. "I'll let you boys be. I'll go make a batch of hot chocolate. Just don't start fighting. If you do, I'll beat both of your asses. And not in that sexy way they talk about in my book club."

"MOM!" both men shouted at once, causing Lily to laugh.

"Oh, lighten up you two. I swear, sometimes I think I raised a couple of prudes," she said laughing, as she breezed back in the house.

****

Shaking his head, Graham stared at the back door. He turned back to his brother, and the two men just held each other's gazes without speaking. When Graham had arrived, he'd almost turned back around when he saw his brother's car. Instead, he'd decided to come in and finish what they'd started. His anger seemed to evaporate as he'd listened to Chris talking to their mom . . . really listened to what Chris had to say.

He hadn't thought about his brother's feelings – not all those years ago, and certainly not now. Chris was charming, easy-going, let everything roll off his back. Graham never stopped to realize how difficult things must have been for him.

The pain in Chris was obvious to him now. He was hurting just as much as Graham was. And whether he wanted to admit it or not, they needed each other.

"Hey," he finally said to his brother.

"Hey," Chris responded.

Sitting down on the steps of the deck, Graham put his elbows on his knees and leaned forward to stare at the big tree, remembering how many times they would climb it just to see how high they could go. He waited patiently as Chris paced behind him for a moment before finally sitting down next to him. "So, what exactly are we going to do?" Graham began.

"Make sure she's safe," Chris responded without hesitation. "More than anything, we need to make sure she's safe."

The anguish in his brother's eyes was evident. Chris didn't care about himself right now. He cared about Izzy.

Graham could see that, and instead of jealousy, he only felt relief. "Finally, we agree."

In the last couple of hours, Graham had been on the phone with Theo and the fire inspector. When frustration had almost gotten the better of him, he comprised a plan – a schedule of sorts – to make sure there wasn't a time when Izzy was alone. She might not want to see he and Chris right now, but he could sure as hell make a plan for her safety. And thank God his brother was on the same page.

Graham calmly explained how they would take turns at the Lakewood, take turns watching Izzy, until they figured out who had set the fire.

"I needed to run this by you to see if you wanted to be involved. I didn't even know when you planned to go back," Graham said with a side glance at his twin.

The war going on in Chris's head showed on his face, his eyes tight, brows furrowed. Graham could feel the conflict vibrating within his brother.

Finally Chris looked up. "I'm not going back. I don't want to go back, Graham. I want to stay here. I'm not happy in St. Louis. The job – it's just . . . it's not me."

"Good," said Graham on an exhaled sigh, enjoying the surprised look that crossed his brother's face. "Look, the truth is that I don't want you to go back. Despite everything that happened today, I've enjoyed having you around the last couple of weeks. This afternoon, I shouldn't have – well, I was upset. Surprised. I'd been sure you wouldn't hurt Izzy, and then I thought that maybe I was wrong, maybe you'd changed into someone I didn't even know anymore."

"I didn't change, Graham. And I would never hurt her. Ever."

Graham nodded and looked at his hands, clasping and unclasping them in front of him. "I know that now. And I'm sorry, Chris. I am."

A slow smile spread over Chris's face, causing Graham to smile back. He felt a deep affection toward his brother, one he'd held back for a long time. He finally felt like he didn't have to hold it back anymore. And just that thought made him feel like a weight had been lifted off of him. He reached up a hand and punched his brother in the shoulder. "You're still a douche, though," he said laughing.

Chris grinned even wider and leaned over to shove his brother's shoulder with his own. "No, you are."

"Here you go, boys, hot chocolate. And fresh cookies." Lily breezed through the back door and set a tray down on the large patio table. The smell of freshly baked chocolate chip cookies wafted over to Graham, and his mouth began to water. Chris was already on his feet grabbing one of the steaming blue ceramic mugs.

"Mom, why don't we help you clean up?" Graham asked, but his mom was already waving him away.

"No, no. You boys talk. I don't have much cleaning up to do, and then I need to get ready for book club."

Graham exchanged glances with his brother and nearly laughed out loud at Chris's smirk. He simply shook his head as Lily walked back in the house.

"I've heard about that book club," Chris finally said.

"Don't," Graham held up one hand as he grabbed two cookies with the other. "I still haven't resolved the fact that Mom reads . . . *erotica*." He said the last word with an exaggerated shiver.

Chris pulled out a chair and plunked down. "You know," he began. "Tessa was at the resort yesterday afternoon and talked about the book they're reading. Apparently, it's a ménage story."

Graham laughed as his brother waggled his eyebrows. Chewing on a cookie, he plopped down in the chair opposite Chris and thought of Izzy reading a ménage story. His arousal was immediate.

"Exactly," Chris said.

"Dude, quit reading my fucking mind," Graham said in exasperation as he reached for another cookie.

Quirking an eyebrow, Chris sipped from his mug. "I'm just saying it's an idea she's open to. I want her, Graham, and so do you. You're telling me the thought hasn't crossed your mind?"

Of course it had crossed his mind. Even when he'd made love to Izzy, he'd thought of how Chris should be claiming her mouth while he was devouring her sweet pussy. But did he really want to admit that? Was he ready for that kind of relationship again?

"You're ready, Graham," his brother said, even better at reading him now that Graham had let his defenses down. "You're ready, and there has never been a more perfect woman – for either of us."

Graham blew out a breath, leaning back in his chair. "Whether I'm ready or not, I just don't know if Izzy would ever be into that kind of relationship. I know she reads about it, but a fantasy is a lot different than reality. Women have a lot of fantasies that they wouldn't want to actually happen."

"Yeah, but we'll never know if we don't try, right?" Chris held his up his mug, in an invitation for Graham to toast.

Tracing the lip on his mug in a moment of hesitation, Graham worried this could go horribly wrong. Except it felt right. After all this time, all his hesitation with Izzy, the thought of the three of them together felt right. Maybe this is what he'd been waiting on.

At Chris's smirk, Graham finally lifted his mug and clinked it against his brother's with a slow grin.

He took a sip from his mug, and was startled out of his thoughts by the ringing of his brother's phone. He watched as Chris looked at his phone and frowned. "It's my boss."

"You going to take it?"

Chris sighed. "Well, I suppose there's no time like the present to turn in my resignation."

Graham was taken aback by the insurmountable joy he felt as he listened to his brother quit his job. Yeah, Chris was back, all right. And the two of them were united. *Watch out Izzy. You're not going to know what hit you.*

Chapter Nine

A new coffee machine was definitely on the agenda for the sheriff's office. Chris was choking down his second cup of coffee that he could damn near chew when Jilly swung through the front door, thermos in hand, and stopped in her tracks at the sight of him sitting at Dustin's desk.

He owed the bubbly redhead a great deal of thanks for taking Izzy to and from book club last night without alerting her to the fact that they were following her. Izzy was smart. They wouldn't be able to keep that up for very long before she finally started to catch on. If she would just cooperate and agree to have an escort, there wouldn't be so much need for subterfuge, but he and Graham both knew she would fight tooth and nail before she'd agree to any sort of protection.

Recovering quickly from her surprise, Jillian gave Chris a slow flirtatious smile. "Well, well, my favorite breakfast right here in the office."

Cocking his head, he looked at her questioningly. "And what's that, darlin'?"

"Man candy," she said with a grin. "It goes great with coffee."

He snorted a laugh as Graham shouted from his office, "Eww, quit flirting with my brother, Jilly."

"Oh, keep your panties on, Sheriff. I'm just teasing. Besides, you two are already taken."

Graham suddenly appeared in the doorway between his office and the main area. "Taken? What exactly do you mean by that?"

With an overly dramatic eye roll, Jillian answered, "Seriously? Come on, everyone knows that you two belong to Izzy just as much as she belongs to you. I just wish all of you weren't so damn pig-headed."

As Graham's mouth popped open, Chris wondered what the hell was up with the fact that every woman in this town was so damn outspoken. And wait a second, they belonged to Izzy?

Quickly recovering, Graham failed miserably at acting nonchalant. "How is Izzy? Have you talked to her today?"

"Not this morning, but Andrea texted," Jillian said as she set her purse and thermos down on her desk and walked out of the room toward the kitchenette in the back of the building.

She returned holding two coffee mugs. "Andi and Iz are working in the big ballroom this morning, setting up all the tables. There are about ten employees in there with them."

Pouring two cups of coffee from her thermos, she shoved one at Graham and set the other one in front of Chris. "But she's not stupid, you guys. You think she's not going to wonder why Dustin just decided to hang out there all morning?"

"I know it's only a matter of time," Chris supplied, taking a sip of fresh coffee and nearly groaning in delight. "But she's nice enough that she won't kick Dustin out of the hotel . . . hopefully."

He desperately wanted to be at the resort himself, but he and Graham had agreed to give Izzy the day to cool off before they invaded her space. It made sense not to crowd her – he knew that. But he would be uneasy unless she was in his arms, unless he and Graham were the ones protecting her.

By late afternoon, Chris had spoken once more to his boss Claude about wrapping up loose ends on the last of his accounts. Once that was finished, he could concentrate on rebuilding his life in Magic. While Claude Stevens had been saddened to lose him, the older man seemed to understand that Chris was never really committed to the company. Claude had thrown incentives at him if he'd close the Lakewood deal, but he'd refused. What he didn't share with his boss was how committed he was to protecting Izzy's land from purchase at all.

Tapping on his computer, Chris brought up the metrics from his latest search. Glancing at Graham's office door, he really hoped his brother was having more luck finding something than he was. Even though he knew Graham would keep him in the loop, he'd decided to set up camp in the sheriff's office all day just to make sure he didn't miss anything.

The creak of the door alerted them to Jilly's return from her afternoon break. When she laid a book down on her desk, Chris knew she'd been to the media center. The door to Graham's office opened and he came out holding his laptop, but stopped short when he spotted the book on Jilly's desk. Just from where Chris sat, he could tell the book cover sported a picture of three men and one woman. Biting his lip to hold back a laugh, he enjoyed the way Graham just shook his head.

"So how was book club last night, Jilly? Everything okay?" he asked the redhead as she sat down at her desk and began flipping through mail.

Her cheeks pinkened slightly as her hands paused. "Oh yeah, everyone really got into this most recent book." She looked from one man to the other as if deciding whether to continue. "The book we just finished took place in a BDSM club, so last night a lot of us dressed up in that theme. It was really fun. Lots of leather." Her eyes cast downward as she tried to hide her grin. "Your mom seemed to enjoy it."

At the thought of Izzy decked out in fetish wear, a streak of desire ran through Chris. Unfortunately, that part of him was immediately squashed by a shiver of downright ickiness as he thought of the leather skirt his mom was wearing when she'd left the previous evening. Suddenly he felt another shiver and looked up to see Graham's expression of horror. He was obviously thinking the same thing.

Before Jillian could discuss the events of last night's book club in further detail, the phone rang.

"Magic Sheriff's Department. How may we protect and serve you this afternoon?"

Graham rolled his eyes at Jillian's animated greeting.

"Oh, hey Viv!" she grinned. Listening for a moment to the person on the other end of the phone, she finally answered, "Are you sure the ghosts took your laundry off the clothes line? It's awfully windy outside today. It might have just blown down."

While Jillian dealt with Vivian, Graham motioned for Chris to come in his office.

"What's up?" Chris asked, shutting the door behind him and plopping down into a chair in front of Graham's desk. "Did you find out anything to help us?"

"I'm not sure," Graham said on a frustrated sigh. His eyes were tired as he leaned back in his chair. "I contacted the insurance company to make sure they had everything they needed from us about the fire, and get a copy of Izzy's policy on the Lakewood. They won't let me access the policy without a warrant or permission from the insured."

A feeling of uneasiness came over Chris. "A warrant? Is that standard?"

"Well, technically yes. But I've dealt with this company on a couple of other cases and they've just handed over the policies." Graham's brow furrowed. "The fact that they won't this time raises a red flag. There's obviously something unusual in the policy. I don't know if it's anything relevant to the investigation or not."

Unable to sit still any longer, Graham rose from his chair and paced the small office. "It's like we're playing a very slow game of connect the dots."

Helpless was not a feeling Chris enjoyed. Luckily this time, he could do something about it.

"What? Why are you grinning?" Graham studied his face.

"There's no reason we have to wait." Getting up, Chris headed for the door. "Just give me about twenty minutes. I seriously doubt the insurance company's files are that hard to access."

"Whoa, whoa, whoa." Graham slapped his hand on the door to stop Chris. "Dude, you are in a police station. Do you understand this?" Graham reached up to smack him in the forehead, but Chris easily blocked his hand.

"So what? Aren't you willing to do whatever it takes right now? What does it matter if I'm bending the rules a little bit?" Putting Izzy first took precedence over anyone's arbitrary rules.

Lifting a hand to his brow, Graham began to rub at his temple. "Or we could just ask her for a copy of the policy. But I like how you immediately jump to the other side of the law," he chastised with a stern look.

"Yeah, it would be a lot easier to ask her," Chris agreed, "if she were fucking speaking to us." Stepping back, he threw his arms up in exasperation. "I don't think she would talk to us if we went out there right now, unless it was to tell us to fuck off."

With a defeated sigh, Graham mumbled, "Dammit, maybe I just want to see her." Running a hand through his hair, Graham's voice was full of frustration. "Look, it's worth a shot. This gives us a legitimate reason to go talk to her. If we can find anything to help us figure out who's trying to hurt her, then I'll face her wrath."

Yeah, Chris wanted to catch the arsonist too, and convince Izzy to give a relationship with two men a shot while he was at it. Was that too much to ask? Maybe Graham was right. This did give them a good excuse.

"Oh, gentlemen, you have a call," Jilly said popping her head in. "Line one."

Graham looked perplexed. "Both of us have a call?"

Jilly nodded, her eyes twinkling. "Yep, she asked to speak to both of you."

She? Chris and Graham glanced at each other. "Izzy," they both said.

"Yep, and I should warn you, she sounds really irritated," Jillian said.

"Well that certainly didn't take her long. I was hoping it would take her a little while to figure out Dustin was there for her protection," Chris said.

They both walked back over to Graham's desk, and he reached over to hit the speaker button on the phone. "Iz, you're on speaker."

The beat of Chris's heart sped up exponentially as he heard a very pissed off Izzy, and he couldn't help but smirk.

"Whose idea was it to assign me a fucking babysitter?" she yelled. "Are you two just going to have Dustin stay here all day? Isn't that a waste of taxpayer money?"

"Izzy, I'm not arguing with you on this." Graham's gruff voice seemed ready for a confrontation.

However, the last thing Chris wanted to do was antagonize her even more. Calming her down should be the first thing they tried to do. "Hold on a second. Can everyone just relax? Izzy, sweetheart, we just want you to be safe. We certainly don't mean to cause any trouble."

"Trouble? Seriously? That seems to be all the two of you do! But if that's how you want to play this, I just thought I would let you know I'm going to use this to my advantage. I currently have Dustin at the top of a ladder hanging up black streamers. And if you two think you're going to set foot in this hotel, I'm putting your asses to work!" And with that, there was an audible click.

A slow smile spread over Chris's face as a spark of hope took up residence in his heart. Graham's jaw was clenched tightly, and he barked out, "What the hell are you smiling about? She's pissed!"

"Oh dear brother, you have to look at the positive. Yesterday, Izzy never wanted to see us again. But today, she told us she would put us to work when we go to the hotel. I would say that's progress, wouldn't you?"

Graham's eyes lit up as he realized what Chris was saying. "I think now would be a very good time to pay Izzy a visit and see if she can't find that insurance policy." Graham opened his office door to usher his brother out. "She can't kick us out for that."

****

Whoever created heels should be shot. Izzy really should have rethought her choice of footwear. She'd been on her feet all day decorating for the party. Now she plopped back on her bed and kicked her heels halfway across the room as she contemplated whether she even had the energy to change into a T-shirt and sweats, or if she should just sleep in her work clothes.

Solitude for the first time today felt damn good. She'd run Dustin ragged, and almost felt guilty about it. Almost. She'd just been starting to calm down a little bit when Theo had swapped him out this afternoon. Since he'd been staring at her almost as much as he did Andi, she knew he must be the latest in her personal team of babysitters.

By the time she was done for the day, it had becoming increasingly difficult not to take her frustrations out on the men, so she was really proud of herself for squelching the impulse to trip Theo when he insisted on walking her to her room. Plus Theo was way bigger than her. If she tried to trip him, she'd probably end up breaking her ankle.

A knock at the door pulled her from her thoughts, and she groaned. Maybe if she didn't answer it, they would go away. She didn't feel like dealing with more adventures in hunky babysitting. When the knocking got louder, she pulled herself up with a sigh and padded over to the door. Looking through the peephole, she was greeted with the sight of two hard-bodied Nolan brothers. The reaction of her body annoyed the crap out of her— the way her heart flipped and her breath quickened.

Closing her eyes, she rested her forehead against the cool door. *Don't open it. Don't open it.* But, damn, she really she wanted to open it. She'd been away from them for less than two days and the ache inside her throbbed more every second without them. Before she could truly think through the situation, she found herself pulling back the chain and opening the door.

Graham's piercing eyes looked right through her, and Chris's face lit up in a smile when he saw her. Izzy almost groaned. The stress and the exhaustion of the last few days pressed in on her, and all she wanted to do was lean on these two men, just fall and let them catch her.

Chris's smile faltered as she just stood there silently, grasping the door for support. "Iz, are you all right?" he asked, concerned.

"I'm fine," she said squaring her shoulders. *Snap out of it, Izzy.* "It's been a long day, and I just want to go to bed." She started to close the door, but Graham laid a hand flat against the door, stopping her.

"Not yet, sweetheart, we want to talk." The command in his voice told her there was no room for argument.

The pull she felt to them was so strong. It crumbled the edges of her resolve until she knew she didn't have the energy to fight it. Did she really even want to? The need for them outweighed the anger in her gut, and if she was honest with herself, all she really wanted was for them to hold her. Backing up a step, she put a hand to her temple to massage out the headache that was starting to form.

That was all her men needed. Graham shut the door behind them, and Chris came over to put his arms around her, pulling her close. He smelled so good, an aftershave of light spice and strong man, which shredded her last strand of willpower as she snuggled into his warmth.

His arms went around her and held her close, and she felt his lips in her hair. Opening her eyes, she saw Graham watching her closely and tried to give him her best stern voice that sounded pathetic even to her own ears. "I'm still mad at you – both of you," she said weakly.

"I know, baby," Chris said gently rubbing a strong hand up and down her back.

"We really did have a reason for coming –" Graham started to say. Izzy looked at him quizzically, but missed the slight shake of Chris's head toward his brother.

"We wanted to make sure you've eaten dinner, sweetheart," Chris said.

Izzy sighed warily. "So you're the next shift in the babysitter club?"

"Maybe," Graham said with a slight smile, his hand coming up to stroke her arm, "but you're in luck. We give the most personalized service."

She couldn't stop her lips from turning up as her insides went a little melty at his words. "You really think someone would come after me now, with a hotel full of people?" she asked with a little headshake. "That's just silly."

"Silly is not a word I would use to describe a situation where your safety is concerned," Chris said with a threat to his voice.

"Iz, I hope we're being overly cautious," Graham said. "I really do. But you have to remember that an arsonist set fire to your office at a time when you were supposed to be in there. We need to find out why someone wanted to hurt you. And until we do. . ."

"I'm on continuous watch," she finished.

"Yes. You can contemplate that while I rub the tension out of your shoulders." Chris pulled away to gently massage her neck and shoulders and Izzy's eyes drifted shut, her knees weakening as she felt the anxiety start to drain out. The warmth of his hands radiated through the thin fabric of her blouse. While her muscles relaxed, her insides tensed in excitement at his touch.

She moaned lightly, feeling not only Chris's warm body at her back, but also a warmth in front of her. When she opened her eyes, she gasped as Graham stood in front of her, his big body taking up all of her personal space.

Suddenly, she couldn't breathe. Graham took one last tiny step toward her until they were toe-to-toe and then reached out to rest his hands on her hips. She instinctively tried to step back. Not because she was scared, but because he exuded such dominance, such power just in his presence, his intensity.

When Izzy backed up, she ran into Chris who had his body pressed up against her. "Whoa baby, where do you think you're going?" Chris's voice from behind her was softer than Graham's, but just as effective. His erection pressed up against her lower back alerted her to his arousal.

She swallowed hard as Chris gently brushed her hair aside, his lips gently touching the back of her neck, kissing lightly, exploring. When she felt his tongue against her skin, her eyes floated shut as her whole body tingled with awareness.

"Look at me," Graham ordered.

Her eyes fluttered open, obeying instantly, and her insides melted under his intense gaze. His callused hand brushed her face, and then wrapped gently around her throat, the rough pad of his thumb strumming the jittery pulse point on her neck.

When he smiled at her reaction, she wondered if he could actually hear the loud drumming of her heart. The power in his smoky eyes had Izzy's gaze sliding away until his hand squeezed lightly around her throat, that imposing touch reminding her that he was in charge, and signaling to her that she was to keep her eyes on him.

"We want you, Izzy." Graham couldn't hide the distinctive arousal in his hooded eyes, the parting of his lips, the rasp of his voice. "We want you to be with us – both of us."

Her mouth went dry as every muscle in her body grew languid with lust for these two men. She was dreaming. She had to be dreaming. How many times over the last few days had she thought about being with Graham and Chris? Dreamed of them taking her together? No, this wasn't real.

The confusion on her face relayed her emotions. Licking her lips, she finally spoke, her voice scraping against her throat, "You can't."

At Graham's chuckle, it was Chris who spoke. "Oh Izzy, we can, and we most certainly *do* want you." His hands ran lightly up and down her arms, and the feeling of their touches made it extremely difficult to think.

"Sweetheart," Graham breathed as his hand moved up to cup her cheek, "we don't want to overwhelm you. We just want . . ." He flicked a gaze toward his brother. "Look, maybe this isn't the right time," he said, dropping his hand.

The loss of his warmth caused Izzy to shiver. No, they couldn't stop. They couldn't leave. Panic seized her at the thought. It should feel weird or wrong to want two men, shouldn't it? But it didn't. If she'd been unsure before, she was certain now. *Tell them! Tell them what you want!*

Before Graham could move away, she stepped forward and reached up to place her hands on the sides of his face, pulling him down to meet her kiss.

****

Her soft lips pressed against his mouth, causing Graham's eyes to widen in surprise. He'd sensed her unease, so her sudden aggressiveness took him aback for a moment. She wanted them? Was that what she was saying with this kiss?

Stepping forward, Izzy pressed her body against his and he groaned at the feel of her firm breasts pressed against his chest. When her tongue hesitantly probed through his parted lips, he would have lost control if it weren't for Chris standing behind her dramatically clearing his throat.

Grasping her shoulders, it took every ounce of strength in Graham to push Izzy away and plant her back on her feet. Her lips were slightly swollen, and her blue eyes had darkened. Before he could catch his breath to speak, a stunned look crossed her pretty face.

"I – I'm sorry. You said this wasn't the right time. Obviously you don't want to – I – I shouldn't have. . ." She trailed off, trying to step away, but both of them reached for her at the same time. Dammit, he hadn't meant to upset her.

Looking to his brother for help, Graham was relieved when Chris leaned into Izzy without hesitation, easing her worry.

"You have to tell us, baby," Chris murmured against her ear. "Trust me, we want nothing more than to kiss your pretty lips until your head swims, but you have to tell us what you want first."

"I don't want to guess wrong," Graham agreed, reaching for her hand and entwining his fingers with hers. "It would be easy for us to just take you, toss you on the bed, make you come over and over." He stepped closer to her as her eyes started to glaze at that statement. "And maybe that's what you want. Us taking you without you having to actually make the decision." He brushed her swollen lips with the pad of his finger. "But it doesn't work that way, sweetheart. You have to tell us what you want."

"But – but – I thought you liked to dominate." Damn, that low, breathy voice did things to him.

He had to bite back a groan. The thought of dominating Izzy, tying her up, spanking that pretty round ass caused him to harden to the point of pain. "Baby, I need to know that you want us – together – as much as we want you. We need your consent, Iz. And once you *do* consent, you should know that we won't go easy on you."

Her jaw dropped open a bit as her eyes dilated, and Graham grinned as she tried to figure out what he meant. Behind her, Chris gave him a sly smile.

"I – I —" she stammered, and then bit her lip and took a shaky breath.

"Deep breath, sweetheart," Chris crooned, his lips finding her ear again. Graham shot him a warning look. If he didn't quit kissing her, she wasn't going to be able to form a thought, much less words.

"I – I want you." Her breathy voice was barely audible, and he stepped close enough to press himself against her, sandwiching her in between himself and Chris.

Taking another long shaky breath, she tried again. "I want both of you – to – to make love to me." The way her milky skin flushed led Graham to believe that she'd never actually said that to a man before, never asked for what she wanted.

Her words empowered him. She wanted them. She was theirs. He leaned forward to take her lips, cupping her face in his large hands so he could tilt her head how he wanted. His tongue traced the line of her lips until they parted, allowing him access. He swallowed her light whimper as his tongue delved deeper. And she kissed him back. Oh how she kissed him back. When her hands clutched at his arms, he eased back, gently nipping her bottom lip.

"Chris," Graham spoke to his brother without looking away from Izzy. "Undress her. I want her naked."

Her breath caught in her throat, and she jerked her head back to look at Chris who smiled wickedly. "With pleasure."

As Graham backed up to allow his brother room, Chris walked around to stand in front of Izzy. He jokingly rolled his eyes at Graham. "He can be a little bossy," he said to her with a wink.

Graham watched as his brother ran his hands lightly down her arms, before lifting her arms over her head. He quickly stripped off her black blouse before tugging off the khaki pants she wore.

When Chris stepped back, he darted a glance at his twin, and Graham could see that his eyes were as molten as he felt inside.

Izzy stood before both of them in only her black bra and panties, looking from one man to the other as their steel gazes swept up and down her body, ravenously consuming every inch of her. When a shiver went through her, Graham reached out to envelop her in his arms. "Are we making you nervous, sweetheart?"

She shook her head, a little smile playing at her mouth.

Chris reached out, needing to touch her, and Graham passed her off to his brother. "Are you sure? I know we can be a little overwhelming."

"I'm sure," she said, smiling at their concern. "Very sure. I need you. Both of you. I want you both so much, so badly. I just . . ." She stumbled. "I um —"

"What, baby? What's wrong?" Graham asked. When her gaze slid away, he lifted her chin up. "Look at me, Iz. What's wrong? You need to be honest with us or I will smack that pretty ass right now."

The brief flaring of her eyes told Graham she would enjoy a spanking, his hand pounding her ass. Now, there was some fun they could have later.

"Do I get a safe word? I mean not that I want you to stop, but if you spank me . . ." She chewed on her bottom lip. "I mean, I know before, you said . . . I just didn't know with both of you . . . oh never mind," she said, turning away, obviously embarrassed.

God, she was sweet. But he really had to buy her some reading material other than BDSM books. "Iz, come sit with us for a moment." Graham led her to sit on the edge of the bed, and Chris sat on the other side of her. Each of them held one of her hands, and he didn't miss how her eyes darted from one hand to the other.

"Sweetheart, you have to get out of your head," Chris said softly.

Graham just frowned at her. "Izzy, I'll say this again. Just like last time, your safe word is 'no.' 'Stop' will also work just as effectively. If either of us do anything that you don't want or that makes you feel uncomfortable at all, you say 'stop,' and everything will cease. Do you understand?"

She nodded gratefully, her shoulders relaxing a fraction.

"No. Answer me," he demanded.

"Jeez, Mr. Bossy Pants," she said with a little eye roll. "Yes. Yes, I understand."

"Mr. Bossy Pants?" he said, holding back a smile. "Watch it, sweetheart."

She opened her mouth to respond, but thought better of it and shut it again, causing a laugh from Chris. "Smart girl."

Shaking his head, Graham squeezed her hand. "Now Iz, I don't mean to scare you with the dramatics, but I have a feeling you've never been with two men at the same time, have you?"

Izzy shook her head, which was answered by a sigh from Graham. Letting go of her hand, he threaded his fingers through her hair and tightened his grip just slightly until he elicited a little gasp from her.

"Answer him, baby. Out loud," Chris said reassuringly.

"Yes, sir," she said hurriedly, causing both men to smile. "I – um . . . not only have I not been with two men at the same time, but before this week, I'd only been with two men period."

A brilliant smile lit Graham's face.

"Good," was all Chris said as he stood up.

"Good?" she asked, looking from one to the other.

Chris tugged his shirt off over his head without bothering to unbutton it, revealing taut abdominal muscles. "You're ours, Izzy. I don't like thinking of you with anyone else."

Running his fingers through her honey blond waves, Graham enjoyed her appreciative expression as she watched his brother. "Let me tell you how this is going to go because I don't want you to be scared. Eventually, we want to take you together."

She looked at him, swallowing hard. "You mean, together together?"

"Yes, baby, by together I mean Chris will take your sweet pussy and I will be buried inside of your tight little ass." As he spoke, one hand moved to her knee, easing her legs apart as he slid his rough palm along her inner thigh. God, he loved the feel of her smooth skin.

Izzy flushed at his explicit words. Her eyes darted to the bulge of his jeans, and Graham detected a slight wince from her. "Is that possible?" she almost whispered. "I mean you're both so . . ."

Chris's laugh eased the tension. "Don't worry, sweetheart, we'll fit. And we're not going to take you together like that tonight. We need to prepare you first. Eventually you'll be ready for us."

"Eventually?" she asked confused. "What do you mean? I thought that we, I mean, I thought that tonight. . ."

Graham smiled sweetly, his hand cupping her cheek. His heart gave a little jolt when she instinctively nuzzled his hand. "Yes, eventually," he said. "Iz, you are not ready to take either one of us anally. That takes some preparation like Chris said."

His brother interjected. "And we will definitely start preparing you tonight."

"P - preparing me?" she stumbled. "Preparing me how exactly?"

Graham just grinned as Chris searched his pocket and pulled out the key card to his room. "I'll be right back."

Chris was out the door, and Izzy began to ask where he had gone when Graham leaned in, gently pushing her back on the bed. His lips found the skin right above her breasts, and he deliberately scraped his chin along the sensitive area, knowing the scratch of his whiskers would cause just the right amount of erotic pain. When her hands clutched at his shoulders, and her hips thrust up in reaction, Graham knew he was right.

As he palmed a full breast, he heard Chris come back into the room, and looked up at Izzy's slight gasp. Her eyes were trained behind him, and before Graham could look, she exclaimed, "Good God, is that a butt plug? That's huge!"

Graham lifted his head and followed her gaze to see the purple silicone plug. He shook his head, laughing, "Izzy, that's the starter size. It's actually quite small."

"Starter size? Seriously?" Her wide eyes were looking from one of them to the other as if they had just gone insane.

Propping himself up on one elbow, Graham quirked an eyebrow. "Think about it, sweetheart. Imagine how big it is in comparison to me." At the way she sucked on her bottom lip, he knew she was thinking about his size. He sure remembered how tight she was as he slid his thickness into that wet cunt. Damn, he needed to be inside of her.

"Well, I - I suppose if you use that comparison, it's smallish," she conceded.

"Exactly." Graham leaned in to suddenly capture her mouth, unable to get enough of her.

****

Chris set the new toy on the bedside table, along with a couple of condoms. Then he sat next to her, enjoying the way she quivered as he slid his hands up her abdomen to those luscious breasts, finding the clasp of her bra. Quickly undoing the hooks, he let her breasts spill free, and he and Graham let out simultaneous moans of pleasure as they each cupped a breast. Chris rubbed a thumb in light circles around her nipple, causing it to bunch up. Izzy's back arched, pushing her breast into his hand as Graham kept a firm hold on her head, his tongue delving, exploring.

When Graham lifted his hand, Izzy panted, a dazed look on her face as their strong hands moved over her body, sliding her bra down her arms. Chris leaned in to take his turn claiming her. One hand wound in her hair, holding her head immobile as he plundered her mouth, his other hand still on her breast, massaging, squeezing.

When he grabbed her thigh, Graham grabbed the other one, and they spread her legs, completely in sync. When his hand slid over her pussy, she moaned into his mouth as he massaged her through her silk panties. He finally broke this kiss, enjoying the way Izzy's lust-filled eyes watched him.

Graham's hand moved to cup her mound as Chris's moved back up to her breasts. Her nipples were hard little pebbles that poked into his palms as they were pinched and rubbed.

"We need to get you out of these panties, baby." Graham's voice was rough with arousal. "You're all wet. God, you're so wet for us, Iz."

As Graham slid her panties down her legs, Chris slipped a finger between her slick folds, playing, caressing, teasing, but ever so carefully avoiding her clit. Izzy involuntarily bucked her hips forward wanting more. Oh yes, they were driving her crazy, all right. The frantic darting of her eyes, the light moaning. When he grinned at her reaction, she practically glowered at him in frustration.

"Just relax, sweetheart," Graham instructed, leaning in for a quick kiss. Chris smoothed his hands down her legs as he stood up to remove the jeans that felt like a prison of torture for his straining cock.

He watched with amusement as Izzy tugged desperately at Graham's shirt. "Off," she commanded breathily. "Too many clothes." She was so far gone, she couldn't even form a complete sentence.

Graham got up to quickly shed his clothes, and Izzy sat up to watch as they both shoved their jeans off, setting their engorged cocks bobbing free. "Oh God," she breathed, looking from one man to the other as if she could eat them up.

The thought of her mouth around him made Chris's cock twitch. How good it would feel to thrust himself inside that soft mouth, feel her throat opening up around him. He needed her so damn much. Izzy reached for him with one hand and Graham with the other.

Leaning in, Chris took her mouth, nipping gently at her lips as her hand went to his broad shoulders.

"Easy," Graham said gently, taking her hand and intertwining her fingers with his. He removed her other hand from Chris's shoulder, and moved both wrists over her head, keeping them immobile in one of his firm grip.

Where the fuck was his brother getting all of his self-control? Chris didn't think he could hold out much longer before he would have to be inside of her. When his fingers slid between her legs, he felt the trickle of wetness as her pussy clenched, sending a jolt of electricity straight to his cock. He could see her yanking against Graham's hold, causing his brother to tighten his grip, holding her more firmly so she couldn't escape.

Both men bent their heads to devour a breast, causing Izzy to cry out. "Please," she begged. "Please." Her entire body was one taut muscle, coiled, needing release. Chris marveled at how responsive she was, how sensitive, and he wondered if they could make her come just by playing with her breasts.

Except he'd rather make her come in a different way. But first, a little teasing was in order. Needing to taste her, he kissed his way down her body, spreading her legs open wide as he nibbled along the crease of her inner thigh.

He growled, "God, Izzy, you smell like heaven." The scent of her arousal caused his dick to swell painfully. He desperately wanted nothing more than to shove his cock into her and fuck her hard and fast. But he was determined to keep his self-control in check because more than anything he wanted this to last.

His tongue snaked out, running up the swollen folds of her labia. Izzy bucked up, so Chris anchored an arm over her abdomen. He watched as her pussy clenched in response. Unable to move her hips or her arms, Izzy was completely helpless to the two men. She whimpered in response, and her arousal told him this was just what she needed. Just what they all needed.

Izzy's swollen clit poked out, begging for attention, but Chris licked up and down, sucking at the folds of her pussy, being careful to avoid the hard knot of nerves. He knew it wouldn't take much to set her off, but he wasn't quite ready yet. He needed her arousal heightened as much as possible for what they had in mind.

God, he loved the taste of her. Izzy's cream was honey sweet with a slight tang — truly the most delicious thing he'd ever tasted. He spread her folds open with his fingers and enjoyed the way her vagina spasmed as if searching for a hard cock. He obliged by thrusting his tongue inside her, mimicking what he wanted to do with his dick. He thrust his tongue in and out, lapping up her delectable cream, enjoying the sound of her muffled cries that were swallowed by Graham's kisses.

He firmly sucked in each of her labia before he finally, as if a little reward to them both, moved up to circle her clit with the tip of his tongue, reveling in the way Izzy's entire body jerked in response.

"Wow, I don't know what you just did, man, but that just about sent her over the edge," Graham said with wonder.

Chris circled his tongue around her clit again very lightly, and held his forearm even tighter over her midsection as her hips desperately tried to arch up to meet his mouth. Her clit was so engorged with blood, hard and swollen. He knew she was close.

"Please, please, please." Her voice was one long plea, her head thrashing back and forth on the pillow.

"Not yet, baby. Not yet," said Graham.

Chris made eye contact with his brother, and Graham nodded to indicate that she was ready for what they wanted to do next. When Chris moved away from her, she literally growled in frustration. "You two are evil bastards!" she shouted.

He bit his lip to keep from laughing, knowing that was not something you said to Graham in the bedroom.

His brother's eyes practically glittered as they narrowed at Izzy.

****

Graham's face darkened as he assessed Izzy. Even though her eyes were glazed over from the ministrations of his brother, he caught a glimmer of worry as she realized what she said.

"What did you just say?" he asked ominously.

"Uh – um, nothing," she stammered. "I- I- I'm so sorry. I didn't mean – uh, I'm sorry, sir." She bit her lip, as she worriedly looked from him to Chris.

Graham almost laughed as he looked at Chris, who had already stood up and crossed his arms, smiling widely, looking as he if he were about to receive a giant present on Christmas morning.

Graham quickly pulled Izzy up and to her feet, and she gasped in surprise, not even able to catch her balance before he grasped her around the waist and sat on the chaise lounge next to the bed, bending her over his lap despite her squeals.

Izzy shrieked in response, and immediately tried to get up, but Chris planted a hand firmly on her lower back, and Graham held a hand on her shoulders, preventing her movements.

When she continued to writhe, Graham delivered a sharp smack to her lovely round ass, grinning at her sharp intake of breath and at the way a pink hand print appeared on her creamy skin. Oh holy God, that was just about the loveliest sight. Izzy flailed her hands, trying to find some leverage so she could push herself up.

Graham made a "tsk tsk" sound and tilted his head at the nightstand. Chris walked over to grab a couple of items he'd placed there as Izzy tried to wrench her head around.

"What are you doing?! Let me up!" Damn, he enjoyed how cute she looked even as she kicked her little legs like a disobedient child.

As Chris held Izzy immobile with his strong hands on her back, Graham grasped her wrists, moving her hands low behind her back. He had the handcuffs snicked shut over her wrists before she even realized what he was doing.

"Graham! Chris!" She jerked at her hands. "What are you doing?" she asked again, her voice growing panicky. "I don't know if this is a good idea." She pulled roughly at the cuffs.

"Sweetheart, you need to calm down. Don't yank so hard against the cuffs." He was ready to slip the key in the lock. If she struggled against the cuffs, it would make them tighter, cutting off her circulation.

Chris held up a hand to signal for him not remove the cuffs yet, and then knelt in front of her, lifting her chin so she could meet his gaze. "Shhh," he soothed, brushing her hair out of her eyes. "Calm down, baby. If you truly want us to stop, you just have to say it, remember? Do you trust us?"

Graham was pleased at the way the panic in her spine eased immediately and her struggling stopped, her hands going limp. "I – yes. Yes, I trust you," she said softly.

"Good girl," Graham murmured gently, making large sweeping motions over her back with his hands as

Chris stroked her hair. Yes, this is exactly what she needed – what they all needed.

****

Izzy immediately calmed at the tenderness in his voice. She did trust him. She trusted both of them. She had expected the hard, dominant male attitudes, but hadn't expected the dominance to be combined with such gentleness and caring. The combination threw her off balance until she couldn't think. And then all that was left to do was to feel, to react. And her heart and body submitted to them without question.

Chris's eyes flickered in front of her as his face filled with . . . love? He nodded at his brother as if to say, "Ready."

Suddenly, Izzy felt something cool trickle down between her ass cheeks. She jerked as she felt Graham spread her cheeks open. When she felt something pressing against her tight anal entrance, she squirmed, loving the way Graham's large hot erection rubbed against her belly.

He cursed softly, "Iz, stop squirming. You're killing me."

Feeling mischievous after the way they'd tortured her earlier, Izzy grinned and squirmed again, making sure to rub firmly against his cock.

"Fuck," Graham cursed, delivering a swat to her upturned ass.

Chris laughed shaking his head at her. "Oh, you are going to be quite the little brat, aren't you, sweetheart?"

Graham seemed to take advantage of her momentary distraction because he pressed again against her tight hole, this time gaining entrance. Izzy gasped, lifting up, and Chris's hands went to her shoulders.

"Keep still, baby. It's just his finger. We want to loosen you up."

That was just his finger? Holy crap, she was in trouble. Graham rubbed her back gently with one hand as if sensing her unease. "Try to relax, sweetheart." He pulled his finger out and thrust back in gently, slowly gaining ground. The slight burning sensation eased as Izzy felt him add more lube.

Chris leaned in to kiss her mouth, and Izzy relaxed into him. As his tongue rubbed against hers, she felt her body begin to go hot and liquid at the thrusting of Graham's finger in her ass. When she inadvertently tugged against the handcuffs, she moaned, wondering if there had ever been anything so erotic.

"She's ready," Graham mumbled, removing his finger. Izzy again felt more lube and then something larger pressing against her anus. She tensed and immediately tightened up until Chris nuzzled her cheek and whispered, "Push back against him, sweetheart."

Izzy took a deep breath and pushed back, and the plug popped in. *There's that damn burning sensation again.* Sucking in another breath, she focused on Chris's calming voice in her ear, telling her how amazing she was, how gorgeous she looked.

Graham slowly fucked the plug in and out, and the burning eased. Instead, nerves lit up that Izzy didn't even know existed, sending a warm jangly sensation shooting up her spine. She bit her lip to stifle a whimper. Who knew that could feel so amazing?

With short gentle strokes, Graham slid the plug home, and her tight sphincter muscle closed around the base, holding it in.

"God, that's so fucking beautiful," he said, admiring his work.

Rubbing his hands over the two round globes, Graham massaged her ass as Chris took her mouth in a gentle kiss before standing up and pulling her up with him. When Graham disappeared into the bathroom, Chris leaned in, brushing the hair out of her face. "How do you feel?"

Every nerve ending in Izzy's body sizzled – from the spanking and the plug to just having their hands on her. "I feel so . . . full."

A grin split Chris's beautiful face. "Just wait, baby. We're going to have you so full that you won't remember a time when we weren't inside of you."

At her little gasp, Chris leaned in to thrust his tongue in her mouth for a mind-blowing kiss, tasting her, taking. God, the taste of him, the fullness, the cuffs on her wrists, the wetness in her pussy. . . Izzy was so overwhelmed with sensation. She wanted them to take her now. Maybe they would . . .

When Graham walked back in, Izzy didn't have time to think before Chris was pulling her down over his lap, his hands steadying her for support. She squirmed trying to get up, but was stilled by several hands on her back. "Wait a second. What else . . ."

"Oh no, you don't," said Graham. "We're not done yet."

Not done? Uh oh. "What – what do you mean?"

She could see Graham's feet as he paced back and forth in front of her.

"I seem to remember you being so rude as to call us evil bastards. I think there is some punishment in store for you."

Who knew feet could be so sexy? Wait, what? "Punishment? You just shoved a plug up my ass. I thought that was the punishment."

She felt Chris's fingers sliding between her folds. "Mmm, and as wet as you are, I would say you enjoyed it a great deal. Let's see how you enjoy your spanking."

"Sp-spanking? You really are going to spank me?" she squeaked. A little thrill went through her, and she wasn't sure if it was fear or excitement, or maybe both. The way her pussy clenched told her it was mostly excitement, need.

"Graham is the one who administers the spankings," Chris said, and she could almost hear him smiling.

Her breath quickened as she felt four hands caressing her back, her ass, her pussy.

"Izzy, I'm going to swat you ten times, and I want you to count, okay?" Graham's voice was stern, but gentle.

She nodded rapidly, as her breath quickened. "Out loud, Izzy," said Chris. "Or he'll add more."

She gasped. "Yes sir," she said quickly. "Yes, I'll count."

"Very good," Graham said.

Hands gently rubbed her ass, and she clenched in response. Tightening around the plug made her entire body respond, her pussy throbbing as if it had its own heartbeat. Suddenly Graham's hand left her, and she heard the swat before she felt the sting.

She sucked in a breath at the sharp bite of pain. "Count, Izzy," he commanded.

"One," she said shakily. The next smack came quickly, landing on the other cheek. Fuck, that hurt. "Two."

Graham spread out the smacks so none of them landed in the same spot twice. On the fourth whack, Izzy was very close to yelling stop. But then something unexpected happened.

The next swat landed low on her right buttock, and the sting melted into a sensual warmth that was like a livewire straight to her pussy. She felt herself go liquid inside, as the heat from her behind seemed to simmer, sparking with every swat.

Izzy heard a low moan and realized that it was coming from her. "Yes," Chris hissed, and she felt him harden even more against her.

"There's my girl," she heard Graham mumble as he brought his hand down again in a short arc. By the eighth swat, Izzy's clit had tightened painfully, and she tried to rub herself against Chris's thigh. He rubbed his hand over the warmth on her behind, lighting up the nerve endings.

"Two more, sweetheart. You're doing beautifully." The ninth swat came quickly, and Izzy panted with need. Graham aimed the final swat right in the center of her ass, and it seemed to push the plug in further. Izzy jerked at her cuffs as a cry escaped her lips. Her body was so close to a release. She needed an orgasm so badly. She thought she would die if she didn't come soon.

Before she could recover from the spanking, or even speak, Chris's fingers slid between her folds, two fingers thrusting hard into her pussy. The intrusion caused the tightness in Izzy to completely fracture. His thumb rubbed firmly over her clit, and she screamed as her entire body splintered. She yanked at the cuffs as Graham held them firmly against her lower back with one hand, and she shuddered over and over as Chris's fingers thrust powerfully in and out of her pussy.

She thought she would never stop coming, had never experienced anything like this. She was coming from being spanked. Spanked! They owned her body, knew what she needed when she didn't. Graham was suddenly in front of her, gripping her hair and pulling her head up gently, forcing her to look at him as her body continued to quake in orgasm.

Finally Chris's fingers slowed, easing in and out of her as he brought her down gently.

"I do think that was the most beautiful thing I've ever seen," Graham said softly, his hand coming up to cup her chin as he took her lips in a soft kiss.

Izzy collapsed against them, completely boneless, and suddenly her two men were lifting her up.

They lay her face down on the bed, her lower half hanging over the bottom, her head turned to the side. She wasn't even registering them, her mind still reeling from the intensity of her orgasm, and the pleasant haze gave her a loopy grin.

Chris was kneeling on the floor next to her, his face even with hers, studying her as Graham stood behind him. "Baby, look at me. Are you okay?"

Izzy's face lit up as she looked into his concerned eyes, and she nodded. "Perfect. I'm perfect. You're both perfect." This warm, floaty feeling was better than any drug, and she wished it could last forever.

As many romance and erotica books as Izzy had read in her life, nothing had ever prepared her for the intense feeling of being with these two men. And she finally understood. She understood what all those romance novels meant. All the emotion, all the love – it was inside of her, and it radiated out for these two men. For Chris and Graham.

"I want you," she said breathlessly. "Both of you. Please. Please make love to me."

This time when she begged them, they didn't tease her. They didn't try to play. No, this was pure and simple and intense. Each man leaned in to give her a quick kiss, and then Graham was standing behind her, spreading her open.

"You know what I've always loved about the beds here, Izzy? The height. They are the perfect height." Thick fingers spread her pussy open, sliding through her cream. When his fingers slid firmly over her clit, that spark ignited again inside of her, the need bubbling up anew.

She saw Chris toss something to Graham and heard the crinkle of foil as he ripped open a condom packet. A moment later, she felt his large cock sliding between her engorged folds. He was so big, and she was so swollen, so sensitive from her orgasm. And the plug in her ass made her feel even more full. All of a sudden, she was aware of how much bigger he would feel with the plug taking up so much room inside her body.

She tensed as Graham spread her open, the tip of his cock swirling in her wetness. "Relax for me, baby," he pleaded.

****

On a groan, Graham pushed forward, entering her gently. It was everything he could do not to pound her hard and bury himself in her. But she was so swollen, and he didn't want to hurt her. He pressed forward as slowly as he could in short thrusts, gaining a little more ground with each one, sliding into her slick swollen tissues. She felt like a silky glove grasping his cock, and his head fell back at the heavenly vise-like grip she had on him.

Once he seated himself in Izzy, she tried to thrust back against him, but he put a hand on her lower back to steady her. "Easy, baby," he said, his control slipping fast. "Just give yourself a minute to adjust."

Chris was on his knees, murmuring softly to her as he trailed kisses on her shoulders.

"I'm so full," she mumbled. And she was. Her ass was filled with the plug, and Graham took up every little bit of space in her pussy. The entire world seemed to center around the part of himself that was buried inside of her, and he knew as long as he lived, he would never forget the feeling of Izzy's pussy throbbing around his hard cock.

He watched as Chris studied her face, making sure she was okay, his hands running through her hair.

"Chris," she gasped out. "Please. I need you too. Please."

****

Izzy sighed as Chris took her mouth again in a deep kiss, his tongue thrusting, rubbing against hers. He kissed her so thoroughly that it left her gasping before he stood. His cock bobbed in front of her, long and thick, and he stroked it slowly from base to tip as she licked her lips in anticipation.

Her instinct was to reach out to him, but the cuffs stopped her, causing a little whine to escape her. Chris smiled wickedly, "I guess you're at my mercy, baby."

Graham's low laugh rumbled behind her, and she felt it to her very core. She tried again to move, to thrust back, and then winced when that earned her a light slap on her already sore bottom. "Be still," he said roughly.

With a little quirk of a smile, Chris stepped forward, his cock moving closer to her lips. Izzy stuck out her tongue to catch the pearly drop of fluid that rested on the tip, and grinned at the groan that erupted from Chris. His hand tangled in her hair as he moved closer, rubbing the head of his cock over her lips, coating them with the drops of fluid that glistened on his erection. She flicked her tongue out over the head of his cock, enjoying his soft groans. Even though she was trussed up, Izzy had never felt more powerful.

She opened her mouth to take him in, and he thrust gently forward. Her tongue circled his rigid cock, tracing the vein that bulged along the side, sucking hard, her cheeks hollowing in as he pulled almost all the way out.

Then Graham began to move.

****

He'd died and gone to heaven. That had to be the case because Graham had never felt anything so good in his life. He started thrusting slowly. Izzy had been tight the first time he'd taken her, but now, with the plug in, her pussy felt like a vise around his cock. The more she moved her hips trying to increase the pace, the slower he went, enjoying her frustrated little cries.

"Oh God," Chris said, his head falling back. "When she groans like that, it vibrates through my whole body."

"Let's see if I can make her groan some more." Graham grasped the plug that was still embedded in her ass and began slowly thrusting it in and out. He felt the drag of the plug against his cock and it was all he could do not to burst inside of her.

Izzy gasped around Chris, causing his hands to tangle firmly in her hair.

Graham began to move faster, alternating his thrusts with the thrusts of the plug. Izzy began to move back against him to meet his pace, her body coiling tighter. He almost came just from listening to the sounds coming out of her, muffled by Chris's cock in her mouth.

He could see his brother trying his hardest to hold back, Chris's willpower obviously slipping as his hands clenched tighter in her hair.

And Izzy was close. So close. Tingles shot through him every time her pussy contracted. Every muscle in her body tightened as her head bobbed at lightning speed over his brother.

Chris looked from Izzy to Graham in a silent plea. "I. can't. last," he bit out.

And neither could Graham.

He reached around to slip his fingers through her folds and felt himself sliding in and out of her wetness. When his fingers brushed across her slick clit, her entire body jerked in response. Graham's fingers circled the tight ball of nerves for just a moment before he pinched it hard. Her pussy clamped down around him, and her taut body stilled an instant before she let out a high-pitched squeal. She flooded around his cock, spasmodically gripping him as her entire body shook, dragging him over the cliff with her. He thrust deeply and held himself still, his balls tightening a heartbeat before his cock jerked against her womb.

And he wasn't alone. He could only imagine how the vibrations of her scream must feel around Chris's cock. Graham watched as his brother tried to pull back, but Izzy's cheeks hollowed, sucking forcefully, her head moving forward, doing everything in her power to keep him from pulling out of her mouth.

"Iz, no, baby, I'm going to —" His words were cut off and he let out a low growl as his hips instinctively thrust forward. Graham could see Izzy's throat working as she swallowed everything Chris gave her.

As he came down from that exquisite peak, Graham's thrusts slowed. But before he even did that, his hands were on Izzy's wrists, releasing her from the cuffs.

Leaning over her, he kissed the cute little dimples on her lower back, and looked up to see his brother. The moment that passed between the two men was one of complete trust and commitment. Graham felt the bond between them so strong, and Izzy was the heart at the center of it.

Chris caught his breath and knelt in front of her, murmuring to her and stroking her hair.

Graham was struck by the love he felt for these two people, his partners. After disposing of the condom, he collapsed onto the bed next to Izzy, completely spent, and wrapped his arm firmly around her.

****

Izzy felt like her entire body was made of jelly. Graham had gently removed the plug, as Chris had sweetly chastised her for swallowing him when he'd tried to pull away. She smiled, loving the way they made her feel, loving them. She curled up against Chris's chest with Graham spooning her back. As she drifted off to sleep, she thought nothing had ever felt so right.

Chapter Ten

When Izzy awoke, it was still dark outside. A cool breeze blew over her skin and she shivered, snuggling closer to the warm man against her. Chris's arm tightened around her, holding her protectively even as he slept. A little smile curled her lips, and she reached back to find Graham, wanting contact with both men, but her hand only found an empty pillow.

Gently pulling away from Chris, she turned and frowned at the empty bed. Where was Graham? Had he left? Izzy looked around the room, and the breeze hit her again. It was then that she noticed the door to the balcony was ajar.

She slipped out of bed, enjoying the way Chris's arm squeezed her as if he didn't want to let her go. Izzy lightly kissed the stubble of his cheek and then slowly slid from his grasp. Shrugging on a light robe, she padded over to the balcony door.

Her breath caught as she laid eyes on Graham through the open door. His back was to her as he stood at the railing. His jeans hung low on his hips, and even in a relaxed state, the sinewy muscles of his back were pronounced. His chestnut hair glinted in the moonlight curling around the nape of his neck, and Izzy found herself wanting to run her fingers through it.

As if he felt her eyes on him, he suddenly turned, his eyes finding hers with a laser focus. The tenseness in his face faded slightly as he saw her. "Iz, sweetheart, I didn't mean to wake you," he said, making no move to reach for her.

What the heck was going on? Only a few hours ago, they'd shared the most incredible intimate experience of her life. If he pulled away now, she might have to take drastic measures. Yep, she'd grab his handcuffs and just chain him to the bed until he talked about what was bothering him.

A brief shiver of fear ran through her. Graham was good at pushing her away. He'd had three years of practice. What if he went back into standoffish mode?

She shook off her doubts. That may be how he reacted before, but it was not going to fly this time around, and she was going to make sure he knew it.

The cool night air chilled Izzy as she stepped out on the balcony.

"Sweetheart, you're shivering. You should go back to bed." But even as he said it, he was pulling her close, wrapping his arms around her. Izzy burrowed into him, the soft hair on his chest tickling her face.

"Mmmm." She couldn't help her sound of pleasure as he lightly stroked her hair. "I don't want to go back to bed. I want you to tell me what's wrong." His hand stilled for just a moment as she felt his body tense.

"What makes you think something's wrong?"

Izzy's eyes narrowed as she leaned back enough to look up at him. "You know, I think I would like to reserve the right to spank you."

His dark brows shot halfway up his forehead. "Spank me? Why?"

"If you're going to lie to me and tell me nothing's wrong, then I think that's only fair. I can play the Dom too," she said, stepping back and planting her hands on her hips. She lifted her chin and brought herself up to her full 5'4" height.

Unfortunately, that didn't seem to be having the desired effect on Graham. His eyes sparkled, and Izzy thought he looked like he might actually be biting his lip to control his laughter.

"Graham, it's not funny!" she said, stomping her foot.

"Oh, but it is." Like lightning, he reached out and pulled her to him. Izzy gasped as his hand came down, delivering a swat to her ass. Frustration immediately turned into heat. Damn her libido.

Attempting to quell her building desire, Izzy took a deep breath. If this was truly going to work, then he was going to have to be open with her. She wanted all of him. "Graham, I want to know what's wrong. After what we just shared, please don't pull away from me," she said softly, looking up at him.

Graham sobered and dropped his hands from her. She immediately felt the loss of his warmth. "I'm not trying to pull away, Iz." Running a hand through his hair, he turned to look back out at the night. "Opening up just isn't something I'm good at."

"Maybe not, but if you want this to work, then you have to try." She really hoped her voice didn't sound as desperate to him as it did to her own ears. What if he didn't want to try? Maybe after a threesome with her and his brother, he'd decided it wasn't what he wanted at all. Maybe he'd looked at her as a novelty, and now that had worn off.

"No, Iz, stop!" He studied her as if he could tell what she was thinking. "This doesn't have anything to do with you."

Oh no, he wouldn't. "Don't you dare say 'it's not you, it's me.' Graham, don't you dare." She could feel the tears prick her eyes. He didn't want her. He was going to dump her. He was going to tell her thanks for the good time, and leave her.

"Dammit, sweetheart," he said, grasping her shoulders and giving her a little shake. "Look at me and get out of your damn head for a second."

She looked up at him with watery eyes, and he let out a soft curse. "Baby, it's really not you." He rubbed his hands up and down her arms, and she reveled in the warmth. "It's just that the last time Chris and I . . . well, it didn't end well. I want this to be perfect. It's never felt so right, don't you see? The three of us, we feel like a family. I don't want anything to. . ."

He turned, scrubbing a hand over his beard in frustration, looking like he was trying to think of the right words to say.

"We are a family," she said softly. "I love you."

****

Her words touched his heart. They made Graham feel like he could fly. But to fly, he had to shed the burden that kept weighing him down.

"Tell her, Graham," Chris's voice came from the door of the balcony. Graham watched Izzy as her eyes turned to take in his brother, glancing down his body appreciatively as she admired his low-slung jeans. Graham smirked when she gave her head a little shake as if to clear her arousal.

Chris didn't miss it either, and he walked over to toss an arm around Izzy, leaning down to give her a hard kiss on the mouth. He left an arm around her shoulders as they both turned to Graham, who enjoyed the pink flush on Izzy's cheeks. Damn, she was responsive.

"I'm guessing this misplaced sense of guilt has to do with Alicia," Chris said knowingly.

"Alicia?" Izzy looked from one man to the other. "She's the woman you shared before?"

Graham's smile faded as he was brought back into the present conversation. Of course she knew that much. The grapevine in this town was legendary, so it shouldn't surprise him that Izzy had heard at least part of the story.

"Yeah, we shared her." He looked toward his brother for backup, but Chris only gave him an encouraging nod. This was something Graham had to get out, and Chris knew it.

Graham turned, looking out at the lights along the lake. In the moonlight, he could just make out the boats bobbing in their slips. It would be winter soon. The harsh weather would take over as it did every year. Just as it had that night so many years ago.

"Alicia wasn't the first woman Chris and I shared," he finally said. "There were a few in college. We tried having relationships separately, but we just always seemed to gravitate toward the same women. Things never felt right when we tried relationships on our own. It never felt . . ."

"Complete," Chris supplied.

"Yeah, complete." Graham turned to look at both Chris and Izzy. "Even so, things were always pretty casual until we met Alicia. Then things were . . . different."

"Different how?" Izzy asked, reaching out to take his hand.

Squeezing her fingers, Graham continued. "Well, for starters, Chris fell in love with her."

"I *thought* I was in love with her," Chris corrected. "I realize now that I didn't even know what love was. But at the time, I thought I did. I think I just wanted a future with someone. I was in love with the idea of being in love, and Alicia was fun, pretty, smart." He sighed, "And I was young and an idiot."

Graham shook his head. "You weren't an idiot." Chris wanted a wife, a family. How could anyone fault him for that?

"So what happened?" Izzy asked. "She wasn't in love with you guys?"

Graham's mouth tightened, but Chris was the one who answered. "She wasn't in love with me. She was in love with Graham." There was no bitterness in his voice, and his matter-of-fact tone relieved Graham.

"But I didn't love her," Graham said, his stomach twisting with guilt. "I was so mad at her. I felt like she drove Chris away. He left because he couldn't even stand to look at me."

"Graham, I was stupid. You did nothing —" But Graham held up a hand to stop his brother.

"No, please. Let me just get it out. I was angry with Alicia for coming in between Chris and me. I tried to let her down easy, tried to push her away, but she didn't seem to get it. She just kept pursuing me. She would follow me around, show up at my place, show up at the station."

Graham closed his eyes, his mouth going dry at the memory of that horrible night. When he opened his eyes, he saw the night as it had been: the snow blowing through the darkness, the lights of the car. . .

Izzy stepped away from Chris and wrapped her arms around Graham's waist, lending him her strength. She said nothing, just waited for him to continue. God, he loved her. He owed her the truth.

Taking a deep breath, he continued, his voice strained. "One night, there was a horrible blizzard. I'd been out helping clear roads, working an accident. I was exhausted. I came back to the station to just get a little bit of rest before I had to go back out, and Alicia was there." He pressed his fingers against his eyelids as if the memory physically hurt him. "She was waiting for me, naked, in my office."

Izzy's mouth dropped open. "Naked? Are you serious?"

Chris leaned an arm against the balcony railing and sighed. "You have to realize, Iz, Alicia was the type of girl who was used to getting what she wanted. She couldn't seem to fathom the thought that Graham didn't want her."

Helplessness was evident in Graham's face. "I don't even think she was really in love with me. I think at that point, she just wanted something she couldn't have." Pausing for a moment, he lightly stroked his fingertips over Izzy's cheek, brushing a strand of hair off her face, as if just touching her would minimize the pain of that night.

"That was the breaking point for me. I couldn't take it anymore. I'd just pulled a sixteen-year-old out of a mangled car. There were so many things that were so much more important at that moment, and then she was there, and I just didn't have the energy to deal with her." Guilt flooded his system.

"That's completely understandable, Graham." Izzy rested her head against his chest again, holding him tightly. "I would have felt the same way."

Oh, his Iz. She was always so compassionate. Would she still be understanding once she knew the whole truth?

"It's okay, man. Keep going." Chris moved over to lean down and kiss the top of Izzy's head, and Graham saw her small smile at the gesture. He took a moment to gather his words before he continued.

"Iz, I didn't handle it very well. I snapped. I told her she was being pathetic, that I didn't love her. I was mad because she wouldn't leave me alone, but I think the biggest reason I was angry was because I felt like she took my brother away from me. I told her to get out. I threatened her with trespassing, indecent exposure." Even when she'd started to cry, he'd kept going. He'd been a monster. "I told her never to show her face anywhere near me again."

"Graham," Izzy reached for him again, "you didn't do anything wrong."

He backed up as if he couldn't stand her touch. He didn't deserve her touch. "Izzy, I killed her."

Confusion crossed her face. "What do you mean?"

"I mean she left crying. She was so upset. I shouldn't have treated her like that." He swallowed against the lump in his throat. "When she tore out of there, I should have gone after her. The roads that night . . ." He shook his head, shame rolling through him. "It wasn't safe that night." He turned away, unable to look at Izzy. "But I didn't stop her. I was relieved to see her go."

The wind picked up, but Graham didn't even feel the chill, his insides already so cold. Gripping the balcony railing, he closed his eyes, wishing he could take back the mistake he'd made. "She shouldn't have been driving. She was too upset. She lost control of her car and it went off that steep embankment out by Viv's place."

When he opened his eyes, he could see it right in front of him – the snow falling in the black night, the lights from Alicia's car beckoning to him from an odd angle in the snow. "I pulled her body out of her car four hours later. I killed her, Iz." His throat closed up and he felt the wetness in his eyes.

The gentle hand on his shoulder startled him out of the harsh memory. Izzy pulled at his arm until he turned to face her. Her blue eyes looked at him, not judging, just offering her love to him. "It wasn't your fault, Graham."

"Iz, how can you say that? I'm as guilty as if I'd driven her car off the road myself."

"Guilty? What did you do that was so wrong? You were honest with her. You told her how you felt. Graham, you weren't responsible for her choices or her actions. She did that all on her own. It was not your fault." Ignoring the way he backed up, Izzy pressed herself to him, her hand reaching up to stroke his beard. "It wasn't your fault."

Graham was momentarily stunned. He wasn't sure what he'd expected. Maybe part of him had expected her to be shocked, disgusted, to blame him the way he blamed himself. But she didn't. Her eyes held only warmth and sympathy.

"You have to let this go, brother." Chris's strong hand clasped his shoulder. "Izzy's right. You didn't do anything wrong. I've told you that, but if you won't listen to me, maybe you'll listen to her." Chris's eyes were filled with remorse as he stood behind Izzy. "I should have been there for you. It wasn't your fault, man. None of it was your fault."

Forgiveness. Had he ever expected forgiveness when he couldn't even forgive himself? Suddenly Graham felt lighter. He'd told the truth and shared his feelings, and the world hadn't ended. The people he loved hadn't walked away. Now, there was only one more thing he wanted to say.

He reached for Izzy, cupping her face in his strong hands, searching her eyes. "I love you," he said softly. "I think I've always loved you, Iz. Do you think you could truly want me, want us?" He still felt a little unsure. "Do you really think you could find it in your heart to give a relationship with two men a try?"

Tears threatened to spill over Izzy's eyes, but she didn't look sad. She looked filled with joy. "Yes. That's all I want." She put her hand over one of his, and reached for Chris with the other "You're all I want. Both of you. I love you. And I'll say it over and over until you believe me. I love you."

Graham's heart leapt with joy. She really did love him. He felt his heart open for the first time in years, and the burden he'd held onto for so long began to ease. Izzy loved him.

He pulled her into his arms, never wanting to let her go, and he looked at his brother who had a big grin on his face.

"It's about fucking time," Chris said, and Graham couldn't help but smile.

"You're such an asshole," he laughed.

"Why do men show affection by punching and name-calling?" Izzy asked with a smile, shaking her head.

"You're right, baby, that's wrong," Graham agreed, his eyes twinkling.

"It is?" she asked slowly, eyeing him curiously.

"Yes, it is. I have a much better way to show affection." As he winked, Izzy let out a little laugh and turned to head back into the bedroom. She paused at the door to turn to the two men and give them both a come hither motion before she slowly dropped her robe. At the looks on their faces, she giggled and scurried to the bed.

At the site of her gorgeous body, Graham's cock sprang to attention. He looked at his brother, and Chris reached down to adjust his erection through his jeans.

Grinning at his brother, Graham had an idea. "If she likes teasing so much, what do you say we show her just how much we can tease her before we let her come?"

Chris chuckled and punched him in the arm. "Good to have you back, brother."

As he watched his brother walk into the room after Izzy, Graham stood there for a moment reveling in the fact that things were finally turning out the way he'd always hoped. He walked back into the hotel room to join his family.

****

Izzy winced as she sat in the large corner booth in The Lounge, smiling at the delicious soreness. She should be exhausted, considering how little she'd actually slept, but instead, she'd never felt more alive. Graham and Chris had made love to her twice more, until they'd all three collapsed into an exhausted heap about two hours before her alarm went off.

Neither man had even flinched when her alarm had buzzed at six-thirty. They probably wouldn't be thrilled that she'd slipped out of bed without their knowledge – no easy feat since she woke up sandwiched in between the two of them.

And wasn't that a way to wake up? If she didn't have so much to do this morning, she would have woken them up by taking each of their cocks in her mouth. A flush stained her face. She missed them already.

Instead, the real world intruded. She'd taken a quick shower and come downstairs so she could catch Josh as he came off the night shift and coordinate a couple of staffing changes for Saturday night. Graham and Chris had both still been snoring when she'd left the room, and she just didn't have the heart to wake them.

Her fingers flew over the keyboard of her laptop as she typed up an email to the head of her catering staff approving the additions to the menu. Considering how many emails she needed to respond to, it was a good thing she was able to get an early start. If she could get everything wrapped up, maybe she could take off early and talk Graham and Chris into spending some time alone with her. Upstairs. Naked.

She bit her lip as she thought of the ways they'd touched her. After they'd cuffed her hands to her headboard, they'd taken turns teasing her until she was begging for an orgasm. She'd been a quivering mess, but they'd brought her to the edge four times before they'd finally let her come, and then her screams of ecstasy had been so loud, it was a wonder she didn't wake every guest in the hotel. Her insides went warm at the thought, and she wasn't sure if she wanted revenge on them for teasing her or if she wanted to beg them to do it again. Hmm. . teasing them would be fun. Satisfaction filled her every time she made them groan under her touch.

"Well, someone must have had a good night," Andi said, setting a cup of coffee down in front of Izzy, startling her out of her x-rated daydream.

Turning to her friend, Izzy's smile faltered. Even though she lacked sleep a good night's sleep, it was Andi who looked exhausted. Dark circles were prominent under her tired brown eyes.

Frowning, Izzy patted the seat in the booth next to her. "Andi, sit down and talk to me. What's going on?"

Pursing her lips, Andi simply shook her head, trying hard to avoid eye contact. "Nothing, Iz. Nothing I can really talk about." She looked on the verge of tears, and it almost broke Izzy's heart. The two women had met a few times when they were teens, and Andi had seemed so happy then. Sure, she'd always been a little shy, but now it was as if she'd completely closed in on herself. What happened to the girl who'd always talked about playing practical jokes on her brothers and giggled at her own silliness?

Izzy reached out to grasp Andi's hand, and her friend locked eyes with her. Those dark eyes held so much pain. Before either woman could say anything, they were interrupted by the buzzing of Izzy's phone. Andi jumped, and Izzy thought of how she seemed startled by the smallest things these days. Nudging the phone toward Izzy, she asked, "Aren't you going to take that?"

Shaking her head, Izzy reached again for her friend. "I'd rather talk to you."

Andi picked up the phone, frowning as she looked at the display. "Iz, you might want to take this. It's Flynn."

Shit. Flynn Davenport, her lawyer. Flynn was another staple of the lake area, working at a law practice that served the southern part of the state. Flynn had been raised in the lake area, and he'd handled her grandfather's legal affairs for several years. Izzy kept going to him because she'd come to trust his opinion. It wasn't often that you found a lawyer you'd describe as trustworthy.

"Maybe he's heard from the insurance adjuster." She took the phone from Andi and tapped 'Answer.'

"Hi, Flynn. What's going on?" The stress of the fire weighed heavy on her, but it helped to know Graham and Theo were following every lead and keeping Flynn updated.

"Hey Iz, I've just received some info that I thought to be a little curious. It seems as though there's been some activity on your insurance policy."

"My insurance policy?" She was confused. Wouldn't that be normal since she'd filed a claim after the fire. "I don't understand. Was there activity on the policy because of the fire? The adjuster came yesterday. I'm sure he filed a report."

"No, no, not that kind of activity. Apparently, there have been a couple of people who have accessed your policy. One is Theo. The only reason I know that is because he left me a message to call him about it. It seems Graham requested a copy of your policy, but he couldn't access it without a warrant. So Theo used his magic fingers to access whatever he wanted. He got a copy of the policy."

Her brow furrowed. "All Graham had to do was ask, and I would have given him a copy of the policy." She still didn't understand why this seemed to warrant a worried phone call from her lawyer.

"Well, that's not actually the thing that worries me." He paused as if he was unsure of how to tell her the next part of the information.

"What?" A sense of dread was starting to take hold in her gut. Andi looked at her questioningly, her dark eyes concerned.

"Iz, the other person, or entity, I should say, who accessed your information was a company based out of Saint Louis. And they didn't just access the basic policy. They also accessed the geophysics report."

"The geophysics report? The oil? Is that what this is about? Someone is interested in drilling for oil?" Izzy almost sighed in relief. She'd been through this before. Her great uncle was at the top of the list of people pressuring her to lease the land for oil drilling. "Flynn, I'm not drilling. I'm not going to ruin this place. I've been over this—"

"No, Iz, you don't understand. It wasn't your uncle who accessed the reports. It was a company called Waddell and Stevens." Izzy's blood ran cold, as Flynn continued. "The company handles —"

"Mergers and acquisitions," Izzy supplied.

"So you're familiar with them? Iz, I'm pretty sure they want your land. Why else would they be accessing that information?" Flynn went over the standard responses she should give anyone who contacted her, but Izzy had already stopped listening.

She was quite familiar with the name of the company that Chris had talked about, where he'd worked his way up for five years. Suddenly, it all made sense. The reason he'd come to town, the reason he'd latched onto her so quickly when he'd first seen her. Tears blurred her vision. She thought of all the questions he'd asked about whether she'd ever thought about selling.

"Flynn, I have to go," she whispered, trying to control her tears.

"Iz, wait, are you okay? I—"

Izzy clicked off the phone while he was still talking. Pain surged through her belly, and she clasped a hand over her mouth to keep from crying out.

"Izzy, what is it?" Andi asked, alarmed.

He'd said he loved her, that he wanted her. And the whole time he'd just been trying to get her land. And Graham had wanted the reports too. If it was for the investigation, he could have simply asked her for them, but he hadn't. Were they working together? Were they both playing her? No, she didn't want to believe it. But what other excuse was there?

"Andi, I have to go." She scooted out of the booth, her breath shaky. She ignored Andi calling her name, as she walked quickly to the elevator. Izzy needed answers. She just didn't know if they would be enough to stem the betrayal she felt.

****

Chris stretched and reached for Izzy without opening his eyes. He patted the body next to him. He certainly didn't remember her chest being so furry.

"Dude, stop feeling me up or I'm going to kick your ass," his brother's sleepy voice said dryly.

Opening his eyes, Chris looked around the room. "Where's Iz?" he mumbled sleepily.

Graham rubbed his eyes and sat up in bed. He called out for her, but there was no answer. The bathroom door was open, so it looked like she wasn't in the room.

"Dammit," Graham said, yanking back the covers. "I thought we made it clear that we didn't want her going anywhere by herself." Both men started yanking on their jeans as Graham's phone rang.

Chris looked up, hoping it was Izzy, but Graham just shook his head. "It's Theo." He punched a button on his phone, and Chris continued to sleepily fumble with his clothes as he listened to Graham's half of the conversation.

"What kind of report? What the hell is a geophysics report?" Graham barked into the phone.

Chris became fully alert in a heartbeat, all remnants of sleep leaving him. A geophysics report. He knew what it was. Around the Midwest, he'd done the acquisition of several pieces of land that were rich with oil. A geologist or oil surveyor tested the land, and the resulting geophysics report detailed the findings. There always seemed to be a tug-of-war with mineral rights to any land in question, especially if oil was involved. If Izzy's insurance policy had a geophysics report attached to it, then her land must be sitting on a significant amount of oil.

"And Izzy knew this? I don't understand," Graham was saying. "She's never mentioned anything about there being oil on the land."

Oh no. Chris's hands shook. It made sense now. Everything made sense. How had he not seen it? He'd been told the client wanted to expand the Lakewood. But that wasn't the truth at all. The bastard knew there was oil. That's why he wanted the place. Fucking Jacobs had been livid when Chris had suggested another piece of land. Now he knew why.

He looked up at his brother and for once, he couldn't read what he was thinking, but he could see that Graham's jaw was clenched so tightly, it was a wonder his teeth didn't crack. When Graham's icy cold stare landed on him, Chris almost took a step back.

"I'll call you back, Theo," Graham bit out before he punched the button on the phone.

His hands fisted at his sides, and Chris could practically see him counting to ten before he spoke. "If you know anything about this, you'd better fucking share it with me right now, Christopher. Do not lie to me."

Glancing at the phone and back to Graham, he wondered if his brother would even believe he hadn't known anything about this. Not that he could blame him. What would he think if he were in Graham's position?

"Well," Chris began slowly. "I know what a geophysics report is. I know it measures for oil."

"Don't play games with me." Graham's voice rose a notch. "Is that why you came here? Is that why you wanted Izzy to sell this place to you? To your company?"

Chris was already shaking his head as he shrugged on a T-shirt. "No. Graham, I swear to you I didn't know anything about any oil. The client who hired us wanted the Lakewood because he said he was interested in lake property he could expand into a nationally recognized resort." Chris sat down on the edge of the bed tugging on running shoes. "I always wondered why he didn't want to start from scratch, why he wanted an existing property."

His hands stilled as a wave of nausea washed over him. "Shit, it makes so much sense now."

Graham came over to stand in front of him and looked hard into his face as if trying to come to his own decision. Finally, his jaw loosened. "You really didn't know, did you?"

"No, I didn't fucking know!" It was his fault, though. He brought danger right to Izzy's doorstep. Someone wanted her land and was willing to take her out of the picture to get it, and Chris had been working for the son of a bitch.

"All I know is this client – this Eric Jacobs – wanted to buy the land under a holdings company. He never said why, but that's not something that's uncommon so it really didn't occur to me to ask." Chris wondered if his boss had been in on the deal too. Suddenly he felt used, taken advantage of. "They used me to get to her. Shit, Graham, they sent me down here because they knew I grew up here, they knew I had an 'in,'" he said, punctuating with air quotes. "Dammit, this is my fault."

Graham slowly shook his head. "You're not the one who did this, man. If it wasn't you, they would have sent someone else. Or hell, maybe they just would have taken her out from day one rather than even trying to buy the land from her first. If anything, you bought us some time. This is the first real lead we've had. You've laid eyes on this asshole." Graham yanked a shirt on. "If he truly is the one coming after Izzy, I highly doubt he's using his real name, but you've got his contact information. We can find him."

As the sheriff in Graham sprang to life, Chris couldn't let go of the sinking feeling in his gut. He might have warded off the bad guys when they thought he was working on Izzy to sell her land, but what about now? He'd turned in his resignation. They knew he wasn't working on it anymore. If he was the only thing buying her time . . .

He jumped up, panic setting in. "We need to find her. Graham, I quit my job. If counting on me was their last hope for to trying to get the land, then there's nothing holding them back now. She's not safe."

Chris was already running out the door as Graham followed him, punching the buttons on his phone. "Theo, I need to know everything you can find out on Eric Jacobs," he said as they ran down the hall.

****

Romero scanned the lobby. He was surprised as he watched Izzy sprint toward the elevators. Her routine was very familiar to him now. Usually she worked for a good couple of hours at the start of every morning before she got up from her desk.

Not that knowing her routine had done him any good so far. He was still pissed off that she hadn't been in her office the afternoon of the fire. She was in her office every fucking afternoon. She should be dead now. But no, the one day Romero made his move, she decided to switch up her day. It was his own fault. He should have checked to make sure she was there before setting the fire. Instead, all he'd done was put everyone on edge, and they'd started a fucking investigation.

He knew he had to keep the heat off his boss or things would not end well for him. Martin Craig was a mean son of a bitch. No, things would go much better for him if he could get the situation under control and get rid of their little blonde problem.

As Milo Livingston followed her to the elevator, Romero grimaced, reminded of how difficult his mission had become. Isabel Craig had a lot of friends – too many damn friends, and they all watched her. Since the fire, she was never alone. Someone was always escorting her, which made it damn near impossible to get close to her.

He'd started to form a new plan over the last couple of days, one that would allow him to take her out without having to be close to her at all. In fact, he was almost ready to make his move.

He looked up as Izzy's voice rose, tears streaking down her face, and wondered what the hell was going on. He tried to look inconspicuous while moving closer to the drama unfolding.

****

"Milo, I don't need a fucking babysitter!" Izzy practically screamed, not even caring how the eyes around the lobby turned toward her.

"Iz, you're upset," Milo said calmly, as if he were talking to a small child. "Just let me call Graham or Chris so they can come down here." He was already punching the buttons on his phone.

"I don't want them here. They did this!" Her voice broke on a sob.

"Did what? Izzy, I don't know what's going on, but please calm down."

The ding of the elevator had Izzy spinning around. She had to get away, had to get out of there. Teetering on the verge of a panic attack, she could barely catch her breath, but the pain in her chest wasn't from anxiety. It was from her heart breaking. How could they do this to her?

When she barreled into the elevator, she collided with a hard, muscular chest. Strong arms went around her to steady her.

"Oh, sweetheart, thank God," Chris's voice was relieved as he held her close. "Don't take off like that, okay?"

But Izzy didn't want to have anything to do with his act anymore. "Get away from me," she cried, shoving away from him. Chris staggered back, his mouth dropping open in surprise as Graham stepped forward.

"Iz?" he asked cautiously. "What's wrong? What happened?" He looked to Milo for answers, but the large man just shrugged his shoulders.

"What happened?" Izzy screamed. "What happened?" She could hear her own voice rising an octave. "You two! You've been working together this whole time, haven't you? You've been playing me!"

Graham was shaking his head. Izzy looked toward Chris hoping to see denial, confusion, anything that would tell her she was wrong. Instead, he swallowed, and shame flickered in his eyes. He understood exactly what she meant.

"I knew it." The tears pooling in her eyes spilled over. "How could I be so dumb?" she asked bitterly, taking a step back. "My land. That's why you came here, isn't it?" She looked at both Nolan brothers, but she addressed Chris. "That's what you wanted? That's why you got close to me?"

When he didn't say anything, Izzy felt rage bubble up inside of her. "Isn't it?" she screamed. "Answer me!"

"Yes," Chris finally said quietly. "Yes, that's why I came here."

Izzy jerked as if she'd been slapped. She wanted to be wrong. She was hoping she was wrong.

The normal buzz of voices in the lobby had come to a halt as all eyes were on them. Milo stepped forward. "I don't know what is going on, but you are not doing this here. Follow me. Now." The look on his face did not invite discussion, and Izzy was reminded of how intimidating he could be when he wanted to. They followed Milo back to the kitchen, where only a few staff remained after the morning breakfast rush.

Milo quickly dismissed them before he spoke. "Does someone please want to tell me what the hell is going on?" He looked between Izzy, Graham and Chris, waiting for an answer. Andi rushed in to stand next to Izzy, her dark brown eyes cold as she looked at the two men. When Izzy felt Andi clasp her hand, she was immediately grateful for her friend's support.

Graham looked at his brother, "You're not even going to defend yourself? Tell her! Tell her the whole fucking truth," he bellowed.

Izzy could read the guilt on Chris's face and just shook her head sadly. "He already has."

****

Graham longed to reach out for her, but when he took a step toward Izzy, she immediately backed up. "No. I don't want you to touch me." Dammit, she was shutting him out, too. He thought even though she was angry with Chris, he would be able to talk some sense into her. He could understand that she was mad, but she needed to listen to reason.

"Izzy, listen to me. You don't know the whole story."

"Like I could believe anything you say," she said bitterly.

Confusion lit Graham's eyes. "What? What are you talking about?" He thought of the way she'd given herself to them the night before. "I know you trust me. Trust us. Izzy, you have to listen to reason here."

"No! There's nothing to listen to. I did trust you – both of you." The pain in her face twisted Graham's heart. "You both lied to me. I know you accessed the insurance reports too, Graham. I know you're both aware of how much oil is underneath this property."

She turned her attention to Chris. "What was your plan exactly? Fuck me until I can't see straight, then get me to sell, sign the papers? How much money would you get off that deal?" She turned her furious eyes to Graham. "Were you in this together from the start?"

"Iz, no," Chris responded quietly. "It's not like that at all."

She shook her head, swiping at the tears. "I don't believe you."

"Iz, I swear I didn't know who you were when I met you. I mean, I knew there was something between you and Graham, but I didn't know you owned the hotel. That first night between us, it all just happened, and it was real. I never even talked to you about selling your land. I couldn't do it. I saw how much you loved this place. I couldn't take that away from you." His voice was pleading, and Graham could feel his pain so harshly that it stole his breath away.

Izzy just shook her head, unwilling to listen.

"Sweetheart, it's true," Graham said. She had to understand. They had to make her understand. They couldn't lose her.

"You came here with the intention of talking me into selling. You said that. And maybe you didn't approach me outright, but I'm not an idiot, Chris. Do you think I missed all the questions you asked about the resort? The history of the property? If I'd ever be interested in selling? Were you priming me?" The accusation in her tone stabbed at Chris, and Graham watched him flinch with every word.

Graham knew that Chris thought he'd done the right thing by never actually bringing up the sale to Izzy. But he could see the truth. She would see it as a betrayal, as a lie because he never told her. If Chris had just been up front with her, she would have adamantly said no, and that would have been that. But now? Jesus, now it looked like Chris had been stringing her along, and she thought Graham was a part of it, too.

"And you!" Izzy turned her fury toward him, jabbing her finger in his face. Dammit, even angry, she was the most beautiful thing he'd ever seen.

"Did you know about this? That he wanted my land?"

Shit, why hadn't he told her when he found out? Why hadn't he forced Chris to tell her? Then he'd let Chris and Theo access the insurance reports and hadn't even told her because he didn't want to worry her anymore. He'd wanted to shield her from harm, and by doing so, he'd pushed her away. Shame flickered across his own face. Yep, they had royally fucked up.

"That's what I thought," Izzy said. But it wasn't said with triumph or even satisfaction. As Graham watched, she just seemed to deflate. The love and hope and energy of their future leaked out of her as if she were a balloon that had just been pricked.

"I didn't prime you for anything," Chris tried to say. "Izzy, I love you. You have to see how much I love you."

But she wouldn't understand. Graham could see the betrayal overwhelmed everything else inside of her.

"But I don't love you. I can't love you." She gasped for a breath as if the very words knocked all the air out of her. "And I don't trust you. Not anymore."

Graham watched as Chris's face went white, and his eyes teared. If Izzy had taken a knife to his chest, she would have hurt him less than telling him she didn't love him. He knew that because he felt his brother's pain, and it compounded with his own. Izzy had seen the hurt too. He knew it. She clamped a hand over her mouth to stifle a sob, and as if she couldn't handle being around them one more second, she turned and fled, with Andrea hot on her heels.

****

Numbness was the only thing that reverberated through Chris's system as he sat on the hotel patio in a daze. He couldn't let anything in but the numbness. They had to keep her safe. That was all that mattered. He tried not to think about her words, but he couldn't help it. Hell, he couldn't really blame her. He hadn't been up front with her. It was his fault, and he knew it. But if he let himself feel, let himself wallow in the misery of having to picture his life without her . . . nope, he couldn't do it. Numb was better right now. He couldn't stay focused if he let all the feelings in that threatened to consume him.

"She didn't mean it," Graham said again, handing him a cup of coffee. He didn't know what made him feel worse – the fact that Izzy seemed to blame Graham just as much as she blamed him, or the fact that Graham pitied him. He could handle it a lot better if Graham just got mad and punched him. That, he knew how to deal with.

"Just don't, okay? Just – not now." He looked through the patio doors. It was almost noon, and Izzy was back in her corner booth, typing away on her laptop. She'd disappeared up to her room with Andrea for almost an hour, and when she'd re-emerged, her face had been a careful blank.

She'd asked Graham and Chris to leave, but they'd refused. Instead of fighting as they'd expected her to do, she'd simply nodded and proceeded to pretend they weren't there.

Graham followed his brother's gaze to stare at her and sighed. "I'm hoping after she has a chance to calm down, she'll see reason."

"She looks pretty damn calm to me," Chris observed with clenched teeth, watching her type, her eyes staring at the screen and looking nowhere else.

"Not really. She looks blank. Just like you, man." Graham shook his head. "Wow, I never thought I'd be the one trying to pull things together."

"She's pissed at you too," Chris reminded him, wondering how the hell his brother was taking all this so coolly.

"True. But after I let everything sink in, I'm smart enough to realize that she's just mad. She'll come around." Graham absently tapped a finger against the handle of his coffee mug. "She has to. Don't let your insecurities get to you. You know she loves you. She loves me. Do you think she would have let last night happen if she wasn't in love with us? She can deny it all she wants, but she sure as hell can't fake it. I know the truth, and so do you."

"Maybe," Chris said, trying to hold onto the kernel of hope. "But anyway, right now, we just need to find out who's after her. The sooner we can put this mess behind us . . ."

"The sooner we can work things out with our girl and spank that heart-shaped ass of hers for flying off the handle," Graham said with a grin.

Chris smiled faintly despite himself. That sounded like a really good plan.

"So, what did you learn?" Graham asked, gesturing toward the computer.

Chris had grilled his boss over the phone and was confident he didn't know anything about Eric Jacobs's grand plan. Then Graham had explained to Claude Stevens that he was obtaining a warrant for all records and information relating to Eric Jacobs. Claude handed them over willingly, and Chris had discovered things were just as they'd feared. "Eric Jacobs doesn't exist."

Graham uttered a curse as he continued. "The information Jacobs gave us for the holdings company is all legit, however it's unclear who exactly is behind it. At the time, I thought it was Jacobs himself, but maybe he was just working for someone – I don't know. Either way, I can say for sure that's not his real name."

Chris turned his laptop so Graham could see the screen. "I tweaked this program so it would cross reference the names we input with birth certificates, death certificates, criminal records, and news articles, just to name a few things. We got three hits on Eric Jacobs. One is a nine-year-old boy in St. Louis, one is seventy-eight year-old man in Jefferson City who is in an assisted living facility, and one is thirty-two year-old Marine who is currently deployed in Afghanistan."

Graham let out a frustrated growl, and stood to pace beside the table. "Well, hell, I had about as much luck as you. I've done background checks on not only every person who was registered at this hotel, but every person I can find who was in town at the time of the attack."

"I'm telling you, we need to focus on the holdings company." Chris had a gut feeling that was where the answers lay. If they could just find out who was behind that, then they would know who was after Izzy.

"There's always a possibility that whoever set the fire doesn't have anything to do with the person who wants the land," Graham mumbled almost to himself.

"But you don't believe that, do you?" Chris certainly didn't.

"No," Graham said with a sigh as he looked in through the doors at Izzy. Chris followed his gaze, and they both watched her for a long moment. She was wearing a red blouse, and she twisted a long blonde strand of hair absently around her finger as she read her computer screen.

As if she could feel their eyes on her, she stilled and looked up. Neither man attempted to hide the fact that they were staring.

Izzy frowned, and she dropped her hands, clenching them into tight fists. Chris watched as she took several long breaths, looking back and forth between the two of them before she lifted her chin in a defiant gesture.

God, how he loved her. "I'm not letting her out of my sight." He only wished their presence didn't cause her more anxiety, that she could see they would protect her to the ends of the earth. But right now, he knew that just amped up her fury.

Graham was thinking the same thing. "So let her be pissed," he said answering Chris's unspoken thought. "We can make it up to her later and help her see reason. I'd rather her be really angry than really dead."

****

Damn, damn, damn. Izzy deleted the paragraph she'd just typed for the fifth time. She was just trying to write emails to past guests who were celebrating anniversaries this month. It was something she did every month, emailing them a congratulatory note along with a coupon for 20% off their hotel stay and a free dinner at The Lounge. But right now, she couldn't even freaking see straight.

She'd tried to throw both Nolan brothers out of the hotel, but they'd refused to budge. And now they just stood there staring at her as she tried to work? Really? They couldn't sit in the lobby? Or at the very least, somewhere that wasn't right in her line of sight? *Bastards,* she silently grumbled to herself.

"Oh, Isabel! I've been looking for you!" Izzy smelled the potent scent of sage before she looked up to see Vivian Warner headed her way. Vivian wore a flowing kimono-type dress and tinkled as she walked, crystals hanging from her ears and wrists.

Izzy smiled despite herself. A lot of people looked at Viv as the town crazy, but Izzy knew her to be a sweet, kind woman who liked to bake brownies and talk about old movies . . . well, that was when she wasn't talking about the ghosts who were out to get her.

"Viv, it's always good to see you. What's wrong?" she asked the distressed woman.

Vivian tucked a silver strand of hair behind her ear. "I've been putting these sage candles all around the lobby. Your grandfather knew this place was haunted. He would have wanted it protected. But someone has taken away all the sage I've left. That Lockhart girl is telling me I can't do my protection spells!" Viv also believed herself to be a bit of a witch, and she was getting more and more worked up as she talked, her arms waving.

"It's no wonder you've had trouble here with the fire. That's how they get you, Isabel. The evil spirits love fire. I'm afraid you have a demon!"

Right now, Izzy was pretty sure she'd take a demon over all of the very human problems she was having. She bit the inside of her lip as she attempted to placate Vivian. The older woman might be a bit misguided, but it warmed Izzy's heart that she was going out of her way to try to help.

"Viv, we really can't have open flames in the lobby." She lowered her voice to a whisper. "People are so clumsy, you know. And with the fire, it just concerns me."

Vivian was nodding vigorously. "I do see the problem. I think I have a back-up idea. It's not quite as effective, but I did bring a box of my homemade potpourri. It contains sage and copal. I have a few bunches of it that we can put all around the hotel. Can you help me grab it from my car?"

"Of course, Viv, that sounds perfect." Izzy looked up to see Chris and Graham engrossed in the screen of Chris's laptop. The memory of Graham's words rang in her ears. *"Don't go anywhere by yourself, Isabel,"* he'd told her sternly.

Well, she certainly didn't want to talk to them to let them know she was heading outside for a minute. She looked around for Milo, but didn't see him. Crap, he must be in the back.

Well, she needed a break. This was about the time she normally left for lunch anyway. Certainly, no one could begrudge her a thirty-second trip to the parking lot and back. Besides, she wasn't alone. Vivian was with her.

She smiled at the older woman, sliding out of the booth. "Okay, Viv, lead the way."

****

Graham blew out a breath, looking over his brother's shoulder. Whoever wanted to hide under a damn holdings company was doing a damn good job. He still didn't even understand what the fuck a holdings company was. But they now had the names of two shell organizations that didn't exist, along with two addresses that he'd bet his right arm were also fakes.

Chris tapped away, laser-focused on the screen, and Graham looked up, not comfortable unless he laid eyes on Izzy about every thirty seconds.

His blood chilled. "Where is she?" Graham stood up so fast that the chair he'd been sitting in fell over. She'd just been there, sitting in her booth, talking to Vivian, and now he didn't see either woman. He looked around frantically. Where had she gone so quickly?

"What?" Chris snapped out of his computer daze. "She was just there a second ago," but Graham was already making his way briskly into The Lounge. He spotted Milo coming out of the back with a stack of coffee mugs.

"Is Izzy back there?" he asked hurriedly.

Milo just stared at him blankly for a moment. "No, she's sitting right over —" He nodded toward the big corner booth where Izzy had left her laptop and all her papers spread out. "Well, hell," he cursed. "I was just in the back for a second."

Graham was already heading to the lobby, looking around. She couldn't have disappeared that fast. "Graham!" Chris had made his way to the front sliding glass door of the hotel, and Graham watched him noticeably breathe a sigh of relief. "She's here."

The tightness in his chest loosened a bit. He moved over to his brother and saw Izzy walking to the parking lot chatting animatedly with Vivian. "Seriously? What the hell is she thinking, going outside?"

Graham watched as Vivian fumbled for her keys and dropped them on the ground. He started to make his way out the door. He really didn't care if Izzy was still mad at him. She needed to understand that she was still under their protection whether she liked it or not, and she couldn't just up and leave the building.

He walked toward the two women as Izzy bent over to pick up Vivian's keys, and was startled by the loud shot that rang out. The scream stuck in his throat as he watched Izzy crumple to the ground.

Chapter Eleven

Izzy heard a man's shout, and wasn't sure who it came from. Chris? Graham? She saw them running toward her, but they seemed to move in slow motion. Vivian was by her side. Was she okay? Izzy tried to raise her arm to the older woman, but let out a strangled cry when pain exploded through her arm, radiating through her entire body.

"Don't move, Isabel." Vivian's gentle voice was firmer than she'd ever heard. Gone was the flighty woman who was sure ghosts were chasing her. This woman was clear-headed and focused as she pressed her floral scarf to Izzy's upper arm.

"Noo…" A strangled cry escaped Izzy as she gritted her teeth from the burning pain. The tangy smell of blood hit her nostrils, causing a wave of nausea to roll through her. When she looked down to see a growing red stain on Viv's scarf, she thought reality seemed splintered. She couldn't be lying here on the ground bleeding.

She opened her mouth to talk, but her voice just came out as a weak moan when Viv applied more pressure to her wound. *Fuck, that hurt.* Izzy's breath came out in shallow pants as her vision began to dim.

Then Chris's face was above hers. Pale. He was so pale. His words were soothing as his hands tenderly explored her body, checking to see where she was injured. But wait, those weren't his hands. Izzy tried to sit up, and her head spun, her stomach pitching dangerously.

"Stay still!" The gruff voice jarred her. Graham's voice, Graham's touch.

Chris eased her back down, his grip firm, but his hands gentle on her face. "Easy, baby," he lulled.

Her men, they were both here – firmness and softness all rolled into gorgeous twin bodies. Izzy looked into Chris's worried eyes and her lips parted to ask what happened, tell him she was fine. But when Graham's probing hands came closer to her upper arm, all she could do was gasp. Her vision dimmed at the pain, and Chris's face swam in front of her.

"Chris," she gasped before blackness engulfed her.

****

That stupid bitch! Ramiro jacked up the heat in his Range Rover, as he took the curve around the lake. He'd been staked out for two hours this morning waiting for Isabel, and he was freezing. Originally from Florida, he didn't think he'd ever get used to the cold weather of the Midwest.

And he couldn't fucking believe the bad luck he was having. With those damn twins checking every person at the hotel, he had to get out of there. He couldn't continue to sit in the lobby. Sooner or later, they were going to realize he didn't belong there. If the sheriff added him to their suspect list and found out who he worked for, it would all be over.

He'd had such a great plan. After the damn fire didn't work, he'd decided to be a little more direct. He knew Izzy left for lunch every day at some point between eleven and one. Even if the fucking Nolan brothers followed her, he'd thought he could get off a good shot when she walked out of the hotel. He'd hunted often growing up — deer mostly. Hunting humans was actually a hell of a lot easier. Usually.

But not today. He slammed his hand against the steering wheel in frustration. He couldn't believe that bitch had bent over just when he'd fired. If she hadn't

been with that old lady who'd dropped her keys. . .
Damn. He'd had the perfect shot, and he took it. He could only hope the shot had hit a vital organ, and the mission would still be a success. He was going to have to wait, though. He couldn't very well go around the hospital and just hang out. And he certainly couldn't go back to the hotel at this point either.

If Izzy wasn't dead, then he was done playing games. No, he wasn't going to sit around with his dick in his hand trying to keep his distance anymore. He was sick of screwing around. If he still needed to take her out, then this time, he would just have to get up close and personal.

****

The smell of disinfectant was starting to get to Chris after what seemed like forever in the waiting room. He hated hospitals. He couldn't set foot in one without being reminded of the awful days he'd spent here when his dad was so sick. The hospital had been updated, but that smell was still the same. Why did all hospitals smell the same? The industrial blue carpet hadn't changed either.

He put down the two-month old copy of *People* magazine and rose to look around the room. What was taking so long? He looked at his phone, and saw that it had been less than an hour, but still, it was a shoulder wound, right? He wasn't a doctor, but shouldn't Reed just be able to take the bullet out and be done?

And why the hell wouldn't they let him back there with her? He'd tried to slip past the nurses' station into the curtained areas where they'd taken her, but a crotchety nurse who looked like Mrs. Voorhees from *Friday the 13th* had dragged his ass back out to the waiting room and threatened to call security.

If he paced anymore, he was going to wear a damn hole in the carpet. He sat again in the worn red chair and wondered if Graham had found anything. After he'd made Chris promise not to leave Izzy, he'd put them in the ambulance and then left with his deputy to comb the area around the hotel. They were already taping off the crime scene when the ambulance left, and Graham had called in the police department in Clinton for backup.

Chris looked at his phone one more time. He should have heard from Graham by now. And if Reed didn't get out here soon and give him an update on Izzy, he was going to fucking walk back there and start yelling until someone answered him, Nurse Voorhees be damned.

As if on cue, Reed stepped around the corner, and Chris leapt up, not giving him a chance to talk. "How is she? Is she okay? I want to see her."

"She's going to be fine, man." Reed adjusted his glasses. "She was so lucky. If she hadn't bent over when that shot was fired, the bullet would have most likely hit her square in the chest."

Chris felt his entire body grow cold. This hadn't been a prank or someone trying to scare Izzy. Someone truly wanted to kill her, to snuff out her beautiful life. The thought sent a rage through him so strong he could barely breathe.

"Where did it . . where did it hit her? There was so much blood. Did you get the bullet out?"

Reed smiled and slapped a hand on Chris's back. "Like I said, she was lucky. The shot hit her arm, and passed right through here." He gave the fleshy part of Chris's upper arm a slight pinch. "So we didn't even have to remove a bullet. There were no major arteries hit, no extensive bleeding. We just got done stitching her up."

The relief that flowed through Chris made his knees go weak. He didn't even realize he'd been holding his breath until he exhaled. She was going to be okay. He just had to keep telling himself that.

"I need to see her." He needed proof. He needed to see with his own eyes that she was all right. And he didn't care if she was still pissed off at him.

"Chris, listen to me. I want to keep her overnight. In addition to the gunshot wound, Izzy has a mild concussion from hitting her head on the pavement so hard, which is why she blacked out. Even though she lives at the hotel, she's still by herself. I would feel better if she stayed here tonight for observation, where we can keep an eye on her and make sure she doesn't have any problems."

Chris was already shaking his head vehemently. "No, I want to take her home. I'll take care of her."

"We'll take care of her," said Graham's voice, as he entered the waiting room.

A relieved smile crossed Chris's face at the sight of his brother. Graham came to stand next to him and crossed his arms, almost daring the doctor to argue with him.

Reed looked from one man to the other and didn't try to suppress a smile. "She's probably going to fight you on this, but why do I get the feeling that you two don't care?"

They were a united front, supporting each other, and taking care of Izzy. She was theirs. Chris damn sure knew that he wasn't taking his eyes off of her from now on, and he didn't care if he had to tie her to his bed all day. . . actually, that didn't sound like a bad idea.

****

Even though the pain pill Reed had given her was finally kicking in, Izzy still winced as she tried to move her arm.

Kendall sighed. Izzy knew the young nurse as a friend of Andi's. Kendall looked to be about her own age, except gorgeous, as far as Izzy was concerned. In fact, she kind of had a girl crush on the nurse. Kendall's mocha-colored skin and raven hair hinted at a mixed ethnicity. And her wide dark chocolate eyes looked very disapprovingly at Izzy.

"I told you to stop trying to move your arm," she said, fastening the sling tighter against Izzy's body, eliciting a grimace.

"This is ridiculous. I'm fine. All they had to do was put on a Band-Aid, for crying out loud," she grumbled stubbornly.

"A Band-Aid and twelve stiches," Reed said as he pulled the curtain back. He walked in, and Izzy's heart skipped a beat as she saw Chris and Graham following closely behind him. Kendall gave her a wink and smiled at the men as she slipped out of the area, pulling the curtain shut behind her.

Izzy felt her bottom lip quiver at the sight of her two men. She'd always considered herself strong. She had gritted her teeth against the pain when the paramedics brought her in and the doctor stitched her up, but her emotions seemed to have a mind of their own right now. No matter how strong she was, the sight of the Nolan brothers made her want to collapse into their embrace. She wanted to tell them that she was so scared, and make them put their strong arms around her. Graham and Chris could make her feel safe.

But she was still mad at them. And they weren't safe. It was all an illusion. They'd betrayed her. They'd lied to her. And that hurt her way more than a bullet ever could.

As if he sensed her need for comfort, Chris moved around Reed to sit on the edge of the Izzy's bed and curl an arm around her, pulling her close. She tensed, warring with herself, needing him, but not trusting him.

His eyes washed over her, taking in her bandage, the sling, her face. Oh lord, she must look a mess.

"Can we take her home?" asked Graham, his voice sounding tired, his eyes never leaving her.

She started to protest, but Chris squeezed her waist gently as if letting her know that no matter what she said, he wasn't going to let her go.

"You can't really argue, Izzy," said Doc Reed, the bastard traitor. She needed a new doctor, dammit. "You have a concussion. I can't let you go home by yourself. If Graham or Chris is going to stay with you, then fine. If not, then I want to keep you overnight for observation."

"No." She wasn't sure which she was protesting exactly – the thought of staying in the hospital or going home with Graham and Chris. She shook her head and immediately regretted it, instinctively grasping Chris's denim-covered thigh to ward off the dizziness, as the room made a spinny loop in her head. "Dammit," she muttered, feeling defeated.

"Easy, sweetheart," Chris said easing her back down. She took deep breaths as she listened to his voice. "Izzy, honey, I refuse to argue with you about this. You're mad at us. Fine. I don't blame you. But you can be mad later. I'm fairly patient, but you're hurt. We're not screwing around here. You're going home with us, end of argument." His normally gentle voice was as hard as granite.

Her mouth opened to voice a protest, but as she stared at Chris, she could see the resolve in his face.

What the hell? He was the easy-going one. She expected Graham to be a hard ass, but not Chris. She looked over at Graham, standing at the edge of the bed with his arms crossed. She couldn't read him, but she could feel the intensity radiating off of him. Yeah, it was pretty obvious he wasn't going to give into her anytime soon either.

She blew out a long breath. "Fine," she snapped. She could agree, but she didn't have to be happy about it. Then a realization hit her and she frowned.

"I take it that means you didn't find anything? You still don't know who did this?"

The muscles of Graham's jaw clenched beneath his beard. He hadn't trimmed it in a couple of days, and it was a bit scraggly. She could still remember how it felt as he slowly dragged his cheek along her breast. Soft and scratchy at the same time, kind of like the man himself.

"We did find where the shot came from. There's a little clearing in the trees across from the hotel. He had to have a scope from that distance. We found one shell casing, so we know it came from a Knights SR-25 sniper rifle. Our shooter didn't stop to pick it up, so he obviously ran as soon as he fired the shot. He must've had a car parked somewhere nearby. We're checking the security cameras in the parking lot at the Lakewood, but I don't expect them to show anything." His tone was clipped, conveying his displeasure with the situation.

She didn't know what she'd hoped for. Maybe for the guy to walk forward with his hands in the air and say 'I did it. Arrest me.' But that wasn't too likely to happen.

"So that's it? No witnesses? Nothing?" The lack of information didn't come as a surprise to her, but her already nervous stomach tightened even more.

"I'm sorry, Izzy. We'll find him," Graham assured her. His aloof tone seemed to betray his words. Oh, she didn't doubt that he meant what he said, but he sounded cold, professional, distant. Was he mad at her? What the hell reason did he have to be mad at *her*?

"Look, you don't have to worry," Graham continued. "We're not going to let anyone hurt you. We'll keep you safe."

Izzy clenched her fist in frustration. After all of their lies, how was she supposed to trust them now? "You'll protect me? Because you're doing such a bang-up job so far," she said flippantly, her irritation caving in on her.

As soon as she looked up at Graham, she regretted her words. His face had gone pale, and he looked as though she'd just punched him. Oh God, what had she said? He'd opened up to her about Alicia the night before. She knew how hurt he was that he couldn't protect her, knew he blamed himself for it. What was she doing?

"Graham, I – I didn't mean—"

"No, you're right." His tone was clipped, detached. "You have every right to doubt us, but I assure you, *ma'am*, this situation is our highest priority." She flinched at the word 'ma'am.' It felt like a slap in the face.

He'd gone into sheriff mode and was talking to her like she was some resident of the town who was fussing at him. She wanted him to talk to her like she was his. Because she did belong to him, really, didn't she?

Realization finally hit her. But had it hit her too late? She *was* his. And now he was backing away. Even before their relationship had progressed, he'd never sounded cold when he talked to her.

"Graham, I'm sorry," she pleaded, tears pricking her eyes. I didn't—"

But he wasn't going to let her speak. "You have every right to feel the way you do, Isabel. All I can do is reassure you that we will do everything to make sure nothing else happens to you or to the hotel. Just please be patient with us. The sooner we catch this guy, the sooner we'll be out of your hair."

Out of her hair? The thought of Graham and Chris not around her every day made her stomach clench, and this time it had nothing to do with nausea. She didn't know what to say. Oh, she'd really messed up.

She lifted her good arm to reach out for him, not trusting herself to speak. But he was already backing away, not looking at her. "I need to get back to the hotel, but I will have Dustin escort you both home." He nodded at Chris and then turned on his heel, and he was gone.

Izzy felt the tears spill over. She twisted her hands together in her lap. Chris was still sitting next to her, an arm around her, but he hadn't said a word. His hand had clenched on her hip, most likely in frustration. She was afraid to even look at him.

Reed had also stood there silently and watched her make a complete fool out of herself.

"Izzy," he said softly, "I'll get your discharge papers ready, okay? We'll have you out of here in about fifteen minutes."

She just nodded mutely, swiping away a tear. As Reed left, he pulled the curtain back to give her and Chris the illusion of privacy.

Izzy stared at her hands, afraid to look up at Chris, afraid that she would see the same coldness in his eyes that she'd seen in Graham's. She didn't think she could handle it. Chris was always so charming, confident. No matter how angry she'd been at him, she couldn't handle him looking at her like he didn't want her.

"I'm sorry," she finally whispered, still staring at her shaking fingers. "I didn't mean that. I didn't. It just came out." More tears spilled over. "I wasn't even thinking."

Chris sighed, his hand gently stroking her back. "Izzy, look at me."

She hesitated before she finally lifted her gaze to meet his. What she saw in Chris's eyes scared her. It wasn't anger. It was disappointment. And that was worse.

****

Chris focused on Izzy's eyes as she bit back a sob. He always loved watching her eyes, the way they danced when she laughed, or went all unfocused when he sent her over the edge into orgasmic bliss. But now, those blue eyes were the color of a stormy sea, and as the tears welled over, they searched his face for something . . . forgiveness. Well, that was something he could give her, even though he knew Graham couldn't. Not right now, anyway.

He let out a breath and softened, reaching up to brush the tears off her cheeks with the back of his knuckles.

"No, you didn't mean it, did you?" He could see that. She wouldn't try to hurt Graham, not intentionally. "Izzy, he's still broken. He puts on a good front . . . well, most of the time. But, he's always felt things deeper than most people. The normal pain hurts him more. I think that's why he likes to be in control most of the time."

Izzy nodded in understanding. "He controls the things he can. That makes sense." She sniffled. "I want to go talk to him. I want to apologize."

But Chris shook his head. "We all need to talk – I agree, but Iz, you have a concussion. You were just stitched up because you took a fucking bullet. The only place you're going now is home, where I'm going to put a fucking guard dog on you if I have to."

She had to put herself first. She had to heal, and there was still a fucking psychopath after her. Nope, she wasn't going anywhere. Maybe Chris couldn't control his brother, but he could damn sure control the fact that Izzy stayed safe.

****

Martin Craig watched his phone shatter as he threw it against the fireplace. Incompetents. This world was full of fucking incompetents! First, Chris Nolan was supposed to seal the land deal, but no, that bitch had batted her eyelashes at him, and he'd forgotten about work and went on a two-week fuckfest with the little slut instead.

Then Ramiro was supposed to take her out, alleviate the fucking problem, and even he couldn't seem to do it. The fire had been a stupid idea. Yeah, he'd hoped Ramiro would make it look like more of an accident, but a fire? That was just idiotic. And then he'd tried to shoot her from sniper range? Martin rolled his eyes. Ramiro really was a dumb fuck.

Storming out of the living room of his high-rise condo, Martin walked with purpose down the hall toward his bedroom. If he wanted something done right, he was just going to have to do it himself. It should have been what he'd done from the very beginning anyway.

He began yanking clothes out of his large walk-in closet. Yes, it was time for a little trip to Magic. A cold grin split his face as he packed a suitcase, a plan hatching inside of his head.

****

Graham made one more loop around the perimeter of the Lakewood, looking closely at everyone he came into contact with. Dustin was manning the station, and Chris and Theo were situated at the hotel. Theo had put three of his security guards on Izzy detail, and their presence made him feel slightly better. He only casually knew the men, but he'd read the files on them along with the background checks that Theo did, and he trusted Theo. Plus, the addition of three more burly guys walking around in black security shirts seemed to make guests feel more comfortable.

As Graham rounded the building and headed back toward the front, the wind felt like an icy cold slap in his face, and he zipped his leather sheriff's jacket to ward off the chill. In the last twenty-four hours, the weather had gone from cool and brisk to downright cold. The bright fall-colored leaves rained down everywhere he looked, and if it weren't for the tightness inside of him, he would have enjoyed the beauty.

Well, it looked beautiful except for the crime scene tape that still outlined the perimeter of the hotel. He'd planned to take it down, but Tessa had convinced him to leave it up, saying it went with the Halloween party décor. He shook his head. Since they'd practically barricaded Izzy upstairs in her room, Tessa had decided to come and help out at the hotel, working with Andrea to put the finishing touches on the party. Andrea was channeling Izzy as much as possible while she managed the place, and he knew she was trying hard to let Izzy rest and not bug her for every little thing.

No matter how hard Graham had tried to stop the party, no one seemed interested in listening to reason. Psychos be damned, no one stopped a Lakewood Costume Ball – or so Tessa had said.

Graham stood at the front door of the hotel as two middle-aged women walked out, smiling and chatting, coffees in hand. After the shooting yesterday, several guests had checked out, but there were still a lot who remained. He'd found that some guests were residents around the lake area, friends of Izzy's and her grandfather's, people who wanted to support her and make sure she didn't lose business.

The thought should have warmed him, but there was a chill in his gut that rivaled the harsh wind. She had friends who would take care of her, friends she could turn to. That should make it easier for Graham to push away from her.

He walked inside and took in the surroundings of the brightly colored lobby before he took a seat in one of the plush chairs near the front. From this vantage point, Graham could see everyone who walked through.

Sitting next to a lighted jack-o-lantern and large bowl of Tootsie Rolls seemed to be the perfect place to set up camp. He loved Tootsie Rolls. Reaching for one, Graham remembered how Izzy had quizzed him on his likes and dislikes, so he knew it wasn't a coincidence that there were bowls of his favorite candies all around the lobby.

Popping the candy into his mouth, he pressed his palms against his eyelids. He needed to keep his distance, but every little thing made him want to run straight to her. Izzy had been home for sixteen hours, not that he was counting, but he hadn't gone up to see her. What she said yesterday at the hospital had been dead on. She hadn't meant to be hurtful – he knew that – but her words held truth, nonetheless, even if she regretted them.

He couldn't protect Alicia all those years ago, so what made him think he could protect Izzy? Hell, it was his fucking *job* to protect Izzy. And what happened? When he was supposed to be watching her, she'd been shot by a maniac. It was only luck that she'd bent over to pick up those keys. If it hadn't been for fate, guardian angels, or whatever the hell you wanted to call it, she would be dead now. And it would be his fault.

Nope, he wasn't going to do that. He wasn't going to put her in any more danger because of his carelessness. He was going to make sure he did everything – *everything* – in his power to ensure her safety. And after he caught this bastard, then he would back off. He was poison to her — he could see that now. She deserved to be happy, and he couldn't give that to her.

He was all kinds of fucked up, and she sure as hell didn't need that. He was moody and dark, and as Chris always said—too fucking sensitive. He sure as hell wasn't going to try to squash the light that radiated out of Izzy. No, she needed someone who would make her happy. She needed Chris. He could make her happy, make her laugh. They could be together, and Graham would support them.

And sooner or later, they would forget that he was ever part of their relationship to begin with. They would get married and have babies, and he would just be the brother-in-law that Izzy had fun with once. Yeah, they would laugh about it someday.

But his stomach rolled at the thought of seeing her married and having babies that weren't his. So he obviously wasn't cool with the idea today, but he would be eventually. He had to be. For Izzy's sake.

At the ding of the elevator, Graham looked up, and bolted out of his seat at the sight of Chris barreling toward him.

"What the fuck are you doing down here? You're not supposed to leave her alone!" Graham rested a hand on the butt of his gun, not as a threat to his brother, but as if entering attack mode in case anyone came near Izzy.

Chris stopped in his tracks, eyeing Graham's gun. "What the hell are you going to do? Shoot me?" He rolled his eyes, unintimidated. "Easy, Rambo. One of Theo's guard dogs is standing outside her door."

Graham relaxed an iota. "Still, you should be with her."

"Try telling her that," Chris said with a frustrated sigh, his hands scrubbing through his already mussed hair. "After I argued with her because she's not eating, she threw me out of her room!"

A smile played at the corner of Graham's lips at the thought of petite little Izzy throwing his large brother out of her room, and he didn't doubt that she would do it.

"She told me not to come back until you were with me."

Graham's smile faded. "I told you to tell her—"

"I know what you told me, dammit." Chris was growing more frustrated. "I'm telling you that she wants to see you, and if you don't go talk to her, she's going to come looking for you, whether we want her out of her room or not."

Fuck. He knew he was going to have to talk to her eventually, but he just didn't know if he was ready yet. Unfortunately, it didn't sound like he had a choice. He steeled his shoulders, hoping he was ready to take on Izzy . . . and then let her go.

****

Scrolling through the emails on her tablet for the third time, Izzy didn't think she'd actually read one single word in front of her. Giving up, she closed the cover on the tablet and tossed it down on the bed next to her. She sank back into the gigantic mountain of pillows Chris had lovingly arranged for her, and mentally kicked herself for throwing him out. But seriously, the man had tried to feed her Brussels sprouts. Brussels sprouts! No one would blame her for throwing him out after that. The fact that he'd admitted he liked them made her seriously question his sanity.

She hadn't wanted to take the pain pill he'd offered this morning either, but he'd threatened to drug her coffee, and she was pretty sure he would have. So she'd agreed to take half a pill, and it had long since worn off, as evidenced by the sharp pull in her arm every time she moved.

Shivering slightly, Izzy slid off the bed so she could adjust the thermostat on the far wall. All the heat seemed to have left the room with Chris, and she really hoped he would be back soon. For a moment, she considered going after him, but she had a feeling leaving the room wouldn't be so easy with the Hulk standing in the hall. That's what she'd decided to name the extra large bouncer outside of her door.

Standing by the window, she looked at the falling leaves. The wind made it look like it was snowing orange, red, and yellow. She loved this time of year, but she found herself ignoring the leaves and looking down trying to spot Graham somewhere. Anywhere. She'd seen him earlier pulling his jacket around himself as she'd looked out the window. She really hoped Chris could find him. But when he did, there was no guarantee Graham would agree to talk to her.

Could Chris convince him? After he'd brought her home yesterday, they'd sat and talked for a long time. Chris had told her more about Alicia. The woman had really done a number on the brothers. It sounded as though she'd manipulated both of them. Chris hadn't said that, but Izzy could read between the lines. Alicia had tried to drive a wedge between the men in hopes of having Graham all to herself. Once she'd gotten Chris out of the way, she couldn't seem to accept the fact that Graham still didn't want her.

He shouldn't feel guilty for not loving her. You can't force yourself to love someone. But he did feel guilty, and Izzy had just made matters worse.

The whistle of the wind drew her attention back outside. She looked around again, but didn't see anyone. Graham probably wasn't out there anymore. He wasn't a big fan of the cold. *You could keep him warm*, said the voice in her head. She'd slide her hands underneath the jacket and wrap her arms around him. Pressing her body to his, she'd lift up her face, run her cheek along his rough jaw, searching for his lips.

Then Chris would press in behind her. She would be able to feel Graham's erection against her belly and Chris's against her lower back. He would brush her hair aside, and his lips would find the nape of her neck. And then his hands—

The snick of the lock yanked Izzy back to reality. She whirled around and her heart skipped a beat as both Graham and Chris entered the room. She could feel the flush rise to her face as she looked from one to the other. As if they could almost tell what she'd been thinking, they reacted. She saw Chris's eyes dilate, his lips parting slightly as his gaze slid down her body. Graham's eyes grew hooded, and that steel gaze was focused on her mouth.

She looked away, almost gasping for breath. The intensity of them, the sexuality that crackled around them practically sucked all the air from her.

"I – I—" She cleared her throat and straightened her back. Taking a deep breath, she started again. "I'm glad you're both here. I wanted to talk to you. We need to get some things straightened out." She looked back up from one man to the other. "Graham, I want to apologize."

He simply shook his head. "Nothing to apologize for." But he stood by the door with his arms crossed. That wall he'd constructed around himself was firmly in place.

She watched Chris's face tighten in frustration. "You should be in bed," he finally said, stepping forward.

"Chris," she started to protest, but he was already leading her back to the bed. As he helped her get settled, careful to avoid her injured arm, Graham simply watched the two of them.

"How are you feeling? Better today?" he finally asked.

That was a start. Maybe he does care about me, Izzy thought.

"Yeah, better. My head still hurts, but it's lightened to more of a dull throb." Chris had slept next to her all night, waking her every couple of hours to check the size of her pupils. By four a.m., she'd wanted to kill him, but the circles under his eyes told her he had most likely not slept at all. He'd stayed up all night to make sure she was okay.

She offered him a warm smile as he adjusted her pillows. As sweet as he was, she still wasn't trying Brussels sprouts.

Her gaze shifted to Graham, and she opened her mouth to offer him another apology when he spoke. "Look, Isabel, the reason I came up here was because I wanted to talk you out of having this ridiculous party."

"Ridiculous party?" She felt as if he'd slapped her. He knew how much this party meant to her. It was her grandfather's tradition. "Graham, I am not cancelling this party. Not this year. The first year without—" She took a deep breath. "I need to have it."

"You need to look at the facts," he said coldly.

Where was the Graham who held her and offered her his support? He really was trying his damnedest to be reserved. And he was good at it. He was a fucking island.

****

Why did she have to look so fucking sexy? Even with her bandaged arm strapped to her body, Graham wanted nothing more than to throw her down on the bed and kiss her senseless until she submitted, until she was begging. The way her hair tumbled around her face did things to him.

When he'd walked into the room, her face had been flushed, her lips parted. He hadn't mistaken the way her breath had hitched when she'd looked at him. He'd instantly become erect with his need to be inside of her. He was so thankful his jacket was long enough to cover the telltale bulge in his pants.

Focus, Nolan. He had to make her listen. She had to understand reason. He squared his jaw. "Isabel, I don't think —"

"Stop calling me Isabel," she snapped, her eyes heating up.

He raised an eyebrow at her. "Izzy." He began slowly. "I don't think having a hotel full of people in costumes – in *masks* – is a good idea when there is someone on the loose who is trying to fucking kill you!" His voice rose an octave as he spoke, his careful control slipping.

"Chris already said the same thing. That's why I talked to Theo. He's going to have the security team checking people into the party. That way, no matter who has a mask on, no one can get in unless they're supposed to be here." She looked pleased with herself, but Graham felt a nerve in his eye begin to twitch.

"Do you mean to tell me that you are taking the security team who needs to be watching *you* and putting them on party patrol?" He turned to his brother to offer an accusatory glare. "You didn't think this little tidbit was important to fucking share with me? Didn't you try to stop her?"

"He's not in charge of me! Neither are you!" Izzy began to struggle off the bed, wincing as she inadvertently rolled on her bad arm.

"Dammit!" both men said at once, rushing toward her at the same time to stabilize her.

"Sweetheart, you have to be more careful. You're going to rip your damn stitches open." Graham realized his mistake as soon as he saw hope flare in Izzy's eyes.

Dropping his hands, he backed away from her as if she were on fire. Hurt quickly replaced every other emotion on her face as he put distance between them.

Chris put an arm around her, but his eyes never left Graham. "You son of a bitch."

Graham's mouth twisted in a humorless smile. "No argument there," he said flatly.

"Graham, please," Izzy said quietly. "I don't want to fight with you. With either of you. I was angry yesterday, but Chris told me everything last night. He told me about this Eric Jacobs person who commissioned Waddell & Stevens to acquire my land."

Eric fucking Jacobs. Still no information on him. The number Chris had used to contact him previously had been traced to a disposable phone, and Graham had worked nearly half the night with Theo digging into every tracking program they could access trying to find something. He knew that Eric Jacobs was an alias, but Graham had long since decided that the man had to be working for someone. He just didn't know who. And it pissed him off that he still couldn't figure out who wanted Izzy's land badly enough to kill her for it.

Graham watched her wince again as she tried to adjust her arm, and fought the urge to reach for her. He watched Chris gently put his arm around her and settle her back. His arm remained protectively around her shoulders as he lightly stroked her hair. He was silently comforting her, knowing that Graham was going to cause her pain, and wanting to prevent it.

Don't do it. Graham could hear Chris's voice in his head as clearly as if his twin had spoken in his ear.

"Well, if you're not going to listen to reason and cancel the damn party, then I'd better go downstairs and make sure everything doesn't go to hell." Graham turned his back to leave, fighting the urge to go to her, needing to get away so he could escape the pain in her eyes.

"That's it?" He heard her soft voice, all the fight gone. "You're just leaving? I know you're upset, Graham, but don't you even care enough to fight? To fight *for* me?"

Didn't she see that he did care for her? He loved her. He loved her with all his heart. That's why he had to walk away. Someday she would understand.

"Isabel. . ." he began in almost a warning tone.

"No, Graham." His brother's voice was almost threatening. "Just go."

"No, I want to hear what he has to say," Izzy said quietly.

He heard Chris sigh. "Okay. If you're going to say something, Graham, then turn around and look at her. Look at me."

Graham turned, shooting a glare at his brother. He knew what Chris was doing. He was thinking – hoping – that Graham couldn't do what he needed to do if he was looking at the two people he loved most in the world. But that's what Chris didn't understand. He would do this *because* he loved them.

"Fine," he said, looking at Izzy straight on. "Isabel, whatever this is," he gestured his hand back and forth between the three of them, "is not going to work. It was fun, but that's it. It's over."

His gut clenched as he watched the color drain from her face, the anger in Chris's rising.

"Fun?" she repeated in a near whisper. "But you said – you said you loved me." Her voice was choked with emotion.

"Yeah, fun," he continued. "I know what I said, and I shouldn't have lead you on. I am sorry about that. It had been so long since Chris and I shared a woman, I thought that maybe . . . well, it doesn't matter what I thought. I was wrong. The point is that we had fun, but that's all it was, and it's over. I just want to focus on this investigation. Once I find whoever is behind this, we can all move on with our lives." His heart was breaking with every word out of his mouth. Did she believe him?

Chris had come off the bed and stood directly in front of Graham. "You motherfucker, don't do this to her. She doesn't deserve this."

No, she didn't. She deserved better, so much better.

"Fun?" her voice caught on the word as she said it again. "But what about. . . what about the other night? When we. . . when you . . ." A tear spilled over.

Graham felt the sick feeling in his gut threaten to take hold. "When we fucked?" he asked harshly. She flinched at the word as her hand clamped over her mouth. Graham barely had a chance to register her reaction before his head snapped back at the punch from his brother.

The strength behind the punch sent him reeling, and he stumbled back to catch himself from falling on his ass. Chris raised his fist to punch him again, and Graham did nothing to fend it off. He deserved it. He wanted to hurt. Maybe the pain would help him get through the numbness that was taking over his body.

"No!" Izzy was scrambling off the bed, and Chris dropped his arm to stop her.

She swayed a bit, shaking her head as if to clear it.

"Baby, you're still dizzy," Chris said gently. He turned back to Graham, his eyes spitting fire. "Get out!"

Graham turned to reach for the door when he heard her.

"Do you mean it?" Izzy asked. "Do you really mean it?"

He squeezed his eyes shut, taking a deep breath and swallowing the large lump that was forming in his throat.

"I do. I do mean it, Isabel." He couldn't look at her this time and remained facing away. "Chris will take care of you. He's the one you want."

"But what about what I want? I want you both. I love you both," she sobbed.

He clenched his hand on the doorknob. He was almost there. One final nail. "But I don't want you, Isabel. I'm sorry, but I don't love you."

As he opened the door, he ignored Chris's curse, and tried to ignore Izzy's soft crying.

Chapter Twelve

Candles appeared to be floating all around the hotel lobby, casting an eerie glow over the marble floors. Chris still didn't know how the candles appeared to float, but by noon today, he had stopped asking questions as he, Tessa, Andi, Milo, Josh, and anyone else they could recruit hung decorations.

Unable to climb a ladder with her bad arm – although she had tried – Izzy had stood and directed. She quickly shut down anyone who tried to talk to her about Graham or the shooting and pasted that ridiculous fake smile on her face that didn't reach her eyes.

Fisting his hands at the thought of his damn twin, Chris wanted nothing more than to wrap his hands around his brother's neck for how he'd treated Izzy. Graham had been noticeably absent all day, even though Chris knew he was at the hotel, peeking in whenever he thought Izzy wasn't looking.

To the casual observer, Izzy looked like she'd been enjoying the decorating. But Chris could see the truth. He could see the circles under her puffy eyes, and how she kept wrapping her good arm around herself as a shield against any more hurt.

When Graham had stormed out yesterday, she'd been inconsolable. The fucker needed a good ass-kicking, which Chris would have happily delivered if Izzy hadn't restrained him. At the look in her eyes, he'd let Graham go. She needed him more. Her heart-wrenching sobs had torn at him, especially when he knew nothing he said could make her feel better.

After her tears had subsided, she'd tried her best to act like she didn't care. And when she'd attempted to push him away, he'd just held her and refused to leave.

Unlike his brother, Chris was completely ready to admit how much he loved this woman. He wasn't going to make the idiotic decision of letting her go.

He'd tried his best to calm her down. She needed to heal from her injuries, those to her body and her heart. Even as she tried to pull away from him emotionally, her little body had burrowed into him as they'd lain in bed. Chris turned on her favorite horror movie to relax her. His mouth tipped up at the thought. A horror movie to relax. His Izzy didn't do chick flicks.

"Just give me a guy in a mask hacking up babysitters, and I'm happy," she'd said. He still didn't know if he should be worried or amused that she'd finally managed to fall asleep to the screams of a teenager being chased by a chainsaw-wielding maniac.

As he walked across the lobby, he sobered immediately as he saw Josh rushing out of The Lounge. The night manager wasn't in costume, and his face looked ashen.

Chris immediately went on alert. "Josh, what's the matter? Did something happen?"

Josh's eyes darted around as if he couldn't contain his anxiety. "Uh, no, no. Izzy just wanted me to change into one of the extra costumes we had on hand for employees." His face reddened, and Chris noticed that he was wearing plain clothes and holding a monster mask. Izzy was very specific that she wanted employees in full costume. Josh knew that, but was that enough to upset him so much?

Wringing the mask in his hands, Josh stepped away from Chris. "Izzy's behind the bar with the others if you're looking for her. I'll be back."

Dismissing the flustered man, Chris moved toward The Lounge to find Izzy. He hadn't seen the final touches of her costume. She'd gone down to the party with Tessa and Andi earlier while he'd still been working. He and Theo had a source at the holdings company who was close to getting them the information they needed. They were so close. Deep down, he knew this information would help him catch the bastard. They just had to do it before . . .

Shaking off the dark thoughts, Chris stepped into The Lounge where the party was already in full swing. He spotted Milo at the bar. The large man wore a werewolf costume as if it were his everyday attire. When Milo moved aside, Chris saw that he was chatting with Izzy. Wow, who knew a zombie costume could be sexy?

Tessa had brought a suitcase full of make-up, fabric, and prosthetics with her this afternoon. Izzy had been a little nervous when Tessa had whisked her away to do makeup. But damn, the result was perfection. Her creamy skin held a greenish tint, and the darker make-up on her face made her wide eyes stand out. The dress was a long flowing gauzy material that was ripped in all the right places, offering glimpses of Izzy's ivory skin. Chris's mouth practically watered at the thought of sliding his hands under that dress.

But it was the make-up that was truly impressive. She was completely dotted with fake blood except for her wounded arm. That was the piece de resistance. He couldn't tell if it was latex or prosthetics, but Tessa had made it looked like Izzy's left arm was ripped off, leaving a bloody stump.

Before making his way over to her, Chris stopped, looking around in awe at how she'd organized The Lounge. The candles sitting on the tables looked to be dripping blood. Ghosts swirled around the ceiling on what looked to be some sort of complicated pulley system, and everything was bathed in a ghostly purple light. The room was sprinkled with jack-o-lanterns.

Several cauldrons, which must have held a ton of dry ice, emanated waves of floating fog.

Everyone was in costume, and he was pleased to see that a lot of the costumes didn't include masks. There was the random Ghostface or Michael Myers, but for the most part, people went with make-up for face decorating, which included some detailed latex wounds. Chris spotted Vivian heading toward the dance floor in a Cleopatra costume, complete with black wig and jewels. She joined an older man dressed as Frankenstein, and Chris smiled warmly in their direction.

"There you are!" Tessa bounded up and linked her arm through his to lead him over to the bar area. "I knew Indiana Jones would be a good costume for you two. You look damn sexy with a whip, Nolan."

He smiled gratefully at her. With everything else going on, he hadn't even thought about a costume. But Tessa had. She'd shown up not only with zombie makeup, but also with a costume for him as well. He would have protested, but the look of desire in Izzy's eyes when he'd perched the fedora on his head made him think he might want to wear the costume all the time.

But wait a minute. Indiana Jones would be a good costume for *you two*? Frowning, Chris was afraid he understood exactly what she meant. "You two?"

Her smile wavered, "Well, I didn't know Sheriff Sexy was going to turn into Captain Douchebag before I ordered the costumes, now, did I? So yeah, you're dressed as twin Indys, but I wouldn't worry about it. Looks like he's trying to keep his distance." She nodded across the room, and Chris spotted Graham in a far corner, fedora crookedly perched on his head, nursing a bottle of water, his eyes laser-focused on Izzy.

All of his anger dissolved as he was hit full force with the amount of pain his brother was feeling. The idiot thought hurting Izzy and pushing her away was the only way to protect her. Chris had to press a hand to his stomach as he felt Graham's feelings shooting through him. It was like he was being ripped apart from the inside out. This was ridiculous.

It was time for Graham to quit feeling terrified at the idea of letting himself be happy. If he was so determined to push Izzy away, then Chris was sure as hell going to make it hard for him. He firmed his shoulders as a plan began to form in his head.

****

Tipping back her glass of champagne, Izzy swallowed deeply. Twin fucking Indiana Jones's? Seriously? As if the Nolan brothers didn't just exude sex on a normal basis, now they had hats and whips? She poured herself another glass of champagne as she felt the liquid heat radiate south.

How was she supposed to forget about Graham when he was just standing across the room looking sexy and not trying at all to hide the fact that he was staring at her? And Chris had his jaw clenched, so Izzy couldn't tell if he was happy to see her or if he was angry too.

Why was she so afraid that Chris was going to be angry with her? He wasn't the one who'd left. He'd been there for her, held her, brushed away her tears. He'd stayed. Why did that scare her just as much as Graham leaving?

Get it together, Izzy. She slowly swirled her glass, looking out over the party. There were at least two hundred guests packed into the space, and she couldn't have been more thrilled with the turnout. Rain threatened the chilly night, so everyone was inside rather than trailing out on the patios as she'd hoped. Yet there were enough activities dispersed throughout the lobby and the ballroom that none of the areas seemed overly crowded.

As she heard a gasp, she turned to see a young couple tentatively peer into the cauldron of punch. Twinkling orange and purple lights surrounded the large bar, and soft wisps of fog drifted by. In addition to the usual libations, Milo was serving "bloody" punch from a large cauldron, ladling it into ornate glasses that boasted skulls and crossbones. Izzy smiled. The bloody punch tasted a lot like cherry vodka. She probably shouldn't have many glasses of that since the champagne was already doing its job. Since she'd decided to lay off the pain pills, she figured this was a good way to self-medicate.

She winced as she rolled her shoulder. Maybe she needed one more glass.

A shy laugh had Izzy turning her attention back to her friends seated at the bar. Andrea was smiling at something Flynn was saying. The brunette had donned a long blonde wig, and a long-sleeved blue dress with a white overlay. The black headband completed her Alice in Wonderland ensemble. She looked adorable.

And Flynn was practically drooling over her. Gone was the lawyer's normal suit and tie. His thick blonde hair was swept back, and Izzy grinned at his mussed button down shirt and jeans. His lean body was covered with newspapers and leaves, and he carried an umbrella that was inside out. Flynn's costume was "guy caught in windstorm."

He didn't seem to notice Theo sitting two bar stools down. You'd never know the two men were friends considering the death stare Theo was shooting at Flynn. It was obvious Theo wasn't crazy about the conversation going on between Andi and Flynn. Not that he could even hear what they were saying, but when Andi put a hand on

Flynn's arm, Theo looked as if he were about to come out of his seat.

The PI had not been happy when Tessa had insisted he wear a costume. They had finally compromised and he'd let Tessa write the word "BOOK" across his face with her eye pencil. Yes, Theo's costume was "Facebook."

Izzy found it odd that Theo and Flynn lavished Andi with attention, yet the woman's husband was nowhere to be found.

"Is Brian here tonight?" she asked her friend. Andi's smile immediately faded, and Izzy could have kicked herself for mentioning the name of Andi's jerky husband.

"Uh – no. He's driving back from St. Louis. He said he'd just meet me at home later," she said hurriedly.

"Awesome!" Tessa piped up, slinging an arm around Andi's shoulders. "So we can get you all liquored up, and there's no one here to complain about it." She handed Andi a martini, and Andi only hesitated a heartbeat before taking a sip.

"Careful, Andi, that's a double," Milo piped up, giving a stern warning look to Tessa.

She rolled her eyes dramatically, which looked quite comical considering her zombie costume was complete with sickly green contact lenses. "Oh, don't go all stick in the mud, Mi. It's a par-tay," she said waggling her eyebrows. "And that calls for a fun drink!" She leaned over the bar so her face was about an inch from his. Izzy was pretty sure she'd had more than one "fun drink" already this evening.

Milo didn't flinch, but stood perfectly still as Tessa leaned in. Her dark chestnut hair cascaded around her shoulders, which was different than her usual bun, and she wasn't wearing her glasses. The ripped dress she wore hugged her hourglass figure. As she ran a tongue over her bright red lips, Izzy was impressed at just how sexy Tessa could make a zombie look.

When Milo leaned in, he was so close that his lips were just a breath away from Tessa's. "And what exactly do you consider *"fun,"* pet?" His eyes sparkled as he eyed Tessa's mouth.

At Tessa's little smile, Izzy had a feeling she knew what was coming. "Sex . . ." Tessa breathed. "On the beach."

Even though Milo practically snorted at Tessa's request, his eyes still glittered with arousal. It was easy to see just how much Tessa affected Milo. Izzy wondered if he could see how much he affected her, too.

She lifted her glass in a little toast to her friends. At least they were having a good time. And she was relieved that the party was a success. She just wished she felt more celebratory. Glancing around again, she blushed as she looked right into Chris's eyes, measuring her, assessing her. He moved closer to the bar so he stood directly across from her.

"Hi." He reached across the bar and took the glass out of her hand. Setting it down, he intertwined his fingers with hers. "You okay, baby?"

Her heart fluttered a bit at his touch. "I'm fine." She glanced in Graham's direction. She'd be better if he weren't here. . .

Sighing, she knew that wasn't true. She'd be thinking about him just as much even if he weren't there. So which was worse? Him ignoring her completely, or standing across the room studying at her as if she were a bug he had pinned to the wall? As she inadvertently glanced in his direction, Chris's mouth tightened as if sensing the reason for her unease.

"Why don't we walk around? I wanted to talk to you," he said, motioning to the hallway that led to the large patio. "It stopped raining, so maybe we can step out and get some air."

She frowned. "I shouldn't. Josh was supposed to be back to help serve drinks and food." Looking around, she still didn't see him. What on earth was taking him so long? "I'll just stay and help until he gets back."

"No, you won't," Milo and Chris said at the same time. Milo was stirring a red cocktail, and took the stirrer out to pop it in his mouth and lick it dramatically before he put it back in the drink and handed the glass to Tessa. Giggles erupted from Izzy and Andrea, and even Tessa couldn't help hide her grin.

"Izzy," Milo continued. "No offense, but you're not going to be much help serving with one arm. You've been on your feet all day, and you need to rest. Go with Chris."

Narrowing her eyes at Milo, Izzy thought about arguing, but the truth was that she really was tired, and the dull ache in the back of her head was starting to throb in time with the music. "Fine," she conceded, placing her hand in Chris's. "I could use a few minutes someplace quiet."

With a relieved sigh, Chris led her out from behind the bar. He stopped to lean in and whisper something to Theo before he put a strong arm around her and led her away.

Several partygoers stopped Izzy to compliment her on the wonderful party, and it warmed her to know that despite that chaos of the last few weeks, she could make her guests happy.

Looking around, she'd lost track of Graham and wondered if he had finally left. The thought made her sag against Chris, who kept his strong arm firmly around her as he opened the patio door, leading her out into the cool night air.

The stone patio formed a large semicircle that was surrounded by a four-foot stone wall. Izzy loved this space because it was more secluded than the smaller patio off of the dining room. She could come here to enjoy a lovely view of the lake and just think – something she seemed to be doing a lot lately. There were a few tables and chairs to accommodate overflow from The Lounge, and a wrought iron gate opened out to the walking path that circled the hotel.

Normally, there were a handful of people on the patio relaxing in the lounge chairs. But with the evening's off-and-on drizzle, all the guests were inside, and she could enjoy a quiet moment with Chris.

Izzy looked out on the lake, and shivered slightly in the night air. It was cool, but she welcomed the chill. The moonlight sparkled off the water and it reminded her of only a few nights ago when she stood on her balcony with Graham and Chris looking out over the water. Everything had seemed so perfect then.

She immediately felt Chris's warm hand on her arm as he turned her to face him. The hungry look in his silver eyes made her knees go weak, and she tried to push her troubled thoughts aside. She didn't think she looked very sexy, even though Tessa described their costumes as "sexy zombies," but the way Chris looked at her made her feel sexy. Wanted. She felt her insides go all warm, but she knew this wasn't the time to give into her desire when she had a hotel full of guests in the next room.

She took a shaky breath as Chris stroked her cheek with the backs of his fingers. "Was there – um – something you wanted to talk to me about?"

Chris opened his mouth to speak, but before he could, the patio door creaked opened.

"Theo said you wanted to talk to me. What —" Graham's husky voice stopped short when he spotted Chris and Izzy. Joy flashed on her face as she saw him. And when he looked at her, his eyes flared briefly before his cool mask slid into place. Izzy felt her insides constrict. He was so cold toward her. She couldn't do this. She couldn't take this from him. Not right now.

Chris's phone buzzed, and she backed away from him so he could look at his texts. "I'll let you two talk. Excuse me," she mumbled as she started to move around Graham to make her escape. But his hand shot out in a flash to grasp her good arm. "I don't think so, sweetheart. Nowhere by yourself, remember?"

Her lips tightened. So he cared now? She looked up, narrowing her eyes at him. "There is a room full of people in there. I think I can make my way back to the party."

"No." His voice was as firm as his grip, and his monosyllabic response only raised her blood pressure.

"Why do you care?" She yanked her arm away. "You made it perfectly clear that—"

"Iz." It was Chris's gentle voice that stopped her. "I actually need to go find Flynn. He just texted. Graham, can you watch her for a moment?"

She thought she saw momentary panic in Graham's eyes. "Chris, I don't think—"

"Great." He leaned down to give her a hard kiss. "I will be right back, baby." Before she or Graham could even react, Chris had disappeared through the doors, leaving them alone.

****

Fuck! The door clicked shut, and Graham was left alone with Izzy. He was pretty damn sure that she would rather be anywhere other than right here with him. One glance at her face told him he was right. Damn, she was sexy when she was angry. Even with that ridiculous mangled prosthetic strapped to her sling, she looked gorgeous as hell.

She squared her shoulders and raised her chin. "I don't need a babysitter. I can make my way back to the party."

The door was still cracked open slightly from when Chris had made his way in, and the low buzz of voices drifted out along with the music. When the newest Ellie Goulding song began to play, Izzy wavered. He'd heard her hum that song a hundred times. It always made him think of her. She looked up at him with those wide blue eyes, and he could tell she was scared.

He could see that she wanted to turn and run, but she firmed her jaw and stared at him. He loved her strength, and she was trying so hard not to let him see how much he'd gotten to her. He'd pushed her away and told her he didn't want her, and now he had to stick to his guns.

That was really hard considering he wanted nothing more in the entire world than to wrap himself around her, drown himself inside of her. Why did he have to be so drawn to her? Why couldn't it be easy for him to let her go? It was the best thing for her. He knew that. Yet the voice inside his head that kept telling him to push her away was getting weaker and more distant.

He couldn't keep doing this to her or himself. When he'd left her last night, bitterness had soured his stomach so badly that he'd immediately started heaving when he got outside. He loved her. God, he loved her so much. But she couldn't know that. He had to channel all his love for her into keeping her safe. That was something he could do without hesitation.

She tried to move away from him, but he stood in front of her, blocking her path back to the party.

"Graham, please," she said shakily. She took a step to move around him, but his hands reached out to tenderly grasp her shoulders. Gently, yet effectively immobilizing her.

"I can't let you go, Iz." *I don't want to let you go.* He watched her eyes grow weary, and she tried to look away. Even though he had resolved to do the right thing, sometimes he couldn't help himself around her. He just wanted to hold her one last time. One last kiss, and then he would let her go.

As he pulled her close, Izzy's breathing sped up, becoming shallower. She swallowed hard, saying nothing as she searched his face for answers.

Graham reached up to brush a stray hair from her greenish-tinted face. He was really glad she didn't opt to have fake wounds on her face like Tessa. Although he couldn't imagine Izzy looking anything other than sexy as hell no matter how she was dressed.

"Graham, you shouldn't . . . we shouldn't . . ." But even as she protested, he felt her body melt into his as his hand gently gripped the back of her neck, immobilizing her as he brought his face down to meet hers.

When he lightly brushed his lips over hers, they parted in response. Tilting her face up to him was all the invitation Graham needed, and he claimed her mouth hard, tasting, teasing, his tongue delving deep as if she was his only lifeline. The little moan that escaped her throat caused his cock to stiffen painfully against her. She tasted like sunshine and chocolate – a light in his darkness. He tilted his head to go deeper, longing to be as close to her as possible, moving a hand to her lower back to pull her more firmly against him.

Her strangled gasp made him instantly drop his hands, and he realized that he'd pressed himself against her bandaged arm. Reality came crashing back to him like shards of ice destroying the fire that sizzled between them. He'd hurt her. No matter how hard he tried to prevent it, he always hurt her in the end.

Graham backed up, quickly severing the contact between them, and Izzy stumbled a bit, unable to steady herself at his sudden departure. She reached out her hand and grasped his arm. "No, don't you dare back away from me. Not this time, Graham. My head is spinning with the back and forth, and you have to stop."

She looked deep into his eyes as if she could see into his soul. "Please. You love me. I know you love me. I can feel it." She grasped his arm tighter. "Whatever you have going on in your head, we can talk about it, we can get through it. Just please don't pull away from me again." Her eyes searched his face. "Please," she begged.

He wanted to hold her and ease her fears, but he couldn't. It would just make it harder to walk away from her. But the pain in her face got to him. At the very least, he owed her some semblance of the truth.

"Izzy, it's never been a question of how I feel about you," he admitted, lacing his fingers with hers.

Hope flared in her eyes. "What about yesterday? You said you didn't love me. Didn't want me." He felt the pain flare in his chest, knowing that's what it must have felt like for her – that sharp pain in his heart. Dammit, she deserved honesty. She didn't deserve to be toyed with.

He slowly shook his head, coming to a decision. "It's not a question of how I feel about you. I was just trying to figure out the best way to . . . let you go." He took a long, slow breath. "Izzy, I just need you to realize I'm no good for you. You're so much better without me.

Chris can give you what you need. He's the one you want." *He doesn't have demons to battle.*

She dropped his hand, startling him with a harsh laugh. When he looked at her, he could tell she was ready for a fight. "Don't you see? I need you both. Chris does give me what I need, but so do you, Graham. You said it yourself once – relationships don't seem to work when you two have them separately. So how long do you think Chris and I will work without you? We need you. We need your strength, your control. And you and I—" She gestured between them. "We had three years, and we never found our way to each other. Chris brought us together. He brought us all together. We need him too."

The way she searched his face made his heart speed up. Could she be right? Could this ever work?

"We're a team, Graham. Don't you see that?"

If only she knew how much he wanted to. Before he could respond, the patio doors opened. Without thinking, he stepped in front of Izzy as protection, but it was Chris, Theo, Flynn, and Tessa who came out. *Dammit, not now.* He wanted to work this out, needed to work this out with Izzy.

Chris looked knowingly between the two of them, the corner of his mouth tipping up as if something made him extremely happy.

Flynn stepped forward. "Graham, we need to talk to you about something inside."

Without a word, Theo jerked his head sideways, motioning for Graham to follow them in.

"Right now?" Aggravation made him want to shove every one of them back through the door and lock it so he could be alone with Izzy. "Can't this wait?"

"No, brother, it really can't." Chris looked steadily at Graham, and then moved his eyes to Izzy and back. *Shit, this was about her. They'd found something.*

"Someone needs to stay with her," Graham said, protectively putting his arm around her, pulling her close. When she looked up at him, there was such trust in her eyes, and he didn't deserve it. "Why don't you come back inside where you're around more people?"

"No, it's okay. I'll stay with her out here if she wants." Tessa piped up. "I even brought some bottled water." She winked at Izzy, and pulled her away from Graham, linking arms with her. Graham heard her whisper to Izzy, "I need to drink a bottle of water between every one of those skull and crossbones concoctions just to make sure I stay sober enough to give Milo a hard time."

Graham looked from one woman to the other. He wondered if Milo knew what kind of trouble he was in for. "Okay, but don't go anywhere," he said finally. "We will be right back."

****

More people had crowded into the party, but most of them were either dancing or milling around by the food tables. As 'Monster Mash' blared over the speakers, the men found a large table in the opposite corner of the dance floor.

As they sat down, Chris wished they'd had better timing. It looked like Izzy was finally getting Graham to open up. He hoped yanking his brother away from the patio wouldn't give him time to shut down again.

"Okay, we're all here," he said to Theo and Flynn. "What did you find?"

"You're not going to like it," Flynn answered. "We just got a call from our source who was digging into the holdings company that wanted Izzy's land so badly. We found out who was behind it. It's Izzy's uncle. It's Martin Craig."

Chris's mouth dropped open just as he watched Graham's lips thin so tightly that they almost disappeared within his face. "Her own flesh and blood," Graham spit out. "Trying to kill her? Fuck! We need to get this asshole." He yanked out his phone, but Theo held a hand up to stop him.

"We've already tried to locate him, but he's not at his condo in St. Louis. He left town unexpectedly, and no one knows where he went." Theo clenched his fist tightly. "It's not like we can do much with this information, Graham. We've connected the dots, but there's still no proof that he's the one who tried to kill her."

"Why, though?" Chris asked, trying to grasp the facts. "Why would her own uncle want to kill her?"

"Half uncle," Graham corrected, shoving a hand through his hair. "And they've never been particularly close." He shifted his steely gaze to Theo. "Are you sure on this? I investigated him, but all my leads were a dead end."

Theo rested his elbows on the table and leaned forward. "Yeah, we're sure. It took some work to figure it all out. He tried hard to cover it up, but we think he had this planned for awhile." He paused as a couple passed the table, and looked around to make sure no one was within earshot. "You see, several years ago, Martin helped his brother conduct a mineral study on the Lakewood and the surrounding land to see if there were any natural resources. As you know from the geophysics reports, the study showed oil under the hotel. A lot of fucking oil. Martin wanted his brother to sell it. He wanted the money."

"But I don't get it," Chris said. He still didn't understand why Martin Craig would care one way or the other whether his brother sold the land. "Why would it matter to him whether or not his brother got rich?"

Flynn answered. "Martin owns ten percent of the land. It doesn't sound like much, but with the amount of money we're talking about, he would make some serious bank off of that much oil." Flynn shifted his eyes to Theo. "But we don't think that was his long game."

Chris shook his head, confused. "What do you mean?"

Candlelight flickered over Flynn's serious face. The music suddenly shifted to something slower, and Flynn lowered his voice so he wouldn't be overheard.

"I've handled the legal documents for Richard Craig and the Lakewood for years. At the time the studies on the land were done, Martin was the main beneficiary of the Lakewood. If Richard died, everything went to Martin."

Understanding began to show on Graham's face. "The land study was done five years ago, right? Richard had already been diagnosed with cancer at that time."

"Exactly," said Theo. "Except then there was a problem he didn't foresee." He looked toward the hall leading out to the patio they'd just left.

"Izzy," Chris and Graham said together.

"Right," Flynn continued. "Izzy came to town three years ago to help her grandpa run the hotel. Two years ago, when Richard began to get worse, he contacted me to have his will changed. I think he realized he didn't have much time left. Izzy was getting a nice chunk of change before, but he saw that she truly loved the hotel as much as he did. He knew if he left it to his brother, then the bastard would start drilling before his body was even cold."

Realization struck Chris. Izzy would die before she'd let anyone touch this land. "So he changed the will, didn't he? Left everything to Izzy?"

"Exactly," Flynn answered. "Martin still owns ten percent of the land, but Izzy owns the rest."

Graham let out a low whistle, and raised a hand to rub his eyes. "Damn, it always comes down to money, doesn't it?"

"But why kill her now?" Chris asked. "What does he hope to gain? Some misplaced sense of revenge?"

Flynn shook his head. "Richard's will stated that if Izzy was deceased at the time of his passing, then Martin would get all of the land."

"So if he kills her, everything goes to him? Her life is worth a few million dollars?" Chris felt the rage began to boil inside of him.

"Except, he'd be mistaken," Theo said, glancing at Flynn.

Confusion marred Chris's face as he looked between Graham and the other two men. "What do you mean?"

Flynn answered. "Martin is under the impression that he still gets the land if Izzy dies. But he doesn't." He exchanged a look with Theo. "Graham does."

Chapter Thirteen

Rarely rendered speechless, Graham just sat there with his mouth open. He would have laughed had the situation not been so serious. He watched Chris's eyes go wide as he sputtered, "You? You get the land?"

"Well, kind of," Flynn said slowly.

Looking from Theo to Flynn, Graham finally gained his composure enough to respond. "You want to explain that, please?"

Flynn nodded. "Izzy was going to tell you, but she said the time never seemed right."

Of course it hadn't ever seemed right. He'd never given her the chance. Every time she pushed closer, he pulled away. Shame filled him at the way he'd treated her for so long.

"If Izzy hadn't made a will, then yes, the land would still go to Martin in the event of her death. That's obviously what he still thinks," Flynn explained.

"So the fucker didn't do his research," Graham grumbled.

Flynn lifted his empty glass, signaling to the waitress a few tables over before continuing. "Izzy made a will almost immediately after her grandfather died. She knew Martin wanted the land for the oil, and she wasn't about to let anything happen to the Lakewood."

Of course she wouldn't. This was her home. "Our girl's smart," he said, not realizing he'd said "our" until he earned a smile from Chris.

"She loves this place," his brother said with admiration. "She would want to preserve it no matter what happened."

Nodding in agreement, Graham thought of her uncle. How he'd pestered Izzy to sell him the land, how he didn't even care enough to stay for the service when her grandpa died. That type of man didn't love anything except money. "That's something her uncle will never understand," Graham agreed.

"So she's leaving the place to Graham?" Chris asked Flynn.

"There's actually more to it than that," Flynn said. "In her will, she leaves the land to the city of Magic, with the stipulation that the hotel can't be torn down. But she left the hotel to one person — the same person she left as a trustee in charge of the land and the money that goes with it." The three men turned to look at Graham.

He shook his head slowly. How could she leave everything she loved to him? He didn't deserve it. He didn't deserve *her*. His voice was thick when he responded. "But I pushed her away at every turn. I wouldn't let her get close to me." How could she put so much trust in him?

"You're lucky." Chris looked at him knowingly. "She sees past all your bullshit whether you want her to or not. Guess you're not as good at hiding as you thought."

Swallowing, Graham tried to comprehend the situation. He'd treated Izzy like shit. She'd pushed and pushed, but he wouldn't let her in. He just shoved back. And what had she done? She'd laid her trust in him. The Lakewood – the one thing that meant more to her than anything in the world – and she trusted him with it.

Suddenly Graham felt as if someone was taking a sledgehammer to the ice around his heart. All of the love he'd bottled up for Izzy for so long began to flow out, and the barriers he'd constructed so carefully began to crumble. If she was going to put her love and her trust in him, he wanted to be the man who deserved it. He owed that to her.

Graham was pulling out his phone to put in a call to Dustin even as he looked at Theo for answers. The first step was making sure her bastard of an uncle couldn't hurt her. "Any idea where her uncle is?"

"I've been running Chris's tracking program," said Theo. "Our buddy Martin isn't using credit cards – at least not in his own name – or we would have found him by now."

"He's off the grid?" Chris asked.

Graham punched in the number on his phone to call his deputy. "Well, one thing is for damn sure. We have this place surrounded, so he's not getting near Izzy. No one can get into the party unless they're supposed to be here." As he half listened to the men, he repeated the details to Dustin and issued an APB on Martin Craig.

****

Shivering in the cool night air, Izzy missed the warmth of Graham's arms around her. Licking her lips, she savored the taste of him. Damn, why did they have to be interrupted?

"Are you cold?" Tessa asked, sipping her bottle of water. "We don't have to stay out here. We can go back inside to the party."

But she didn't want to go back. She was glad the guests seemed to be enjoying themselves, but right now she craved time alone with Graham and Chris. Graham had been on the verge of coming to his senses. She just knew it. When he and Chris were done talking to Flynn and Theo, they would come back. And this time, Izzy wasn't letting either one of them leave until they all finally admitted the truth in their hearts.

"No, I'd rather wait here," she said taking a seat in one of the patio chairs, listening to the low thrum of music coming from the party. "Do you know what was so important? What did Theo and Flynn want to talk about?"

Shaking her head, Tessa took a seat next to Izzy. She took another long swig of water. "I saw Theo and Chris talking pretty intensely, and then they came out here. I just followed them. When I saw Chris without you, I was worried that you might be alone somewhere."

An almost sad smile played at Tessa's mouth, and Izzy wondered if she knew how beautiful she was, even in green zombie makeup. "I should have known they wouldn't leave you alone. You're really lucky, you know? Graham and Chris are both amazing. And they love you so much, Iz."

Izzy thought of how Chris had refused to leave yesterday. She'd cried and tried to push him away, her pain too great after Graham had left. But Chris wouldn't leave. He wanted to share her burden, ease her pain. And she'd finally let him in. But Graham . . .

"I don't know, Tess." She shook her head. "Graham has done his best to pull away from me." She'd tried so hard for so long with the belief that Graham really did love her, and that he was just too afraid to admit it. When he'd finally made love to her, she thought that was finally it, and that she'd finally broken through. But now . . . maybe he really didn't love her. Maybe she'd just been too hopeful to see the truth.

"He told me yesterday he didn't love me," she admitted quietly.

A snort came from Tessa's pretty mouth, and she looked down, intently studying the cap of her water bottle. "And you believed him?"

When Izzy didn't answer, Tessa turned to look at her, and her smile turned into a look of almost disbelief. "Ohmigod, Iz, you *do* believe him. Seriously?"

"That's what he said, Tessa." Izzy sighed, wishing Graham weren't so baffling. "Yesterday, he's pushing me away, and then today, he . . ." She blushed as she raised a hand to touch her lips, still slightly swollen from the scrape of his beard.

"He kissed you, didn't he?" When Izzy said nothing, Tessa just grinned. "Yeah, he doesn't want you." She rolled her eyes to punctuate the sarcasm. "Whatever! Izzy, he's scared. Can't you see that?"

Izzy stood up and walked to the edge of the patio so she could look out over the lake. "I know he's scared. I'm scared, too. I don't think he realizes that. Tessa, I don't know what to do. I haven't done this before – a relationship with two men. I don't know how this is supposed to work." She ran her fingers over the concrete ledge. "It's not like this kind of relationship is exactly conventional."

"Then tell him how you feel." Tessa stood, leaning against the half wall next to Izzy. "And who cares about "conventional," she said using air quotes. "Jeez, Izzy, no two loves are the same. Everyone is different. It's always been so funny to me that society tries to confine everyone into these little boxes of normal and conventional, when the reality is those things don't exist. I hate to tell you, baby, but none of us are normal. So you sure as hell better not ever let that be your deciding factor. Besides, you have one hot man who doesn't seem to care about that. Chris certainly doesn't seem scared of moving forward. That boy is all over you."

Smiling at the thought of Chris, Izzy nodded. "Chris is sure of himself. I really envy that about him. He never seems to question what he wants. He just goes for it."

Tessa narrowed her eyes as she contemplated Izzy. "And that's a problem why, exactly?"

Izzy gave a slight shrug with her good arm. "He wants a relationship to work with the three of us."

"But that's what you want, too," Tessa said slowly. "So why does it scare you?"

Taking a long breath, Izzy looked out over the lake before sharing one of her biggest fears. "He's said twenty times how a relationship has never worked for him unless Graham's a part of it. So what if Graham never comes around? What if he walks away?"

"You're afraid Chris will walk away too, aren't you?"

Tears pooled in Izzy's eyes as the thought hit her of life without those two men. "I can't lose either of them, Tess." She loved them more than she could vocalize. At the thought of her life without Graham and Chris, Izzy felt like she couldn't even breathe.

"Then you have to go after them, Izzy. You have to fight," Tessa said fervently. "Time is too precious. You're so lucky. Do you know how many people live their whole lives and never find one person to truly love? You've found two, Iz! Two incredible men! And they love you. So what do you do? You grab them and hold on with all your might. Don't let go of them. You fight for your love because that's the only thing that's worth fighting for. Fight for your men, Izzy."

It was rare to see Tessa so serious. Izzy didn't realize she'd begun to cry until Tessa reached up to wipe a tear off her cheek. Then that notorious spark came back into Tessa's eyes. "And if anyone judges you for loving two men, then they can just go fuck themselves. And that's exactly what I plan to tell everyone."

As another tear fell, Izzy laughed and grabbed Tessa with her good arm for a fierce hug. She was lucky, and not just because she was in love with two incredible men, but also because she had the most amazing friends.

When she let go of Tessa, she backed up to tell her just that, but a sound coming from the bushes next to the patio gate behind her caught her attention. The crunch of leaves sent a cold shiver up her spine. "What was that?" she asked, hearing a soft 'poof' sound.

When Tessa didn't answer, Izzy turned back to look at her. "Tessa?" Tessa's face was frozen for a split second before blood began to bloom near her stomach. For a brief moment, Izzy thought it was some kind of zombie makeup, but then Tessa slumped forward and Izzy lunged to catch her, the pain in her right arm barely noticeable as she struggled out of the sling to steady her friend. "Ohmigod, Tessa!" Izzy screamed as she lowered her friend to the ground.

"Quiet!" A voice said sharply. Izzy looked up to see Josh step out from behind the bushes.

Josh? No. No. This didn't make sense. Izzy opened her mouth to scream, but it froze on her lips as Josh leveled the gun at her head. "I said, 'quiet.'" He was calm, too calm. She'd never seen him like this before. Usually he was fumbling and nervous, always happy to help. This man had a hard face and dead eyes. "If you scream, I will put a bullet in your skull before either of your boyfriends get out here."

Izzy leaned over Tessa as if to protect her friend from more harm. Josh smiled a cruel smile. "Better yet, why don't we finish off your friend here? The world would be a better place without such a slut in it anyway."

As Tessa began to stir, Izzy squeezed her arm tightly as a warning for her to keep still. She leaned over her friend, and buried her face in Tessa's hair. On a sob, she whispered, "Don't move. Be still and just don't move. Please, Tessa."

When she lifted her head, she turned to look straight at Josh. "She's already dead, damn you!" She cried. "You killed her!" Izzy's tears of anguish were quite real. If Tessa didn't get to a hospital soon, she would die. She needed help. Her eyes darted around frantically, looking for something . . . an escape, an idea, someone to help. But there was nothing.

A humorless chuckle escaped Josh. "No one is coming to help you. Not this time." There was a glint in his eyes that she'd never seen before. He was truly crazy. She prayed that Tessa would remain still so he wouldn't shoot her again. Izzy shifted in an attempt to block Tessa's body with her own so he wouldn't see she was still breathing.

"Now," he said in a dangerous voice, "Get up, bitch. You're coming with me."

Izzy shrank back. She couldn't let him take her away. No, they'd never find her. She shook her head. "You are out of your mind if you think I'm going anywhere with you."

Josh had opened the gate to walk onto the patio, and Izzy saw that he was still wearing his hotel uniform of a black shirt and khakis. She had a fleeting thought of how annoyed she'd been that he hadn't been wearing a costume.

His black shoes clicked on the stone of the patio as he walked over and stood only three feet from her. Oh, please don't let him see that Tessa is still breathing. Izzy moved her hand to grasp Tessa's wrist, keeping track of her pulse as her eyes stayed on Josh.

"I don't think you understand. I'm not asking you, Izzy. If you don't seem concerned with me shooting you, then how about we just wait here? I'm sure Sheriff Dickhead and his brother will be back out soon looking for you. They'll be hysterical when they find the bodies of you and Tessa. In fact, they probably wouldn't be expecting someone in the shadows to take them out." He pointed to the silencer on his gun. "And with this little baby, no one will even hear the shot."

Everything inside of Izzy went cold. No, not Chris, not Graham. At that moment, she knew she would do anything she could to protect them.

"N-no." Her voice shook. "I'll do anything you want. Just please don't hurt anyone else."

"Good, I'm glad we understand each other." His smile turned into almost a snarl. "Now, get your ass up, and come with me. We're going to take a little ride."

As Izzy began to rise, she felt Tessa's hand squeeze tightly around hers. Tessa could hear him. Oh, thank God. She would be able to tell them it was Josh. Even if Izzy didn't make it through this, they would know it was him, and he wouldn't be able to hurt anyone else.

"Where are we going?" she asked as she rose shakily.

"No time for questions," he said, reaching forward to grab her harshly by her bad arm. Izzy cried out as pain exploded through her at his tight grip.

"I can hurt you a hell of a lot worse than that," said Josh, shoving the gun into her side. "Now do what I say so you don't have to find out just how much."

As Josh took Izzy's arm in a steel grip, she clenched her teeth, warring with the haze of pain that started to blur her vision. Finally, he adjusted his grip, and she gasped for breath in relief.

As he tugged her to the patio gate, she turned to take one last look at her friend. Oh please, someone find her soon. Izzy was worried about the amount of blood that was pooling around Tessa. It was too much blood. She had to be okay. She just had to. *God, please send someone to help her.*

"Come on!" Josh said in an irritated voice as he shoved Izzy through the gate. He wrapped his arm around her waist and jammed his gun in her ribs so hard that she winced. His eyes darted around, making sure there wasn't anyone out there to pay attention to them.

With the day's rain and the cold weather, everyone was inside. The guards that were positioned outside were most likely at the front by the main doors. And even then, they wouldn't give Josh a second look. He was supposed to be here. He was on the approved list. She looked around for some form of escape, but with only one arm to work with, she didn't have many options. The hope in Izzy started to drift further away.

Josh led her straight toward the front parking lot, and kept Izzy anchored close to his side. Light streaked over the dark lot. He could kill her right now if he wanted too. No one inside would hear. He could shoot her and just leave her for dead.

Izzy's thoughts were beginning to drift as Josh led her to her own car, a black CR-V. Her brow furrowed. "I – what are we doing at my car?"

"Do you really think I'm going to drive?" Josh released her for a moment to pull keys out of his pocket. "Here, I had copies of your keys made last week."

He opened the driver's door and started to shove her in. Never go to a second location. Izzy knew if she got in the car with him, any hope she had of survival was very slim. *Dateline* had taught her that. She turned her body so he wouldn't be able to shove her in so easily and braced herself against the car.

"Why should I go anywhere with you? You're going to kill me anyway. Just do it here," she said defiantly. If she was going to die, she didn't want to be lost somewhere. She didn't want to be one of those people you read about on the news who went missing for months until some hiker found their skeleton in the woods. No, she wouldn't do that to the people she cared about. Her breath hitched. She wouldn't do that to Chris or Graham.

"This is not a debate, bitch! Get in!"

"I don't think she's going to listen, Ramiro."

The dark voice startled both Izzy and Josh. She whirled to look at the person walking around the side of the car and was flooded with momentary relief. "Uncle Martin!" She started to step toward him, but halted as he rounded the car to face her, a gun in his hand.

Was he aiming at Josh? She looked into his grim expression, and then back at the gun. No. He was aiming at her. "That's who you're working for," she said almost to herself rather than Josh.

"You always were a smart girl," Martin said condescendingly. "And you," he said, looking at Josh, "You should have had her out of here by now." While Martin was talking, he stepped to the back of the car, and hit the button to pop open the trunk of Izzy's SUV.

"Well, she wouldn't get in the damn car. That's a good idea, though," Josh said, shoving her forward toward Martin. "We can put her in the trunk. I brought duct tape so we can tie her up." He stepped back from Izzy and turned to rummage around in the trunk.

"Oh, that won't be necessary, my boy," said Martin.

Josh turned to him looking confused. "Well, we can't just let her roam free."

At the evil glint in Martin's eye, Izzy suspected what he was planning. In a split second, the gun that was trained on Izzy was all of a sudden pointed at Josh. The younger man's eyes widened in surprise as Martin pumped two bullets into his chest. Josh's face froze, forever locked in a stunned expression as he fell backward into the trunk.

Izzy opened her mouth to scream, but Martin was wrapping an arm around her, his hand moving up to cover her mouth and nose firmly. She couldn't breathe. She struggled, needing air, but Martin only held her tighter.

"Now you listen to me, you little bitch. I'm not playing games. You will do exactly what I fucking say."

Izzy began to panic, struggling to be free of his grip. Her eyes bulged.

"You get in that fucking car and drive, or I will kill you and everyone left that you love." She could feel his harsh breath on her ear. "Don't fuck with me."

Finally, he released his hand over her face and Izzy gasped in deep breaths, bending over in relief as the wonderful air filled her lungs. Martin slammed the trunk with Josh's body inside. Before Izzy could get her bearings, Martin had a grip on her arm, dragging her around and shoving her in the passenger side of the car. He followed her in, his grip on her arm never wavering as he thrust her behind the steering wheel.

Izzy was still trying to catch her breath as Martin pushed the keys in the ignition and sat back to unscrew the silencer from the barrel of his gun. In the back of Izzy's mind – the part that was having trouble grasping the whole situation as reality – she wondered if there had been a sale on silencers.

"Don't really need this anymore, do we?" Martin asked, tossing it aside. He pressed the barrel of the gun hard against Izzy's temple.

"Drive, Isabel. Now," he said calmly.

With a shaky hand, Izzy started the ignition, and prayed that somehow Graham and Chris could save her.

****

They needed to do everything by the book to make damn sure every charge against Martin Craig would stick. It should be a hell of a lot easier to catch the son of a bitch now that they knew who they were looking for. Except a couple of things still bothered Graham.

"I want to make sure we have everything laid out in an official capacity before we bring in Izzy and tell her everything. And I want to find out who else is working for Martin." What would it do to Izzy once she knew that the only family she had left was trying to kill her?

He looked at his brother. They were her family now. She completed them. No matter how much the information about Martin hurt her, they would be there for her to make sure no one ever caused her pain again.

After confirming with Dustin, Graham knew that Martin had alibis for the time of the fire and for the time Izzy was shot. "He has alibis, so this means he's got somebody doing his dirty work."

Graham felt the unease start in his gut again, and he longed to lay his eyes on Izzy. It had been a few minutes since she'd been outside with Tessa. And he just had the urge to look at her, make sure she was okay. He knew that no one could get by security if they didn't belong at the party, but the thought didn't comfort him now. He looked at Chris, and his brother nodded, an unspoken understanding passing between them.

They both began to rise when Flynn spoke to Theo. "You never said why it took so long to find out Martin Craig was behind this?"

Theo responded, "That was the hard part. We kept running into roadblocks with the shell corps listed behind the holdings company. That was where the red flag immediately went up for me. Someone was going to a lot of lengths to hide their identity, including setting up more than ten shell companies under a false name."

Andrea walked over with a tray in her hand and leaned in to set drinks down in front of Theo and Flynn, eliciting smiles of admiration from the two men.

Theo turned back to Graham, "Does the name Joshua Ramiro mean anything to you? That was the name behind the shell companies, but we couldn't find any information on someone with that name, so it's most likely an alias."

The gasp that came from Andrea had all the men's attention turning toward her, and Graham's uneasiness turned into a sense of dread as he watched all of the color drain from her face, the empty tray slipping out of her hands.

Flynn rose to snatch the tray before it hit the ground as Graham stepped over to Andi, gripping her arm harder than he intended. "You know him?" he barked, inadvertently causing her to flinch.

"Hey, easy, Nolan," Flynn said, shoving at Graham's chest with one hand, as he put a comforting arm around Andi.

"I know him," she said in a shocked voice. "Josh. It's Josh."

"Wait, what do you mean Josh?" asked Chris. "You mean night manager Josh? We looked into him. His last name is Capello."

Graham watched his brother's eyes roll upward as he tried to recall information. "Joshua Robert Capello. Parents are Jim and Donna Capello. They live in St. Charles, Missouri." Chris shook his head. "What makes you think he's Joshua Ramiro?"

"His computer," Andrea said, swallowing. "He was having problems logging into the computer at the front desk. When I helped him, he gave me his password." Andi spoke so softly, the men had to strain to listen. "Ramiro. His password was Ramiro. He said it was his grandmother's maiden name." Suddenly she looked at Graham with dread on her face. "Graham, I haven't seen him all night." Panic filled her voice. "He was supposed to help serve, but he never showed up. I don't know where he is."

But the men were already running. Izzy. They had to get to Izzy. He darted around people in the ballroom, heading in the direction of the patio. Never did he think the person trying to kill her was someone who was close to her, someone who had been under their noses every day.

He ran down the hall, his throat closing off. Izzy. She had to be okay. She had to.

Chris reached the patio door a heartbeat before Graham did. When they wrenched the door open, Chris let out a strangled sound at the bleeding woman lying on the ground. The world seemed to come to a halt. The gauzy dress, the zombie makeup. Graham stopped breathing.

Somewhere behind him there was a scream, and Andi pushed past him to kneel next to her friend. "Tessa, Tess." Tears streamed down her face.

Tessa. It was Tessa. Dark hair, not blonde. It wasn't Izzy. A slight modicum of relief hit Graham. It wasn't Izzy. As the world started to spin again, he yanked out his phone to call for an ambulance. "We need a bus. Now!" he shouted into the phone.

Milo pushed past, "What's going on? I heard a scream. Where's —" When he noticed Tessa, his eyes widened, and he looked like all the blood drained from him. He collapsed at Tessa's side. "Ambulance. Call an ambulance."

Milo gathered Tessa to him. He was more gentle than Graham had ever seen as he tenderly cradled her head in his arms. "Baby," Milo whispered, "don't leave me." A sob escaped him.

When Tessa's lids fluttered opened, Graham breathed a sigh of relief. She was alive. But where was Izzy?

"Tessa." He knelt on her other side, trying to avoid the growing pool of blood. "Tessa, look at me."

She struggled to sit, gasping, and moving a hand to her abdomen where the blood bloomed out. Milo eased her back down, already yanking off his bar apron, pressing it to her wound. She screamed as he pressed, and Graham tried to divert her attention.

"Tessa, please, please, where's Izzy? Do you know where she is?" he begged. If Tessa was shot, then Izzy could be . . . no, he wouldn't let himself think it.

Tessa's pale lips held a slight blue tint and she took short gasping breaths. "Josh," she panted out. "Josh, he – he had a gun." She panted again, choking on a laugh. "Fucking ob-obviously, right?" she said, wincing as she attempted to gesture toward her stomach.

Milo smirked as he stroked her hair. "Always time for sarcasm, isn't there, pet?"

"I don't know where —" She grimaced. "I don't know where. He said—" Her eyes started to drift shut.

"Stay with me, Tessa!" Milo practically yelled, startling her to open her eyes. "You stay with me," he said more softly.

"He said what, Tessa?" Chris asked. "Did he say where he was taking Izzy?"

She shook her head slightly. "Said he'd kill her. Said he'd finish me off." Her words began to slur. "Parking lot. Told her to come with him."

"Thank you, Tessa." Graham just hoped they weren't too late. He didn't take the time to unlock the gate off the patio. Instead, he hopped the concrete wall, and ran as fast as he could to the front lot. . . just in time to see Izzy's car speeding off.

"They're in her car!" he yelled at Chris, who was right behind him. "Come on!"

Graham ran to his police car, followed by Chris, and stopped in his tracks. "Mother fuck!"

His hands fisted as rage filled him. All four tires on his patrol car were slashed to shreds. Izzy was gone, and he couldn't save her.

Chapter Fourteen

"It's not just you. All of the tires in the employees' section of the lot have been slashed." Chris clenched his fists. "Fuck! He had a plan to get her out of here, and we can't follow him." Circling like a caged animal, he tried to control his anger so he could think.

"We're losing time, dammit." Graham was hastily checking tires on cars, and Chris had no doubt he was ready to commandeer the first one he found where they were intact.

"What happened?" Andi asked, hastily running up, followed by Flynn. She still had tears in her eyes, and her blue and white dress was covered with Tessa's blood.

"They're in Izzy's car, except we don't have a way to follow them." Chris ran to look in the next row of the lot, hoping he would have more luck than Graham, who uttered curse after curse as he searched.

"Let me check mine," said Flynn. As he turned to run to his car, a large red truck pulled into the lot blocking his path.

An angry-looking man jumped out, his brown hair mussed, and his icy gaze focusing on Andi. The smaller woman flinched back as Flynn's face tightened, immediately putting a hand on her shoulder.

"Brian," Andi said in a near whisper. "What are you doing here? You weren't supposed to be home until later."

Brian Milton reached out to grab his wife's arm as she cowered back into Flynn.

"Andrea," Brian stepped toward her. "I told you not to come here tonight. You were to wait for me at home. We are leaving. Get in the truck. Now."

Flynn opened his mouth to respond as Graham came rushing up, badge in hand. Flashing it at Brian, he said, "We need your truck." He motioned at Chris. "Get in."

Brian's eyes flared slightly before his lips thinned in anger. "But – but, you can't just take my truck."

"Oh yes, we can. Out of my way, Milton." Graham effectively shoved past the gaping man, climbed in the truck and threw it in drive. Chris jumped in the passenger seat as Graham barreled out of the lot, and he hoped they weren't too far behind Izzy.

****

The gun pressed harder against Izzy's temple, making her wince.

"Turn left, and drive faster!" Martin ordered.

She took a deep breath in a futile effort to remain calm as she turned. He was taking her up the mountain. At the end of the Lakewood road, you could either turn right and drive through town, or you could turn left and head up into the Ozark Mountains. Izzy did not like driving on the twisty mountain roads in bad weather. Especially now when she had a gun to her head and was steering with only one arm as a steady rain pounded on the windshield.

She snuck a glance at Martin. He looked nervous and kept checking the mirrors, looking out the back window. It was a small comfort that he seemed concerned someone would come for her. And they *would* come for her. She knew they would. She just had to buy herself some time. Slowing the car more than necessary around a curve, she could feel her uncle's frustration as the gun jerked against her temple.

"Why are you going so slow? Hurry up!" he demanded.

"I'm trying not to get us both killed. The mountain roads get terribly slick in the rain, and I only have one hand to steer with here, or did you forget?" Her sling had been left behind at the hotel, but Izzy tucked her left arm close to her body. From the throbbing of her upper arm and the blood on her sleeve, she knew her stitches had ripped open where Josh had grabbed her earlier.

Casting a glance at Martin, Izzy bit her tongue to keep her sarcasm in check. Making him angrier probably wasn't a smart idea. "I can't go much faster right now unless you want me sliding off the road. It would also help if you told me where we're going."

"Just drive." He flicked a glance behind the car once more.

Thinking maybe she could try a different tactic, Izzy asked, "Why are you doing this? Why are you trying to hurt me?"

Martin's smile came off as an evil sneer as he let out a laugh. "You don't get it, do you? You thought just because you strolled into town three years ago, you could take what was rightfully mine?"

Her brow furrowed in utter confusion. "What are you talking about?"

"My land, you stupid bitch." Martin seemed manic, going from laughing to nervous to angry. He really was insane. This wasn't the man she remembered. The Martin she knew may have been a little sleazy, but he was always quiet and non-threatening. And now, Izzy wondered if there was any way she could reach a shred of sanity in him.

"It should have gone to me." He spoke again. "I put in the work on all those studies. I'm the one who discovered how much the resources on that land are worth. Richard didn't even care. He could have been richer than his wildest dreams, and the bastard didn't even care. But he was sick, so I waited patiently. And then what happens? He leaves it all to you!"

Her grandpa left it to her because he loved the Lakewood and didn't want it destroyed. Martin would never understand that. Izzy took another curve slowly as the rain began to pummel the car even harder. "What does all of that matter now?" she asked.

"Don't you get it? In the event of *your* death, the land goes to me. All this," Martin waved the gun around in a wide gesture, "goes to me. My land. My money. Sorry I don't have a more grandiose reason, little girl, but in the end, it's all about the money."

Realization hit Izzy with full force. He didn't realize she had her own will. He didn't get the land. The city inherited it. Graham inherited it. This time she was the one who laughed, a hysterical giggle bubbling up before she could stop it.

"What? What's so funny?" His annoyance with her was palpable.

"You," she snorted. "Well, I don't know if funny is the right word for you. Maybe dumbass. Dumbass is a better word." She glanced over to see Martin's face grow red as she slowed the car even more, buying herself precious seconds.

"Watch it, Isabel. You don't want to make me angry," he said in a warning tone, gripping the gun tighter.

"Make you angry? You're going to kill me," she said with disbelief. "Does it really matter what I say now?" Fury began to replace the fear inside of her. And without waiting for an answer, she continued. "You're going to be really angry when you realize this was all for nothing."

"I wouldn't call a few hundred million nothing. And if you're so smug because you think your boyfriends have me all figured out, then think again. I covered all my tracks, Isabel. I have an alibi for the time you were shot and an alibi for the fire. Your sheriff knows someone was trying to buy your land, but a holdings company is the only firm ever listed as the party attempting to make that purchase. If they dig a little further, they'll find that the companies behind it are all in the name of Joshua Ramiro."

"Josh?" She still couldn't process the fact that someone she'd worked so closely with had tried to kill her. "You think you're setting Josh up? They're never going to believe he was some criminal mastermind."

"Oh, I think they will. You see, you and Josh are never going to be found. Maybe they'll think Josh killed you in a jealous rage. Or maybe they'll see you for the little slut you are and think you ran off with him. Either way, they're never going to find your bodies. And me? Well, I'll just be the poor, grieving uncle."

Bile surged up in her throat. She would never see her men again. Never look into those steel blue eyes. Never hear Chris's laugh, or feel Graham's strong hand cradling her head as he kissed her.

She looked at her uncle, this evil man who wanted to take everything away from her. She wasn't going to let him do it without a fight. A cruel smile crossed her face. "Poor uncle is right. Because you're not going to be inheriting shit, you worthless goon."

Narrowing his eyes at her, Martin couldn't hide his frustration. "Of course I am. What are you talking about?"

"You're such an idiot," Izzy said angrily. "Do you honestly think I wouldn't have my own will? Yeah, if I died and there was no will in place, you would have gotten the land. But I drew up my own will right after my grandpa died. You get nothing, Martin. The land goes to the city of Magic, not you. Oh, and don't get the bright idea of trying to buy it because there's a codicil in my will to make sure no one tears down the hotel. So good luck with that."

Izzy almost wanted to laugh at the way the color drained from Martin's face making him look older than he was.

"You're lying," he bit out, disbelievingly.

The car fishtailed around a curve, and Izzy hit the brake. *Slow down,* she told herself.

She shot a glare at her uncle. "No, you imbecile. I'm not lying. They're going to figure out everything you did. You're going to fry for this, and when you do die, you're going to die penniless."

A sound that couldn't be described as anything other than pure animalistic rage came out of Martin. He seemed to snap, his face a twisted mask of fury. As he screamed at Izzy, he brought the butt of his gun down hard on the side of her head.

Stars swam in front of her vision as the car swerved. Blinking, she jerked the steering wheel, but her vision dimmed, and she was unable to right the car. A scream tore from her throat as the car plunged over the embankment into the trees below.

****

Raindrops struck the windshield like little fists hammering in frustration on the glass, echoing the pounding of Graham's heart. Where was she? Where the hell was she?

"They couldn't have traveled far," Chris said in answer. He gripped the armrest tightly as Graham sped toward the main road, but didn't ask him to slow down.

Graham knew his brother was just as anxious to get to Izzy as he was. They had to find her. They had to get to her before anything happened to her.

When they reached the main road, Graham paused and looked at Chris. He knew Martin wouldn't take her through town. Someone might see them. The only other way to go was left through the mountains. The memory of finding Alicia off the side of that mountain came into his head, but Graham quickly pushed it aside. He turned left and gunned the engine. The only thing that mattered right now was Izzy. *Just please let her be okay. Please please please let her be okay.*

The two men were silent as Graham maneuvered the treacherous roads. The only thing he could think of was how he'd pushed Izzy away. When he thought of the nasty things he'd said to her the night before, he felt nauseated. She had to know he didn't mean it. *I love you, Izzy.* He tried to send her silent strength. *I love you. Just hold on.*

When he found her, he was never going to let her go again. She was going to have to put up with him every day for the rest of her life. And if she didn't want him, then he would still be there for her, watching her, protecting her.

He noticed Chris staring at him. "She knows, man. Deep down she knows how you feel."

Clenching the wheel, Graham forced himself to take a deep breath. "I couldn't handle something happening to her and her thinking that I . . ."

"Don't say that. Nothing's going to happen to her. We're going to find her," Chris said adamantly.

Just like his brother, Graham couldn't handle the alternative. He couldn't think about what might happen if they were too late. *We won't be too late. We won't.*

The truck skidded as he took a sharp curve at high speed. "We've got to be catching up to them. No way Josh could be going that fast. He doesn't know the area that well."

"And Izzy would stall him if she could," Chris agreed. "She'd do everything she could to slow him down."

As the road curved again, the guardrail to the side disappeared. Graham was familiar with this area. Way too many accidents occurred at this junction – too many cars that took the curve too fast.

"There!" Chris shouted, pointing.

Graham's blood went cold as he saw the skid marks going off the side of the road into nothingness.

The bottom fell out of his stomach. "No, no no no," he chanted as he pulled to the side. He told himself the skid marks might not be fresh. But deep down, he knew.

As he and Chris swung open the doors on the truck, the smell of burnt rubber confirmed that the skid marks were recent. Both men rushed to where the skid marks went over the side, and without hesitation, the brothers began making their way down the steep hill, sliding down as they tried to gain footing.

When they got about halfway down, Graham began yelling. "Izzy! Isabel, answer me!"

****

Pain pulsed through Izzy's temple. She tried to move, but that just caused the ache in her forehead to throb. She moaned as she opened her eyes. Wetness trickled down the side of her forehead, and she reached up to swipe the rain away with a shaky hand. Her fingertips came back red, and she realized it wasn't rain, but blood that was dripping into her eyes.

She took several deep breaths trying to stave off the nausea that threatened. Forcing herself to move, Izzy cried out as pain stabbed through her left side. The door handle was jammed into her ribs, and when she moved, the agony in her side almost took her breath away.

The air bag, there was an inflated air bag. Then why was her head bleeding? Sucking in shallow breaths, Izzy gave her head a little shake, trying to gather her thoughts. Looking to her right, she saw Martin Craig slumped forward in his seat, and it all came rushing back to her. She had been driving, and she'd angered him. He'd been so mad that he'd hit her in the head.

She reached up again to touch the right side of her head that was bleeding. That's where he'd hit her with the gun. Then the car must have gone over the embankment.

As the fog began to clear from her brain, Izzy looked around for an escape. She had to get out of here. Looking at Martin, she couldn't tell if he was dead or just unconscious. He was slumped over the dash with blood wet on his face, and his door was hanging open at an odd angle. He hadn't been wearing a seatbelt, and his head must have hit the windshield.

She didn't have time to contemplate whether or not he was still alive. She just knew she needed to get out of there. She reached for her handle and pulled, but nothing happened. She bit her lip against the pain in her ribs and her left arm, and shoved hard against the door, but it didn't budge. "Shit! Shit crap dammit fuck!" She said in a loud whisper.

If she couldn't get out of the driver's side door . . . . she looked over at the open passenger door that loomed just a few feet away. Only a few feet. She just had to get past Martin. She could do this. She had to. She thought of Graham and Chris. She had to get back to them. The thought of her two men gave her the strength she needed. She unhooked her seatbelt, and took a deep breath, wincing, and swiped at her temple one more time. Reaching over with her right hand, she gripped Martin's arm and firmly pulled him back against the seat. His head lolled back and she thought she heard a light groan. Shit! He wasn't dead. She had to get out of there before he woke up.

Stifling a whimper, Izzy scooted as far over to him in the seat as she could. Taking as steadying breath, she swung a leg over to straddle him. He groaned again, and she froze. *Please don't wake up.*

She moved her left leg out of the door to gain footing on the ground, and used her good hand to brace herself on the side of the door before dragging her right leg slowly across Martin's lap. *Almost there.*

With a grunt, his eyes opened. He looked dazed, and Izzy scooted as quickly as she could out the passenger door. Realization came quickly for Martin, and before she could get her leg completely free, he grabbed her ankle, sending her tumbling to the ground, landing hard on her rear. A cry stuck in her chest as Izzy used every ounce of strength she had to push the pain aside.

She kicked at Martin's hand. "Let go of me!"

With a growl, he gripped tighter onto her ankle, leaning over to reach for her. Izzy took a deep breath, bent her left leg, and kicked out as hard as she could. Her foot caught Martin in the side of the face with a heavy thud. She didn't know if she'd actually hurt him, but she startled him enough that he let go of her ankle.

This was the opportunity she needed. She scrambled up as quickly as she could and half ran/half stumbled toward the trees. The rain was coming down a bit lighter now, but Izzy slipped on the mud as she went, feeling as if the ground was sucking at her feet. She was almost there, almost to the trees.

Skidding on the mud, she fell on her bandaged arm, unable to catch herself, and she gasped for breath, stars swimming in front of her vision. She heard a loud crack as a bullet pinged off a tree. "Get back here, you bitch!"

He was shooting at her. *No. She wouldn't die here.* Almost to the trees. She could hear the wet stomping footsteps. How close was he? She didn't take the chance of looking back, and managed to get up and duck behind a clump of trees as another bullet zinged past. She paused for just a moment to catch her breath before zigzagging from one tree to another. She needed a plan. Where was she going? *Think, Izzy.* She moved to another tree, and then another, praying that he wouldn't be able to make out her footsteps in the darkness.

"Isabel, oh, Isabel," came Martin's sing-songy voice. He was on her left, only a couple hundred yards away. She paused to take several breaths and tucked her sore arm around her side in an attempt to protect herself from any more injury.

"Isabel." His voice was getting closer. "Let's work something out. Let's talk about this." Talk? He really was crazy. She wished she had some sort of weapon. Searching the darkness, she tried to find something, anything she could use.

And then she remembered her phone. Tessa had fashioned a pocket on their dresses to look like a bloody zombie wound. *Even zombies need a place to carry their lipstick*, she'd said.

Oh, thank God for Tessa. Izzy reached into her pocket, fumbling for her phone when she heard the stomping footsteps getting closer. Not wanting Martin to close the distance, she sprinted to the next tree, and then the next, making her way further into the forestry.

She peeked around the tree, and didn't spot Martin anywhere behind her. Getting her bearings, Izzy realized she was near Vivian's. If she could just get to the older woman's house, she knew Vivian had weapons, knew where her spare key was. But first she had to get a hold of Graham and Chris, had to alert them to where she was. *Oh please, let me get a signal on this damn mountain.*

As she fumbled again for her phone, she heard footsteps, except in front of her this time. She froze. Oh no, he'd circled around. Instead of following her, Martin had circled around the clearing. She clicked her phone on. She could still call her men. Even if she couldn't talk, they'd be able to hear her, to trace where she was.

Before she could dial, music exploded out of her phone. *"So what. I'm still a rock star, I've got my rock moves, and I don't need you."* She gasped, trying to silence the phone, but it was too late.

Martin rounded the corner, his gun in one hand raised at her head. In his other hand, he waved his cell phone at her. "Did you forget I had your number?" An evil smile lit his face. "Got you, bitch."

****

Halfway down the embankment, Chris flinched at the loud crack. He could swear his heart stopped. "That was a gunshot. Fuck, Graham, that was a gunshot."

He caught site of his brother's pale face before the two of them slid the rest of the way down the embankment. A gunshot. He couldn't let himself think they might be too late. *Hang on, Izzy. Just hang on.*

When they reached the bottom, they spotted Izzy's car. The driver's side was wedged against a tree, the windshield cracked and splintered, airbags deployed. And it was empty. She was still alive. "Either she ran, or Josh took her," Chris panted as he tried to catch his breath.

Graham shook his head, his grim face set, staring at something near the back of the car. "No, it doesn't look like Josh took her anywhere."

Chris rounded the car and followed Graham's gaze. The trunk to the SUV was open, and Josh's body was half out, eyes open and dilated.

"Looks like a gunshot wound," Graham said, as he quickly reached down to feel for a pulse.

Chris shook his head, confused. "If it's not him, then who . . ."

"Martin," Graham said. "Fuck." He ran a hand through his hair. "Martin's got her."

As the two men made their way to the passenger side of the car, they found the door open, and two sets of footprints leading away.

"This way," Graham said, pointing to the trees, running.

At the tree line, both men stopped at the two diverging sets of footprints. Chris breathed a momentary sigh of relief. Maybe she got away. "These are Izzy's footprints. They have to be. They're smaller." He began to start in the direction of her footprints, but Graham didn't move.

"Wait." Graham held a hand up to stop him. "He's circling. He saw her footprints too, so he knows which way she went. He's circling to head her off."

Chris felt stuck, not knowing what to do to save her, and he looked to his brother for help. "What do we do? Tell me what to do."

Graham unholstered his gun. "You follow Izzy's footprints. Go after her, but be quiet. If Martin hasn't gotten to her, you don't want to attract attention. I'm going to go this way and see if I can get to him before he finds her."

Unspoken emotion passed between the brothers. They both knew this was it. Either they saved Izzy now, or it was all over.

"Be careful, brother," Graham finally said, and despite his strong, professional demeanor, Chris knew the truth. He knew that Graham was dying a little inside at the thought that they could lose Izzy.

Chris swallowed hard and gave Graham a short nod before turning to follow Izzy's tracks. They were hard to follow in the dark, but he had Graham's extra penlight, which made it easier. Tree to tree in a zigzag pattern. His girl was smart.

As he quickly moved along, following every track, he heard a voice, but not Izzy's. He stopped cold.

"Isabel. Oh, Isabel."

The sing-songy voice was coming from the right, and not that far ahead of him. Chris moved slowly, not wanting the crunch of his footsteps to be heard. Where was Graham? Had he made his way around yet? As Chris moved silently, he thought he saw movement up ahead, and he turned off the penlight so he wouldn't be spotted.

Suddenly, he was startled by the song from Izzy's phone. It was directly to his right behind the tree. *"So what, I'm still a rock star."*

He moved quietly and quickly, the noise from the phone covering the sound of his movements until he was at the next tree.

At that moment, the clouds seemed to clear, and the light of the moon glinted off the leaves, almost illuminating Izzy. Except she wasn't alone. Eric Jacobs stepped in front of her. Eric Jacobs was Martin Craig. "Got you, bitch."

He aimed the gun at Izzy. And at that moment, Chris stepped forward. "Not so fucking fast."

Startled, Izzy spun around to face Chris, her back to Martin. The older man took the opportunity to grab her. His arm went around her neck, squeezing, his gun pressed to her temple. As he yanked her against him, she cried out, her face twisting in pain. "Back the fuck up, Nolan. Or she's dead."

Chris held his hands up to show that he wasn't armed. His eyes focused on Izzy, and he winced at the blood drizzling down her forehead. Her eyes were wild, and she was so fucking pale. What had that monster done to her? "Sweetheart, look at me. Are you okay?"

He watched as Izzy took a shaky breath. "I'm okay," she said weakly. But he could tell she wasn't. Chris inched closer, and stopped immediately at Izzy's gasp as Martin pressed the gun harder against her head. "I said back up, Nolan. Don't fucking come any closer. I will kill her. Do you think I won't?"

Chris stopped. If ever in his life he needed to sweet talk someone, now was the time. All he had to do was stall. Graham was here, coming around the clearing. He would come up on them from a different angle. Chris just had to keep Martin talking until he arrived.

"Don't hurt her!" he yelled. If Graham was anywhere close, Chris wanted to make sure he knew exactly where they were.

****

Chris's voice was like a beacon to Graham as he made his way through the trees. He could hear his brother talking loudly, asking why Martin had felt the need to dress up like Eric Jacobs. *That's it, brother. Keep him talking.* As he came up on the group of trees, he could see that Martin held Izzy in a tight grip.

Graham's hands tightened as he saw Izzy very clearly. Her blonde hair was stained with blood, and her face looked pale. Too pale. Her left arm was bloodied, and she clutched it against her side in obvious pain. As red clouded his vision, Graham forced himself to calm down. He couldn't let his rage lead him, or he would get them all killed.

Switching into cop mode, he assessed the situation. Martin had an arm around Izzy's neck, and a gun pressed to her temple. *Shit.* The way they were positioned prevented Graham from getting a good shot. He was almost to the side of them. If he tried to move behind them, the tree blocked him from Martin completely, and if he moved in front of them, he couldn't take a shot without the danger that he might hit Izzy. *Dammit.* He either needed them to move forward, or he needed Izzy to move away from Martin completely before he could get a shot. If he could only get her attention.

"Why drag Josh into this? What is he to you?" Chris was asking.

That's it, brother. Keep going. Martin seemed almost happy to talk about what he'd done, proud. It made Graham sick to listen to him brag about how he'd set up the shell companies to con Izzy.

Sweet Izzy. Her dazed look told him she was going into shock. He'd seen it before. *Stay with me, baby. Just stay with me a little longer.* He needed her to calm down. He couldn't do this without her help. The way Martin had her positioned, her head was in the crook of his arm. She was almost facing Graham. He might be able to get her attention without alerting Martin.

As he moved more into the clearing, the moonlight glinted off the barrel of his gun, and he waved it slightly in the light, trying to get Izzy's attention.

****

Chris's voice was the only thing that kept her from panicking. Izzy knew that if she died right now, at least she wouldn't be alone. Chris was here with her. She got to see him one last time. She only wished Graham were here too. She almost sobbed. She hoped he knew she forgave him for pulling away. She knew he loved her, she could see it, feel it. He'd been scared, but it was okay. Her fear was that he would blame himself for this. It wasn't his fault.

She tried to squirm, but Martin's grasp only firmed around her neck, nearly cutting off her air. She stilled, making sure she could get in a breath. Her body had gone numb now. She was grateful she couldn't feel the pain anymore. Her legs felt weaker, and she knew she was starting to fade.

Chris kept Martin talking, asking questions about every detail of his plan. Chris almost acted as though he admired Martin, and her uncle was eating it up. *Smug son of a bitch.*

But why was Chris talking so loudly? Maybe her perception was off. Maybe his voice seemed louder than it was. Or maybe . . . was he trying to get someone's attention?

Graham. Oh God, Chris wouldn't come here by himself. Suddenly Izzy knew. Graham was here. Chris was stalling. Her eyes sharpened, and she tried to look around as best she could. She locked eyes with Chris, and just barely caught his slight head tilt to her right. Izzy's eyes flicked sideways, and she saw the glinting of a light, or was it a light?

A gun. It was the metal from a gun. Graham stepped out of the shadows just enough so she could make him out, silently catching her eye. Relief flooded through her. Both her men were here. No matter what happened to her, they were both here, they'd both come for her. She felt her heart swell with love, and tears pooled in her eyes.

Her uncle's words snapped her back to reality as his arm tightened once more against her throat. ". . . kill your girlfriend, and you're going to watch her die."

"There's no point, Martin," Chris said calmly. "You told me everything. You're not going to get away with this."

"Oh, I'll get away with it. And I'll make sure you don't tell anyone anything. You can die knowing this was all your fault, Nolan. If you'd done your job and purchased the Lakewood like you'd been hired to do, everything would be fine. The land would be mine, and Isabel would be safe. You did this, not me."

"No," Izzy choked out. She couldn't let Chris think that, not even for a second. If she was going to die, she had to make sure Graham and Chris knew the truth.

"Shut up," Martin spat out at her.

"No, this is not Chris's fault," she gasped out. "Chris, don't you believe that. I love you. And I love Graham. You make sure he knows that." Her breath was coming in short pants now. "Neither of you did anything wrong."

"I said shut up," Martin yelled, slapping at the side of her head with the gun, causing her to whimper.

At the impact of the gun, Chris practically growled, and stepped closer to Izzy. "I will fucking kill you," he said, a dangerous spark in his eyes that she'd never seen before.

"Stop!" Martin yelled at him.

This is it, she thought. What did she do? She couldn't let Chris die trying to save her. And Graham couldn't get a clear shot, could he? She looked back toward Graham, and he had moved closer. Izzy saw that he had moved to a position where the tree wasn't in his way, and now she was the only obstacle between him and Martin. She was the only obstacle between Graham getting a clear shot.

She looked toward Graham again, her eyes on his. He was still hidden in the shadow, but she could make him out easily. *What do I do, Graham?* She pleaded silently. *What do I do?*

As if in answer, Graham pointed his gun in her direction and then pointed down. Again, he pointed toward her and pointed down. Martin held her tightly. She couldn't move right or left, but . . .

"I. . . I don't feel well," she stammered.

"What?" Martin said, his attention shifting between her and Chris. "What are you mumbling about?"

"My head. It's spinning." That definitely wasn't a lie. Izzy gave into her nerves and let her knees start to shudder. Now she just let it all go. "I don't think I can . . . I don't think . . ." She took a breath and went limp.

Martin's arm cut off her air briefly as he tried to hold her up by her neck. Even though Izzy was petite, it was much harder for him to hold up dead weight, especially when he was only using one arm. Martin struggled momentarily to keep her limp body upright, but he lost the battle. It was either let her go, or topple to the ground with her. He stumbled and let his grip on her go, steadying himself.

As Izzy tumbled to the cold ground, a loud shot rang out, then another, then another. She looked up to see Martin's eyes go wide, and the gun fell from his hand as he fell back.

Chris and Graham rushed to Izzy's side, both men collapsing to the ground beside her, gathering her in their arms. They were all around her, surrounding her, and Izzy's body started to shake.

She opened her eyes and looked into their twin steel gazes listening to their words of comfort as they held her, their strong hands gentle on her body. "It's going to be okay, Sweetheart. You're okay. We love you. It's over now. It's all over. You're fine. We're not leaving you. Never again, baby."

Their words ran together, and she wasn't quite sure who said what, but it didn't matter. She snuggled closer as she released the sobs she'd been holding back, and they held her as she cried. She reveled in their warmth, breathing in their scent.

She loved these two men. And they loved her. She knew that unquestionable truth above all else. And she didn't care what anyone else thought. She loved them, and she was never going to let them go.

Chapter Fifteen

Six weeks later

Snow swirled around the cars lining Main Street, covering everything in a fine powder. With the Christmas lights lining the old buildings, Izzy thought it looked like the picture from a Norman Rockwell Christmas card.

"Did they say what kind of surprise?" Tessa asked, stirring another spoonful of sugar into her coffee. She and Izzy sat by the window of Magic's newest coffee shop – aptly named The Coffeehouse – and watched the snow falling outside.

"Nope, Graham just told me to wait here, and he'd pick me up after he finished his shift at the station." She smiled as she thought of Graham's explicit instructions. He'd seemed so nervous. "He said they had a Christmas present for me, but they couldn't wait, so I get it early." She smiled in giddy anticipation as she raised her coffee to her lips.

"Well it's about damn time. Six weeks, and they haven't even double-teamed you yet. Maybe that's the big surprise," Tessa's loud statement caused Izzy to suck in a breath, choking on her hot coffee. Several heads turned, the other patrons looking up from their laptops or magazines to stare at the two women by the window.

"Ohmigod, keep your voice down," Izzy laughed.

"I'm serious," Tessa grinned, lowering her voice. "What is the hold-up exactly?"

In the weeks since the ordeal with Martin, her men had been very protective of her. They wouldn't touch her sexually at all for two weeks afterward, fearing they would hurt her. Doc Reed had finally given her the okay for physical activity, attesting that her injuries had healed well enough that she could make love without a problem. Then her men had definitely made up for lost time.

She could feel her face flush as she remembered the previous night. Graham had held her in his arms as Chris had brought her to ecstasy twice with his very talented tongue and lips.

At Tessa's raised eyebrow, she just said, "Trust me, things are moving along quite nicely in that department." Even so, they still hadn't taken her together. They seemed so afraid of hurting her these days. Not that she didn't enjoy their gentle lovemaking, but she missed the dominance they'd shown the first time the three of them had made love together.

"Nicely? Nice is great, sweetie, but it's not earth shattering," Tessa observed, adjusting her glasses.

Twisting her mouth, Izzy circled the rim of her coffee cup with a finger. "I just feel like they're holding back. I need to make them realize that I'm not made of glass. I mean they've been "preparing me," which they said is necessary." She used air quotes to punctuate her statement. "But I'm pretty damn sure I'm prepared enough." She winced at the small anal plug she currently wore.

"Then maybe you should tell them that. No holding back, anymore, right? Isn't that what you said?" asked Tessa.

Izzy sighed. "You're right, Tess." She was exactly right. No holding back. She smiled, hoping her honesty would get her rewarded by her men.

Studying her friend, Izzy noticed that although Tessa seemed to be back to her normal self, there was still a spark missing. It was something she'd hoped to talk to her about. "So, how are you Tess?" As Tessa opened her mouth to speak, Izzy said, "And before you say "fine," I mean how are you really? You seem like you're doing well, but something's not right. Is your stomach still bothering you? Are you having nightmares?"

Tessa abandoned her coffee, and pushed her glasses up her nose before clenching her hands together. As she stared out the window, she looked like she was contemplating exactly what to say.

"I'm okay. Really." She shrugged a shoulder. "I've just been having trouble sleeping. No nightmares, not really. It's just every time I close my eyes, the wheels in my brain keep turning, and I'm not sure how to get them to stop." She took a shaky breath. "Doc Reed actually suggested a psychiatrist, but I haven't called him yet." She unclenched her hands and clenched her coffee up instead, looking up at Izzy as if to seek approval.

"Tess, I think that's a great idea. Did he suggest Doctor Murphy?"

Blinking, Tessa said, "How did you know that?"

"Because that's who he recommended to me too. I actually have my first appointment on Tuesday. That's nothing to be ashamed of, you know. I hear he's really good."

Tessa breathed a sigh of relief. "Yeah, I researched him. He seems to get great reviews from patients. I guess I'll give it a shot. We can be crazy together." She winked.

"We always have been, so why should now be any different?" Izzy asked, smiling as she reached for Tessa's hand.

The two women sat in silence for a moment as they shared each other's strength, listening to the wind whistling outside. Izzy decided to broach the next subject she wanted to talk about. "So my other question to you is why haven't you come out to The Lounge since

Halloween? I mean, I'm sure it has to be difficult for you after the shooting, but is that the only reason?"

"Wow," Tessa said, leaning back in her chair. "You sure aren't holding back with the questions."

"No holding back," Izzy repeated. "That applies to you too."

When Tessa said nothing, Izzy took a deep breath and steamrolled ahead. "I miss seeing you. And I know Milo misses you too."

Tessa turned to look out the window again, but not before Izzy saw the tears pool in her eyes.

"Tess, you know I don't mean to upset you. I love you." The two women had been close before Halloween, but that night had sealed a bond between them that would never be broken.

Tessa just nodded, lifting her glasses to swipe at her eyes. "I just don't know if pursuing anything with Milo is a good idea. And I don't feel right leading him on."

The fact that Tessa refused to admit she had feelings for Milo confused the hell out of Izzy. She didn't know why Tessa was running from it, but it was easy to see that getting close to Milo scared her to death.

"You know, he came to see you every day when you were in the hospital." Tessa had been in a coma for three days after the shooting. Izzy had been in the room next to her for those three days. The doctor wouldn't let her out of bed to go in and see Tessa, so she'd taken matters into her own hands.

When Graham and Chris had walked in to find Izzy trying to maneuver a wheelchair with her wounded arm and a broken rib, they had given in and simply carried her to Tessa's room. Milo had been there the whole time. Tessa had been hospitalized for two weeks before she'd recovered enough from her internal injuries to go home. While she seemed like herself to the casual observer, those who knew her well could tell that her usual light had dimmed.

"I know," Tessa whispered, looking back at Izzy. "I appreciated him being there. I told him that." She blew out a long breath. "He just wants more than I can give."

By her tone of voice, Izzy could tell that now was not the time to push her any further on the subject. "You know, you can always come out and say hi without leading him on. Just don't order a blow job shot," she said with a wink.

A bubble of laughter escaped from Tessa. It was good to see her smile.

"Have you heard anything from Andi?" Tessa asked changing the subject.

Izzy's smile faded and she let out a frustrated sigh. After Halloween, Andi's husband had made her quit the Lakewood. Oh, Andi hadn't said that, but when she'd called to give her resignation, Izzy could read between the lines. No one seemed to know what was going on with her. Even Andi's brothers hadn't seen her, and she was ignoring everyone's calls.

"She hasn't returned my calls for over a week now. I even stopped by her house, but either she wasn't there or wasn't answering. I'm really worried about her."

Nodding, Tessa agreed. "Me too. I even asked Reed, but he hasn't heard anything either. Have you hired anyone to replace her?"

"I just hired a new day manager, but not a new night one." Izzy was holding out hope that Andi would come back, so she was hesitant to fill all of her open positions. "We've all been taking turns working nights to pick up the slack."

"Oh, I'm sure Graham and Chris love that," Tessa said sarcastically.

"Yeah, not so much," Izzy smiled as she thought of the men working the front desk. "They've been helping me run the desk at night, you know."

"Oh yes, I've heard," Tessa laughed. "Chris charms the hell out of everyone. I think half the women in this town want to bed down with him. And Graham just scares them all away."

Izzy could feel herself grinning like an idiot as she thought about last week when a few reporters had come in snooping for a story. Chris kindly threatened to kill them and hide their bodies somewhere remote. Graham had just growled, and they'd backed up so fast they'd practically knocked each other over.

The tinkling of the bell over the door had them both looking up. "Well, speak of the devil," Tessa said. "There's one of your protectors right now."

Graham walked up to their table, his hungry eyes taking in Izzy. She felt herself blush down to her toes as he bent down to give her a quick kiss, lightly running his tongue over her lips.

"Hello, Sheriff Hottie," said Tessa, causing Graham to back up before he devoured Izzy.

He rolled his eyes Tessa's direction and smiled. "Hello, Tess, staying out of trouble?"

"I do try," she said, grinning. "By the way, Izzy said your sex life is 'nice.'"

Graham pulled out Izzy's chair and raised an eyebrow at her. "Nice?"

Giggling, Izzy reached over and gave Tessa a small shove. "That is NOT what I said, you troublemaker."

Wrapping a muscular arm around her, Graham pulled her close. "Just wait 'til we get home, sweetheart. We'll show you nice."

Izzy felt her insides go molten at that velvet voice he used on her.

"Oh, goodness," Tessa said, pushing her chair back. "It is really coming down out there."

Izzy looked out the window, surprised to see how heavily the snow had started falling. It looked like giant puffy cotton balls were falling out of the sky.

"Come on, Tessa," Graham said, reaching to pick up her messenger bag. "We'll take you home first. It's too slick out there for you to be walking."

****

After dropping Tessa off at her apartment and making sure she made it inside safely, Graham leaned over and dropped a kiss on Izzy's mouth.

"Nice, huh?" He smiled at the pretty pink color in her cheeks and loved the way she sucked on that bottom lip as he moved lower, his beard lightly scraping her neck as he placed a soft kiss right below her ear.

He grinned at Izzy's little whine as he backed away from her. "You have to wait until we get home," he said patting her denim-clad thigh, enjoying the way her thighs automatically parted in response to his touch.

"You are such a tease," she grumbled.

Maneuvering his truck out of town, he headed in the direction of the Lakewood, asking Izzy about her day, and loving the way she talked animatedly with her hands. When they passed Lakewood road, it took her a moment to realize it.

"I tried to get Tessa to come out to the Lakewood, but she – hey, wait a second, where are we going?" Izzy looked out the window, her cute little brow furrowing slightly.

Graham took a curve slowly, once again admiring the newly installed guardrails. They had made a lot of safety improvements on the roads over the last month.

He glanced at Izzy to see if she'd figured out yet where he was headed. She had her cute little brow furrowed and finally said, "This is the way to Vivian's. Why are we going there?"

Vivian had moved into town two weeks ago with her son who had recently moved back to Magic. "Is there a problem at her house?"

"Not a problem really – just something we need to check out." He couldn't wait to see the look on her face when he and Chris surprised her.

****

After adding another log to the fire, Chris lit a few more vanilla-scented candles on the long coffee table. He and Graham had rushed around all week to try to get at least the downstairs of the house in perfect condition to surprise Izzy.

The front foyer led to a big farmhouse kitchen where the men had made a few custom improvements that he couldn't wait to show Izzy. On the left side of the front hall, was the large homey living area where they'd brought in Graham's leather furniture. They'd decorated the room in the reds and golds that Izzy seemed to love so much.

As Chris looked around, he took in the open space next to the brick fireplace where they would soon put up their first Christmas tree. This was a room where he could see children laughing and playing. But first, they had to make sure Izzy wanted the same thing. Tonight was huge.

Embrace your confidence, Nolan. Turning at the sound of a truck driving up, Chris straightened his gray suit jacket and adjusted the silver tie that matched his eyes. He placed a red plush couch pillow on the large Oriental rug in the middle of the room and took a deep breath, standing next to it.

"Graham, what the hell?" he heard Izzy's voice. "Why is Chris's car here? And what's with the flickering light. Oh good lord, there really is a ghost!"

Stifling a laugh, Chris waited quietly as Graham unlocked the door.

****

Thank God for Graham's hand on her lower back guiding her into the room or Izzy would have just stood still in shock. Chris stood there dressed in a suit and tie, with candlelight flickering over his gorgeous body. Wow, he was beautiful.

"Seriously, man? A suit?" asked Graham, tossing his keys on the coffee table and shrugging out of his coat.

Rolling his eyes at his brother, Chris took a step toward Izzy, holding out a hand.

"Chris? What's going on? Why are you at Vivian's? Why are we here?" She looked back and forth between the two men, feeling incredibly exposed as their eyes focused intently on her face.

"We have something we want to talk about, Iz," said Graham, pushing up the sleeves of his red plaid shirt.

"Um . . . okay." She started twisting her fingers, her nerves taking over.

"Don't be nervous, baby." Chris took her hand and moved closer to brush a light kiss over her mouth.

"Welcome home," he whispered against her lips.

"Home? What do you mean? This is Viv's place." Confusion flickered through her as both men shook their heads. Their faces warmed, and Chris released her hand to slide off her black leather coat and toss it over the arm of the couch before returning to her and taking her hand. Graham took her other hand entwining his fingers with hers.

Exchanging one last glance with his brother, it was Graham who finally spoke. "Baby, Viv decided to move into town with Lane. She put the house up for sale, and we decided to buy it."

Her mouth dropped open as he continued. "You can decorate it any way you want, we can make any renovations you want. We just thought you deserved a nice home. It's close enough to the hotel that you won't be driving very far. And it's big enough for all of us."

"For all of us?" Hope flared inside of her. They had enjoyed every day with each other over the last few weeks, and Izzy had no doubt that her men loved her since they told her every day, but they hadn't talked much about the future.

"Vivian raised three children here . . . despite the ghosts," Graham smirked. "It's time this house saw a family again."

In unison, the men took a step back and sank to one knee right next to each other on the giant pillow. Izzy felt as though someone lit sparklers inside her body, the tingles shooting through every cell.

As Graham reached for her hand, Chris pulled a small velvet box from his lapel pocket.

"Ohmigod, ohmigod." She clamped her free hand over her mouth as Chris opened the box to reveal a platinum band with one large diamond nestled in the middle of two smaller ones. "Ohmigod," she said again, causing both men to smile.

"Iz," Chris began. "I was honestly to a point in my life that I never thought I would find true love. I didn't think it really even existed. And then you walked into my life. When I met you, the world suddenly made sense because I'd finally found my place in it – with you. I'd finally found my home. You are my home, Isabel Elizabeth Craig."

"And you're mine, too," said Graham. "I've loved you for so long, but I was too scared to do anything about it, scared of what my life would be like if I let you in, scared of what it would be like without you. And then I finally realized that you are my life, Izzy. Without you, I have no point in this world. I need you. I love you with my whole heart, baby. You're my family." He looked at his brother. "You two are both my family. You told me once, Izzy, that we're a team, and you were right. So, Isabel Elizabeth Craig . . ."

Chris accepted the handoff. "We want you to become Isabel Elizabeth Nolan."

Both men took a deep breath and said together, "Will you marry us?"

Her hands trembled as she looked from one man to the other, tears welling in her eyes. "Ohmigod, ohmigod."

Graham rose from the floor and grasped her shaking hands, looking intently into her eyes. "Ohmigod, what, Sweetheart?"

"Ohmigod, yes. Yes! Of course I will marry you! Both of you! I love you so much!" Izzy jumped up and down, unable to contain her joy.

Both men exhaled a sigh of relief, and Chris rose before letting out a whoop of joy and grabbing her to pick her up and spin her around. He kissed her fiercely and set her on her feet in front of Graham who kissed her with just as much fervor.

Chris took her left hand and slid the ring on her finger, as a thought occurred to her. "How will this work? I mean, legally—"

Graham shook his head and reached up to wipe the tears of joy off her cheeks with the back of his knuckles. "You'll marry one of us legally, and we can draw straws or something. It doesn't really matter."

"No, it doesn't," Chris said, pressing himself in behind her. "Because we will both be your husbands, so whatever it says on a piece of paper doesn't make a difference."

"You'll be married to both of us," said Graham. He leaned down to take Izzy's lips in a kiss that started off sweet, but deepened as she moaned into his mouth. She felt Chris's hands moving up to cup her breasts, brushing his thumbs over her tight nipples through her fuzzy pink sweater.

Suddenly Graham pulled back, "Hold on just a second," he said, his eyes darkening. Chris's hands stilled, leaving Izzy wanting more.

"What?" Izzy's voice was so husky that she barely recognized it as her own.

Graham's eyes gleamed wickedly as he smirked. "I seem to remember Tessa saying that you described our sex life as "nice."

"Nice?" Chris exclaimed loudly. "Seriously, baby?" he said, his fingers tightening on her nipples.

****

Enjoying her gasp at his tight grip on her nipples, Chris rubbed them to ease the slight pain, smiling at the way color rushed to Izzy's face. "You wanna explain, sweetheart?" he asked, watching her flush grow deeper.

She looked down, biting that lower lip, but he could see Graham wasn't having that. His brother brought his hand lightly around her throat to remind her of his dominance, remind her of who was in charge. "Eyes on me, Iz."

She looked up, and Chris could see those blue eyes had darkened. He could also feel her heart beating rapidly beneath his palm.

"Talk to us, baby," he said in a gentle command.

Taking a deep breath, she forged ahead, her voice breathy as Chris lightly caressed her nipples, and Graham stroked the side of her throat with his thumb. The double assault made her breathing quicken to a pant, and her words came out husky.

"It's just – you guys have been so . . . careful lately."

"Baby, you had a broken rib," he said gently.

"And a gunshot wound to your arm," Graham reminded her.

"I know that," she said, nodding. "But I'm fine now. I just don't want you to hold back anymore. I miss the way you . . . take control." Her cheeks grew pink at the confession, and Chris grew painfully hard as he understood her meaning.

Graham's thumb stilled on her neck, and Chris knew what his brother was thinking. Was she ready? Was she ready for them to take the control she was so willing to give them? Was she ready for them to finally take her together? He knew the answer, could feel it in her. Her body was practically vibrating with need.

"Graham, I think maybe it's time we showed Izzy some of the improvements we've made in the kitchen," Chris suggested.

The lines at the corners of Graham's eyes deepened as a smile lit his face. "Yes, yes, I do think we should."

"The kitchen? What's in the kitchen?" Izzy asked, looking back and forth between them.

"Oh, you'll see, baby. Graham and I have made some . . . improvements to better fit our lifestyle." Chris laughed as Izzy's eyes widened. He backed up and took her hand. Glancing at Graham, he said, "Do you want to grab a blanket?"

As Graham retrieved a fluffy red blanket off the couch, Chris took Izzy's hand, leading her down the hall. The kitchen was big and open, lined with dark granite countertops and walnut cabinets. A large island stood in the center of the room covered in the same granite, and was lined with four leather barstools. Chris could just imagine Izzy there. She loved to cook, and he could visualize her blonde hair pulled back in a ponytail as she made dinner, or baked those brownies she loved so much.

Chris grinned at the way Izzy's eyes widened when she spotted the new addition to the kitchen. The large walnut dining table was the centerpiece in the expanded breakfast nook. Izzy walked over and ran her fingers along the smooth wood.

"Wow," she breathed. "This is incredible." Turning toward them, Izzy eyed Chris and then Graham who was noticeably blushing beneath his beard. He couldn't help but smile at his brother. Graham used to love woodworking to relax, but he'd stopped years ago. A month ago, he'd taken it up again when an idea had ignited in his head.

Talk about a truly inspired idea. He couldn't wait to see Izzy's reaction when she realized this wasn't a run of the mill dining room table. The four legs on the solid rectangle table jutted upward into ornate columns. They were higher than the platform of the table, making it resemble a four-poster bed. The decorative columns curved outward, and Chris knew that the curved design would anchor ropes quite well.

"Did you make this?" Izzy looked at Graham with wonder. He leaned in and gave her a quick kiss and then winked at Chris. "I did. Now let us give you the grand tour."

Izzy eyed Graham curiously as he spread the large blanket over the table. As he prepared the space, Chris moved to stand in front of Izzy.

"Strip, baby." He felt himself instantly thicken at the way she sucked in a breath, her eyes dilating.

****

Both men watched with intent gazes as she took a step back and reached for the hem of her sweater. Taking a breath, she quickly pulled it over her head and slid her jeans over her hips. She felt her insides heat up at the way two sets of steely eyes radiated approval and need. My God, even fully clothed, they just screamed sex. How did she ever get so lucky to deserve these men?

Looking at her lacy bra and panties, Chris raised an eyebrow. "Everything, Izzy."

She shivered and quickly shed her underwear, standing in front of both of her men completely exposed, open, and trusting. God, how she loved their dominance, their control, just in the way they looked at her. She needed that control, craved it from them. And they were more than happy to accommodate her.

"Good girl," said Graham, reaching for her and lifting her up on the table. The way he laid her out on the blanket made her feel like she was their own personal buffet. And she was, she was all theirs.

Each man took one of her hands and she felt them placing something around each of her wrists.

"What are you doing?" She tried to look back, but they were already spreading her arms out wide apart above her head.

"Let's just call these your new bracelets, custom made for you," said Graham with a wink.

Those bracelets looked like leather cuffs, but they were soft against her wrists, the insides lined with what felt like fur or something. She caught a glimpse of metal and realized that each cuff came attached with a carabiner hook. Each man opened a hook and attached a rope to it before looping the ropes over the large curves of wood at the corners of the table.

"Wha – how did you —?" She yanked on her arms, but they were firmly secured.

Chuckling, Graham ran his hands down her body. "Like we said," he kissed between her breasts, "we made improvements." He kissed above her belly button, and Izzy moaned lightly as his tongue circled her navel, the scratching of his beard on her sensitive skin making the feeling all the more erotic.

He pulled her down the table as far as her bound arms would allow so her butt rested right at the very edge. Izzy felt herself becoming even wetter at his deep growl. "Our measurements were right, Chris. She is just the perfect size." He bent over sliding his hands up her arms until his face met hers. "Just perfect," he whispered before taking her lips.

Arching up, Izzy spread her legs even more, wrapping them around his jeans-clad hips. She wished Graham would take his clothes off, but the roughness of his jeans against her pussy had her yearning for more. He pressed against her, and she could feel his cock bulging. God, she wanted him inside of her. When he broke the kiss and stroked her cheek with a calloused finger, she said, "You're overdressed. I want you naked. Both of you. I want you —"

"Now, now, do you think you're in charge of this, baby?" She heard Chris ask from behind her.

"Um – I –uh, no." She stammered as Graham rubbed his erection right *there*. "Ohgod!" she whined, arching up. She was so close. She just needed him to rub a little harder, a little more, right *there*, and she –

As if sensing she was close, Graham backed up, chuckling, lightly running his hands down her body.

"You sadistic bastard!" she yelled without thinking.

****

Biting the inside of his lip, Graham tried to control a laugh. Chris was standing on the opposite side of the table behind Izzy, smirking as he watched her writhe around, yanking at her bonds.

"Be still, sweetheart," Graham said with a sharp slap to her inner thigh, bringing her out of her head.

Izzy gasped, her entire body jerking before she immediately stilled. Graham could tell from the way her eyes softened that the sharp sting had already dissolved into an erotic heat that shot straight to her pussy. He also knew that every time she lightly yanked at the bonds, her arousal rocketed up another notch. Her submission of that control to him was what he needed, what they all needed, and every tug at the bonds reminded her of that.

He ran a finger from one full breast down to her thigh and back up again, loving the way her muscles quivered beneath his touch.

"Now, baby, I'm going to leave your legs free, but I want you to stay still." He bent her knees and brought her feet up, anchoring each of her heels against a corner column, effectively spreading her legs wide.

Soon, he would tie her legs down, but not tonight. Right now, he wanted her to choose to follow his orders. He was also still concerned that having her stretched and bound too tightly would pull too much at her ribs. With her spread open, he could see that her pussy was already glistening. Knowing how aroused she was made him even more careful with her because she was too turned on to realize if something hurt too much. Luckily, Graham was becoming an expert at reading her facial expressions and interpreting her body language.

Without a word, he nodded at Chris, and both men shed their clothes, enjoying the way Izzy's hungry eyes darted around to watch both of them. At the sight of their cocks, her mouth immediately opened, her tongue darting out to touch her lips.

****

Chris erased the distance between he and Izzy, and bent to claim her mouth as he tugged on the blanket, dragging her whole body up until her head rested on his hand rather than on the table.

"I want your mouth on me, Iz." He flicked a glance at his brother and smiled. "Your mouth on me while Graham has his dessert." Her hips wriggled in response, but stilled instantly at his brother's low growl.

Holding Izzy's head in his hand, Chris leaned over her so their eyes were even. "I'm going let your head drop back, but I want you to tell me if this is uncomfortable, okay?"

She nodded, sucking in a breath, and Chris looked down to see Graham trailing his tongue along the top of her thigh.

"What if – What if I – ohgod!" Her eyes shut as she arched in response to Graham's mouth so close to that spot that would send her into the abyss.

"Talk to me, baby," he said, stroking her hair. "What if . . .?"

She cleared her throat and tried again. "What if I'm uncomfortable, but my mouth is full?" she asked, causing a snort of laughter from Graham.

Grinning, Chris tapped her swollen lips. "Can you hum Jingle Bells for me?"

"Jingle Bells? Yes." As if to prove herself, she closed her lips and began to hum.

"Good girl. If you want us to stop anything and you can't *say* stop, you just start to hum to me, okay?"

A look of relief flickered across her face as she nodded.

Standing up, he gently let her head fall back, but made sure he kept his hand on the back of her head so it didn't bang into the side of the hard table. That also gave him the added benefit of being able to control her movements.

****

As Chris's cock bobbed in front of her face, Izzy marveled at how beautiful he was. Like steel covered in fine silk, his gentle strength sent a shiver of need through her. She wanted him. She wanted to taste him, his musky scent making her mouth water. She licked her lips and opened her mouth, allowing Chris to guide his cock into her, enjoying the way he groaned as she sucked him in. In this position, she was able to suck him in deep, his swollen head nudging at the back of her throat. His hand fisted in her hair, holding her, directing her movements.

The sweet control sizzled inside of her, and grew to a flame as he leaned over and slowly licked at a hard nipple, causing Izzy to give an instinctive yank on her bonds. The reminder of how they owned her body caused her to involuntarily arch up, wanting more.

That was met with a firm hand on her belly. Graham was working his mouth up and down her inner thighs, and now he drove her crazy as he scraped that beard along the sensitive skin, closer to her center. Suddenly she felt him blow lightly on her exposed pussy.

The contrast of the cool air on her burning fire made her moan in response. Her growing arousal made her work even harder at pleasing Chris, swirling her tongue around his thickness, sucking him firmly, trying to take him deeper into her throat, only to have him pull back, and then thrust in again. As his breathing sped up, Izzy sucked harder, wanting to taste him, wanting to please him. With a groan, he pulled out of her mouth.

"Noo," she practically whined. "Why are you stopping?" She felt a tug on the blanket as Graham pulled her back to where her head rested once again on the tabletop.

"You feel way too good, sweetheart," Chris panted. "I want to come deep inside of you . . . with *both* of us deep inside of you."

Understanding his meaning, Izzy smiled. "I want that too. So much." She'd actually thought of little else over the last couple of weeks.

Nerves lit up as she felt tugging on the anal plug that Graham had lovingly inserted a few hours before.

"And you kept this in just like I asked," his rough voice said. "Good girl." He kissed right above her mound as he thrust the plug gently in and out. She clenched and released her hands as her eyes dilated.

Chris cupped a breast, rubbing her nipple. She was so swollen and aching for need. Her body involuntarily arched upward as her breasts yearned for more attention. "Yeah, she's definitely ready for us." Chris leaned over to take a nipple in his mouth, sucking firmly as he gently pinched the other.

Tugging at her hands, Izzy's head began to writhe back and forth. She couldn't take the sweet torture any longer. "Please," she begged. "Oh please."

****

In response, Graham finally gave into her wanton need and let his tongue snake out to swirl around her swollen clit. She raised her hips, trying to press herself into his mouth, silently wanting, begging. He knew that as soon as he touched her, she would go off like a rocket.

As he swirled his tongue around her clit, he traced a finger along her slick labia. When he surprised her by thrusting a finger deep inside of her wetness, he was glad he had placed a hand on her stomach to hold her down because her hips jerked up violently. Chris still worked over her nipples, loving on her breasts, and their double assault had her moaning incoherently. Graham couldn't hold back any longer. He needed to feel her come.

He added another finger, thrusting hard into her pussy. He curved his fingers upward as he sucked her clit into his mouth, holding it firmly between his lips as he flicked it back and forth with his tongue. Izzy let out a squeak and her writhing stopped. Her entire body stilled and went rigid for just a moment before she jerked against them and let out a high-pitched scream. Her vaginal muscles clenched tightly around his fingers as her body dissolved into spasms. She cried out some incoherent form of their names as Graham continued to firmly suck on her clit, her satisfaction flooding his hand and his mouth. God, she tasted exquisite.

He brought her down slowly, gently lapping, his tongue circling around her clit, occasionally stopping to run firmly over the softening nub just so he could feel her involuntary shudders.

Finally, he lifted his head. Izzy glowed with the beautiful flush of orgasm and lay there softly panting. Graham met Chris's eyes and the emotion of the moment silently passed between them. Their woman, their fiancé, their wife. This moment, like every moment with her was a treasure they would both cherish forever.

****

Izzy felt like her whole body had melted into Jell-O. Somewhere in her hazy, satisfied brain, she realized that Chris had unhooked her wrists and was removing the cuffs. She felt Graham slide the plug out of her and move to the sink. Closing her eyes, she stretched her arms, wondering if she could just sleep here in the kitchen. Why not? It was her house, right? A giggle escaped her.

"I think she's a little loopy," Graham said with a chuckle. "Come here, sweetheart." He pulled her up to sitting position and immediately took her mouth. His tongue delved deep, thrusting. She could taste her arousal on him, and just when she thought she was completely spent, she felt the surge of heat shoot through her body once more. Her hands went up to tangle in Graham's hair, enjoying the silky slide of it through her fingers.

When Graham pulled away, Izzy saw Chris sitting on a bar stool facing them. Her breath caught at the look in his hooded eyes. Those deep eyes, the color of a stormy night, saw through to her soul. She trembled in response, and without a word, Graham helped her off the table as Chris opened his arms to her.

His cock looked painfully swollen, as did Graham's. She wanted to please them, to show them how much she loved them. She reached out to both men, her hands finding twin velvet rods, and watching their faces as she stroked them both gently, from base to tip.

"Good God, I think she's trying to kill us, Graham." Chris put his hand at the nape of her neck and pulled her in for a kiss. As Izzy returned his eagerness, his hands firmed on her hips. She started to straddle him, but Graham stopped her.

"Wait, baby, I need to get the condoms." He grasped her hips to stop her, but Izzy grinned and shook her head.

She couldn't believe she'd almost forgotten her own surprise for them. "I talked to Doc Reed today at my check-up, and he said the shot should be effective now. So, we're good. No condoms." She couldn't wait to feel both of them inside of her with nothing holding them back.

The joy that lit the men's faces made her heart swell. "You're sure, sweetheart? I mean, Reed is sure?" asked Chris.

She nodded vigorously. "Very sure. I don't want anything keeping us apart now. Nothing between us." Tonight, it would be the three of them with no barriers. Her hands rested against Chris's chest, and the thundering beat of his heart told her that he was just as ready as she was.

Graham pressed in behind her, steadying her as she straddled Chris. Izzy felt his hard cock bump at her entrance, but the four strong hands on her hips kept her from sinking straight down onto him like she wanted. She was so desperate for them, needing to please them, needing to feel them inside of her.

She felt Graham's arm curl around her stomach, and his large hand slid lower, his finger circling her clit. She curved her back in response, her head falling against Graham's shoulder, revealing her neck. Chris took immediate advantage and moved in to nibble at her slender throat.

"Oh, oh." Her body was already hypersensitive from her orgasm, and every touch, every nip from her men drove her higher. When she reached the point of breathlessness, the twin grips on her hips pushed down, and she sank to take Chris's full length into her pussy, both of them groaning at the feeling. Big, he was so big. But she wanted more. She wanted to be fuller. She reached behind her for contact with both of her men.

"Graham, I need —" she mumbled breathlessly.

"I know, Iz. I know exactly what you need." He stroked up and down the sides of her body, one hand going up to gently squeeze her breast. "Are you sure you're ready?"

"I'm more than ready," she said on a gasp as Chris thrust up.

"Okay, I want you to lean forward for me, and put your hands here." He moved her hands to grip the edge of the granite island behind Chris.

At Graham's command, Chris leaned back, resting against the counter, allowing Izzy to more easily lean forward, exposing her to Graham.

Suddenly, she felt something cold drizzling down between her cheeks. Lube? She didn't see him get out lube. But then, she hadn't seen them get out cuffs earlier, so she was pretty sure there was a drawer somewhere in this kitchen that had lots of toys that weren't for cooking.

A sharp swat to her rear had her tensing up around Chris's cock, both sensations melting together to send her arousal higher.

She felt Graham's hand flat on her lower back, and then felt his fingers at her back entrance. Two fingers slid into her, causing nerves to flare into a jangly sensation that traveled up her spine. His fingers thrust and twisted, scissoring, stretching. She moaned as he murmured in her ear for her to relax.

"You're ready for me, baby." Graham nipped at her shoulder as he removed his fingers. She felt empty for a moment until she felt something thick and hot pressing against her anus. "I want you to take a deep breath and press back against me, okay? Flatten your back."

Chris's hands on her hips steadied her as she pressed back against Graham's hardness, feeling the plum-sized head of his cock pop inside. So big, he was so big. She bit her lip and tensed up, squeezing her eyes shut.

"No, look at me, Iz. Open your eyes." Chris's gentle voice was like a caress. She opened her eyes to see his brow furrowed, studying her. "Graham, wait, we're hurting her. She's crying."

She felt Graham go still. Crying? Chris wiped a tear from her cheek. She hadn't realized she was crying. "No, don't stop. I'm not – it doesn't hurt. I've just never felt something so intimate. Please don't stop. Please."

Graham nuzzled against her ear and didn't say anything for a long moment. "You're sure?" he finally asked.

"Yes, yes, God yes!" she pleaded frantically.

Relieved, Chris pulled her forward again to kiss her as Graham pushed in further, slowly in short thrusts. Surprisingly after the initial shock, it didn't hurt. When she felt Graham's hips against her buttocks, she knew he was all the way in, and she felt full, so deliciously full. She didn't want to ever let them go.

Graham fisted a hand in her hair, and pulled her head back so he could have his turn claiming her mouth. She felt Chris's mouth at her nipple, and the firm sucking to the hard pebble almost did her in. When she started to move, four hands went to her hips to hold her still as the men began a slow rhythm. Graham slid out, lighting up those nerves again, and Chris pressed in. Then Graham surged back in as Chris lifted her up so just the head of his cock remained inside before thrusting her back down.

A moan escaped her as the intensity of the sensations confused Izzy's senses and had her soaring up, up, up. Her body responded immediately, and she knew she was seconds away from a forceful orgasm. She could tell the men weren't far behind her as their thrusts became more powerful, deeper, harder.

Graham's hands gripped her hips so tightly that it caused a wonderful flutter of pain, as Chris moved his hand around so his thumb could find her clit.

She gripped the edge of the counter so hard that her knuckles were white, and her shallow breaths came out in pants as each thrust drove her higher up that mountain. Higher she rose, and as Chris pressed firmly on her clit, she felt the tingling start low in her belly, except this time, it was so intense that it scared her, the feelings so strong, so extreme.

"I – I don't know if I can —" she stammered out. "It's too much – too much."

"You can take it, Izzy," Graham groaned in her ear. "I want you to come again. You're right there, ready to explode, aren't you, baby? Come now, Izzy. Come now for us."

His command drove her to the edge of that peak, and then Chris pinched her clit hard, the bundle of nerves igniting. Izzy's entire body shuddered violently as she flew off that cliff, every cell inside of her exploding, fireworks shooting off from her very soul. She heard a scream and realized it was her own. Her men gripped her hard, sandwiching her tightly in between them as she shook and quivered. Their rhythm sped up, thrusting harder into her swollen tissues, every drag of their cocks causing her nerves to spark like a frayed wire.

With a loud grunt, Graham slammed hard into her ass, and she felt his release in thick hot jolts of fluid.

Chris's movements became jerky, and he groaned her name as he thrust up into her pussy, filling her, releasing burst after burst of come.

As Izzy came down, her forehead lolled against Chris's shoulder, Graham's arms around her as he kissed her upper back.

He gently pulled out, and she let out a soft moan at the loss. "It's okay, baby, let me clean you up," he said softly. Chris moved so his cock slid from her, and she winced at the empty feeling.

Graham returned with a warm cloth, cleaning her gently as Chris caressed her face, watching her reaction.
*

"Are you okay, Izzy?"

She felt the tears come again at the sweetness in his voice. Graham reappeared at his side, and reached out to stroke her hair. "Baby, you really can't cry every time we make love to you. You're going to start scaring us."

She laughed weakly. "I'm fine. That was just perfect. I'd imagined it so much, so often. In all of my imagination . . ." She shook her head. "This was better," she finally said. "Way way better."

"I love you, Izzy," said both husky voices in unison. Damn, sometimes she really loved their twin sense.

Before she could respond, she heard . . . was that music?

Chris looked up. "What on earth? That sounds like it's coming from upstairs."

Graham's mouth dropped. "But there's no one up there, and it sounds like . . ."

They strained to listen, and Izzy's eyes grew wide. "Is that 'Here Comes the Bride'? How is there music? Did one of you . . ."

As both men shook their heads, she thought of all the time times Vivian had talked of her ghosts and told Izzy about the music that would come from the attic. "Ohmigod, everyone always thought Viv was crazy."

"You don't mean to tell me . . ." Chris started. "No way!"

They both looked at Graham. When he finally closed his mouth, he looked up again as the light tinkling of music continued to come from upstairs. He grinned. "This is going to be fun."

Oh, it certainly was.

The End

www.njyoungauthor.wordpress.com

Evernight Publishing ®

www.evernightpublishing.com